THE HOUSE
ON THE
SUNDERSTRASSE

§

Frank Spiller

TIDAL BOOKS

TIDAL BOOKS PAPERBACK FICTION

Canadian Cataloguing in Publication Data

Spiller Frank, 1922 -
    The house on the Sunderstrasse : a novel

ISBN 0-9684298-0-7

    I. Title

PS8587.P524H68 1998   C813'.54   C98-901029-5
PR9199.3.S64H68 1998

Printed and bound in Canada by DocuLink International

TIDAL BOOKS
Ottawa, Ontario.
<tidalbks@aol.ca>

for UNA,

§

ONE

1938

1.

Peter Gray puffed up the pillow, trying to capture a few more minutes of restful sleep before facing his parents. Moving shadows, patterns of the early morning sunlight, filtered through the leaves of the larch tree outside the bedroom window - the tree he'd helped his father plant as a sapling. He felt anxious, but then he always did when he was at home. Ordinarily there wasn't anything specific he could attribute it to, other than the fact that his behaviour came under constant scrutiny, but this time there was a particular reason for his unease. He pulled up the soft sheet, sinking into the generous layers of blankets, a luxury unknown in the cramped environment of His Majesty's Ship Saram, the naval minesweeper he'd left the day before.

He dozed, for how long he couldn't tell. It was the scrape of a chair in the kitchen that awakened him, then he heard his parents talking. The smell of frying bacon wafted into the room. They had probably finished breakfast.

He glanced idly at the clock on the night table and then sat up abruptly - squinting, disbelieving, It was nine thirty! He tried to remember. What time had Helga said? Wide awake now, he looked for her last letter. He found the blue envelope on the floor. It must have fallen there when he unpacked his things. He pulled out the single page, searching for a time. Ten thirty, she had written. He looked at the clock again, not wanting to believe he'd slept in on the one special day that he had awaited all year. He leapt out of bed, and rushed down the hall to the loo, his footsteps made louder by a squeaky floorboard.

He relieved himself, and yanked twice at the chain before the cranky cistern did its job and flushed the toilet. He stood in front of the mirror above the grotesque white porcelain washbasin with the cracked glaze, regarding for a moment the tired blue eyes and the regulation close-cropped fair hair, and then he turned on the tap, holding his finger in the flow, hoping it would be hot enough for a shave.

There was a knock at the door and he opened it.

It was his mother, Elizabeth.

"Here, I brought you a kettle," she said.

The pale blue eyes in the angular face were as lively as ever, but she had visibly aged he thought, especially in the last few years. There were silver streaks in the fair hair now, bearing testimony to the fact that she was approaching her mid-fifties.

"Thanks Mum."

He poured the scalding water into the basin, gave her back the kettle, and added cold water to create a comfortable temperature. It was a ritual he'd grown up with, his father having refused to bear the cost of a hot water heater.

"Breakfast'll be ready soon, don't be too long."

Her footsteps faded and he lathered his face. Picking up his new safety razor, he attacked the fuzz on his jaw line. It hardly justified attention, but it made him feel more manly, more comfortable with his peers in the Navy.

Feeling freshened and a trifle more relaxed, he went to the wardrobe, happy at the sight of his old sports jacket and the grey flannel trousers. He dressed hurriedly, finding a creased open-necked shirt and a pair of old brogues to complete his attire. He left the bedroom and came out onto the landing, stopping for a salutary glance at the old etching of a sailing ship, HMS Carotyne, fighting her way through rough seas. It was his father's memory of his training in the ships of the old navy and he seldom failed to remind Peter of the tyrannical routines and the poor food - salt pork and biscuits; 'laced with maggots,' his father would add, implying that the modern navy was a picnic by comparison with the hardships of his times.

He pulled himself erect, steeling himself for the paternal

encounter. He went to the top of the stairs. His mother was talking and he waited, trying to decide if he should interrupt.

"D'you think there'll be another war?" Her voice sounded troubled.

"How'd I know? For God's sake stop worrying . . ."

"Harry. He's only nineteen!"

"If there's another one, the Navy's the best place to be."

Peter bounded down the stairs, making sure he was heard, appearing suddenly at the kitchen door like a trapeze artist who had just completed his turn on the high wire.

"What's this about the RN?"

His father's face revealed a fleeting glimpse of discomfort as though he had something to hide. There was still the familiar shyness in the brown eyes set in the rounded face, the shyness that gave him a deference to authority which Peter hated. He regarded the tanned face, the bushy eyebrows, and the generous head of brown hair which, lacking any signs of grey, belied his age. He had just turned sixty the year before.

"I was telling your mother. It's a good career . . . "

"Makes a man of you. Isn't that right?" Peter couldn't disguise the frostiness in his voice. Good career indeed? More like his father's prescription for a son who needed toughening up. Yet it was his mother who, when he was thirteen, had taken him to London for a medical examination. It was all a hazy memory now, as though he went innocently to some kind of bondage. He remembered his mother's discomfort. No doubt she was carrying out the plan against her will, succumbing to her husband's notion that the navy would make a man of him. They had stayed with his maternal grandfather in Rotherhithe, close to the Thames and the bustling docks. It was an experience he would never forget.

"Wind it up and put the needle on the edge of the record." His grandfather, with a twinkle in his eye, had introduced him to the gramophone and 'Easter Parade' the hit song of the day. There had been other delights too: listening to him play the violin, taking walks in the nearby park, and trips down the Thames. The river was particularly exciting. It had the smell of the sea and ships. With his grandfather's encouragement it was easy to imagine far away places, out beyond the extremity of the river, where the river reached the North Sea and joined the oceans of the world, from whence came the big ships with their exotic cargoes of teas and spices.

Staying with his grandfather had been so astonishingly different from living at home with his father's stoicism. But it all came to an end too soon to be replaced by the rigours of a naval school, and afterwards, entry into the Royal Navy, the real navy, as a boy seaman, just like his father wanted it to be, the father who faced him now with a soulful stare. Peter waited, not knowing what to expect, and his father turned away, burying himself in his morning paper.

"That's true, Dad," Peter spoke slowly and deliberately. "It's a good career, the navy . . . Makes a man of you."

Peter looked at his mother, hoping she had caught the sarcasm that his father had missed, or had chosen to ignore, but she hadn't even heard. "Where's your uniform?" she said, adding fried bread to the bacon and eggs. "I like to see you in your uniform."

He rolled his eyes.

"Mum, I'm on leave. Time for civvies."

Peter took a sip of tea, nearly choking when his father yelled unexpectedly.

"Bloody hell!" he pronounced, slapping the newspaper on the table. "There's a German ship coming in - the *Joachim*. I wonder they've the cheek to come here?"

Peter felt his heart race. "That ship . . . "

He hesitated. Could it be that his father knew about Helga? This was no time for speculation, however, and desperate to overcome the silence of conjecture, he continued.

"That ship . . . It's been here before,"

"I **know**, but why now?"

6

"Why not?" His voice sounded more argumentative than he intended.

"For God's sake, don't you read the papers?"

Peter dropped into the nearest chair - he felt reassured. If his father had known about Helga, he wouldn't have failed to disclose it. "Just the other day I read about the Berlin Olympics," Peter's voice was more tranquil, his confidence returning. "Very impressive I thought,"

"What the hell's that got to do with it . . . That was nineteen thirty six, two years ago?"

"It wasn't just Germans involved. It was international."

"Yes, well, all Hitler's propaganda . . . " His voice faded, but then rose suddenly to a shout.

"Two hours I was in the water! A German torpedo! We never even saw the bloody submarine - sneaky bastards!"

"But that was war . . ."

"Which they started, just like they'll start the next one. Well - that is, if there's another one," he spoke sheepishly, sneaking a sideways glance at his wife.

Peter had heard it all before. His father seldom recounted his exploits in the war, but when he did he displayed a level of emotion rarely seen on other occasions. His voice would get louder and louder as he waved his arms and thumped his fists on the table to simulate the sound of shells bursting. Like so many others of his generation he had been harmed by war, the nightmares testified to that. Peter, as a child, remembered only too well being awakened in the night by the sudden shouting and screaming which sent a shiver through him as he lay terrified, feeling that some dire fate was imminent. Small wonder that his father would nurse this hatred of everything German.

"How often do they hold the Olympics?" his mother looked up from the stove.

Peter doubted that she actually cared. It was her way of seeking to lower the tension as she placed his breakfast on the table.

7

"Thanks Mum." He eyed the lavish helping of eggs and bacon. "Olympics? . . . every four years. Next one should be in nineteen forty." He took a generous mouthful. "Don't get meals like this in the Navy."

She smiled appreciatively, but turning away with a frustrated look, which Peter recognized as a wish to be alone with him, she glared at her husband.

"Going to see what's readying in the garden, Harry?"

She poured herself another tea and brought it to the table.

"Harry?"

"I heard you."

His father got up slowly, reluctantly.

"Keep the tea warm!" he mumbled.

"It'll last till you get back,"

He gave her a foul look and, jamming a battered straw hat on his head, he made for the large vegetable garden at the back of the house. As the door closed behind him, she reached for the teapot, holding it over Peter's cup.

"A little more?"

"Please."

She filled his cup, and then her own.

"Let's go in the living room. It's more comfortable there."

He sneaked a quick look at the clock on the wall - he needed to leave immediately - but she was motioning him to follow her.

The living room was at the back of the house and through the large bay window, beyond the larch tree and the small lawn, he could see his father selecting some rhubarb. There was no time to lose.

"I think I'll walk to the harbour this morning. Take a look at that ship, the *Joachim* . . . "

"Your father's not going to like you going off alone. It's his day off. I'm sure he was hoping to spend some time with you. Anyway, why do you want to look at a German ship?"

"Curiosity I suppose."

"I thought you would've gone to see Harriet?"

"Oh, come on Mum, she was just a schoolmate. . . . "

"Not like Helga," he mumbled to himself.

"What?"

"Nothing . . . Look, I don't want to explain my actions to Dad - Just tell him I went out."

"Wait, Peter . . . "

He went into the hall, grabbed his coat, and left by the front door.

The road was deserted. Not much traffic came this way. The adjacent houses were of mixed vintage. Those opposite, below the base of a steep hill which was a favourite spot for hikers, were built around nineteen hundred, whereas those occupied by Peter's family were more recent, only some ten years' old. They were two-storey houses with bay windows in the front and back, constructed quickly and not very soundly, modest accommodation for working class families who had retired to this small village near the Dorset coast.

It was about a mile along pleasant footpaths to the beaches and the small harbour entered from the sea between two piers which jutted out into the bay. The port was once known for its shipbuilding, but that was in the days of sail, now it was a small fishing port. As well, it was able to receive the small coastal steamers that plied between England and European ports.

The weather had been overcast all morning, but as he reached the harbour the sun broke through. By the time he'd walked out onto one of the piers, the *Joachim* was in sight. She was a three-masted, diesel-powered, vessel. Well down in the water she had a large deck cargo of timber. A small crowd had gathered to watch her arrival and he had to stand on tiptoe to see above the heads in front of him.

"Bloody Jerries, what do they want coming here?"

The voice startled him and he turned to the lined and unshaven face of a scruffy-looking elderly man whose battered briar gave off an acrid cloud of tobacco smoke.

"We must have agreed," said Peter.

"What d'you mean - agreed?" He turned on Peter with unexpected hostility.

"To let it come here."

"More fools us, I'd say. Just like we let them in the Rhineland. Now it's Austria."

Peter eased himself away from the old man and the crowd, quickening his pace a little to match the ship's speed as it advanced between the piers.

Then he saw Helga. He stopped and stared, awed by the truth of her presence, unable to take his eyes off her. She was dressed in worn overalls and standing next to the helmsman in the open wheelhouse. Her tall athletic-looking figure was unmistakable and her flaxen hair was being teased by the breeze. She spotted him and waved, a spirited sweep of her arm which was accompanied by a broad smile. He raised a hand, discreetly acknowledging her greeting.

He allowed the ship to draw ahead of him, not wanting to get in the way of the workers and the mooring lines, thankful for a chance to calm his excitement. Besides, he didn't want to be too conspicuous. He watched as the ship was secured and a gangway run out, and then he hastened towards the stern on which bold letters proclaimed its identity and port of registry - *Jocchim, Hamburg*.

When he came abreast of the ship, she was waiting. The vessel was close to the jetty now and a small gap separated them. She came towards the rail, blue eyes twinkling in the same pleasant face,

"Peter! *Mein* Peter!"

"Helga! You came," his voice was tremulous and he felt flushed.

"I promised"

"I didn't think . . . "

She laughed.

"I make it happen."

10

Her accent charmed him, as it had the first time, and her smile banished his confusion. She beckoned him to come closer.

"I missed you." He shouted across the gap.

"It has been very - *lang* . . . "

She struggled to find a word, but failed, and she spread her hands apart in an effort to convey her meaning.

"Too long?" he suggested.

"*Ja.* Too long."

She looked behind her, then leaned slightly forward.

"The *Kapitän* - he is new," she whispered.

"A problem?"

"*Nein.*" She shook her head, her hair falling over her brow. "*Vater* asked him. He did not refuse to take me."

"But if your father owns the ship?"

"The *Kapitän* . . . "

She placed her hands together as if in prayerful obedience.

He certainly understood the extent of a captain's authority. Still, it gave him comfort to know that her father had approved of the trip.

"Can you come ashore . . . Now?"

"Peter . . . you must wait. I think . . . today . . . at two o'clock."

He stood unmoving, fighting his eagerness, not wanting to leave.

"You had better go now. I will arrange it."

"I'll be here . . . At two."

She looked away as if expecting the Captain to appear.

"I cannot promise," she said.

"I understand."

He walked towards home, taking the longest route to extend his private elation. Helga! Dear, beautiful Helga! How lucky he was, she was here and nothing else mattered. Still, the old man on the pier and his talk of the Rhineland was bothersome.

He arrived at the house just before noon and went up to

his room to look for photographs. His mother had made his bed - damn, he had intended to do that. The folder was on the bedside table. It contained the pictures that they had taken of each other during her first visit. Those he had sent on to her. The date on the back was April 7, 1937 almost exactly a year earlier, yet he couldn't remember them talking about the political situation at all then. What a difference a year had made. Earlier, there had been little talk of war; now it seemed hard to avoid. Besides, their first meeting had remained a secret. Somehow his parents had been less intrusive then, glad that he was enjoying the lonely trips to the seaside with his camera, a present from his mother.

"Lunch is ready!" his mother called.

"Be there in a minute," he answered, wondering if she had read Helga's most recent letter.

It was difficult to leave after lunch. He didn't want to make more excuses, so when his mother went into the kitchen he jumped up from the dining room table, hating his artfulness, but determined nonetheless to escape.

"I'm going out," he called, making an unseemly rush to the door before she could ask any questions.

It was a sunny afternoon, like the morning only warmer now, with a light breeze stirring the signs of spring growth. He kept up a brisk pace along the path to the harbour. When he arrived at the gangway, unloading was in progress and he had to dodge the stacks of timber being swung out on the derricks to the waiting lorries. Helga was talking to the Captain but she caught his eye, motioning him to join them.

"Peter - Peter Gray - *Kapitän Ernst Hopp*," she said.

Captain *Hopp* was of a medium build with an unruly mop of grey hair which protruded around the edges of his peaked cap. The weather-beaten face made it hard to deduce his age. His eyes were a deep blue and when he turned to Peter their gaze was steady. Peter held out his hand and the Captain clasped it in a firm grip.

"Pleased to meet you, sir," Peter said.

The Captain shook Peter's hand and then looked at Helga. He appeared to be waiting for some explanation.

"*Wir wollten nur einen Spaziergang machen,*" she said.

The Captain hesitated, holding Peter in a prolonged stare, causing him to think that he was about to be sent away.

"*Seid um sechs Uhr wieder zurück!*" he replied, turning his gaze to Helga.

He looked at Peter again, nodded, turned on his heel, and disappeared down a hatch. The dismissive gesture, for that's how Peter interpreted it, seemed to signal an uneasy beginning to their reunion. He looked with dismay at Helga.

"Do not worry . . . He said, Yes."

"But what did *you* say?"

"I told him we would walk in the country. He said to be back by six."

"Is he upset?"

She shook her head, appearing mildly impatient with his consternation.

"It is . . . arranged," she said, taking him firmly by the arm.

He looked back at the ship, trying to see if the Captain was watching, but she drew him away.

"Does he know we met last year?"

"*Nein* . . . I did not tell my family."

"Neither have I," Peter confessed.

"I told my *bruder* Gunther. We are good friends."

"What did he say?"

A long pause.

"I am . . . *anfreunden* . . . with the enemy."

He tried to fathom a likely interpretation.

"Ah . . . Fraternizing with the enemy?" Peter laughed, "Maybe you are?"

"Do not joke, Peter." Helga's voice was sharp but he

13

caught the hint of sadness.

"Sorry . . . "

"I told him about you and the Royal Navy. Günther is to go to the navy too . . . The *Kriegsmarine* next year."

"He's older than you?" It didn't seem that important, it was just that he felt he had to acknowledge her brother, a brother who might not take kindly to his sister's new English friend and whose existence made him uncomfortable, as though he were a rival suitor.

"No younger, a year under, he is seventeen."

"Ah," he said, trying to sound interested as he indicated the route he intended to follow.

They left the harbour area, taking the road which skirted the beach, passing a little café with an assortment of cakes displayed in the window. Next to it was another shop selling a jumble of nondescript objects, funny postcards, and a collection of spades and buckets for the expected younger visitors to the beach. He felt suddenly irritated with his father's gloomy view of the future. There was nothing here that gave any cause to believe that this would not be a summer just like any other.

"Oh Peter . . . I am lucky to come again."

She leaned on his arm.

He wished it could always be like this, having Helga near, but the pleasant musing was replaced by the persistent thought of his father and his attitude to Germans, and to the Olympics.

"Did you go to the Olympics?" he said.

She looked surprised.

"We all went. The family went for a day . . . to Berlin . . . *Wunderbar!*"

"I wish I could have been there with you . . . But that was the year before we first met?"

"*Ja* . . . I remember when the English entered, carrying the flag."

"The Union Jack?"

"*Ja . . . Ja.*"

She became pensive and he considered asking her how the English had been received by the crowd. But the opportunity passed and as they emerged from the shadow of the buildings the sun dispelled any trace of gloom.

"You like my dress?"

He held her at arms' length.

It was a white dress with large red spots. Over it she wore a white sweater. Around her hair was a red ribbon. He looked at the tanned face and the lively eyes.

"Very nice."

"I buy for you." She hesitated. "Nice? Nice? What is Nice?"

He kissed her fingers and waved his arms. "*Wunderbar!*"

"Peter! *Du sprichst Deutsch!*"

"*Nein*," he said, becoming self-conscious. She moved towards him and he caught the scent of her, her soft hair brushing his face. He whispered in her ear.

"Helga. Darling Helga . . . you're so beautiful."

She looked into his eyes, her face colouring slightly.

"Oh Peter! Peter!"she cried, hugging him tightly.

"What shall we do today?" he said, as his cheek touched the softness of her neck.

"The walk - the Tea Room, and a . . . cream tea?"

He leaned back, regarding her with satisfaction.

"You see. You did like it." His face erupted in a smile. "I knew you would."

"Very rich . . . but very *gut*." She slid her tongue over her lips, a delicate gesture of approval, a reminder of her last visit and how he had introduced her to an English afternoon tea.

They started up the narrow path ahead which led steeply to the top of the cliffs to the east of the harbour. It was the walk they had taken the first time, but there was less of a breeze than before. Then it was impossible to speak against the wind, but now it posed no problems. When they reached the top, they sat resting on a wooden bench, gazing out at the distant horizon. He

15

put his arm around her and she snuggled up to him.

"I can't believe you're here."

"I would like to stay Peter. Stay here with you always, but I know I cannot, my *Vater* would not . . . He would be offended. I would not wish to hurt my parents."

He had often fantasized that she would stay. It was unrealistic, of course, but now that she had confirmed the impossibility it took away a little of his dream. They meandered along the same leafy lane of the year before. He drew her to him, held her tightly and kissed her. Her lips were soft and yielding.

"Peter . . . I . . . " Very gently, she pushed him away.

It was not the first time he'd been given a mild rebuff, a polite reminder of the responsibility entrusted to her by her parents and by the Captain's willingness to put faith in her good behaviour.

"I'm sorry."

"*Nein, Nein* . . . not to be sorry, Peter."

They strolled hand-in-hand towards the small village with its quaint old houses with thatched roofs. The Tea Room was in one of these buildings and the owner recognized them from the previous year, surprising them by asking if they wanted the same order as before. And, seeing her memory of them as an endorsement of the feelings they shared, they readily agreed.

When the order arrived, they tucked into the sweet morsels and sipped contentedly at their tea. He reached across and touched her arm.

"Happy?"

She nodded.

"Will there be other days?"

"*Ja*, Peter . . . Tomorrow, and tomorrow, and tomorrow. I think for six days the *Joachim* will be here."

Billowy white clouds were scattered in a blue sky when he went down to join his parents at breakfast. His father was about to leave for the local estate where he was employed as the head gardener.

"Got to work, no time to spare . . . not like yesterday," he said sternly.

"Dad . . . When did Germany enter the Rhineland?"

"About two years ago . . . almost exactly . . . Why?"

"Just . . . sort of wondered."   He tried to sound indifferent.

"Yes . . . we let them do it,"   his voice was despondent. "Just like Austria."

He shook his head and for a moment Peter expected a hostile outburst, but he finished his tea, kissed his wife, climbed on his ancient bicycle and, with a quick wave, rode off.

"He's pretty upset you didn't spend time with him yesterday . . . Why were you away so long anyway?"

"I . . . I went down to the harbour, like I said I would, watched the ship come in . . . then, well . . . I took a walk, ended up in the tea room in Bradstor, and came home."   He squirmed inwardly at the half-truth.

"I've got a couple of classes today, so you're going to be on your own again."

His mother did a few days each week of part-time teaching at a local school. She obviously enjoyed it, but he sometimes wondered if it wasn't an escape into a world she craved, a world of social and intellectual challenge, a satisfaction denied to her at home. He remembered when he was younger. It was a time when her friends from London - those she had once worked with in the City - came to visit for the summer. Their feminine laughter would brighten the warm days. They would tease him about all the girls he knew, and he would blush, proud that they granted him the potential of female association. All these things embarrassed his father, like the immense care his mother took to entertain them with a generous table. But even he would join his wife when she played old music hall songs on the piano. Peter remembered too, her delight in the drab winter months, when she took him - his father never came - to see

17

Gilbert and Sullivan operas put on by the local Amateur Operatic Society. Then there were the nights, which maddened his father, when she managed to sneak away for a game of Whist. But all this had faded with time and she had become more subdued, her lightness of spirit overwhelmed by the cares of daily living. But these reflections could not erase the guilt of his own lie.

"Mum . . . I . . . "

"What?"

"It's nothing."

"Well, you must have had something on your mind?"

"No, no . . . Nothing important."

She got up and put on her coat.

"Supper at six."

He gave her a kiss and she left, going out through the garden, taking a short cut across the fields into the town.

Peter was climbing up the path on the West Cliffs with Helga when it dawned on him that it was already the fourth day of her visit. The ascent was less demanding than that of the cliff on the east side of the harbour and his thoughts drifted to what had they had done with their time together?

The second day it had rained and they went to a cinema. The third day he took her eastwards, along the coastal road by bus, to spend the day in Weymouth. There had been a steady drizzle, but it had not deterred them from strolling along the promenade. He had shown her the sculptures on the beach, intricate designs fashioned in the fine sand by a family who had been working there for as long as he could remember. It was the day they had fun dodging the waves. The day they carried their shoes, leaving imprints in the sand with their bare feet, and then having difficulty drying their feet and getting rid of the fine particles. The day that he took her to an afternoon tea dance, when even his clumsiness on the floor was masked by her grace and the inspiration of Glenn Miller tunes, the day they almost missed her appointed time of return to the *Joachim*.

"Peter."

"Uh."

"You were away somewhere?"

"Just thinking of all the things we've done."

"I remember the first time we met." She laughed. "You were very shy. I thought. He is an *Engländer*."

She made a face, and he felt himself blushing.

She clasped his arm.

"I make fun. Sorry."

He turned and held her tightly and kissed her and she folded into his arms.

"It is not so . . . what I thought, " she whispered.

His excitement building, and with longing fighting with the need for restraint, he moved back, seeking the safety of her hand to continue their climb up the cliffs. The desire she awakened perturbed him. He wanted her, but did she want him? When they reached the top, they followed the path along the edge, stopping now and then to look down at the sea. The sky had cleared after all the spotty rain of the last two days and the sun had made an appearance.

After some twenty minutes the path veered inland across a broad meadow. The view then changed again with a copse up ahead bordered by a hedge.

He helped her over the stile, and she ran away, laughing, her long blonde hair streaming behind.

Something unsettling gripped him, a fear of loss perhaps, for the nearness of her was suddenly replaced by a distancing. In a flash he was possessed with the need to bring her back, to feel the physical and emotional closeness which now seemed to be slipping from him.

He ran after her, wildly, shouting, Helga! Helga! And his plaintive call startled her so that she slowed, and he caught up with her, and they fell tumbling forward and over into the long grass.

And the constraints of propriety were replaced with the

now unbounded forces of desire, a need to confirm what they felt but which they had restrained. They saw in each other a depth of feeling wanting expression and they came together, becoming as one, no longer able to hold to the unnaturalness of convention.

For a blissful space in time the world was shut out. And they lay together, happy and fulfilled, thinking only of the moment.

They dozed in the sweet-smelling grass, arms around each other. It had been a spontaneous and tender experience and the warmth of the sun added to the pleasure of the moment.

It was the cry of a lark flying high overhead that invaded the quiet. Peter opened his eyes, looking across at her, motionless by his side.

"I love you, Helga," he whispered.

She leaned over and caressed him. Her eyes were moist.

"I love you, too, Peter."

She rolled on top of him, smothering him with happiness. "Peter! Peter! You are *mein* Peter, *Ja?*"

"*Ja*," he said.

He felt fulfilled. All his preoccupations had evaporated within the magic of her presence. Then gradually, in the distance, he became aware of the sound of the sea, the sea of waves and tides and movement and change, and he sat up, disturbing her.

"What's wrong, Peter?"

"Are we mad Helga? You'll be going again soon. It'll be another year of waiting?"

"I do not know . . . "

"Isn't there some way . . . Maybe? I could visit you?"

"In *Deutschland?* . . . I do not think . . . "

He felt despondent now.

"Probably not, but I have to hope."

"Peter . . . we must enjoy today. We are together. Do not worry about the future."

He put his arm around her shoulders, blissfully aware of

her presence, content now to comply with her wishes to savour the moment.

It was five o'clock when they reached the *Joachim*. He waved a farewell and set out for home.

The next afternoon was as filled with sunshine. There was a light breeze. He arrived at the *Joachim* a little earlier than usual but she was waiting. Even before he got close to her he could see her sombre expression.

"Peter . . . Oh, Peter, this is our last day."

"I thought it was tomorrow! Surely it's tomorrow?"

"Tomorrow I leave."

He stood, staring. The unwelcome news shattered his complacency.

"I see . . . well . . . "

Pushing the truth aside, resigned to the inevitable, he took her hand and they retraced the route of the first day. They picked primroses and bluebells and in the shade of the lane the cool air brought colour to their cheeks. When they arrived at the Tea Room again, the owner asked if she could put their flowers in a vase. He looked at Helga, her face mirroring the happiness he felt.

"Yes please," he said.

The owner departed with a knowing smile, returning with their flowers neatly arranged in a pair of china vases. Then she served them cream teas.

"I hope this is what you want?" Her whimsical smile left no doubt that she knew that it was.

Delighted, they began what he recognized might well be their last cream tea. The finality of it stabbed at his heart, but he fought it off, seeking hope and optimism from the agreeable atmosphere which they shared.

As they left, taking the flowers with them, they paused in the doorway to exchange kisses, but as their heads were coming together he heard his name being called, and before he could compose himself he was accosted by one of the regular churchgoers, Annie Gilbert.

"Hello Peter, so nice to see you. I heard you were on leave."

It was then that he realized that she was with her friend, Rachel.

"Hello . . . Mrs. Gilbert . . . Mrs. Samward . . . I . . . We were just having a tea . . . "

There was a pause while they waited for him to identify his friend.

"Ah, yes . . . this is Helga."

"Hello Helga," they spoke in unison, offering their hands in greeting.

Helga shook them in turn, appearing shy, nodding without speaking, an omission for which he was eternally grateful.

Another pause.

"The wildflowers are so nice at this time of year," Mrs. Samward, already intrigued by the bunches they both held, was looking intently at Helga as if trying to will an answer.

Helga just smiled.

"Well then," said Annie Gilbert, breaking the uncomfortable silence. "We'll have our turn inside . . . So nice to meet you both."

With that they entered the tearoom.

He took Helga's arm and hastened her away from the site of the encounter.

"Annie Gilbert and Rachel Samward . . . widows who live not far from us . . . now my parents will know about us . . . "

He managed a nervous laugh, and he thought how fortunate it was that the meeting had occurred on Helga's last day.

His hand moved from her arm to grasp her hand.

"Nothing to worry about," he murmured, trying to deny his consternation.

"Are you sure?"

"No . . . but then my parents would have found out. This is a small village. People talk . . . But, I'm not going to think about it."

They went back towards the harbour, but instead of going directly to the *Joachim* they went to the beach. They sat on the pea-sized shingle, picking up handfuls, letting the small stones trickle through their hands. Occasionally, they selected individual stones, admiring the range of colours and shapes, fascinated by the smoothness that the sea had wrought.

"I'm going to take some home," Helga scooped up a handful.

Unsure at first, but then recognizing that she was serious, he took out his handkerchief and she filled it.

He tied the four corners and handed it to her. Happy now, she held it up triumphantly. "It will be a memory . . . "

He felt both sad and happy. Sad because he would soon be alone again; happy for all they had been able to share.

They collected their flowers and made their way back towards the *Joachim*. They were both silent, but soon a lingering curiosity, which he had been unable to shake, claimed his attention.

"You've had a difficult time? . . . with the Captain?" he said.

He wanted her answer to the tenseness he had been feeling each time he had seen them in conversation.

"You . . . ?"

Peter nodded.

"He might tell my father . . . "

"About us?"

"*Ja* . . . "

She seemed to want to go on, but couldn't.

"Will your parents be angry?"

"I think . . . *Ja*. They will be angry. I must decide what to do . . . "

23

A pause.

"I will wait to see what the *Kapitän* does . . . "

"Is that a good idea?"

"I do not know . . . "

It was evident that she didn't want to pursue the matter any further. It appeared likely that the Captain would report to her father, but then perhaps he was just prepared to keep the decision - for he allowed them to meet - to himself. Peter thought then of the problems that he would have to confront, now not so different from those of Helga, especially after the unfortunate meeting with Annie Gilbert and her friend.

"My parents are concerned about a war?" He wanted to change the subject but he instantly regretted what he had said.

She looked surprised.

"The *Führer* does not want war with England."

"How can you be so sure? . . . Germany has just occupied Austria."

"It is good in *Deutschland* . . . people have work . . . the *Führer* made this happen. Why would he want war?"

"But why did he invade Austria?"

"Everyone agreed . . . it was part of the *Vaterland*."

"Part of Germany?"

"*Ja.*"

The conversation was getting more awkward than he intended, but there were things he had to know.

"Are you in the Hitler Youth?"

"We must join . . . girls in the *BDM, Bund Deutscher Mädchen* - boys in the *Hitler Jugend.*"

"It must be awful?"

"Peter!" She seemed astonished. "It is fun, Peter. Günther goes on hikes, goes mountaineering . . . it is being outdoors and healthy."

"I hope you didn't mind my asking?"

"I am . . . confused. You are very serious."

"Sorry . . . It was on my mind."

He wanted to drop the subject. Perhaps Helga did too? Nothing was said until she broke the silence.

"Will you write Peter?"

"Just like before . . . until you come again next year."

His attempt to create lightheartedness only seemed to intensify the gloom that enveloped them. They got up and headed slowly back towards the harbour. Within sight of the *Joachim* they sat on an upturned boat. Their silence caused him to become acutely conscious of the passage of time, a preoccupation that was intensified by a growing nervousness. It was all coming to an end and he was seized with a mood of desperation.

"Helga!".

She was watching a couple of fishermen mending their nets.

"*Ja?*"

"Will you marry me, Helga?" His voice betrayed his apprehension. He waited for her reaction.

She turned slowly and faced him. There was a discernible sadness in her eyes. He thought he glimpsed tears and, as if to mask them, she brought her face to meet his, brushing his cheek with her lips. He flung his arms around her and she hugged him tightly. He felt a sob and when he kissed her their tears ran together. The passion they felt swept them up in its grip. "We must get away from here," he said.

He found a deserted timber warehouse. It was musty and dark. The only light was from a beam of sunlight caused by a hole in the roof, but this was sufficient to confirm that it hadn't been used recently. It was full of piles of old planks and as they walked on the earthen floor the dust rose, animating the ray of sunlight with visible particles. Off to their left there was a smaller area in which were bundles of straw. Some had been pulled apart, perhaps by other trespassers?

It no longer mattered where they were, only that they were alone. Unable to contain their yearning they struggled to free themselves from restraining garments, and they made love on a bale of hay. Unlike the first time, they reached another level of fulfilment, at once more tempestuous and more satisfying in its intensity.

They stood up, brushing the hay from their clothes, trying to restore their former decorum. They looked at each other and seeing the flushed cheeks and the tender eyes, they laughed and embraced again and again, until time allowed them no more opportunity.

They returned to the upturned boat, trying to contain their ardour, and he asked again.

"Will you marry me, Helga?" He was feeling reckless now, and repeating the question increased the realization of his vulnerability. He waited.

She appeared to delay a response, regarding him patiently, displaying an air of longing, but it was tinged with anguish.

"Dear Peter . . . How can it happen? Our parents will not agree."

"But Helga . . . if we want it?"

"I do. I do, Peter." She struggled to go on. "But the time is not right . . . we must wait."

"Must we wait?"

"I think it would be best. When we are . . . of age . . . our parents cannot stop us."

"You're convinced they'll be against it?"

"Your *Mutter* and *Vater* will agree?"

No . . . "

"*Mein*, will not."

There was a finality about her words, a sense of resignation.

"I *can* wait Helga . . . as long as it takes."

She studied his expression, taking her time.

"Dear Peter . . . I can wait too."

She took his hand and squeezed it. "I will wait."

He gripped her arms as he felt his tears. So many happy hours were already becoming memories.

"I must go, Peter. It is time."

They wandered back to the *Joachim*. At the gangplank, he kissed her and she started to go aboard, but then she turned and rushed back into his arms. There were more tears, his own and hers, and they hugged again and she turned and climbed the slope to reach the deck. She waved, holding aloft the white handkerchief bulging with shingle, before she went down the hatch. He waved back. The Captain was in the stern, smoking his pipe. Peter felt his face colour, the closeness of authority troubled him, and he turned quickly away, not looking back.

When he reached the upturned boat, their flowers were still there. He thought about taking hers to the *Joachim*. He picked them up, hesitated, and then moved slowly towards the edge of the quay and dropped them into the harbour. He watched as the outgoing tide began to carry them seawards. He didn't know why he had disposed of them in that way; he hoped it was not a symbol of the end, hoped that it might be a way of committing a memory and an expectation to the care of the sea, the sea which had brought her to him.

He turned away, and when he was safely clear of the sight of the *Joachim* he slowed down - home offered little sanctuary for his feelings.

2.

Peter's father was sitting in his usual place at the head of the kitchen table, but there was no newspaper to moderate the demand in his question.

"What's going on?"

Peter felt himself blushing.

His mother brought his breakfast to the table and sat down.

"I met this girl . . . "

"So I've heard . . . " His father's voice sounded bitter now.

"Mrs. Gilbert?"

"Yes . . . bloody embarrassing when your neighbours know more about things."

My God, the gossipy bitches didn't waste any time. But his father was waiting. He would have to reveal his secret. He took a deep breath.

"It was when I was on leave last spring. She was on the *Joachim*. It had come in the first day I went to the harbour. She invited me on board for a visit, and we became friendly. We spent part of each day of her stay together. When it came back, she was on board - she promised me she'd try and return."

"My God, she's German?" His father admitted to the unthinkable.

"Yes . . . her name is Helga - Helga *Jansen*."

"That's where you've been?"

"Yes."

"Bit underhanded, isn't it?"

"I didn't think you'd approve?"

Harry looked at Elizabeth.

"Did you know?"

"No . . . No . . . " Her attempt at evasion only heightened the feeling that she knew something. Peter thought of the letters on the table, and the bed his mother had made up.

Harry brightened.

"But the *Joachim* left - so it's all over?"

"No, we plan to keep in touch."

"You must be out of your mind," his father was aghast. "You mean you've been conned by a foreigner you don't know - know nothing about. My God, she could be a spy . . . and you're in the navy - the Royal Navy - that might have to defend the country against such people."

"Dad . . . I've not been conned into anything. She's a human being, just like us. She doesn't want war any more than you or me."

"How old is she?"

"Eighteen . . . she's studying at the University of Hamburg . . . Her father owns a shipping company."

"So that makes it all right . . . She's still a German, for God's sake!"

His mother shifted uneasily.

"I forbid you to have anything more to do with her!" he said.

"Harry," His mother jumped in. "Aren't you being a little drastic?"

"I'm not the one who's drastic . . . "

Peter stood up.

"I don't think it's any of your business. It's between me and Helga."

"Helga!" He spat out the word. "Good name for a German wench!"

"I'm going to my room. I'm not going to sit here and listen to this."

He ran upstairs to his room, slammed the door, and collapsed on his bed.

An hour later there was a knock on the bedroom door.

"Who is it?"

"Me," his mother answered.

"Don't? . . . "

She entered and placed a cup of tea on the bedside table.

"You must have known your father would react this way?"

"I suppose, but I expected a little understanding. Instead, I was treated like a child."

"Well, let's just let things settle down a bit."

"I'm sorry, Mother, but I have to decide what to do."

"Peter - I knew all about it."

"How could you?"

"I saw the letters on the table here - I noticed the German stamps and the Hamburg postmark . . . I didn't read them but, well, it wasn't hard to put two and two together . . . "

"You told Father?"

"Of course not . . . It was Mrs. Samward, then . . . well, you supplied him with the rest."

"Has he gone?"

"Yes."

"Mother - before we go any further. I've decided to leave after lunch. I'm going to stay with my navy friend, Stephen, in Cornwall. I'll take the bus to Axminster and catch the train there - it's a much faster route."

She slumped down into the nearest chair.

"Must you do this? - I know your father was pretty tactless, but underneath all the anger there's a genuine concern for your welfare. It saddened him you were not with him at breakfast."

"But has he apologized? No, he has not. Will he listen to me - try and understand my point of view - no? He never has and he never will . . . "

She started to interrupt but he went on. "Mother. I have to do this for my own sake. I know I'm hurting you but I don't see a way out. Perhaps, after a few days I'll be able to put it all in perspective - I don't know. All I know is I must leave now."

She fidgeted.

"Please don't try and stop me."

"I . . ."

She turned away and left, unable to mask a frantic searching for her handkerchief.

It was a difficult lunch. Peter wanted to get it over with and when he was finished he went upstairs to pack. When he came down his mother was waiting in the hall.

"I'm going to the bus with you," she said firmly.

It was a short distance to the centre of the village. Unlike the day he'd arrived, when they were full of happy chatter, they were both quiet, a light rain and fog contributing to their introspection.

The bus appeared and they stood staring at each other, not knowing what to say. Tears came to his mother's eyes and, overcome with remorse, he hugged and kissed her.

"Promise me you'll stay with us for a few days before your leave ends?"

He felt terrible, but the difficulty of dealing with his father overcame his compassion for his mother.

"I can't promise because I really don't know - I have to think . . . "

He kissed her again and climbed aboard.

The bus started to move and he waved from the window until she faded from view.

3.

The *Joachim* arrived in Hamburg in the early hours of the morning. It had traversed, in darkness, some ninety-five kilometres of the Elbe river, southwards from the point where its estuary joined the North Sea. The dawn was breaking, lighting up the spire of St. Michael's Church, the sighting that all sailors welcomed as confirmation that they were home and soon to be rejoined with their families. They passed the Fish Market and reached their berth in the inner harbour. A company car had been dispatched by her father, Rolf, to take her to the ferry dock, Helga having decided to travel to her home in Blankenese by the water route. She took her leave of *Kapitän Hopp*, thanking him for letting her make the trip, wondering what he had thought of her liaison with Peter and whether word of it would get back to her father.

An hour later, as the sun rose higher in the clear sky, Helga sat on the upper deck of the ferry out of Hamburg as it made its way back down the Elbe towards Blankenese, retracing the way the *Joachim* had come in the early morning darkness. There was a cool breeze off the river and she could have gone below instead of subjecting herself to the exposed deck, but she liked the feeling of space, the rush of air caused by the boat's forward motion contributing to a sense of freedom. It was the invigorating feeling to which she had become accustomed aboard the *Joachim* as, far out at sea, it had rolled gently in the swell or headed steadily into a stiff wind.

The view from the top deck of the ferry was always impressive. Once clear of the quays of the busy port, the city was soon left behind and the near bank, although still showing signs of habitation, took on more of the looks of the country.

The tree-covered shore became steeper, rising up from the narrow stretches of beach where families would soon frolic in the summer sun. The chestnut trees were showing signs of blossoming, whites and pinks beginning to dot the canopies of foliage, and she thought of Peter and England, and she wondered what he might be doing. More than likely he was back aboard his ship, or perhaps he was sitting on the beach where they shared their last hour together, gazing out to sea as he ran the shingle through his hands, looking at the fine stones, thinking of her, counting the days to the next reunion.

She looked ahead, to the high point of land which they were approaching. She could understand why her father had picked this location. From the top of the hill there was a commanding view of the vast river. To the left was the last stage of the journey of the merchant ships making their way into the Port of Hamburg. To the right, disappearing into the distance, was the ribbon of water which eventually broadened into the Elbe estuary.

Blankenese hove in sight, a collection of houses nestling among the trees. Her eyes scanned the peaceful scene, quickly locating the family house with its distinctive cupola from where her father, binoculars in hand, would watch the ships plying in and out of the Port. His captains were well aware of his habit, especially on weekends or in the long summer evenings, causing them to be a trifle more precise about departure and arrival times.

She could see the whole house now with its distinctive red-tiled roof capping the three stories below. The cupola rose above the line of the roof so that it provided an unobstructed view of the river and the surrounding land. The third level had extensive balconies facing towards the river and the windows on the second level offered a pleasant view of the slope down to the shoreline. There was a large garden at the back with apple and pear trees, a once favourite spot where Helga and her brother played.

The ferry slowed as it approached the dock and she could see the waiting crowd, the blacks and browns of the uniforms of a few boys from the *Hitler Jugend* contrasting strongly with the colourful spring dresses and the wide-brimmed hats of the women, and the more restrained but informal sports-like attire of the men - the informality being epitomized by the demeanour of a group returning from a round of golf. She spotted her mother and father, standing erect as they always did, she smartly dressed in a patterned dress and sweater and holding a parasol, he, businesslike in a dark blue suit, giving the impression that a special mark of respect was called for. It was her mother Ilse who spotted her first, waving and pointing, distracting her father Rolf from his preoccupation with the docking process. Now he was waving and Helga waved back before collecting her knapsack and disappearing below the deck on her way ashore.

There were hugs of greeting and then they all strolled over to the Mercedes parked beyond the ferry dock. Heinrich the chauffeur saluted smartly, took her knapsack, and opened the doors.

"Is Günther home yet?" said Helga as they began to move off. Her preoccupation with the coming reunion had bothered her all day. She hadn't seen her brother for some months before departing for England as she had gone to the *Joachim* directly from the University. She felt close to her brother and this closeness would make it difficult to disguise her feelings. She knew he would want to know why England had become such an attraction.

"He's expected this afternoon. He insisted on hiking in from Hamburg," There was a note of pride in her father's voice.

"I don't know why." Ilse didn't share her husband's enthusiasm.

"Does him good? Besides, all his friends did the same."

Rolf *Jansen* was a tall man with an imposing presence. Slightly older than Ilse at fifty-two, he was a natural leader, somewhat cold and aloof and impatient with incompetence, a man of the old school, but to Günther and Helga he was a loving father. Ilse was, by contrast, warm and understanding and with a strength of character usually well able to cope with the restlessness which went with Rolf's ambitions. She was only slightly shorter than Rolf, with a slim athletic figure which belied her forty five years. Adding to her charm was a pleasant angular face, with blue eyes and fair hair. In great measure she resembled her daughter.

Helga was in her bedroom on the third floor unpacking her knapsack when Günther arrived back. She heard the commotion and started down to greet him. Her parents were already at the front door.

"Heil Hitler!"

She stopped on the second landing, startled to see Günther's raised arm. The gesture didn't seem appropriate in the family home. Nevertheless, tanned and fit, a tall strapping figure with fair hair and blue eyes, with his knapsack still on his back, he held his arm outstretched, waiting for a reaction.

There was an awkward silence. Rolf looked questioningly at Ilse and then with calm deliberation extended his hand in a conventional greeting. Günther hesitated, then lowered his hand, took his father's hand in his, and shook it politely.

It had been a tense moment and Helga could feel Günther's relief when he looked up and caught sight of her. With a few gigantic leaps he came up to greet her as she continued down. The meeting almost precipitated a fall and Helga had to restrain them both by a tight hold on the banister. With demonstrable joy he hugged and kissed her.

"Helga! I hoped you'd be here." He turned to look down at his parents.

"I'll just get rid of this gear."

"Freshen up dear and then come and get some lunch," said Ilse.

"Yes, Mother."

He continued up to his bedroom while her father, motioning Helga to wait, came up to accompany her to the living room on the second floor.

"What do you think of your brother?" he said, and the implication that there might be some cause for worry troubled her.

"He looks the same as ever," she said.

"I'm glad you think so."

Ilse came in with cups of coffee. Helga took one and sat quietly, taking in the parental behaviour and thinking how different things were from life at the university.

"I thought you might need this," her mother smiled as she offered Rolf a cup.

"He doesn't lack enthusiasm," Rolf observed.

Her mother settled opposite them. "I would call it commitment."

Rolf put his cup on the table. "I wish there was a little less gesturing."

The conversation was conducted as though Helga wasn't there, yet it was obvious by their side glances that they wanted her to hear, perhaps it was their way of testing her reaction without having to admit they valued it.

"It's what he's been taught Father." As much as she disliked Günther's actions, it bothered her to hear her parents talking about him like this.

"I know Helga, but it's new to your mother and me."

Günther could be heard descending the stairs and her parents stood up, as if wanting to mask their covert conversation. Helga got up too and they all moved off towards the dining room. If Günther noticed their discomfort, he didn't reveal it.

Seated at the table, Helga felt happy to be with them all again although the tenseness provoked by Günther's greeting remained. With Minna the housekeeper fussing over them, the talk turned to the activities of the Easter holidays. Helga listened with keen interest to what her brother had done.

"We went by train to Goslar. Then we had four days in the mountains - Wonderful!"

"How many of you?" asked Rolf.

"About forty all together. No one from around here though, except Mark, the fellow I met last year. He lives in Hamburg."

"You didn't mind the discipline?"

"It gets a bit tough, but you have to be organized."

Rolf's questions seemed stiff, lacking warmth or genuine interest.

"How was England Helga?"

Günther's question caught her by surprise. She had been thinking how hard her father and mother were trying to come to grips with Hitler's new programs for young people.

"It was very different. The spring is later there."

"You don't sound very enthusiastic?" said Günther.

"I'm tired . . . it was very pleasant . . . I enjoyed it."

"I'll bet you did." There was a sharp edge in Günther's voice.

Helga felt herself blushing, but Günther continued.

"Must be a boyfriend?"

"It's . . . " She felt hot and confused. She had no idea how to confront her brother's assault for that's how it was beginning to feel.

"None of my business . . . is that what you're going to tell me? Well, it is my business when my sister is stupid enough to lust after an Englishman."

Helga struggled to regain her composure, unable to think of a response, appalled by her brother's attitude.

"Günther, that's enough," Ilse spoke sharply. "You're making accusations that are false."

Helga faced her mother's questioning eyes. She had the impression that she wanted to hear her denial, and not wishing to lie she turned away. Günther looked towards his father as if to seek support, but Rolf was either disinterested or anxious to avoid a family conflict.

Helga found the silence that followed unbearable. She wanted to escape to her room to deal with her own contradictions. Fortunately, Minna came in to clear away the places. In a calm voice, suggesting a normality which didn't exist, Ilse spoke.

"Minna - Would you bring the dessert. And we'll have the coffee in the study."

She turned back to her family.

"I hope you like it. I made it myself - *Streuselkuchen.*"

4.

*H*is Majesty's Ship, Saram, had been in commission for some six months. It was a brand-new minesweeper and Peter and Stephen had joined it shortly after it had completed its acceptance trials. Presently, she was berthed alongside the naval dockyard in Devonport on the south coast. She looked prim in her new coat of paint, the result of the labours of the crew prior to the commencement of the leave just ending. The painting exercise was a much debated subject. Most of the crew members regarded it as an unnecessary undertaking given that the ship was barely in service, but their Captain apparently felt it important to keep the sailors occupied until they moved into active minesweeping operations.

Peter strode up the gangplank and faced towards the stern. He saluted the White Ensign fluttering majestically in the light breeze.

"Good leave then, Gray?"

The Duty Quartermaster gave a look that suggested the fun was over and it was now time to buckle down to some hard work. If only he knew how tumultuous a leave it had been.

"Stephen Trantor's 'bin looking for you," he said.

"He's back already?"

"Yea, one of those keen types."

Peter went forward to his mess on the starboard side. There was no one there so he dumped his things on his locker and sat down, silently reflecting upon the events that had marked the end of his leave. His sudden departure from home and the flight to Cornwall to see Stephen had not been as rewarding as he had hoped. Stephen, like Peter's parents, had questioned the wisdom of his association with Helga, even inferring that lust had driven his actions and that it would be anything but a lasting relationship - something best forgotten. Bitterly disappointed, he had returned home to a still intransigent father, and a mother despairing of what was happening to the family she had worked so hard to prove was normal and happy. He got up and, trying to shake off his pessimism, set out to find Stephen. He was in a generating room on the deck below, lying on a work bench.

"Loafing again are we? . . . what's up?"

"Pete!" Stephen peeped out from behind the covers of the Zane Grey Western he was reading. "How'd the leave end?"

"Not bad . . . Hell, that's not true. Father's being difficult."

"The Fraulein?"

"You mean, Helga?"

"Jesus, Pete. Who the hell d'you think I mean?"

"I'm sticking with my commitment."

"Sometimes you're so fucking stuck up . . ."

Peter ignored the taunt. "I intend to marry her."

"It'll pass . . . "

"Christ, Stephen, you're a bastard!"

"A bloody realist."

"Well, you can sink in your bloody realism."

Peter strode away and Stephen called after him.

"Heard the buzz?"

"What?"

"Minesweeping exercises start earlier."

"The Captain's in a God-damned hurry?"

"It doesn't bother you - Helga and all? I thought you'd be pissed off?"

Peter stopped and shrugged. Whatever happened wouldn't change his feelings for Helga, and how could a long spell of sea duty matter? It would certainly be better than being stuck alongside the dockyard.

"If you want to natter . . . " Stephen appeared apologetic.

"It's all right . . . "

40

Peter kept on walking. He didn't need any more of Stephen's 'sage' advice.

The next day he received a letter from his mother.

Dear Peter,

I was saddened by your abrupt departure and so was your father, although he will never admit to feelings like that. I hope you come to see us before your leave ends, but if you don't, just remember that we care about you and don't want to see you unhappy, but neither do we want to see you make a fool of yourself.

However much you are attracted to this girl you must consider the impossibility of it going anywhere. You are young - look for an English girl, someone you can settle with, who will share your own values, not someone from another country - especially Germany.

I don't want to preach but I do worry about you.

If we don't see you this leave, make sure you come at Christmas.

Your loving mother

It was more of the same and unexpected. His mother had not mentioned the letter when he went home again, after Cornwall, before his leave had ended. Perhaps she was embarrassed by it, but she had written it, it was after all a reflection of her thoughts. His mother, whom he had thought was on his side, had apparently placed herself among the growing body of sceptics. Well, no matter what they thought or said he was in love with Helga. Still, he wished he had received a more positive letter from her, one which offered him a little support.

41

It was not until the end of the month that a letter came from Germany. He found a quiet spot and opened the familiar blue envelope.

Dear Peter,

We arrived in Hamburg after a calm trip. We left early because there was fog. We did not see the piers much because of the fog and rain. Later the wind was stronger and the sun came out. It stayed all the way. I am at the *Universität* in Hamburg again. I stayed with my parents in Blankenese before returning to Hamburg and the room I share with three other girls.

Dear Peter, I always remember our days together. It is like a dream now but I know it was not. I can't forget your arms around me, the warm kisses. Every moment of our time together is full of sunlight and flowers. Like an *englischer* spring.

Life is, like always, full of problems we read about in the papers. I don't believe that *Deutschland* wants war and England must understand that but I am still afraid.

My darling, please write soon.
Love,
Helga.

He reread it. Although excited by her display of affection, he was bothered by the clear signs of the mounting political crisis which neither of them could avoid. He had just read in the daily newspaper that a high German official had implied that the masses feared war. But what did that mean when the politicians seemed confused about Germany's intentions? He felt uneasy about the concessions that were being made to assuage Germany's territorial ambitions even though they appeared to have a certain logic about them.

He looked at the picture of Helga which he kept in his wallet. There was little opportunity for privacy aboard ship, and he had not told any of his mates - except Stephen - that his attractive girlfriend was German.

That night, as he lay in his hammock, he composed a reply.

Dear Helga,

It was difficult to go back to the daily routine after your visit, it was just like the first time all over again, but I have the memory of those glorious days with you. We had fun, didn't we? I'm looking at your picture and the sun glints in your hair. I love everything about you - your eyes and your smile, your wonderful sense of humour and your passion for life and living. We must find a way to get back together and I wish, like you, we didn't have to contend with all this political nonsense that's going on.

I keep thinking how strange it is that Günther will soon be in the Navy like me.

Please darling, don't worry about what others think, or trouble yourself with world events. I'm sure everything will work out all right.

All my love,
Peter.

He put down his pen. The last paragraph was ridiculous. How could she not be affected by world events, just as he would be? Nevertheless, he decided to leave it. They both needed some hope no matter how unrealistic it might be. He addressed the envelope, and was reminded again of the geography and the ideologies that separated them.

The next morning he went to the post box, deposited his letter, and returned to the mess. He considered writing to his parents, he owed them a letter, but he wasn't in the mood. In any event, Stephen arrived with an Illustrated London News, an old one published in 1936.

"Look at this, Pete."

Peter took the magazine reluctantly. It was open at the double centre page which showed what was purporting to be the New German Navy, an impressive array of new and old vessels.

"Makes you think, mate?" Stephen stood waiting for his reaction but he had none. He just stared into space and Stephen, annoyed by his lack of response, turned away.

"You can keep it," he shot back.

Peter looked again at the illustrations. What did it all mean? Were these the ships of the navy he would fight? He'd never given much thought to actual war, and combat and dying. He'd been pushed into the Royal Navy by his family. It was not that he hadn't always been attracted by the sea. It was the furtive way he had been committed to serve. There had never been a full explanation of why they did it, nor had there been any serious attempt to find out what he thought of the idea. Lately though, he had to admit that he was beginning to accept, in spite of his father's continuing practice of deciding what was best for him, that there was some esteem in being a member of Britain's Senior Service. But now, the enemy of boys' story books and of those who died - the names engraved on war memorials - the focal point of annual remembrances - took on another meaning. And this so-called enemy was not nameless anymore. He was in love with a person called Helga *Jansen*, and they had kissed and made love and shared a common emotion and a common fear - that war might come between them.

He felt dejected, a pawn in some risky game being played out by politicians, those that had little sympathy for love between persons of different cultures.

5.

$\mathcal{I}$t was a Saturday in mid June and Hamburg was crowded. Helga had left the University in the morning, having suggested to her mother that they meet to do some shopping. The real reason for the meeting, however, was to be revealed later.

Her mother joined her at an outdoor café on the *Jungfernstieg,* the upscale shopping district overlooking the Lake, and they had toured the stores all day, stopping only for a light lunch. It was around four in the afternoon when they caught the train back to Blankenese. By this time her mother was showing signs of weariness.

"I'll be glad to get home," Ilse said, as she settled into her seat.

"You're not the only one Mother," Helga sat beside her.

"It's nice to have a good shop though . . . and, I bought a new hat." Her mother cradled the large cardboard box.

"Will Father like it?" Helga feared that he might not even notice it.

"I don't care what he thinks . . . Anyway. I'll tell him you like it."

"Mother! Helga admonished. " I do like it, but . . . "

Ilse gave a self-satisfied smile.

"I'm so glad you get home from university now and again."

It was nice to be so near home, and to be able to be with the family, but there were times when the closeness felt like an unnecessary obstacle and this was certainly one of those occasions.

"It's not like I'm far away, Mother." Helga knew she sounded irritable but the time for pleasantries was passing rapidly; she had to deal with her problem. Her mother was rambling on.

"But it's not home . . . "

Ilse paused, adopting a penetrating stare that usually marked the beginning of a few well-considered questions.

"Is there something wrong . . . you've been, well . . . preoccupied?"

"It's nothing."

"I hope you'll tell me if it's anything I can help with?"

My God, Helga murmured silently. She had forgotten her mother's uncanny ability to read her mood.

The train stopped at a station and more people clambered aboard.

"You know," her mother began, as if to try and lower the tension. "When we first moved out to Blankenese, the trains were never this busy. We built the house because it was near the water. It was what your father wanted."

"You've told me Mother," her voice reflected agitation.

"I suppose I have, but I remember when we moved . . . I was living in Hamburg then . . . "

Helga plucked at a strand of her hair "When will father be home?"

"Probably late. I've asked Minna to get dinner for six o'clock . . . why do you ask . . . are you anxious to see him?"

"Yes . . . ah, no . . . I thought you and I could have a talk?"

"So there is something?"

Of course there was, her mother had known it all along, so why must she feign ignorance, but this was not the place to discuss it.

"I knew there was something . . . "

"Mother, please." She had to think and she needed more time. "Can we wait till we get home?"

Ilse reached over and touched her hand and Helga turned away, unable to cope with her gesture of sympathy.

46

They took the short walk from the station and, when they neared the house, Helga hastened on ahead and then stopped, waiting for her mother to catch up.

"Don't wait for me." Ilse motioned her on.

She ran ahead, opening the door, making for her bedroom on the third floor, almost colliding with Minna who was sweeping the hallway.

As she started up the stairs, she heard Minna talking to her mother.

"Is there anything wrong Ma'am?"

"It's all right. We'll have some coffee and cake . . . in the living room."

When Helga came downstairs to the living room on the second floor, her mother was sitting on the sofa reading, so she sat down in the armchair opposite her.

Minna came in with the tray.

Ilse handed Helga a cup of coffee and she added sugar.

"A piece of cake?"

Helga shook her head.

"So, what is it you want to tell me?"

Helga stood up slowly and walked towards the window. There was no easy way, and the enormity of the confession to come was too daunting. When she turned to face her mother, tears were trickling down her face.

"Mum . . . I'm pregnant!"

"Oh! No!"

Ilse almost dropped her cup, the coffee splashing over her dress, but she ignored the damage, staring back in disbelief.

"How could you possibly be pregnant?"

Helga watched her mother dab her dress with her handkerchief.

"Who's responsible? Is it a student at the University? - God, I never wanted you to go to Hamburg on your own."

"He's in England!"

"What! . . . Of course, another thing I was against - letting you go on the *Joachim.*"

Helga slumped down in the armchair. It was not the time to say that she was grown up and able to take care of herself. Or more truthfully, to say that she had welcomed the chance to escape the constraints of home.

"Don't tell me that you have some insane notion that this Englishman will come here - live in *Deutschland* - become your husband?"

"He's in the Royal Navy. I don't see how I can expect that mother."

Ilse sighed. "This will finish your father."

"I'm sorry. I didn't mean . . . " She didn't know what she meant only that she wanted to get it all out, have done with it.

"But you let it happen. Unless you were raped?"

For a brief moment she thought her mother hoped that she would agree.

"No . . . No. It wasn't like that."

"Do you realize what you've done? The shame you're bringing to our family?"

Helga stood up, her face mirroring her determination.

"I love Peter. I want to marry him."

"But how do you know he'll marry you?"

"I believe he will - we made promises to each other."

"What about your studies? God, Helga, you're only eighteen!"

Ilse stood up. There was a large coffee stain on her dress.

"I'll have to change."

She turned to go but then looked back.

"Your father will have to be told."

"I know," she sighed.

It was her father's response that she feared the most. There had never been a crisis of this magnitude in the family and she had no idea how he might react.

Helga was in her bedroom when her father returned. He was late and she heard him trying to counter her mother's frustration. She got up from the bed, closing the door silently, reaching the stairs, descending slowly, one step at a time, listening to the animated conversation.

"I'm sorry dear. I couldn't get away. Three ships were leaving. The captains needed my instructions . . . "

"But Rolf. You promised . . . "

"Ilse!" His voice had a note of despair. "Haven't you heard the news? The French have stated again that they will stand by Czechoslovakia. The English will probably join them."

"There'll be war?" Ilse worried.

He held up his hands in a despairing gesture. "I don't know."

Ilse sat on the bottom stair, her head in her hands.

Helga ran down the last few stairs.

"Father!"

He held out his arms and she rushed into them, and he hugged her and held her at arms' length.

"You look well Helga. University life must agree with you."

She blushed and turned away.

Nothing was said about her problem over dinner, the talk turned to the political crisis and what it might mean, but she felt sure that her father had already sensed that something was amiss. After the coffee had been served, her mother took her aside.

"Your father's in the study. I suggest you go and talk to him."

"Have you? . . . " she began, hoping to find out what had been discussed, but her mother gave her a gentle push. When she knocked on the study door there was only silence. She thought of Günther and how much she missed his presence. She needed his brotherly support. Even his anger would be acceptable - although she knew he would have taken his father's side in the matter - at least they could have talked and argued on

49

equal terms, not like this where the weight of parental authority threatened to crush all hope of a meaningful discourse.

She was just about to knock again when her father called her in.

He was sitting behind his large oak desk. He seemed to become more formidable in this setting. With the rows of books behind him and the bulwark of oak in front of him, he was emotionally apart from her, ready to wield his authority. She walked over to the window which looked out over the river. The reunion with Peter seemed so far away now, so far removed from the innocent and protected life she had led here.

"What do you want to talk about Helga?"

She turned towards him, but when she opened her mouth to speak, the words wouldn't come and she felt her eyes moisten. Her father got up, responding quickly to her distress, abandoning his remoteness. He rushed over and hugged her.

The gesture only heightened her discomfort. The tears came more freely and she sobbed, losing control, her whole body shuddering. He led her to a chair and then he poured some *Schnaps*. She took it reluctantly.

"Take your time," he said, sitting in the chair beside her. "Just talk when you feel able . . . I'll leave you alone if you like?"

"No," she said, fearing aloneness, "I'll be all right in a minute." She sipped at her drink and then placed it, her hand shaking, on the table beside her. She looked into his eyes.

"Father," she began, but his kindly eyes were too disconcerting and she looked down, avoiding his gaze, putting her hand to her forehead.

"I'm pregnant!"

He downed the rest of his drink.

"I see," he said, as if responding to a legal matter. He got up and poured himself another drink, then he walked over to the window, not looking back at her. She continued.

"I met this boy . . . in England . . . we became friendly

and . . ."

"More than friendly it seems?" He was angry now.

"We were intimate . . . It happened just before I left . . . we're in love?"

He turned towards her, eyes blazing.

"My God! Don't you understand? We could be at war with England? . . . "

"I don't understand . . . the *Führer* doesn't want war."

Helga felt stunned, betrayed, war was not a possibility she had considered.

He swung around.

"But war it might be!"

"I love him Father."

"Was it love or merely physical desire?"

"It wasn't like that."

He toyed with his drink.

"Whatever it was, we now have a family crisis to face. Does this boy know?"

"No - I've written to him but I didn't know then."

"Would he marry you?"

"Yes - he'd marry me." The strength of her reply, given her father's resistance, surprised her.

"But how could he . . . unless of course he came here or you went to England and it's ridiculous to think of that, especially now, at a time like this!"

"He's in the Royal Navy. He couldn't come here without deserting."

"The *Englische Marine*?"

"Yes."

"No, No!" He banged his fist on the table, appearing to be bothered more by the Royal Navy than her predicament. "You must end the relationship . . . now."

Helga felt the tears welling up again and he walked over and stood beside her.

"It's for the best." He spoke softly now.

She felt only outrage and looking up, held his eyes in hers.

"I love him and I want to marry him!"

He got up and moved back behind his desk.

"It's a noble gesture, but it's not acceptable. I want to discuss this with your mother. Go upstairs Helga . . . get some rest. I'll talk to her tonight. You'll have our decision in the morning."

"Don't I have a say in this?" She was indignant now.

"Leave it to us Helga."

His authority restored, Helga realized that it was useless to argue. She dragged herself towards the door, not looking back, closing it quietly behind her. She considered trying to get in touch with Günther, but he was in Cuxhaven undergoing an interview for acceptance into the *Kriegsmarine*.

That night she slept badly. Contemplations about her condition were swept aside by thoughts of war and what it might mean. At one point she awoke calling for Peter and then in the darkness she waited to find out if anyone had heard, but the large house guaranteed a sleeper's privacy, its vastness stifling the sounds of her distress, and no one came. In the morning when she went down for breakfast, she was feeling dreadful. Her mother met her at the bottom of the stairs.

"I've put your breakfast out."

Before Helga could ask any questions, her mother motioned her to follow. They headed towards the dining room.

"This is Father's doing?"

Ilse ignored her question.

"When you've finished, go to his study."

Helga looked at the freshly cut breads and the cold meats and she pushed the plate aside, opting for the coffee. She felt very alone, a prisoner waiting for the jury to announce its verdict. What she wanted was a chance to talk, to unburden herself. It wasn't a question of explaining, for she couldn't explain what had driven her to act as she did. It was an impulse that she had succumbed to.

She sat quietly. She was in no hurry to face her parents.

There was a knock at the door.

"Have you finished?" It was her mother.

"Yes, Mother."

She didn't get up immediately. Like an actor waiting to go on stage she was suddenly seized with the terror of exposure. She gritted her teeth and walked towards the door.

When she entered the study, her parents were already seated. Her father was behind his desk, her mother sitting opposite him. Beside her was an empty chair. When Helga was seated, her father began.

"Your Mother and I feel you have let us down . . . have failed to live up to the confidence we placed in you in allowing you to make the trip to England."

Helga moved to speak, but her father continued.

"I've thought of dismissing *Kapitän Hopp* whom I entrusted with the task of looking after your welfare."

"No, no," Helga pleaded.

Ignoring her protestation, her father continued. "But I have decided not to do this. He told me he felt he could trust you, but you broke that trust by your irresponsibility. I had assumed that my daughter had high moral standards, but it appears that I was mistaken. I considered you old enough to be trusted and you've misplaced that trust."

"We are very sad you allowed this to happen," said Ilse.

"He's very nice, kind and gentle, I'm sure you would like him," Helga pleaded for understanding. "I'm in love with him,"

"Love is no excuse for bearing a child out of wedlock," her mother said. "Or for that matter giving yourself so freely to someone you hardly knew, and whom you may never see again."

"Marriage and the bearing of children are sacred commitments no matter what views you have been fed at those BDM meetings," said her father. "What you face may seem like a justifiable penalty for your actions . . ."

"But I want the baby - it's mine and Peter's."

"You may feel that way, but the child will be illegitimate and that's what we have to think about."

He hesitated as if reluctant to go on.

"We want you to have an abortion."

The import of the blunt statement didn't immediately register, but when it did Helga was possessed by a terror that was beyond containment. She leapt out of her chair and ran from the rocm crying and screaming.

When she reached her bedroom she bolted the door and flung herself on the bed.

6.

$\mathcal{P}$eter looked forward to Helga's letters. Ever since his return to HMS Saram they had arrived with unfailing regularity and he had responded, keeping up the flow of correspondence, but as the summer advanced and he had begun to think about a spell of home leave, they had stopped. It was more than a month since he had heard from her. Then a letter came at the end of July.

Dearest Peter,

You can see that I write from *München*. Three weeks ago I went home to see my parents in Blankenese and we had a fight. I am sorry it was about you. *Vater* says that I must end it but I don't want to. *Mutter* tried to get *Vater* to change his mind but he didn't. They sent me to *München* to live with my *Grossmutter* here.   I will probably go to the *Universität* here.

I want you to know that I love you and that I will always love you. I will write you when I can and let you know how I am. I hope that you will write to me.

Vater also says that I should not write to someone in England because it will cause difficulties if someone finds out. I think that is nonsense.

I am going to look at your photo again and to read my diary of my visits to England.

Love,
Helga.

It was a distressing letter. Given the disagreement with his own parents, Peter felt more isolated. Surely she must feel the same. Yet the letter was confusing. Why was she being sent to Munich?   Helga was not telling the full story. He hadn't much time to speculate on the cause before he left for his summer leave.

His mother met him at the station. She looked weary and he felt responsible for it. His last leave had been especially disruptive. The disagreement with his father over Helga had not, as he had hoped, been confined to the two of them. He could sense that his mother, having taken his side in spite of her own reservations, was caught in the middle, trying to be fair to both aspects of the argument.   It had taken its toll on her health, he could see that, but he was reluctant to draw her out on the subject.

The sun was high in the blue cloud-flecked sky, a beautiful summer's day. There was a refreshing breeze blowing across the open field as they took the usual footpath home. The high sweet scented grass awaited mowing. The scene reminded him of happier, brighter times, a spring with Helga, gone now like the change of seasons.

"He's so moody these days," she said.   "He works too much . . . doesn't eat well, shuns conversation."

"Is Dad unwell?"

"No, No . . . it's not that. I think he's still angry with you."

"I'm sorry . . ."

"I don't think he's right, but neither do I think you're being very sensible."

Not wanting to be lured into another inconclusive argument he remained silent, and they trudged on, their feet kicking up little swirls of dust which testified to the lack of rain.

When they arrived home, his mother made tea and they sat in the living room.

"I've had a long talk with your father. He regrets his outburst."

He sighed, a deep intake of breath and a noisy expiration.

"That doesn't mean he's changed his mind about things, but he admits that he was too quick to condemn."

"I'd like to believe you, Mother."

"Well, I'm not saying any more. It's up to him to deal with the matter."

It was evident that his parents were intent on reopening the issue. He went up to his room and waited.

Peter and his father sat in the living room with glasses of sherry. It wasn't Peter's favourite drink but he felt he had to show some flexibility if the reunion with his father was to start on a positive note.

"Peter. I want to apologize for my outburst."

Peter made a move to speak but his father motioned him to wait.

"You were quite right - it's none of my business, but I can't see the point of it. I know how you feel but, well . . . because of the way things are with Germany it's hardly the time to be getting involved . . . "

"With a potential enemy?" Peter interjected.

"I'm not saying it's going to happen, but the present situation has all the signs that I remember from the last war."

"I don't think you have any idea of how I feel. Anyhow, I intend to correspond with Helga, to weigh the conditions as they arise, not jump to conclusions."

"That's your decision. I'm not going to interfere."

"In other words, you don't agree?"

"No. I don't agree, but I've tried to be reasonable. I don't want to argue about it. I hope you'll also understand I don't want to hear anything more about it."

"You're washing your hands of the whole thing?"

"Quite frankly, I hope you'll come to your senses . . . now let's forget it."

His father proffered his hand and Peter shook it as if

concluding a deal to change their relationship without getting a divorce.

Over the next few days he tried to put aside further thoughts about the subject.   He told himself that the matter was now closed and that things could once again return to some kind of normality.   But relations with his parents were still difficult.   He couldn't overlook what they had said about his association with Helga.   Most of all he saw it as an unwarranted interference in his personal life.

For days on end he took lonely walks on the beach.   Each day would be different.   The sea could be rough, the waves rolling in to crash with a thunderous roar, stirring up the shingle and creating a sound like rough sandpaper being drawn over a wooden surface.

Some days he took bags of stale bread, selecting pieces to throw to the seagulls who would emit piercing cries as they fought over the choice morsels.   Other days there would be no wind, the sea like a sheet of glass, with the water lapping quietly at the shoreline.   When the rain at last broke the long dry spell he bundled up warmly, enjoying the wetness and looking out to sea, trying to pierce the mist, fantasizing that the *Joachim* would emerge with Helga aboard.

He knew his actions were upsetting his parents, and during the last few days of his leave he tried to be with them more, making polite conversation and joining his mother for endless cups of tea, but the effort was too forced to be of much help.

His mother saw him off at the station.

"It's been difficult, Peter, I know.   But you have to believe we love you."

Peter was overcome by a rush of affection.

"I'm sorry Mother. I've not been in the best of spirits."

He looked into her eyes, and when he saw the despair he felt a compassion which swept away his reclusiveness.

He hugged her tightly.

"I'm so sorry."

"It's all right dear. I understand."

He knew then, that in spite of everything, he loved her dearly, knew most of all that it was her quiet strength that kept the family together.   In that moment, he was almost ready to promise he would never see Helga again, but in a way he didn't understand, his love for his mother gave him a confirmation of his love for Helga.

He kissed her and climbed aboard as the train started to move.

On the journey back to the Saram he had great difficulty in believing that his leave had passed and he couldn't remember what he had done with most of the time.

When he arrived back at the ship after his summer leave, another letter awaited him.

> Dear Peter,
>
> I am now settled in *München* with time to study. I am helping my *Grossmutter*. She is a very nice lady and my parents have sent me to a good place for my punishment for being in love with you, an *Engländer*.
>
> I wish you were here with me or me with you. As I write, you seem so far away, but it is really just a little piece of *Ozean*. I am not near the coast anymore, but *München* is a beautiful city. There are libraries, museums, *theater* and lots of nice shops. I know you would like it.   There are no tea rooms but if so I would go there trying to remember all we did.
>
> Please write soon - to my address in *München*.

Take care of yourself my darling.

All my love, Helga.

He had expected to be enlightened about Helga's reasons for being in Munich but the letter only increased his confusion. There was the suggestion of being there to help her aging relative, coupled with the notion that it was some kind of banishment from the family for associating with him. There was not even a direct confirmation of her being at the university, only a reference to time to spend with her books. He felt frustrated, unable to get a satisfactory indication of what was happening.

It was on a Saturday when he had some afternoon leave. He went by himself, not wishing to involve Stephen, determined to handle his own problems. He went to a matinee at the local cinema and saw 'Lost Horizon' a mystical tale which had the effect of heightening his growing belief that he and Helga were living in a dream world.

It was after he came out of the cinema and was making his way through the crowd that he accidentally bumped into a young woman.

"Sorry."

She turned to face him and for a moment he had the impression that it was Helga. She was tall, and her long fair hair reached down to her shoulders.

She smiled.

"No damage done."

His eyes strayed from her face to her protuberance. He turned a deep red as he realized that she was pregnant.

She smiled again and walked off, and he was left standing, trying to cope with the shock of the encounter and the inference that it had presented.

By the time he'd returned to the Saram he was

convinced. It had all become painfully obvious. Helga was pregnant. Why hadn't he thought of it before? It would certainly explain the sudden shift to Munich. He tried to calm his rapidly beating heart, but it was no use, he felt a swell of consternation which inhibited logical thought. He got up and walked around the upper deck. After half an hour, he searched for some paper and a pen.

Dear Helga, he wrote.

Thank you for your letter. I'm sorry for the long delay in replying but life at sea has been quite demanding - no time to spare. I'm glad to hear that you are established in Munich. I have to be honest though and make it clear that I am totally confused as to what is going on. For example, I cannot understand why you have been sent to Munich. You say that you are serving some kind of sentence - but a sentence for what - for meeting me - becoming my friend - a friend who has professed his love for you and to whom you have professed your love?

Or is there a more serious reason? Are you pregnant? If you are, please tell me because it is our child, a child conceived in love.

Have your parents forbidden you to tell me, or is this your decision? I want to know Helga, and if you love me you must tell me. We must be completely honest with each other.

I want you to become my wife. I want our baby to know who its parents are and to be loved and cherished by them. I know our present separation is difficult but it cannot last. There has to be a solution and I will do all I can to seek it.

If I am mistaken about a pregnancy, please forgive me, but in the present circumstances, with confusing information at my disposal, I have to think of this possibility which does not frighten me. On the contrary, I feel proud if I am to be a father and you are to be the mother of our child.

So, please Helga, write soon and tell me all.

All my love,
Peter.

Standing by the post box, he hesitated. Was he doing the right thing? Was he making unjust accusations? But he had to know. He had to risk her reaction. He dropped the envelope in the box.

7.

$\mathcal{H}$elga, settling into the life in Munich, had not been in communication with her parents since she left Hamburg in July, over a month before. She had left hurriedly. She had fought with her parents, refusing to have an abortion, working herself into such a frenzy that they had been forced to capitulate. Their solution was to banish her to Munich, her grandmother Eva having agreed to provide her with a place to live. Her father forced her to abandon her studies in Hamburg, insisting that she continue them in Munich. She felt they had completely disowned her. In these circumstances her thoughts turned frequently to Peter. She wondered how he had received her letter, particularly as it would have reached him after an unexplained gap in their correspondence.

Although she did not convey any of her thoughts or actions to her grandmother, her grandmother didn't ask her any questions. She was always kind and considerate, fussing over her like a long lost daughter. She gave no inkling of her feelings about the pregnancy, but it was obvious that her parents had told her everything before she agreed to her staying there. It was mainly because of her grandmother's support that she hesitated to raise the issue herself, and because her grandmother did not appear to invite any discussion they carried on as if the pregnancy was quite normal, and her stay there a natural circumstance.

However, as she pondered the wisdom of her stance with Peter she decided to confide in her grandmother. It happened one morning at breakfast.

"*Oma* ... Could we have a talk?".

"What did you have in mind?"

"I'd like to talk about my situation."

"Very well," her grandmother answered. It was said without the slightest hint of resistance, or of her potential attitude to the matter.

"I realize I've disappointed my parents. It's through your generosity that I'm sparing them public humiliation for what I have done."

"You're in love with the father of your child?"

"Yes, very much in love." She looked at Eva and felt the tears. "Oh! *Oma*. I miss him so much."

"But he is in England, the England we fought, the England that wounded my husband and caused his eventual death."

"Yes, but the facts of history do not enter into the reality of our feelings for each other."

"Your father, my son, is a man of high moral principles and I admire him for that. Sometimes he may seem too dogmatic, but he believes strongly in his religious faith and in the rightness of his actions. Furthermore, he believes that others, especially his family, should accept and practise what he regards as a rightful code of behaviour."

"Yes, *Oma,* I appreciate all that, but I met a man I love and I'm glad to be having his child."

"Someone from another country you came to love in less than a week?"

"Yes."

"How do you know he won't desert you?"

"I don't . . . but I don't think he will . . . in fact I'm sure he won't. I'm sure he loves me as I love him."

"The glorious innocence of young love!"

Helga felt the blood rising in her face. So here was yet another critic. Another example of a generation that would not accept the genuineness of her faith and commitment to another person.

"What would you know of my feelings with your strict moral judgement - your unwillingness to believe my sincerity?"

64

"I don't doubt your sincerity . . . I might doubt your wisdom, question your impulsiveness, but only because I understand."

"How could you understand?"

Her grandmother smiled, a kindly smile, and Helga couldn't interpret her reaction. Where she expected hostility, she found only graciousness.

"Dear Helga. How little you know of me or me of you. You've given me the gift of your honesty and the least I can do is to reciprocate. I met my husband, your grandfather, before the First World War. He was a sailor, an officer in the Imperial German Navy and, being a sailor he travelled. There were long periods of separation, like the time he spent in China, a period exceeding two years. I didn't see him in all that time, there were only letters, but they didn't relieve my loneliness or my feelings of abandonment. I was young and pretty then and men friends were not difficult to find, but I was faithful to my marriage vows - that is until one day I met a man who was visiting Hamburg from France. He was handsome and debonair and he made me feel like a woman again."

Helga leaned forward, anxious to catch every word.

"We were very much in love and we enjoyed a passionate affair. I became pregnant and he wanted to marry me, but I refused. You see, even with my unfaithfulness I couldn't desert my husband."

"Did he find out?"

"Call it fate or good luck . . . perhaps even bad luck . . . but I suffered a miscarriage. He never knew, and my brief affair with my only true love ended."

"Oh, *Oma*, I'm sorry, I was very rude."

"You've been entirely honest with me and I've told you something I've never told another living soul. It's been my secret all these years."

"Why didn't you leave your husband and marry your lover?"

"It wasn't possible. My family wouldn't have agreed and I could never have lived with the breaking of my marriage vows."

"You had a tragic life?"

"No, I don't agree. My husband took care of me. He stood by me through all the trials and tribulations of bringing up my son."

"But he was not your lover?"

"No, but love of the intensity I experienced is difficult to sustain. The experience of it lifts you to great heights and the memory of it . . . as it was for me . . . can enrich your life forever."

"Was he unfaithful . . . your husband?"

"It was never an issue for me. He never neglected me nor left me in spirit until he died many years after the War. He had been seriously wounded in the Battle of Jutland, the great naval battle with the British Navy."

"*Oma* - I'm so sorry."

Eva smiled.

"Age does bring room for perspective, wisdom perhaps. It allows for forgiveness, brings a degree of humility . . . an appreciation of human vulnerability. Experience is a great teacher. It taught me that life should be lived to the fullest possible extent. In that way we get to know ourselves, even to bestow our gifts on the human race . . . "

Helga, her eyes moistening, kissed the lined face and held the worn hands.

"Dear *Oma*."

"Now then, enough of this, we have to decide what to do today."

"What will happen to me, *Oma*?"

"I don't know, but you'll manage. You have the courage and strength of your beliefs. Follow your own intuitions and you won't go far wrong."

The talk with her grandmother had brought her to question the wisdom of the letter she had written to Peter. She disliked her dishonesty even though she still felt her earlier judgement - withholding the truth because of the fear that Peter would resort to some rash action - was justified by her mood and her concern at the time of writing. Now, she wasn't so sure. She considered writing another letter telling him the whole story, but she rejected this option, feeling that it might only add to Peter's confusion. She decided to wait, hoping he would write again.

When Peter's letter arrived, she hastened to read it, anxious to discover his reaction to her letter. At first, she was surprised by his exasperated tone, but reading and rereading its contents again and again she was forced to concede that she had been wrong in withholding news of the pregnancy. Why wouldn't he be concerned? He could only make the inference that something was very wrong. After that, reaching the conclusion that she was pregnant with his child was the most logical outcome. It was not, therefore, his disinterest that she should be encouraging by withholding the truth. She should be celebrating his love for her. A love that shone through his frustration and disappointment at her failure to be open and honest with him. She had to follow her own intuition as *Oma* had suggested. She would write to Peter and explain everything.

The actual task she set herself proved to be more difficult than she had expected. Telling the truth could still prompt some precipitous action by Peter. She had to try and reason with him while being totally honest. She struggled with many versions of a reply, alternately engaging in bouts of optimism and despair. When the unexpected news broke over Germany in September - *Royal Navy Mobilizes*, the newspaper headlines screamed - she was galvanized into action. She wrote a letter to Peter and posted it the same day.

8.

*W*hen the Royal Navy was ordered to resort to war mobilization on the morning of September 28, the Saram put to sea. After seven days they anchored in Portland harbour on the south coast, not far from Peter's home. It was here that the ship was to take on extra crew members.

Over pints of ale in the Sailor's Arms they sat silently. Peter, pondering their future, was at a loss for words and it was Stephen that broke the impasse.

"It's war, mate. Take my word for it. A fucking war." It seemed as if he just wanted to say it - get it out in the open.

"Bloody hell, my mum's going to have a fit." Peter could visualize his parents arguing over his fate, his father maintaining that the Navy was 'the best place to be', and his mother fretting over the dangers of what she considered to be her son's premature enlistment.

"Dad thinks it'll happen," Stephen responded. "Mum, well, she doesn't listen."

"Like my parents . . . Mum just gets scared. Doesn't like me being at sea."

Peter tried to shrug off the unpleasant recollections.

"Hell! I'd rather be on the briny than in some frigging shore base."

"Bloody right." Stephen looked down at the polished table top and his voice became more subdued. "Still got a crush on the Jerry?"

Peter's face tensed. "I'm going to marry her, Steve."

Stephen turned away as if seeking time to fashion a reply. When he turned to face Peter, he looked flustered.

"Sorry, mate . . . you see. Oh, hell, Good luck." He held out his hand.

Peter took it, shaken by the unexpected gesture, feeling a swell of emotion.

"Thanks Stephen . . . Thanks . . . " Embarrassed, he got up quickly. Stephen followed, and they made their way back to the jetty to catch the returning liberty boat. In their silence, Peter wondered what the Navy had in store for them.

As they waited at the dockside, Portland looked grey and dismal. When they boarded the pinnace, a light drizzle started. The misty rain obscured a good forward view as they journeyed back to the ship. Suddenly, the Saram arose out of the gloom, a dull grey silhouette at first but gradually assuming a shape and form. She was high-sided with a single funnel and mast. In the stern the massive mine-sweeping winches could be plainly seen.

Peter and his fellow seamen climbed the companionway onto the quarterdeck. He saluted towards the stern and the White Ensign drooped forlornly in the still air. The Quartermaster was casting a disciplined eye over a small group assembled on the quarterdeck.

"Get this through yer 'eads, you're now in the real Navy," he was telling them. "You're going to 'elp us get us up to war complement. Saram's a new ship. Next few months will be chocker with exercises, getting up to snuff."

Peter and Stephen sauntered back to the messdeck.

"Like Nelson's speech before Trafalgar?" Stephen whispered.

"It's the real thing?" Peter felt a hopelessness overtaking him. Any thoughts of seeing Helga again were fast fading.

"What we joined for, mate."

He was tempted to point out that not everyone was given much choice, but what was the use of that?

"The King's Navee," he said, mimicking the tone of Gilbert and Sullivan, and he went for a pee.

It was a shock when Stephen was unexpectedly transferred to a cruiser, the Eurander, which was completing a refit in

Devonport. Peter and Stephen had spent so much of their service time together that Peter had never thought much about the possibility of their being separated. They managed to get ashore for a last pint but their usual banter was missing. Peter was struck by the uncertainty of the times they lived in and Stephen, trying to make light of the situation, ended up sounding even more melancholy.

"Who knows, either one of us may be at the bottom of the briny in a year, sunk by some fucking U Boat."

"Christ! You're a bloody pessimist."

Stephen didn't answer. His silence made Peter feel he was impatient with what he saw as his naïveté.

It was not until some weeks after Stephen's departure that Peter struck up a friendship with Tom Raddle. Tom had some three years' service seniority over Peter, but it was his happy-go-lucky demeanour which brought them together. Not only that, he was a cut above the average seaman, an avid reader, who liked to spend his leisure time with the classics, or seeking out the local repertory theatre when they were in port. He had already acquired a fond reputation as a 'lower deck lawyer' because he always appeared to come up with an answer to suit every situation.

Tom arrived on the scene when Peter was still lamenting the loss of Stephen's friendship, and also trying to cope with the worsening political situation and its affect on his relationship with Helga.

"You're one of those responsible bastards, bit stuffy too," Tom delivered his verdict on the morning that Peter was still worrying about his performance the day before, during a minesweeping exercise, when he almost lost a marker buoy because of his inattention. "Won't do you any bloody good? You need to get pissed now and then, live it up a bit."

"Suppose you're right . . . "

"You know damned well I am."

Over the next few weeks, Peter was beset by thoughts of impending doom. He was listless and irritable, unable to concentrate. He felt trapped, as though in a cell awaiting execution. He always thought of himself as an optimist and now he was possessed with a crippling sense of failure, as if the threat of war was his fault and his dalliance with Helga had tempted fate.

It was Tom who cornered him one morning.

"What the hell's up? You've been looking like death warmed over."

"It's nothing . . ."

"Tell that to the marines."

"Just a little down that's all."

"Come on chum, we need a natter."

Peter followed Tom to a quiet spot on the upper deck, in the bow, below the muzzle of the forward gun.

"Let's hear it then," Tom squatted on the deck and Peter sat beside him.

Peter found it difficult to begin, but once started the whole story of his relations with Helga gushed out. When he had finished, Tom looked at him, appearing visibly stunned. After a while he recovered his sense of humour.

"And I told you to lighten up," Tom, laughing now, suggested that Peter's adventures had put his idea of 'letting go' far beyond his wildest imaginings. He got up and walked to the rail, looking out to the sea beyond. Peter joined him.

"One thing about the sea," Tom became philosophic. "It clears the head . . . but we need a fucking good gale to deal with this."

Peter managed an uneasy laugh, "So?"

"She's gotta be pregnant," he paused. "I think it's over."

"You're telling me to walk out on her?"

"She may be trying to tell you to leave things alone for a while."

"I can't do that."

"It's a bit of a mess then, ain't it. Might be better to sit on it? Parents may force her to get an abortion."

"Christ!"

"Besides, there ain't a hope in hell that you can get anywhere near Germany until this mess blows over . . . or blows up."

"You think there'll be war?"

"Don't you?"

"I don't think Germany wants war, any more than we do."

"Then why are we still mobilized? We're not out of the woods yet, not by a long shot."

Peter wanted to fight back, deny his fears, put his mind at rest, but it was no use. He had to go and see her, but Tom was right, it was out of the question in the light of the present crisis. Or was it? What if he simply deserted? But that would be treason or close to it - at a time when the Navy was mobilized an act presumably punishable by death. Hardly a rational course to follow to pursue a relationship.

"I'll leave it to you, mate." Tom headed down below.

Peter appreciated Tom's acceptance of his need to be left alone. That's what he liked about him, he knew when to back off.

Peter gazed at the distant horizon. Perhaps Tom was right. It was tough medicine but Tom's view certainly coincided with the majority. He needed to think. At least that would be a step forward. Until talking with Tom he hadn't been able to get his brain working.

9.

$\mathcal{A}$ few days after Helga had posted the letter to Peter, Munich was abuzz with rumours. The Prime Minister of England was meeting with the *Führer* to work out a plan for peace. And then suddenly it was all over, a Peace Pact had been signed; there was to be no war. There was jubilation in the streets. The *Führer* had done it again. He had proved that he didn't want war, only a just settlement for Germany. Helga had visions of Peter receiving the news, remembering her words. 'You see,' she would have said if he were with her now, 'The *Führer* does not want war with England.'

Sitting with her grandmother at breakfast the next morning, Helga felt a happiness unknown in the past few weeks. It encouraged her to share some confidences.

"I've written to Peter."

"I know." Her grandmother smiled.

"Dear *Oma*. I can't keep secrets from you."

"Not all of them."

"Do you think it was wise to tell him I'm bearing his child?"

"Honesty required it, but you . . . "

Her words were interrupted by a knock at the front door. Helga got up to answer it.

It was Günther. Dressed in civilian clothes, a sports jacket and colourful trousers, and smiling broadly, he held out his arms.

"A surprise, is it not?" He hugged her tightly.

"Come in," said Helga. "You must have some coffee? . . . some breakfast?"

"No thanks . . . Ah, *Oma*. How good to see you on this

happy day. You see, England backed down. The *Führer* was right. They will not fight."

They all moved into the kitchen. Helga, feeling the chill of Günther's words, abhorred the belligerence they conveyed. She wondered why Günther had come; was it to admonish her again?

"I'll join the *Kriegsmarine* in January." Günther spread his lanky frame over the kitchen chair, tilting it back, creating a posture for expansive gestures. "I had my second interview this week in Cuxhaven. They want committed sailors like me."

"I'm happy for you," said Helga, feeling a little nauseous, finding it hard to muster much enthusiasm.

"So!" Günther looked at Helga, placing his hands behind his head. "You are to bear the Englishman's child. Poor Helga, my innocent sister I love in spite of everything."

It all seemed so hollow, so insincere. It was hard to believe that this was the brother she had grown up with. Her outrage rising, she wanted to hit him.

"I love, Peter," she said defiantly. "I'm happy to bear his child."

"Even if it brings shame to our family?"

He sounded like her father, although she couldn't imagine her father, in spite of his strictness, to be so utterly devoid of compassion. Günther appeared caught up with some notion of honour and ideology which eliminated feeling. It was like he had lost a part of himself, a gentle caring part, that she remembered.

"I won't bring shame to the family. I will honour my responsibility to my child and to the father of that child." Helga delivered the rebuttal in a calm firm voice, eyes glaring, holding Günther's eyes in hers in a withering gaze. Then she sat quietly, unmoving.

Günther was silent. His sister's sudden fury had unnerved him. He shifted uneasily and, looking down at his cup said, between clenched teeth, "Depends what you mean by responsibility."

Helga was about to answer when Eva cut in.

"There may indeed be several interpretations of honour and responsibility. I suggest you think about yours." Her grandmother's words, delivered forcefully, and directed at Günther as he sat, looking cowed now, marked the end of the discourse and the end of Günther's visit. He caught the afternoon train to Hamburg.

10.

The Munich Agreement was greeted with relief aboard the Saram. Still, there were sceptics, especially among the old hands who had served in the first war. In Britain as a whole it also began to expose conflicting views among its people, the press, and the political parties. The Royal Navy, while easing back from the brink of preparedness for war, nevertheless remained alert and ready for any eventuality. For Peter, looking at the world through the narrow lens of his love for Helga and still struggling with the harsh advice from Tom, it was an occasion to celebrate a hope for a renewal of their tryst.

Nevertheless, he couldn't escape a feeling of despair. The events of the last few months had demonstrated the uncertainties of life. And he still needed some explanation from Helga. He had to make a more concerted effort to cement the relationship with the woman he loved, but how?

It was at the beginning of October that her letter arrived.

Dear Peter,

I was not truthful. I am sorry for this but I was very worried about your reaction. I am pregnant and our baby is expected in January.

He stopped reading, conscious of the perspiration breaking out on his forehead. Anticipating her condition was one thing, having it confirmed was quite another. No wonder she had been sent to Munich. He gasped at the thought of the confrontation that must have occurred with her parents. My God, I'm to be a father! The reality of what they had done caused him a great deal of trepidation, but it also evoked an excitement. It was their child, conceived in love. He picked up the letter again.

> My parents know all about it and so does my *Grossmutter*. *Vater* and *Mutter* are angry, but I think *Mutter* understands. They asked me to get an abortion but I told them that I wanted to keep the child and that we want to be married. They don't like the idea, which is why they don't want me to write to you.
>
> Peter. I love you. I love you more than ever now, but don't do anything rash. We have to think of the baby. I think it best if you don't try to come here. It will make it more difficult with my parents. Please Peter, believe me, this is best for us, for you and me. I will tell you when everyone has calmed down again. We can think more clearly about what to do after the baby is born.
>
> Please do as I ask Peter. Believe me. It will be the best.
>
> Please write soon and tell me what you think. Take care of yourself my darling.
>
> All my love,
>
> Helga.

It was a quiet evening. The sun was setting in a blaze of red, promising good weather for the day to come. It was hard to comprehend that he had fathered a child, and he was overwhelmed by Helga's determination. She had refused an abortion, defying her parents, risking everything to save their child. And now, even after her gallant struggle, she was living in a country that might soon be England's enemy again. He had to think clearly. His first impulse was to throw caution to the winds, ignore Helga's advice and head for Germany. He had to see her, console her. She needed him at her side, not hundreds of miles away.   But how could he accomplish this?

The cost of getting to Germany was way beyond his means unless he borrowed money from someone.   But who had such resources to spare?   Another alternative would be to cycle the whole way, camping along the route, but that would mean an extended period of time and a leave of say even three weeks would be out of the question, unless he could offer a compassionate reason?   And what would he do when he got there?   As Helga had implied, the difficulties she faced with her family were bad enough without his sudden appearance to heighten the tensions, especially at a time when she faced the unknown complications of the birth.   Her suggestion that it might be wiser to address the matter of a reunion after the birth, certainly made good sense.   But all these issues were reasons for delay, not for immediate action.   He had to do something now.

It was a blustery morning, the wind whistling in the rigging and Peter, suffering from a week of sleepless nights, reached a decision. He would write immediately and ask Helga for a phone number.   He had considered getting in touch with her parents in Blankenese, convinced that they would have a telephone and would know if there was one at the grandmother's house in Munich.   But phoning her parents was out of the question given their attitude to the relationship.   No, he would write to Helga and ask for a phone number. That still left him with the question of how to locate a phone to make the call.   The best time would be when he went home for Christmas leave.   The local family dentist lived close by and he would probably be willing to allow the use of his phone, although whether he would take kindly to a call to Germany was of concern.   As for the larger question of making an actual trip to Germany, if he cycled and camped it might not be too expensive.   He would ask his mother if she could help him financially.   Leave from the Navy would be difficult, but not impossible, he convinced himself. He would apply immediately for a passport, stating that his reason was to undertake a visit to France.

Feeling better about the entire situation, he wrote to Helga. The first priority was to get her phone number in Munich, if indeed there was one, and then to explain his overall plan.

Helga's reply was received at the end of October. There **was** a number in Munich, and yes he could phone her. Throughout November, they exchanged a series of letters again. Hers were bright and chatty, telling of her life in Munich and the ups and downs of her pregnancy. His were guarded. He talked of his desire to see her but refrained from specific details. He wanted to be sure that he had a workable plan before raising her hopes. Besides, he wanted to talk to her about it in person.

At the end of November, Peter decided to confide in Tom again. This time, faced with Peter's determination, Tom did not attempt to dissuade him, and they were soon poring over maps, seeking a suitable route into Munich.

"Stay in France as long as possible. Go to Strasbourg and cross there," Tom pencil in hand was busy calculating distances.

"D'you think I'll be able to cross the border?" Looking at the distances involved, Peter was acutely conscious that the whole journey might be for naught if the authorities barred his entry into Germany.

"Might get in, but not out?"

"It's a good plan Tom." Peter brushed aside Tom's caution. "I'm going to work on it."

As Christmas approached, Peter began to feel less certain of the practicality of the trip. There was mounting talk of the possibility of war and daily references in the press to Britain and Germany's rearmament.

He was about to depart to go home for Christmas leave when he received a gaily decorated Christmas card. *Fröhliche*

Weihnachten und Ein Glückliches Neues Jahr. It was signed, Love, Helga. He held the card in his hands, daydreaming how she must have selected it, taken it home, and written her message. He felt a discernible closeness to her and an intense longing to be with her, to be able to share Christmas with the woman he loved. Instead he had to face his parents, and he had no idea if or what he would tell them about the latest developments.

11.

*P*eter was jammed into a window seat in a crowded compartment. The train from Weymouth was full of other sailors headed home for Christmas. The air was thick with smoke and the smell of alcohol, and the talk, made louder because of a liberal intake of the latter, was of pubs and girls, wives and girlfriends, the last two regarded in a less ribald fashion than the first. He went out into the corridor and lowered a window, letting in some fresh air, inhaling deeply.

He had taken a bus from Portland with Tom earlier in the day and when they arrived in Weymouth they went for a beer. Peter had just over an hour before his train left and Tom, heading up north, to Yorkshire, was due out some thirty minutes later so they had plenty of time for a chat.

"So, what's up now, Peter. You've been a real drip lately."

"I've got tough decisions to make."

"Thinking of deserting," Tom tried to lighten the mood.

Peter winced. If only he knew how close he'd come to stating the truth.

"Christ, Tom! I'm not looking forward to meeting my parents."

Peter's fear was obvious. Now that he was actually on the way home the immensity of the plan he had set himself, and the dilemma it and Helga's pregnancy had created, was daunting.

"Want to talk about it," Tom, had that look of understanding which Peter had come to expect in difficult situations.

He silently thanked Tom for his sensitivity. He welcomed the opportunity to talk with his trusted friend. He told him about the conflict with his parents, something he had not mentioned before, and the seeming impossibility of resolving it.

"I still aim to try and see Helga. Perhaps it's crazy, but I have to give it a go. The catch is I have to ask my mother for some cash."

"Whew." Tom reeled. "That's quite a handful." He took a swig of his beer, wiping his mouth with his hand.   "What would I do? Oh, I dunno, probably the same, but I wouldn't tell my parents any more than you have already."   He thought for a moment.   "Couldn't you just cadge your way, you know, cycle, tenting? Scrounging your meals from farms, like?"

"Like a tramp?"

"Why not, if it gets you there and back?"

"Take too long Tom,"   Peter tried to dismiss such suggestions from his mind; they were too humbling to consider. "Besides, I'd end up being 'Absent Without Leave' a deserter."

"Hell, I'd ask for compassionate leave. Cook up a good story, family problems or something. Ask for three weeks."

All this might be fine for Tom, Peter thought, but I'm not sure I could carry it off. He glanced at his watch. "Christ! I have to go, Tom."   He fumbled for some change.

"Forget it, Pete. It's on me."

"Thanks Tom."   He grabbed his kitbag and started for the station.

"Have a good leave!"   Tom shouted after him.

His mother was waiting. The weariness was still there, just as before, but she managed a broad smile and a lingering hug.

"It's Christmas Peter, time to forget the Navy for a while."

"I'm going to give you a treat," Peter slung the kitbag over his shoulder and took her to the front of the station. "We'll take a taxi home."

They drove through the town, past shops decorated for Christmas. He looked across at his mother, happy to be able to surprise her with the unexpected ride home.

"How's Dad?"

"Your father's better than the last time, but don't expect miracles."

Peter thought of the conversation with Tom, wondering about the wisdom of informing his parents about Helga's pregnancy and his plans to visit her.

"You seem like you've something on your mind?" His mother was eying him, troubled by his sudden silence.

"I have to talk to you." The words came quickly, spontaneously, defying caution.

"I see," she reacted guardedly, as if expecting an unpleasant surprise.

The taxi arrived at the house and he paid the fare, remembering to add a small tip.

There was a pleasant relaxed feeling as Peter and his mother sat down to tea and cakes in front of the living room fire.

"So, what's this mystery you have to reveal?"

He took a sip of tea and he noticed that his hand was shaking. He felt his face reddening as he took a deep breath.

"Helga's pregnant," He paused. "I intend to go and see her."

His mother's face turned a ghastly white and he thought she might faint. She passed a hand over her forehead.

"Is there no end to this?" Her voice was strained, the weariness in her face seeming to intensify.

Peter thought of Tom again. Perhaps he should have taken his advice and kept the matter to himself.

"I don't suppose there's any stopping you?" There was the suggestion of an appeal in her question.

"No, I'm afraid not." There was no going back now. "I thought I should be honest with you."

"Yes, yes," she shrugged off his gesture of openness with visible impatience.

"What will your father say?" she said, speaking to herself as much as to him.

"I didn't plan to tell him."

She stared at the fire and without turning, murmured. "I suppose it would be best."

She got up quickly, knocking her cup and saucer onto the floor and breaking the handle off the cup.

"Oh God," she wailed. "My good china."

She moved to pick up the pieces, but he brushed her aside.

"I think it can be fixed, Mother." He looked up but she was gone. He heard her going up the stairs and then the bedroom door closed.

Regretting his confession, and feeling utterly dejected, Peter presented a sad spectacle to his father when he arrived home an hour later.

"Hello, son." His father looked around. "Where's your mother?"

"She went upstairs. I don't think she's feeling well."

"Another one of her bouts, I imagine."

He didn't seem at all concerned as he ushered Peter into the living room. He poured himself a sherry. "Like one?"

"No . . . No thanks, Dad."

"So how's life aboard the minesweeper?" His father plunked himself on the sofa, adopting a man-to-man demeanour.

"Good . . . "

"Hell, it's got to be dangerous!"

"It's all very organized. We know where the mines are. It's not as risky as it sounds."

"You mean our mines? You've been sweeping our mines?"

"Yes, that's right. Minefields that are being removed."

"Be a bit different if they were German, wouldn't it?"

"I suppose."

"You bet it would. They wouldn't advertise where they were?"

"International Law requires it?"

"And you think Hitler and his gang would care two hoots about that?"

Peter felt the blood rushing to his head. It was the same old thing, back to fighting the enemy, the enemy that he had dared to associate with. He wanted none of this and he felt his anger would soon explode. Then he heard his mother coming down the stairs. She went straight into the kitchen and he got up and joined her.

"Anything I can help you with," he said.

"You could peel some potatoes."

Over the next few days' Peter removed himself as much as possible from home. It was a repetition of the last visit. He found his mood steadily worsening as he retreated more and more into himself. His withdrawal appeared to cause a strong reaction in his father who became more irritable with his wife. Mostly, he shunned Peter, but such silent encounters as they did have, resulted in a meeting of two pairs of angry eyes. Where once Peter had seen disappointment, now he saw a degree of disdain amounting to outright rejection.

The climax came one evening when they were all seated around the dinner table. They had just finished the meal, which had been notable for the absence of conversation, when his father turned on him.

"Look, son, you've got to pull yourself together. Stop behaving like a spoilt child."

Peter stood up, trance-like. He picked up his plate, hurling it across the room, narrowly missing his mother, as it smashed into tiny pieces against the wall behind her.

"Now look what you've done! Just three days before Christmas!" His mother yelled at his father as Peter rushed out the door and into the hall, grabbing his coat and making a clumsy exit through the front door.

It was raining heavily, with a gale force wind blowing, as he ran across the fields to the harbour. He struggled out onto the pier, the wind and rain lashing at his face. It was difficult to move forward as he met the full force of the wind driving in off the sea. All he could think of was to fight the demons that assailed him. Large waves were hitting the end of the pier, sending huge mounds of water sweeping down its length. He was soon swamped by one of them, unable to keep on his feet, being borne along, rolling and bumping on the hard surface. After it had passed, he struggled to his feet, gulping in air filled with clouds of stinging, salt-laden spray. Another wave hurled him to the ground and he rolled helplessly, not knowing where it might take him, suddenly possessed by an intense fear that he would be washed into the boiling sea.

The lights were still on in the house. They could be seen as one turned the bend in the road, the road that led from the path to the harbour. It was well after midnight. Peter staggered on, weaving unsteadily, having the appearance of a drunk. He barely had the strength to stand erect, let alone to propel himself forward, and when he finally reached the front door, he had to steady himself to collect enough energy to rap on the door. His father opened it.

"Christ," he yelled, as Peter stumbled into the light of the single bulb illuminating the front hall.

"Lilly! Lilly!" His father called out as he stood staring. Peter shivered. He was soaked through, his clothes feeling like a suit of medieval armour.

"You must be crazy to stay out in this," his father was saying.

His mother rushed forward, taking Peter's arm and propelling him upstairs.

"Harry!" she yelled. "Get the copper boiling. He needs

a hot bath!"

It was over an hour before the ancient copper, which they used for boiling water for baths and washing clothes, and which was heated by old newspapers and sticks, delivered sufficient warmth and quantity. Then the water had to be carried upstairs to the bathroom in buckets kept for the purpose.

Peter lay in the warm water, his circulation improving, the chilling subsiding, and he thought how close he had come to being swept into the sea and drowned. He couldn't believe that he had been driven to such a rash act. And he thought of Helga and how much he owed it to her and the child to stay alive.

His mother rapped on the door.

"When you're through, come and get some hot cocoa."

Sitting in the kitchen with a blanket wrapped around his pyjamas, his arms bandaged and his face full of red blotches, the scrapes made by his rolling on the pier, he sipped the warm liquid.

"I'm sorry Mother. I didn't mean to cause all this trouble."

"I know." The tears showed in her eyes and she reached over and touched his hand.

"Oh, Mum!" Fighting his pain and exhaustion he reached over and hugged her. "Why is Dad so against me?"

"He's not against you . . . in his own bumbling way he thinks he's trying to help you. What he thinks is caring comes across as aggression I'm afraid."

"Where is he?"

"I told him to go to bed."

Christmas came and went. It was the strangest Christmas that Peter had ever experienced. He went to church with his father and afterwards they all sat down to a traditional roast beef dinner, followed by his mother's homemade Christmas pudding. Throughout it all there was little conversation, the confrontation with his father was too recent to expect any trace of normality to return. The result was that each of them seemed wrapped up in their own thoughts. He wondered how his father reconciled his religious faith with his actions. Maybe he felt cleansed after the service, but if he did he conveyed none of this. Perhaps he regarded their attendance at the service as some sort of opportunity for Peter to mend his ways. His mother said little, steadily working away, trying to make the holiday reminiscent of those that Peter remembered as a child. But all it did was to worsen Peter's sense of loneliness. He prayed at the service, but it was not for his immediate family. It was for Helga and for the expected child. The matter on his mind, which occupied his thoughts throughout the holiday, was the very subject he dare not mention.

It was the morning that Peter was due to return to his ship. He had arisen early and after a wash and shave he began packing. Now that his leave was ending, he felt conscience-stricken by his behaviour. Nevertheless, he consoled himself with the belief that there had been a reconciliation of sorts, but even this was measured by the lack of expressed hostility rather then by any sign of understanding or forgiveness.

At the station, he bade goodbye to his mother. He had exchanged handshakes with his father before he left for work that morning. His mother hugged and kissed him and he climbed aboard. He waved once or twice, and then he closed the window and sat down. There was no one else in the compartment and he closed his eyes. He awoke when the train stopped at the junction and he alighted to await the express to Weymouth. It was then that it struck him. He had not asked his mother for a loan to get to Germany and, worst of all, in spite of his preoccupation with Helga, he hadn't phoned her.

TWO

1939

G ünther was in the midst of packing. He was in his bedroom on the third floor of the family home in Blankenese. Tomorrow he was to leave for Kiel to report to the *Kriegsmarine* to begin his basic training. It was mid-afternoon on a Sunday in early January and he heard his father coming down from his favourite rooftop observation point, the cupola high above the roof, with its unobstructed view of the Elbe. Perhaps this was the opportunity he had been waiting for? His mother was out and they would be alone together? However, he hesitated, weighing the wisdom of what he intended to do. Then he heard the sound of the piano. His father was playing - one of his favourite Beethoven sonatas. This was usually a sign that he was seeking relaxation, or a deliberate diversion from the worries of the day. He would only play to achieve a polished rendering, which meant that all else was pushed from his mind. Günther stood in the doorway, watching and listening, marvelling at his father's dexterity with the keys. His father stopped playing, sensing Günther's presence, appearing pleased that his son had witnessed his prowess.

"Ah, Günther, all packed?"

"Yes."

He sat on the sofa, and his father left the piano and sat opposite on the high-backed chair.

"Coffee?"

"Please."

His father called for Minna and she soon came with coffee and cakes, placing them on the small table nearby.

"We'll look after the rest, Minna."

They helped themselves and settled down to enjoy the afternoon treats.

"Is there something on your mind, Günther?" His father fixed him with a questioning stare.

Now that the opportunity he wanted was being offered, he felt reluctant. He wondered if he should even admit to his concerns, but his father was waiting.

"I know you're not happy with my joining the *Kriegsmarine* as a seaman, but it's what I feel most comfortable with."

"But it's such a waste of your talents. You have the necessary educational qualifications to enter as an officer candidate."

"I know Father, but starting at the bottom will give me a broader experience. It will allow me to advance when I'm ready to take on more responsibility."

"We've discussed all this before. I reluctantly agreed with your choice," he sounded vexed, "that was providing you seek advancement at the first opportunity." He held Günther's gaze. "But this isn't what you wanted to talk about, is it?"

Günther had never been able to hide things from his father. He was quite right, there was something else, and it was far more difficult to divulge.

"Some cake?" his father said, as if to give him more time to reply.

"Thanks."

"Now what is it?"

"I'm not sure I can ask."

"Try."

"Well, it's your attitude . . . to the *Führer* and his policies." He was uneasy, doubting the wisdom of his question, "I . . . I feel you don't agree."

His father laughed. "Because I refused to acknowledge your *Nazi* salute?"

"There was that, but there's more than that . . . " He wasn't sure how to continue.

"Let me help you." His father interjected. "I believe the

92

Führer has done much for the Fatherland. We have become a prosperous nation with work for everyone. Hitler has brought us out of a great depression that the nations who conquered us in the war imposed, dreadful reparations that brought us to our knees, and which caused a lasting hatred between the German people and the victors . . . "

Günther felt vindicated. His father was on his side after all. But he was continuing.

"All that I accept, what I am worried about is the means we're now employing to reestablish our position as an independent nation. We're becoming more warlike, more aggressive, more narrow-minded to issues of race and culture, we who pride ourselves on having a highly civilized society."

"But we have to be strong. Our enemies have not shown us mercy. It's the only way, Father."

"Is it the only way? That's what I question. That's what gives me cause for concern."

Günther reached for his coffee. What his father had said was certainly rational. There was no doubt that it was a sincere and intelligent questioning of the philosophies being advanced by the *Führer*. But what he had said also constituted grounds for an unacceptable opposition to the policies of the *Third Reich*. People like his father were those who advocated a slowing of the exciting changes sweeping Germany. It was a rejection of the power to get things done, to move towards the emergence of a new vibrant nation that the whole world would respect. No, Günther could not accept his father's way. It was not the way of the future.

"You are suddenly quiet, Günther?"

Yes, he was quiet, but not because he was lacking an opinion, it was the extent of the disagreement with his father that was troubling him.

"Yes." He sought to avoid an open clash of beliefs. "I am thinking of what you have told me. It's something I have to think about too."

In truth, he had already made up his mind. He had faith in the *Führer*. He believed implicitly in all that he had been taught in the *Hitler Jugend*. He had savoured the thrill of being part of a growing body of people who saw Hitler as a saviour. It was all real and alive to him, not old voices from the past that preached conservatism and moderation.

His father was studying his expression, and Günther could see the disappointment in his face. Günther was discouraged too, sad that the gulf existed, but he had to move on with the courage of his own convictions.

"How do you explain our actions towards the Jews, the attacks on Jewish businesses?"

"Don't you see Father?" They are depriving Germans of food and work?"

"What nonsense you speak, Günther. Herr Rosen, our neighbour, whose children you grew up with, are they not Germans?"

"They are Jews, and Jews have to be punished."

Rolf's face reddened. "I can't believe that a son of mine can utter such hatred."

Günther was silent. What his father was saying was not only dangerous, it constituted grounds for turning him into the authorities.

There was mutual relief when Ilse returned unexpectedly and joined them. She had been to see her friend Kirsten.

"She asked me about Helga," she said, looking at them both.

"What did you tell her Mother?" Günther still believed that Helga's behaviour was inexcusable. To deliberately become involved with a likely adversary was beyond Günther's comprehension. England was, after all, Germany's potential enemy. How could she ignore that? The mere thought of what she had done, aroused his ire. He hated her for being so stupid and for bringing shame to the family, but she was still his sister and deep down he could not deny his love for her.

"I merely said she was well and enjoying her studies in Munich."

Günther was well aware that his mother had never forgiven him for his harsh criticism of Helga. As well, he couldn't forget the scene which had erupted between him and his sister during his ill-fated visit to Munich, a visit he had not revealed to his parents. It was not a subject he wanted to talk about.

"Are you in favour of my joining the *Kriegsmarine*?"

It wasn't a prudent question. He knew that his mother had purposely stayed out of any discussion of the differences of opinion between him and his father, and that she would not openly contradict her husband. Still, it annoyed him that she hadn't given him her private support and encouragement for his decision to join the *Kriegsmarine* as a seaman.

"It's whatever you and your father agree upon. I don't know enough about the matter to give an intelligent answer." She flashed an angry glance at Günther.

"I understand," he said meekly, unhappy now that he had embarrassed her.

He stood up.

"I must go and finish my packing," he said.

Smartly outfitted in his new uniform of dark navy blue with black boots and a rakish cap, Günther stood at attention on the parade ground at the Naval Training School in Kiel. It was the first Sunday parade and the latest contingent of draftees was drawn up for inspection by the Commanding Officer. He walked between the ranks, stopping now and then to talk to one of the trainees. When he reached Gunther, he asked him his name and where he was from.

"Günther *Jansen*. Blankenese."

"Your Father. He owns a shipping company, I believe?"

"Yes sir."

The Captain nodded acknowledgement and continued

down the ranks.   When he had finished, he addressed them:

"You will be with us for twelve weeks, twelve weeks of intensive training. All of you have already received some seamanship training in the *Hitler Jugend*, but here it will be much more extensive. On completion of your course here, you will be sent to a training ship.   The next twelve weeks will be tough and I will expect loyalty and commitment to your training.   The navy demands this of you.   The *Führer* demands it of you."

Heil Hitler!

The whole assembly erupted into a spontaneous response. With his arm outstretched, Günther acted in unison, chanting *'Sieg Heil,'* which was repeated in a rising crescendo. When they were dismissed, he could barely hear the command. The parade dispersed, breaking up into small groups and Günther, free now of the duties of the day, could look forward to an afternoon of relaxation before the start of the first week of training on the morrow. He drifted into a circle of trainees.

"My father was in the *Kriegsmarine,*" one was saying.

"Mine too," said another. "I'm from Cuxhaven."

"And where are you from?" said another, as Günther joined the group.

"Blankenese," said Günther, proudly.

"Blankenese! Home of the rich shipowners!" The shout came from a thin figure on the edge of the group. "Blankenese! He repeated his gibe, holding his nose and throwing his head back.

The whole group joined in nervous laughter.

"Yes, **Blankenese**," said Günther, raising his voice. The laughter died and Günther strode off alone to his dormitory. He hoped that the offensive character would not be in the same building. He brushed off the incident. He was in no mood for idle nonsense. He felt possessed of immense personal optimism and power. The enthusiasm and patriotic fervour of the last few minutes confirmed again, in his mind, that he was privileged to be part of a great nation, building and expanding, sweeping away old ideas. There was nothing they could not accomplish. The *Führer* would lead them to victory over those who dared to oppose them.

2.

When Peter arrived back aboard HMS Saram, Tom was already there.

"Good leave?"

"It was God awful.   You know what, I forgot to phone Helga."

"Getting cold feet, are we?"

What if Tom was right?   No, he dismissed the thought. How could he have phoned, even if he had remembered, in the state he was in while at home?

"No way I'm backing off," he said, indignantly.

Tom thought for a moment. "Let's go to that hotel. You know, where the pub is. Old George, the owner, will let you use his telephone."

George Hale was a textbook image of the jolly publican; he was short and rotund. The large head with its generous mop of grey hair topped a reddish countenance. Married with two children, he ran a prosperous business the year round thanks to the presence of the Royal Navy. He enjoyed his work and his family and he presented a happy-go-lucky demeanour to his patrons.

George was unexpectedly sympathetic to Peter's needs.

"Look laddie, " George said. "I don't care if you phone Buckingham Palace, as long as you pay the bill. The phone's in my office, go ahead."

The ease with which the deal was concluded surprised Peter and he went to the phone in a state of mild confusion.   He had remembered to bring Helga's number, but now that he was faced with an actual conversation he felt nervous.   He waited a while to collect his thoughts, then he picked up the receiver.

"What number please?"   The operator had a crisp cultured

voice.

"Ah . . . Munich, Germany."

"You have the number there, sir?" she said, with trained patience.

"Um . . . Yes."

"May I have it please, sir?" She sounded so matter-of-fact. He could have asked to call the North Pole without causing her to show a trace of surprise.

"Ah . . . yes." He read off the digits, carefully articulating each one, and she repeated them back to him.

"Yes, that's correct."

"One moment, please."

He heard a series of clicks, then the sound of static, like rushing water, then more clicks, until finally it became a dialling sound. A voice answered.

"*Guten Abend.*"

Good Evening? He waited, not knowing quite what to say, realizing that it was not Helga's voice.

"*Wer ist da?*" the voice said.

"Oh, ah . . . Can I speak to Helga *Jansen*?"

"*Einen Augenblick, bitte.*"

Peter waited as footsteps told him the person was moving away from the phone, then there were more footsteps, getting louder.

"*Hallo!*"

"Helga." Peter shouted.

"Peter! Peter!"

"Yes, it's me."

"Oh Peter, I'm so happy. You didn't phone at Christmas. I worried . . . "

"I couldn't . . . I'm sorry." No sense in telling her he forgot. "Are you well, Helga?"

"*Ja,* Peter. *Gross,* very big . . . our *Kind* . . . our baby."

"Helga! It's ours. Our child."

"*Ja,* Peter, ours!"

Peter was finding the conversation much more difficult than he had expected. He wanted to be there, to touch her, hold her in his arms.

"I must see you, Helga. I must visit you." He couldn't mask the note of desperation in his voice.

"I am afraid, Peter. It is difficult. I do not want you to be in trouble."

"I'll be careful. I'll come, after the baby. Just like you said."

"It would be wonderful, Peter . . . but I worry still."

"I will come. Helga . . . we must be married."

"I do not know . . . "

There was a hissing, crackling sound, and Helga's voice faded and the line went dead.

"I'm afraid we've lost Munich," the operator came on.

"Is there no way?"

"I would have to try again, sir."

"No. No . . . It's all right."

Peter hung up the phone. He was at once excited and disappointed. He had talked to her as he had promised. She was well and happy and excited to hear from him, yet the experience had exemplified their physical remoteness.

He sat reflecting on what had happened. After planning this for so long it seemed painfully short. He couldn't quite remember what he had said, or even much of what she had said. Her voice sounded the same, although there was worry in it. Worry about his welfare? Had he expressed concern about her and the child? He had forgotten? Everything had happened so fast.

He stumbled out of the room, fumbling in his money pouch.

"If I give you a quid?" he said to George. "If it's any more, let me know."

"That's OK, son. If it's less, you get some back. If it's more and you run out on me, I'll get your mates to find you." He laughed, pocketing the one-pound note.

Tom joined him.

"Let's go, Tom," he said. "I need time to think."

3.

It was early in January, a few days after Peter's phone call, that Helga was sitting in the kitchen with her grandmother, Eva. They had finished their breakfast and were nursing their second cups of coffee when Eva told her.

"Your mother phoned yesterday. It was when you were out. She wanted to know if you wanted her to come here, to help with the baby."

Helga flinched. Her first thought was that her mother had somehow found out about Peter's call. But the only other person that knew was Eva and she wouldn't have told her mother. She hastily dismissed the idea. She had not really thought about her mother at all; she was so comfortable with her grandmother that all thoughts of the parents who deplored her indiscretion had been set aside. As for her father, well, she didn't expect to hear from him, and given the hostility shown by Günther it was unlikely that he would call, so that left her mother, and even now, when Ilse had at last decided to break the silence, the message was delivered via her grandmother. She was embittered by her parents' neglect, but she couldn't bring herself to hate them. In many ways she could identify with their dilemma, even though she was saddened by their actions. Eva was waiting for her answer.

"I don't know, *Oma*. I really don't know," she paused. "I think it is up to mother to decide."

"Will you talk to her?"

Helga felt herself tensing. "*Oma*," she said firmly. "Perhaps I am wrong but, if you don't object, I think my answer should be received in the same manner as it was sent."

"You want me to tell her?"

Helga nodded.

102

"Are you sure?"

"Yes, *Oma*, I'm sure."

"Very well."

In the days that followed, Helga, still heartened by her conversation with Peter, awaited the birth of her child. The expected date was during the third week in January, and the midwife, called in to check on progress, found no evidence that the event was imminent. It was not until February 1, that the first pains awoke her in the early hours of the morning. She called out to her grandmother, seeking reassurance, and she came immediately, sitting by her bed and taking her pulse.

"We must start checking. Tell me when and how often the pains come?"

"I'm frightened, *Oma*," Helga struggled to accustom herself to another deep pulse of pain unlike anything she had experienced before.

"Of course you are," her voice showed understanding. "You just have to remember that it's natural and normal, and keep telling yourself this."

Helga relaxed a little, half dozing, relieved that the pain had passed. Eva waited, holding her hand.

"Oh! . . . Oh!", Helga moaned as the pain came again.

"They're about thirty minutes apart," Eva said, her voice steady and confident. "Plenty of time, but we'll call the midwife."

By the time the midwife arrived the pains were occurring every ten minutes. Water was boiled on the kitchen stove and towels made ready. Eva stayed in the bedroom, holding her hand and wiping the perspiration off her brow. The pains came steadily now and Helga's voice rose and fell, railing against the forces in control of her body. At one point she yelled for Peter.

"We must get Peter. I want to talk to him. I want to know that he loves me!"

"It's all right, Helga," Eva kissed her forehead. "I know

he loves you and so do you."

"Yes, yes," she gasped against another stab of pain.

It was around noon when the baby's head appeared, and with Eva and the midwife calling for a last magnificent effort, Helga pushed and strained, gulping in great breaths of air, marshalling her strength for the last effort. But they called for more and more, until she felt she could give no more, and yet she could give, until she felt its release and heard it cry. And then they handed her the small red body still wet from the womb, its breathing strong and rapid, and she was overcome with joy, her happiness stemming the exhaustion that suffused her body.

"It's a boy," Eva said.

Helga nestled the tiny gift in her arms, feeling clumsy, listening to its cry. She looked up at her grandmother and smiled.

"Its Peter," she said. "Hans-Peter."

Ilse arrived in Munich a week after the birth. Helga dreaded the meeting, regretting now that she had acted so hastily in snubbing her mother's desire to be with her at the actual birth. Ilse came into the bedroom as she was nursing the baby. Her mother looked tired as though the events of the past few months had depleted her of her usual vitality. They faced each other, united for the first time since Helga's banishment from Blankenese. Ilse sat silently on the bed watching.

"Do you want to hold him?" Helga spoke spontaneously, reacting to the desire she saw in her mother's eyes.

"Yes," she said, her face brightening.

Helga handed her the child and she took it in her arms, gently, lovingly, as if it had suddenly become her own.

Helga watched her, and tears formed in her eyes. The powerful surge of emotion caught her by surprise. Drawn by the tenderness in her mother's eyes, and seeing her unabashed joy at the presence of a new life, she imagined herself in those same arms and felt the strength of her mother's love, the love she now felt for her own child. Helga let out a sigh of pleasure, sinking into the soft pillows. She felt contentment, accepted as woman to woman, having a shared experience with her mother.

"He's lovely, Helga," her mother said. "You must be very proud."

"Oh, Mother! Mother! Helga reached awkwardly across the bed, hugging her mother, the tears running in rivulets down her face. "I love you."

Ilse kissed her back, her own eyes tearful and the baby, between them, appeared to look up, as if wondering about the unusual commotion.

For the next two weeks, Ilse and Eva fussed over the infant to such an extent that Helga began to feel she was losing possession of her child. It was a wonderful time of sharing which brushed aside all the past difficulties. It seemed that for a blissful two weeks the past anger had been buried. It was when Ilse was preparing to return to Blankenese that a change occurred. It was Helga's own doing, for she knew that what she had to say represented a risk.

It was in the afternoon when the baby was asleep and they were all enjoying coffee and pastries and conversation in the living room. Helga took a deep breath, and faced her mother.

"I want to keep the baby and bring him up myself," she said.

"How can you do that? Ilse reacted quickly and angrily, dismayed by her daughter's audacity. "It means a continuing interruption of your studies, negating all the planning we did to arrange a prudent way for you to have the baby and then return home. Besides, if you do bring him up how would you support yourself?"

"What's the alternative mother?" She paused, her pulse quickening, challenging her mother for an answer. "I suppose you want me to give him away, or you will remain prudent, as you say, and hire a nanny to look after him?" There was a bitterness in her voice and she was breathing hard, "not in Blankenese of course, that would be too obvious. You've banished me . . . why not the baby as well?"

Ilse looked crushed as Helga continued.

"Well, I'm not going to accept that - no matter what father thinks!"

"I don't know what the answer is." Ilse's voice sounded weary. "I'll have to discuss it with your father."

"It's an easy way out isn't it - to invoke the myth of collective wisdom." Helga was furious now. Nothing had changed. Still, the same outworn prejudices remained. "What you really mean is that you know the answer already, but you don't have the courage to tell me to my face?"

Ilse stood up. Her face was red. Her lips were trembling. "If you think I know, then I can only conclude that you have an idea of what you expect the answer to be?"

"Yes I think I do. It goes like this - don't bring the illegitimate child to Blankenese. That would embarrass us all. After all, we sent you away to retain our prestige in the community. If you want to keep the child, you're on your own. **In other words, fall in with our wishes or we disown you?**" Helga was shouting now, expelling her built-up frustration, and the baby, sensing the conflict, cried loudly.

Ilse spoke firmly, slowly. "Look, Helga, I'm not going to get into this without talking to your father!" She stamped her foot and turned on her heel and walked towards the stairs to be stopped by Eva's words.

"She can stay with me," Eva spoke in the calm measured tone of voice which she always seemed to muster in the midst of a crisis. Helga, hesitated, surprised, then she rushed over and hugged her grandmother while Ilse turned back towards them. She seemed confused - her lips moved but no words came and she turned again towards the stairs. When she reached the bottom step, she turned again.

"I'm going to pack now," she said. "My train leaves in two hours." She had difficulty going on. With her voice breaking and her whole body shaking, she appeared to reach down into herself, searching for and finding another part of her being. She took a faltering step towards Helga.

"Helga, dear." She paused to draw breath. "Take good care of your baby."

Helga felt a momentary sense of shock, and then she rushed forward, embracing her mother, and they both cried. Helga knew then that her mother's aggressiveness, so uncharacteristic of the preceding days, was but a rehearsal for the meeting with her husband and the ordeal yet to be faced. Rolf would not have changed his views and Helga did not envy her mother's dilemma.

Helga stood in the doorway with the baby in her arms. Eva was by her side. Her mother climbed into the waiting taxi and the driver closed the door. Ilse wound down the window for a last wave, and Helga shouted, "Good luck . . . I love you," as the taxi moved off.

4.

Peter received the telegram on February 3.   It had been transmitted to the Wireless Office on board the Saram so that its contents, although personally addressed to Peter, were soon common knowledge throughout the ship's company.   The Wireless Telegraphist who brought it to him as he sat in the mess talking to Tom over a cup of tea, couldn't hide a grin.   Peter, blushing now, waited for him to leave before reading its contents.

LIEBSTER PETER.

BABY BOY, HANS-PETER, BORN AM 3RD FEB.
3.8 *KILOGRAMME.*
ALLES IN ORDNUNG. (All well)
ALLES LIEBE. (All my love) HELGA.

He handed it to Tom.
"Bloody hell, mate," Tom exclaimed. "You're a father!"
Tom proffered his hand and Peter took it.   His actions were automatic, as dazed and disorientated he tried to absorb the reality of what had happened.
"How many pounds in a sodding kilogram?" Tom, pencil and paper in hand, persevered with the conversion.
"About two something pounds to a kilogram I think."
"It's a big one. Must be eight or nine pounds?"
Peter wasn't listening.
"I must phone her, Tom."
"It's back to the pub then."

The next available shore leave was not until the following

afternoon. By supper time, his messmates, as if by some sleight of hand, had produced cigars and an ample supply of rum.

"Time for a celebration, Dad," said Ray Kurdish, always the ringleader in any excuse for a party. The Duty Mess Cook had prepared a celebration cake with 'Daddy Gray' emblazoned on its creamy surface. Peter, unable to hide his embarrassment and uncomfortable with the zest of his shipmates, was prevailed upon to cut the cake as the hoarded rum flowed and the conversation increased in intensity and loudness. He listened to songs and bawdy jokes about marriage and parenthood. Surprised by the camaraderie of his fellow seamen and getting into the mood of the moment, Peter sang and laughed until his consciousness faded in a blur of cheerful faces.

The next morning Peter awoke to the call of 'Rise and Shine' as the Duty Petty Officer went his rounds, whacking hammocks with his hand to encourage some action from the sleeping occupants.

Peter's head seemed to be floating clear of his body at first, then the throbbing began. By the time he had managed to get out of his hammock he barely had time to reach the heads to dispose of a goodly portion of the content of his stomach. He staggered back to the mess to have Tom thrust a cup of strong coffee into his hand.

"Should perk you up a bit, Dad?"

Tom fluttered around him like a mothering hen, helping him to regain some semblance of a connection with the real world.

"Got to get ashore today," Tom said, "time to make that call."

"Christ! What time is it?" Peter felt confused as he tried to get his befuddled mind to focus.

"You've only just got out of the sack. There's lots of time. Just wanted to get that head of yours in working order."

The second phone call was easier. George was, as before, immensely helpful. He hadn't yet received the cost of the first call but that didn't prevent him from allowing Peter a second opportunity.

Helga sounded excited. She described the baby, telling Peter that it looked like him.

"He has fair hair and blue eyes. He is *glücklich* . . . happy."

"Just like his mother," Peter tried to visualize the two of them as the old yearning to be there, sharing the moment, returned.

"Listen. Peter . . . Can you hear him." All Peter could hear was a sucking, gurgling sound.

"He's feeding now," she said, and he had visions of her exposed breast and the baby kneading the soft skin that he had once fondled and kissed in a time lost to dreams.

"I hear him, Helga."

"*Mutter* came," she said, "And she is happy . . . happy for me, Peter."

"Helga, I must see you. I will try to get there."

"Peter, please don't come if there is risk. I love you. You must be careful."

"I will. You take care of our son."

It seemed such an inadequate remark, so lacking an expression of how he felt. The difficulty with the telephone was that it was only voices and sounds and imaginings, there were no eyes to look into and take comfort from. The telephone tantalized, tore at one's memories, played with unattainable closeness while all the time exemplifying distance and remoteness.

He bade her farewell, and she started to cry.

"I love you, Helga," he said, gently replacing the receiver before his own voice failed him.

After offering George another pound, which he promptly

refused, he joined Tom for a beer.

"I've got to get there, Tom. I must see her."

"On with the plan then."

"I suppose."

Peter didn't feel too confident. The difficulties of getting into Germany were becoming all too clear.

"No time to lose," Tom ignored his gloom. "Get in that request to see Jimmy." *

"Compassionate leave," Peter mouthed the words as if to own the hope they represented, but it didn't work. It only reminded him that he had always associated compassionate leave with illness and death, never a birth.

A few days later Peter was called to see the First Lieutenant.

Peter had worded his fictitious request with the utmost care, describing his mother's unexpected illness and the resulting strain on his ailing father. He was needed at home to render assistance until some additional help could be found. He had requested three weeks leave.

Peter waited outside the First Lieutenant's office. He was beginning to doubt the wisdom of his actions when the door opened.

"Come in, Gray."

Lieutenant Braden-Hallet was a young energetic officer with a boyish face and a disarming manner which encouraged confidence, but which also hid a total commitment to strict naval discipline. Peter saluted, and he motioned him to sit. It was a small office with barely room for a desk, least of all a chair, and the closeness of his superior officer made him uneasy.

Bruce-Hallet studied the file in front of him and Peter could see that it was his service record. On top, held by a paper clip, was his written request for leave which the Lieutenant glanced at before looking up to confront him with a steady unwavering gaze.

"You wanted to see me?"

"Yes sir, I . . . I wanted to ask if I could get some special leave."

"Compassionate leave?"

"Yes, sir."

"Your mother is unwell?"

"Yes, sir . . . " Peter shifted uneasily.

"Some quite serious ailment, I believe?"

Bruce-Hallet waited for an answer as Peter's face paled, his confidence failing him. How did he ever expect to be this dishonest? He couldn't go through with it, couldn't involve his family in the fabrication. His elaborate gamble disintegrating, Peter tried to think of another alternative, desperately trying to salvage something from the wreckage, but there was no where else to go but to tell the truth. The Lieutenant's steely eyes held his.

"I . . . I think I would like to withdraw the request, sir."

"The situation has improved, then?"

"Changed, sir."

"I see, well, I'll consider this particular matter closed."

There was something in the way he said 'this particular matter' that made Peter believe that Bruce-Hallet had an inkling of the real reason. After all, the whole ship's company knew of the birth of the child, knew that the mother of the child was in Germany. It would hardly be surprising if the subject was now part of the wardroom gossip as well. Probably, even the Captain knew. His suspicions appeared to have some validity as the Lieutenant continued.

"Gray, as First Lieutenant aboard this ship, I am concerned with the welfare of each member of the crew. If you have a problem that you wish to discuss, you can request to see me at any time."

"Yes, sir. Thank you, sir."

"You are dismissed, Gray."

"Aye, Aye, sir."

Peter stood up, saluted, and stumbled out of the office.

The devastating encounter left Peter doubting his own sanity. If he had even stopped to consider what he was doing he would have realized the implications of making such a foolhardy request. The trouble was, he hadn't thought it through on his terms. It was what Tom would have done not what he, Peter, could carry off. He wanted to see Helga so badly that he had been prepared to resort to any subterfuge to make it happen. He was angry at his foolhardiness and he hoped his rashness had not eradicated all hope of another, more truthful attempt. The common knowledge among the crew of his association with a *foreign national* - it sounded so dehumanizing - a German no less, led him to wonder if it would be forever held against him, marking him as a person of doubtful character, not to be trusted with the added responsibilities which came with any future opportunities for promotion? On top of his parent's objections, and Stephen's earlier scepticism, was now added the potential rejection by his superior officers.

The more he pondered his fate, the more it increased his resolve to do something. The next opportunity would be during the Easter leave. Although this would only give him seven days to make the trip to Munich, it would mean that he would not have to obtain special leave. As he was already in possession of a passport, the outstanding problem was to raise the necessary funds. He had ruled out the possibility of cycling and camping his way there. The short time now at his disposal made this impractical. The only stumbling block was whether he could enlist his mother's support to fund the trip.

"So, you blew it," Tom looked dejected, probably suffering as much from what he regarded as his bad advice as Peter's failure of resolve.

"I'm sorry, Tom. You could'a winged it. I couldn't."

"Too bloody pure," For a moment Tom looked disdainful, but then he brightened. "Try the honest way?"

"I think it's worth a go."

"If I can help . . . " Tom started, but then he stopped.

"Better stay out of this."

"It was a gambit we lost, that's all. I still need your support."

"You have it."

The letter to his mother was a struggle. On the one hand he felt bad about involving her in his scheme, particularly as his father would reject any help and blame his mother if he found out. Still, he had to risk that, he had no other potential benefactors to turn to. After several attempts, he settled for a straightforward approach.

Dear Mother,

I have to ask you for a favour. You will remember that I told you that Helga was pregnant and that I intended to go and see her. Well, the baby, a boy, was born on February 3. He is to be called Hans-Peter and weighs about eight pounds. Helga tells me that she and the child are doing well. My only opportunity to make the trip will be when my Easter leave comes due at the end of March. This will give me a week, and if I'm to get to Munich and back in that time, I need to go by ferry and train into France and then into Germany.

Can you help me financially? I could probably manage it for about £50. I know this is a lot, but I will pay you back. It's just that I need the help now.

I'm sorry to be burdening you with this request but I must try and see Helga and my son.

Your loving son,
Peter.

P.S. Could you send my civvies? You know, the sport's jacket, trousers and shoes, plus a couple of sport's shirts.

He read it again. It seemed terse but he couldn't think of any other way of softening his need and his determination to get into Germany. He sealed the envelope and posted the letter.

5.

$\mathscr{I}$t was the beginning of the second week in March when Peter received a letter from his mother. It was not what he had expected. It was written in a barely legible scrawl, as though the hand that held the pen was trembling, making the formation of the words and letters extremely difficult.

> Dear Peter,
>
> I have not been well of late and I have had to stay in bed for a while. But I am feeling much better now. I was pleased to hear about the baby and that everything is all right. It will be nice if you can get to see Helga. You must let me know when you will be going. You must bring back pictures of the child for me to see.
>
> Your loving mother.

Something was very wrong. Not only had she completely ignored his request for financial help, the writing itself, its scrawl undoubtedly connected with the unexplained illness, was almost unrecognizable from the usually clear confident script that he had come to expect. He felt weak and guilty. His bogus request for compassionate leave, the case he couldn't go through with, had now suddenly become a dreadful reality. He was being punished for his dishonesty.

He struggled with conflicting emotions. Should he resubmit the request for compassionate leave, and then try and combine a visit with his mother with the planned trip to Germany? He couldn't decide. Tom wasn't much help either.

"Go for the compassionate leave again. See how your

mum is, and then off you go to see Helga."

"I can't do that. What if she's really sick?"

"Well then, it's either one or the other . . . or nothing at all." Tom sounded dismissive, as if he wanted to abandon his role as resident advisor and Peter pushed him no further.

Peter awoke the next morning after a fitful sleep. He was sitting in the mess finishing his breakfast when Tom rushed in.

"Heard the news?"

Peter shook his head absentmindedly.

"Hitler invaded Czechoslovakia!"

"Christ," Peter groaned, holding his head in his hands as the loudspeaker blared, 'Sea duty men close up. Prepare for leaving harbour.'

They were at sea for four days carrying out minesweeping exercises in the Channel which most of the crew members felt was an excuse to get them out of harbour, a response to the political situation which had suddenly darkened the days of optimism which had followed the Munich Agreement.

As he participated in the complex procedures of streaming and recovering the minesweeping gear he thought of Helga. What must they be thinking in Germany? It was hard to understand how Hitler's actions could receive the unanimous support of the German people. But their faith in the *Führer* was not in question, not in Peter's mind. Not after what Helga had said. Perhaps it would all blow over? He had to assume that it would and that somehow his plans could still proceed. Then he thought again of his mother. He would write to her as soon as they arrived in harbour.

Dear Mother,

I was surprised to hear that you have been ill. What exactly is the problem? Could you please explain what has happened? While I am happy to

117

know that you are feeling better I worry about you and don't want you to overdo things. Please write soon and tell me all.

And then he added.

> I'll be home soon. Easter leave is coming up. Until then, take care of yourself.

> Your loving son,
> Peter.

He was preparing to go home for a late Easter leave in April when a parcel arrived. It contained his civvies. He didn't recognize the handwriting in the address at first. In fact, it was the return address that established that it was his father's writing. This seemed rather odd, but he assumed that his mother had asked his father to post it. He felt a ripple of dismay. This could only mean one thing, that he had read the letter. The very incident he had tried so hard to avoid had happened - his father knew of his plans to see Helga and, worst of all his request for money.

The next day a letter arrived. The post was distributed in the mess during supper. When his name was called he raised his hand and the plain white envelope was passed to him. It was his father's writing again. He felt his pulse quicken. His father never wrote to him. It was always his mother.

He couldn't bring himself to open the letter in front of his messmates so he stuffed it in his pocket.

"Must be from a tart?" Someone yelled from the other end of the table and Peter managed the suggestion of a smile.

As soon as he could, he left the table, searching for a quiet place where he wouldn't be disturbed. All the heads were occupied but the washrooms opposite were empty. He stood in a corner and opened the envelope.

Dear Peter, it began.

Your mother passed away on March 26th.
It was very sudden. The funeral was on March 30th.
I thought I should tell you. I'm sorry.

God bless you.
Your loving father.

P.S. I hope you received the parcel.

Peter stood gazing at his father's unfamiliar handwriting.
It all seemed like a cruel joke, a simple assembly of words that
he couldn't absorb. The terms 'passed away' and 'funeral'
belonged to some other time and place, it couldn't possibly apply
to the mother who greeted him short months ago, and who had
written to him barely days ago.   He leaned against the
washbasins, feeling unsteady, wanting to ignore the truth which
he held in his hand.

As he reread the sombre statement its full import seeped
into his brain, and he stared absentmindedly at the empty
washbasins. In his bewilderment his eyes focussed on the water
droplets clinging to the sides of the washbasins. There was the
odd bar of soap left behind, perhaps awaiting the return of its
owner. It was suddenly like the bathroom would be at home he
thought, only there it would be all that was left to announce his
mother had been there and would never return.

He read the letter again and he felt offended. Why hadn't
his father told him?   But he was never any good at knowing
what to do. He remembered his mother's words, 'He thinks he's
doing the right thing.' For God's sake though, didn't he feel that
his only son should be told?   She was not only dead; she was
already buried! She was gone from his sight forever.

He went up on deck, and leaned on the rail, gazing at the
horizon. Funny thing about horizons, people disappear over
them like Helga had done.   His mother had passed over a

different horizon, into another world beyond, whatever that meant? He looked out to where sea and sky met, the line of demarcation that looked like the end of one's world, but it wasn't, it was only an illusion, like thoughts of immortality. He thought of Tom's words 'One thing about the sea,' he had said, 'It clears the head. But we need a fucking good gale to deal with this one.'

He was glad that Tom wasn't with him now. He just wanted to be alone. Part of him wanted to weep, but the other part, the disciplined navy part, rejected any thought of it. He had no intention of humiliating himself in front of his crewmates; neither had he any intention of going home. Facing his father after this would be tantamount to condoning his father's actions, confirming that he, Peter, was too young to deal with death. Of course he could deal with death; he would carry on as usual, gritting his teeth, putting all his energies into his work, seeking advancement. He would show his father what he was really made of.

It was a question of getting back to work and resuming his efforts to see Helga - no point in telling her either. He moved away from the rail and he felt a sudden lump in his throat. His mother would no longer grace his life, greet him at the station, show concern for his health and well-being, no longer parade him proudly in his uniform to all her friends - that part at least would not be missed. He told himself that it was just the biting wind that stung his eyes, making the tears flow, besides it was getting cold. He wiped away the wetness and braced himself to rejoin his shipmates.

The next day, the Prime Minister, speaking to the House of Commons, pledged Britain's support in the event that Polish independence was threatened. The stage seemed to be set for war. The chance to see Helga was diminishing fast. In any event, he still had no financial resources to make the trip.

6.

Günther's course at Kiel ended at the beginning of April. A week before its completion the class was told that they were to be sent to the training ship, *Mullenburg*. It was stationed near Wilhelmshaven. However, before reporting for duty, they were to be given ten days of leave.

The twelve weeks of training had been unexpectedly demanding. It wasn't the physical requirements, but the mental strain of living and training in close company with men from a wide range of social and economic backgrounds, many of whom regarded Günther as something of a snob. Unlike the *Hitler Jugend*, where the associations had developed over a longer period of time and most often grew out of being in the same school, in the same district, here men were drawn from all over Germany. There had also been an unrelenting pressure to conform, to become part of a team, forced to work together in unfamiliar circumstances for the first time. But there was one redeeming aspect for Günther. Some three weeks into the course he had made a friendship with Siegfried *Holmann*. Siegfried's family, who lived south of Hamburg in Neuengamme, farmed a marshland area famous for its high yields of vegetable crops. Siegfried was a tall, robust, easy-going character whose life on the land made him view with disdain the petty squabbles among the many conflicting personalities attending the training course. He loved the outdoors, and it was here that he and Günther found a common interest. They first met as crew members of a sailing cutter taking part in class races on the Weser river. They both liked sailing. Günther remembered fondly how, during his growing up years in Blankenese, his father had a small yacht which he sailed on the Elbe. Günther and Helga, often joined by Heinrich, his father's chauffeur, were his enthusiastic crew. Ilse, his mother, was less keen but she still came along, especially when they went for a picnic on a nearby island.

Those were the carefree years, but now Günther was uncertain as to how and where to spend his leave. With the political situation worsening, he felt he owed it to his parents to visit them even though he still retained a considerable discomfort over the disagreement with his father and the unhappiness that he had caused with his mother.

He was sitting in the canteen with Siegfried, relaxing over coffee on the day before they were due to start their leave, when breaking a long silence, Siegfried asked.

"Do you think there'll be war?"

He was surprised by the question. He had never really considered it a serious possibility.

"I don't think England will go to war," said Günther. Why would they protect Poland? It is just a bluff. They don't want war. If they did, it would have happened before now."

"I hope you're right."

Günther didn't share Siegfried's pessimism even though it bothered him. Anyhow, he was much more concerned about what he would do tomorrow. "I'd like to go home," he said "I'm sure father would like to hear about the training but . . . "

Over the course of the last several weeks, Günther had told Siegfried of the family dilemma, the problem that Helga's indiscretion had created, and the disappointment his father felt over his joining the Kriegsmarine as a seaman.

"See your parents. If they're like mine, they'll want to see you no matter what you've done. They're probably less upset than you think. It can't do any harm to go. But how about your sister, shouldn't you visit her?"

"No," said Günther firmly. "I'm not ready for that. She has the child now. The Englishman's child. I've been against it. I still am."

"Are you being fair? Surely she needs your support at a time like this, especially when your parents have sent her away."

"*Oma* is protecting her," Günther said. There was resentment in his voice. "I don't see why I should change my view."

"Racial purity? Allegiance to the cause?" All of a sudden, Siegfried was speaking in a threatening tone of voice and Günther was shocked. "All very noble, Günther, but she is your sister."

Still trying to comprehend the reason for the sudden outburst, Günther responded instinctively.

"Who's been very stupid?" He resented Siegfried's challenge. He shrugged his shoulders and glared back at him, wondering if his new friend was as loyal to Germany's cause as he had assumed and then, unable to let the issue pass, he held Siegfried's eyes in his.

"You do believe in the *Führer?*"

Siegfried matched his stare.

"I believe in a strong Germany," he said firmly. "I have enjoyed the healthy life in the *Hitler Jugend*. I'm excited about being in the *Kriegsmarine* but, like my father, I sometimes wonder where it's taking us . . . especially now."

"You sound like my father."

"I think it's very difficult for the older generation. They don't have our unquestioning faith. The consequence of their wisdom and experience is often great caution."

Günther was struck by Siegfried's willingness to question. It was not a practice that was encouraged these days. It could be construed as treasonous. Yet his words reminded Günther that he had long ago ceased to question, suppressing or rationalizing any misgivings he felt. Besides, life was good, the country was prospering, it required commitment from everyone to sustain it. There was no time for doubters. Such people were not contributing to the attainment of the *Führer's* lofty ambitions. He was pondering all this, trying to frame a suitable challenge, when Siegfried changed the subject.

"Like to spend some of your leave with my family?"

"I." Günther was unprepared for the question. He was still trying to deal with Siegfried's opinions. "I . . . I would like to," Günther stumbled over his words. "Are you . . . well, sure?"

"No problem. I'll tell you how to get to the farm."

Günther went directly from Kiel to Hamburg and then on to Blankenese. He had not warned his parents that he was coming, but they were glad to see him. Sitting in the living room with his father, Günther recounted his experiences.

"Next step is the *Mullenburg*."

"I know that ship. Old Great War cruiser, now an anti-aircraft gun ship."

"It's operating in the Bight. Wilhelmshaven will be our base."

"You may be firing those guns at the enemy soon!"

"You think there'll be war?"

"I don't like the way things are happening . . . "

"England won't fight?" Günther needed the benefit of some of that generational wisdom which Siegfried had talked about.

"Don't be too certain. They can be stubborn when provoked."

"The *Führer* knows what he's doing," Günther tried to give himself some assurance.

"Hitler is a gambler. And like any gambler, he can make mistakes." Rolf showed his resentment now, his fear of a miscalculation plainly evident.

Ilse, entering at an opportune moment, as though she had been listening all along, had Minna with her.

"Here's some coffee," she said, motioning Minna to put it on the table.

"Tell me about this friend of yours," Ilse said looking at Günther.

"He lives in Neuengamme. His parents have a farm. Very pleasant fellow, Siegfried *Holmann*. We get along well together."

"Farmers are they," Rolf said, as if determined to identify their class. "Do you know anything about the family?"

"Not a thing," said Günther.

"Should be interesting to stay with them," Ilse said, "how about Helga? Are you going to see her and the baby?"

"I don't think so." Günther was surprised that his mother had raised the subject.

"That's best left alone," said Rolf, quickly ending any further discussion.

Life in Neuengamme started early, earlier than in the *Kriegsmarine*. Siegfried's family lived in a large building that housed not only his father and mother, two younger brothers and one younger sister, it also provided quarters for the workers. Siegfried introduced Günther to his father and mother and his brothers and sister. His mother and father were industrious people who conveyed the impression that they had never heard of idleness. They were both robust and healthy and it was not difficult to believe that Siegfried was their son. In fact, the same looks and demeanour could be seen in Siegfried's brothers' and sister. His sister, approaching fifteen, the youngest member of the family, had the strong features of her father and the good looks of her mother. It was a happy family and Günther felt at home right away. It seemed natural to help with the farm activities but Günther and Siegfried also had ample opportunities for long walks, or swimming in the Elbe. There were plenty of pretty girls in the area so that their leisure was brightened by feminine companions. There were sexual opportunities too, but Günther, taking a cue from Siegfried, who like himself displayed a shyness about the opposite sex, quickly sensed the caution required in a small community where news and gossip travelled fast to both enhance and threaten reputations. Still, Günther's youthful desires were reflected in a chance remark by Siegfried. They were walking together on the path along the top of a dyke near the Elbe.

"Ever been to the *Reeperbahn?*"

"It's crossed my mind," said Günther.

"That's all."

"I did go once . . . by myself. Checking out the girls - just looking."

"Ah!" Siegfried smiled.

"It was nothing," Günther was in some haste to explain. "I looked at the girls in their cubicles. I wanted, well . . . I just looked."

"That was it?"

"I didn't have the money or the courage. I worried about what my parents would think."

"We should go together. Give each other confidence."

"My God," said Günther, "I'm getting excited just thinking about it."

The *Mullenberg* was an unimposing sight. It looked old in spite of its fresh paint and the bristling array of new anti-aircraft weapons seemed out of place. It was anchored in the German Bight near Wilhelmshaven and the pinnace taking Günther and Siegfried and the rest of the class from Kiel rolled gently in the swell as it made its way towards the gangway. The *Mullenburg* was to be their new home for at least six weeks while they learned how to cope with life aboard ship.   It would be worthwhile putting up with the strict training program for, at the end of it, it would be on to the real navy, an active seagoing warship. Günther, like Siegfried, looked forward to that day.

7.

$\mathcal{I}$t was June and the Saram was returning to Portland after a minesweeping exercise. Peter was leaning over the rail watching the approaching Dorset coastline. He thought how much the peaceful scene belied the worsening political situation - Italy's invasion of Albania in mid April, and the British Government's introduction of conscription in late April when they called up all males of twenty years of age.

He thought of his mother and how devastated she would have been by it all. Perhaps her death was fortuitous? His mind rebelled at his callousness. But then his father had reduced the family tragedy to a few terse words on a piece of paper. He had acknowledged his father's letter after a considerable delay, but his aggravation caused him to confine himself to what amounted to an expression of sympathy and informing him that he'd been unable to be home for Easter leave. He hadn't told Tom of his mother's passing and Tom, apparently sensing that something was wrong, had not attempted to question his long silences or the lonely trips ashore. However, he needed to confide in Tom.

"Sorry for being in the dumps." Peter joined Tom on the upper deck on the evening of their arrival in Portland harbour.

"I figured you didn't need my gabbing on . . ."

Peter moved to speak, wanting to defend his actions.

"No need to explain."

"How 'bout a natter."

"Shoot! I'm all ears."

"It's Helga . . ."

"Nothing wrong, is there?" Tom reacted as though Helga's welfare was as much his concern as Peter's.

"No . . . No, it's just . . . I've decided to make the trip in July. During summer leave."

"Couldn't understand why you didn't go at Easter? Christ, you didn't even go on leave. Saving the coppers, I bet?"

"Yea." Peter choked off the question. "I'm going by train and ferry," he said, and then uncertain how to continue, played for a moment with a flake of rust on a nearby stanchion.

"Tom," he said, looking up. "Could you do me a favour?"

"Depends."

"I've written a letter. It's addressed to Jimmy. It explains what I'm doing."

"Christ, you're not going to tell 'im?"

"No. It's in case I don't return on time."

"Won't make any bloody difference? If you're 'Absent Without Leave' they'll throw the book at you."

"I know, but I'd feel better."

"Pure again, " he hesitated. "Sure, I'll do it."

"Thanks Tom. I really appreciate this."

It felt good to be talking to Tom again, so good in fact that he almost relented and told him the whole story of the events of the past few weeks, but he didn't; it was all behind him now he told himself and he didn't want sympathy even from Tom. Besides, telling Tom that his grandfather had agreed to help him financially was out of the question as it would only prompt questions about his mother.

8.

*H*elga answered the telephone. It was Peter. As he had not phoned at Easter, she had already come to the conclusion that his plan to attempt a visit had been abandoned.

"Where are you, Peter?"

"I'm coming to see you. I begin my leave in two weeks."

"How can you Peter? How is this possible?

"I will come Helga, but I have to ask if you can help."

"What is this, help?"

"Can you come to the border at Strasbourg?"

"Strasbourg? *Mein Gott!*"

"It would help, Helga. I wouldn't have to travel as far."

"I do not know, Peter. With the *Kind?*"

"Yes, with the baby . . . if you can?"

"I will try, dear Peter. I will try."

"I'll meet you in Germany. I'll cross the Rhine into Germany at Strasbourg. We could stay in Kehl or some other town near the border?"

"You are coming, Peter?"

"Yes, yes, really I am. Can you meet me at the border?"

"Peter. I will try. I must see you, Peter."

"I'll be there at noon, midday, on July the fourth. Can you be there?"

"July the fourth. I write it down. Twelve o'clock. I will try, Peter. I will try."

Helga hung up the phone, her emotions caught between happiness and fear and then the tears came and Eva, hearing the sound, came to see what was wrong.

"Peter is coming, *Oma,*" she said, wiping her eyes.

"Coming here?"

"To Strasbourg."

"You have to get to Strasbourg?"

"*Ja . . . Nein*, the border at Strasbourg. He will come to Germany."

"I think we had better talk about this when you're calm."

She stood up, her self-possession restored. "*Ja, Oma.* We will make it happen!"

It was after a day or so had elapsed, and her excitement had subsided enough to allow rational thought, that the immensity of what Peter was planning to do sank in. Getting to the border would probably not present any particular problems; there being regular trains from Munich to Strasbourg. However, she had no idea whether Germany's current state of military preparedness would restrict her ability to travel. She did not, as Peter had suggested, need to cross the border, so that meant leaving the train before the Rhine was crossed at Strasbourg. This could be the first difficulty, she thought, as the fast trains might not stop close to the border and this would necessitate changing to a slower train, perhaps at a place like Ulm or Freudenstadt, and hoping that this train could bring her close to a border town. Even then, she had to get to the actual border point and hope that the German officials would both allow her to wait for Peter and, more critically, to allow his entry into Germany. All this was also predicated on the French officials allowing him to leave France, as well as to return. Furthermore, the whole plan had to be achieved on a specific date and at a specific time. It was a monumental gamble that had as much chance of failing as succeeding.

Eva, far from resisting the scheme, took a delight in becoming involved. She studied maps and train timetables, discussing with Helga the various options that could be explored.

"I wonder why Peter didn't give you his phone number. You have no way of getting in touch with him." Eva, pencil in hand, worried over this omission.

"I think he'll call again, *Oma* . . . but if he doesn't, I must still go."

Eva nodded. "We'll go to the station today and work out the train times."

On June 29, two weeks after large numbers of officers and men of the Royal Naval Reserve had been called up, and after the Saram had returned to Portland, Peter and Tom went to see George.

"Another call, then?"

George had spotted Peter as he entered the pub and as all eyes turned on him he wished George would be a little more circumspect with his comments. Peter nodded, hastening to the small office behind the bar.

"Go ahead, son," said George, poking his head into the office, but Peter was already waiting for Helga to answer.

"*Hallo.*" Damn, it wasn't Helga. It was her grandmother again.

The exchange that followed succeeded only by dint of perseverance by both parties, given Peter's lack of German and Eva's lack of English. However, it was established that Helga was out, but should be returning in about half an hour. Peter gave George's number to Eva and said he would wait for her to ring.

"Relax Pete." Tom sipped at his beer while Peter sat staring into space beginning to fear that his plan was about to go awry. He was annoyed now because he hadn't given George's number to Helga when he made the first call.

When the phone eventually rang, Peter leapt to his feet, never for a moment doubting that it would be Helga.

"It's you!"

"Peter" she exclaimed. "It is arranged. I will be at the border at twelve o'clock on July the fourth. The train from *München* to Strasbourg stops at Kehl so I'll be able to stay in Germany.

"Wonderful! *Wunderbar!* I love you, Helga!"

"Oh, Peter. It has to happen," she said, leaving him with the uneasy reminder that a daunting array of problems, many of them yet to be discovered, had to be overcome to achieve the reunion.

"It will happen, Helga," he said, as much to convince himself that the plan would work. Then, mustering a hint of confidence, he said. "We'll soon be together."

"I love you, Peter. Whatever happens I will always love you."

"Dear, dear, Helga. Take care of yourself and our baby."

"*Auf Wiedersehen, mein* Peter."

"*Auf Wiedersehen*, dear Helga."

He hung up, and turned as George entered.

"Everything, OK, son?"

"Yes. Yes. Thanks, George."

On July 1, Peter left the Saram to begin the big adventure. He handed the letter, addressed to Lieutenant Braden-Hallet, to Tom.

"Hope's I don't have to use it," he said, pocketing the envelope.

Peter shook Tom's hand and then went down the companionway to the waiting pinnace. 'I hope so too,' he thought, rapidly arresting any drift towards pessimism. He had to get there first. Only then would him worry about getting back.

He stopped in the pub to settle his debts with George and to change into his civvies, then he took the bus to Weymouth for the train to Newhaven.

9.

By the time Peter reached the Ferry Terminal at Newhaven it was already mid afternoon. The lines were cast off at three and the ferry headed out into the English Channel. Soon they were in the open sea heading towards Dieppe.

He was on the upper deck, looking out to the horizon, seeking the area where he thought the outline of the French coast would soon appear, when he became conscious of another presence.

"Off to France, or somewhere beyond?" The voice was decidedly Oxford ish, and Peter turned to see a pleasant face crowned by a jaunty cap. He wore a windbreaker over a sweater and navy blue trousers, giving the appearance that he had just vacated a yacht.

"Ah, yes . . . France," said Peter, taken off guard by the question.

"John Barclay." He extended his hand.

It was a firm handshake accompanied by a confident stare.

"Peter Gray. Nice to meet you."

"Driving down to Zurich, myself. Got to get things in order before the balloon goes up. Where in France, Peter? Looking for fun in the south?" He eyed Peter as if trying to determine his pedigree.

"Well, no." Peter, summoned an attempt to match the tenor of the discourse. "Actually, I'm going to Germany."

"Good God, Man. That takes some guts!"

"My . . . My lady friend (he was going to say girlfriend) is there. She's just had our baby."

"Well, that's very honourable. Your going there, I mean. Must be a quite special relationship?"

"It is." Peter wished he hadn't been as forthcoming with the information and he sensed that John had registered his discomfort.

"Like to join me?" John adopted a breezy tone. "I'm going to get a bite to eat, and a midday nip, of course."

They went below to the restaurant, Peter hoping that he wouldn't have to foot the bill, and settled into a generous lunch. He soon learned that John owned a prosperous electrical company outside of Reading and that he had amassed considerable earnings from investments in Europe which were now held in Swiss banks. Peter, feeling obliged to tell his story, embellished it a little by not declaring his status as a naval rating, and inferring that he had some loosely defined assignment as a commissioned officer which he couldn't, of course, discuss. He wondered if John accepted the fabrication, but it didn't appear to matter. John, obviously something of an adventurer, and perhaps given to stretching the truth, was much more interested in Peter's immediate plan to enter Germany and having learned the details was quick to offer assistance.

"Look, Peter. I'm driving to Paris. Are you fixed up with a place to stay?"

"Well, no . . . not yet."

"Tell you what. I'm going to Montparnasse. There's a small hotel near where I stay. How about my taking you there?"

Peter had the impression that a lady friend was awaiting John's arrival. But that was his business. It was an offer he couldn't refuse.

"That's very kind of you."

"No problem, Peter. As a matter of fact I'll drive you to Strasbourg the next day. I've got to pass it on my way to Zurich so it's no trouble."

John paid the bill and they moved towards the car deck.

"By the way, how long do you expect to be in Germany?"

"Perhaps two, maybe three days."

"Tell you what. I'll give you my telephone number in

Zurich. Phone me when you decide to leave. I can pick you up in Strasbourg again."

"But how about your plans?"

"I'm flexible. Only thing is, I'll want to stay in Paris for a while on the way back," he winked. "It's where my lady friend is. So, you'll have to make your own way from there."

The deal was quickly concluded. Peter couldn't believe his good fortune. It was all working out much better than he could have ever imagined.

They arrived in Strasbourg on the evening of July 2, a day earlier than Peter had planned. John insisted on driving to the French border post at the bridge crossing the Rhine, arguing that Peter should get his bearings. Then they searched for a hotel by the river's edge, running into an unexpected difficulty when accosted by soldiers who informed them that the area immediately adjacent to the river was a restricted zone. They eventually found a modest establishment on a street nearby. Then John bade farewell. Obviously, as in Paris, he had other plans for the night.

Peter was awakened the next morning by a knock on the door.

"*Votre petit dejeuner, monsieur.*"

"*Ah, Entrez,*" He managed to get by with his limited vocabulary.

She brought in strong coffee and croissants, hardly the bacon and eggs he craved, but it had to suffice.

Once dressed, he headed towards the bridge, deciding to scout the area. There were ample indications of military readiness. Soldiers were very much in evidence and traffic passing through the control point appeared to be subjected to lengthy inspections. He tried to move closer to the control point, attempting to look directly across the bridge, trying to see what circumstances prevailed on the German side, but he was stopped by fully armed soldiers who asked to see some identification.

There were military fortifications on both sides of the river, all of which appeared to be manned with armed troops, most of whom seemed to be reservists. It did not bode well for an uncomplicated crossing. He had some difficulty in explaining why he was in that particular place, the British passport being a cause for suspicion. However, he decided to claim that he was just a tourist, not wishing to state his real purpose until it was absolutely necessary. It seemed to satisfy them. However, he hoped that the same soldiers would not stop him when he undertook the actual crossing.

He returned to the hotel and ordered coffee. What if he had come all this way for nothing? Still, the big issue was what he would say to the French and German authorities? Yet there was nothing he could say but to state the truth of his intentions and hope that it would be acceptable. By the third cup of coffee he was becoming more jittery. He went up to his room and lay on the bed, but unable to settle down he went out for a walk, ambling around the old narrow streets, avoiding the river and the military presence. He found a small restaurant and ordered a sandwich, a large crusty roll filled with Camembert. He avoided coffee, taking mineral water. He sat outside under a large parasol watching his fellow Diners, two large men, effusive, sharing a bottle of red wine; a young couple, oblivious to anyone but themselves; and a lone girl, reading a book and eating what looked like a salad. She had dark hair and eyes and painted red lips, her Gaulish countenance completing an effect which gave her an air of sensuousness. Feeling suddenly lonely he had a strong desire to catch her attention, but she too, like the lovers, was oblivious to her surroundings, absorbed by her reading.

There was nothing in the peaceful scene to suggest the nearness of the danger exemplified by the military preparations down by the river. Life seemed normal and the summer sun, dispelling any tendency to pessimism, restored his composure. Why would there be any difficulty? Tomorrow he would be reunited with Helga.

In the afternoon he walked some more, returning to the hotel for a wash before dinner. As the sun set and the darkness of night brought the day to an end, he felt his discomfort returning. He wished that he'd set the rendezvous for today. It would have been achieved by now, instead of having to suffer this prolonged waiting. The military situation was far more ominous than he had expected. Being in England, separated from the Continent by the English Channel, isolated one from the immediate sense of danger that prevailed here. Sitting across the Rhine from Germany was altogether different. Two nations faced each another, looked into each others eyes and waited. He began to ponder again the wisdom of his venture. Not only could it fail, it might result in something infinitely more drastic? What if he was detained, imprisoned even? And what of Helga? Would his actions get her into trouble? He went down to the dining room, only to discover that his appetite had failed him. He ordered a glass of wine and went to bed early.

In the morning he looked forward to the coffee and the croissant. He was hungry now. In spite of his anxiety, he had slept for at least five hours. He had a bath, shaved and dressed, and then he walked towards the bridge again. It felt a little like sauntering to the edge of a cliff, getting used to the idea of jumping off the end. He was careful to stay clear of the troops, wanting to see the bridge again, trying to imagine himself crossing it, trying to summon up his courage for the impending task.

He returned to his room and wrote two identical notes in English, one for the French authorities and the other for the German.

> I am an Englishman who wishes to meet the mother of his child at the German border and then to spend some time together with them in Kehl. Afterwards, I wish to return to England. The total visit will last no longer than three days.

He went for an early lunch and then, collecting his small valise, he headed for the French border post.

"*Votre identification s'il vous plâit?*"

Peter handed the French official his passport.

"*Le purpose du votre voyage?*"

"Ah . . . *parlez vous, anglais?*"

"*Oui, un peu.*"

Peter handed him the note and he studied it. Then he shook his head, not understanding it, obviously unable to read it.

"*Une moment, s'il vous plâit.*"

He disappeared into the adjoining office and Peter could see him showing the note to his superior officer. Presently, they both came out. The officer spoke.

"*M'sieur.* You can pass from France, and return to France, but I cannot say what will happen in Germany. It could be *très difficile pour vous* and *votre femme.* It is, of course, your decision. I cannot guarantee your safety."

Peter tried to weigh the implications. He was heartened by the officer's helpfulness but disturbed by his concern, especially about the matter of personal safety. There was no going back now.

"I will go," he said, and he held out his hand. "*Merci.*"

The officer responded. "*Bonne chance,*" he said. Then he added. "We will accompany you to the border."

With an armed soldier on either side of him, Peter was taken to the centre of the bridge. He looked to the left and right at the rapidly flowing river, trying to visualize a demarcation line between the two countries, but he was distracted by a couple of boaters taking advantage of the current and the summer sun, oblivious to territorial exactitude. He saw the German soldiers watching them, their grey uniforms reminding him of paintings from his Father's War. They were holding their rifles at the ready. It was a fearful sight that Peter, leaving the friendly escort, moved towards.

About five yards from the German border, he was ordered to stop and then to advance, slowly. He wished now he hadn't been escorted by the French. It gave him an aura of mystery and intrigue. 'My God,' he thought, 'Perhaps the French are being deliberately provocative - or is it just a game?'

He handed over his passport and the handwritten note. In a repeat of the earlier procedure, the soldier, unable to read it, took it into an adjoining office.

This time he couldn't observe what was going on in the office. The wait seemed endless. Meanwhile cars were crossing from each direction, their occupants being subjected to lengthy questioning. In many cases the cars were examined thoroughly, although it was unclear what the search was intended to achieve. There were no other individuals crossing on foot so he couldn't decide whether his treatment was abnormal.

He began to feel like a victim of some international conspiracy and his discomfort set his mind to thinking how he might reverse the whole process, simply asking for a cancellation of the entire plan. Then the soldier appeared. He beckoned Peter to follow him. Ushered into the office, he was immediately confronted by an official who appeared to be some sort of border policeman. The soldier departed leaving Peter to his fate. They eyed each other and then, as if in a dream, the official smiled. Peter, blinked, trying to erase the dreamlike image, but it was true, he **was** smiling. And then, suddenly, Helga leapt into his arms, hugging and kissing him, while the official watched with a disciplined amusement.

"Peter! Peter! Dear Peter! You came."

He felt the tears gushing from his eyes. He was incapable of speech and he felt dizzy with excitement and the release of tension. The impossible had happened. They were together again.

"Peter!" Helga was calling and pointing. Pointing to a wicker basket and the small figure lying in the blankets. "This is Hans-Peter. Our *Kind*, Peter!"

The officer recalled the soldier, who in turn motioned them to follow him. They were ushered into a large German staff car. Peter felt another moment of dread. 'So, it was just as he had been warned. They were being arrested.'

"Peter! Peter!" Helga was calling again, urging him out of his confusion. "They take us to a hotel."

They were driven to a small hotel where they were greeted by the owners, an elderly couple. A flag, bearing a large swastika in all its stark reality, hung over the doorway. There was no doubt where he was and he wondered again what trouble he might be in.

The car drove off, and they were shown to their room by the wife. It was a pleasant room on the second floor of the old three-storied house. It was quite spacious with two windows overlooking a carefully kept back garden. He could easily have been looking out over his father's garden at home. There was one large bed, and in the corner a small cot.

"*Möchten sie zu mittag essen.*"

"*Ja. Danke,*" Helga said, handing Peter the child. "She'll bring us some lunch."

Peter reacted awkwardly to the small bundle in his arms and Helga laughed. "Oh Peter, you have to practice being a *Vater.*"

He managed to manoeuvre his son into a comfortable position, feeling quite proud of the results as Hans-Peter gurgled and chuckled, looking up at him.

"He's very contented," Peter said, not quite ready to call him handsome.

"Not all the time. Especially not when he is hungry. But I fed him before you came."

Helga took the child and laid him in the cot. "Now I want a kiss," she said.

Peter felt a swell of desire. Her words had freed him from a preoccupation with the strange circumstances of their meeting. He studied the blue eyes and stroked the flaxen hair and he kissed her tenderly, gradually inching his arms around her, enveloping her in his love.   There was a knock on the door. It was the wife of the owner with the promised lunch of soup and *wiener schnitzel* and coffee.   She placed it on the small table and left.   Peter looked at Helga and she laughed and she pushed him onto the bed and slid on top of him and they made love while young Peter slept.

"Our lunch will be cold!"   Helga, laying beside him, got up.   "Come on Peter, we must eat."

The food was delicious and they ate eagerly, celebrating their reunion, but his mind returned to his preoccupation.

"I don't understand, Helga.   How did all this happen?" He waved his arms to emphasize their being here, at this place.

"I came by train to Kehl and walked to the border.   It was yesterday.   I made mistake."   Peter thought of the irony of his being a day early.   "I explained that I was to meet you and the official found this place for me."

"They brought you back to the border, today?"

"*Ja*.   Do not look so troubled, Peter."

He **was** worried.   All this military involvement was the last thing he expected and he couldn't get rid of the feeling that they were hostages. But perhaps it was all quite innocent? Why couldn't the officials be kind and considerate?   But it wouldn't fit with the images he had of the *Third Reich*.

"The official who arranged this was one of the *Grenzpolizei* . . . the border police. The soldiers are from the *Wehrmacht*.   They are reservists.   Don't be distressed Peter."

The fact that he was not contending with frontline troops allayed his fears but did not lessen the reality of the tension he had felt at the border crossings.   But Helga would not permit further discussion of the subject. She pulled him down onto the bed, and they lay together in each other's arms.

"You are funny, Peter.   You worry so much,"   She laughed and tickled him and soon her sense of fun overcame his anxiety and they talked of personal things, but he avoided any mention of his mother's death.   She told him of her family and her life in Munich and the birth of Hans-Peter.   And he told of his loneliness without her, his frequent visits to the seashore.

"I have memories," she said. "Remember the shingle. I carry some with me always."

She sat up and reached into her purse and gathered a few of the small stones.

He took them, examining the variety of shapes and colours. He remembered the day that she left on the *Joachim*. The day he had made a bag with his handkerchief. The day she held her treasure high as she waved to him that last day on the ship.

"Those are for you. They're very special. I've cared for them."

He put them in the small pouch in his belt.

"I'll keep them safe."

She lay beside him again, running her hands over his face.

"I know you will."

She held his eyes in hers.

"What's wrong?"

"There could be war, Helga."

She gripped his arms and kissed him hard on the mouth.

"We must promise, Peter. For the next two days we will not even think about unpleasant things. We are together. We must celebrate that."

"I promise."

He gave her a lingering hug. Then the baby awoke and began to cry.

"He probably needs to be changed," Helga said, picking him up and soothing him while she changed his nappy.

Kehl was a moderately sized town situated in the low-lying area adjacent to the Rhine. Behind it, to the east, was a range of mountains rising steeply from the valley. It was a warm day and the sun shone brightly over the red-tiled roofs, creating pools of shadow in the streets below. Everyone was enjoying the summer weather. The shops were plentifully stocked with goods of all kinds and in the market area one could feast one's eyes on what appeared to be an inexhaustible range of foodstuffs. The hotel proprietors had produced a pram for Helga. It looked like one their own daughter might have used and they were obviously pleased to be able to offer it.

Peter had awakened early, lying beside Helga and listening to her steady breathing, thinking how beautiful she was even in sleep. Then, when she awoke and she caught his gaze, they made love as though it was now the most natural expression of his feelings for her and her feelings for him.

They breakfasted around nine. There were only two other guests in the hotel, an elderly man and his wife who were quick to explain that they were visiting relatives in the area, as though confessing one's motives removed any misunderstanding.

The breakfast consisted of boiled eggs and various breads, with butter and meats and cheeses, washed down with cups of strong coffee.

After returning to their room to change young Hans, they set off to explore the town. Strolling down the busy streets, pushing the pram, Peter felt elated. They were a happy family enjoying a holiday. It was hard for him to imagine anything more preferable than this. He was proud of Helga. Proud of his son. Life had suddenly become a new and enriching experience, a larger emotional space beyond himself, a reaching out to share the delights of just being alive. He looked at Helga.

"Happy?" he asked.

She reached over and touched his hand.

"*Ja,* Peter."

They walked in a nearby park, sitting watching the ducks on the pond, gazing at the passage of the townsfolk, happy young couples with children decked out in summer colours, elderly men and women, some together, others alone, many of them dressed in sombre blacks or greys. There were a few soldiers and some boys dressed in the dark shorts and brown shirts of the *Hitler Jugend*. He remembered Helga's first description of life in Germany from which he had conjured up his own images and now the reality was unfolding before him. It was different from what he had expected. In this small town there was no dramatic evidence of a different ideology, other than the flags, with their swastikas, standing out stridently. Without the flags, he could just have easily been strolling in a small English town. It was only the sounds of voices speaking in another language that gave it a different colouration. The grass and the trees and the abundant flowers, where bees hummed busily in the summer sun, reminded him of the England he had left.

They returned to the hotel for lunch; Hans was fed, and soon asleep, was laid in the cot. Peter lay on the bed with Helga.

"We must be married, Helga," he said, expressing both desire and urgency.

"I want that, Peter." She hesitated and then continued, leaving no doubt of her need for sanction. "But I want our parents to agree."

Peter thought of his father, alone now, but still, he was sure, adamant in his opposition to everything German. If only his mother hadn't died. She had possessed the gift of understanding.

It came out without preparation.

"My Mother . . . she died."

Helga caught unawares, turned sharply.

"Oh, Peter! . . . When?"

"A few months ago."

She threw her arms around him.

"Why didn't you tell me?"

"I didn't . . . I couldn't . . ."

He looked into Helga's face and seeing the sympathy there, he was overcome with great sadness. All his stoicism vanished to be replaced by an outpouring of suppressed grief. He wept, and Helga cradled him in her arms.

He awoke early the next morning to find her watching him.

"I want to marry you, Peter. But we must wait."

He nodded sadly, reluctantly accepting her conclusion, his nagging worry still present.

"If there is a war, Helga, we must . . . "

"Do not speak of war, Peter. You promised. If it happens, we will survive it. I know we will. Nothing will break us apart."

"You aren't afraid?"

"I am very afraid, Peter, but I love you and that is all that matters."

They made love while Hans slept, and then they dozed, arms around each other as the rays of the summer sun shifted around to the west. Hans awakened them with his cry and when he had been changed and fed, they set out again. Peter felt a wholeness, his relationship with Helga consummated. He felt that he was now her husband and she his wife, committed to each other without the ritual of religious ceremony, not to part until death.

Helga, seeming to sense his thoughts moved closer, her hair brushing his face. She suggested that they stop for coffee and cakes and Peter, unprepared for the sweet treat that awaited him, wondered how he could have ever thought a cream tea was the ultimate delight for the palate.

"Tomorrow, we will go to the mountains, Peter. To the *Schwarzwald* . . . the forest."

She spoke assuredly, seeking his hand, her face lighting up with the energy he had first encountered in that small port by the sea, the sea of his childhood. A place that seemed so distant now, a place becoming part of another time and memory, before Helga. It was as if growing up without Helga was as unthinkable as war intruding upon this peaceful place.

The following morning they took the bus to an adjoining town, the departure point for the smaller bus which would take them to the forest. The cook at the hotel had prepared a picnic lunch for them, some meat sandwiches, with *Münster* cheese on the side, as well as fresh bananas and apples, and a thermos full of coffee. Hans was carried in the small wicker basket in which, in addition to the sheets and blankets and the picnic lunch, was a supply of clean nappies.

Reaching the smaller bus, involved a walk through the centre of the town. Upon leaving the first bus, Peter took one side of the basket, which had convenient handles for this purpose, and Helga took the other, making the task of transporting Hans much less onerous. It was as they were walking together, with the child gently swinging between them, that Peter realized that it was the same basket Helga had used to bring the child from Munich.

Peter took an admiring sideways glance at Helga, silently applauding the energy that she brought to everything she did. It wasn't difficult for him to understand what enormous enterprise it had required for her to travel by herself from Munich with Hans to an unknown town. The complexities of that aspect of the task were daunting enough, but then she had to face the unpredictable circumstances inherent upon meeting a *foreign national* at a border crossing controlled by German officialdom. Helga was looking at him and smiling.

"You worry again, Peter?"

"No . . . " Caught unawares with the truth, he found another truth. "No, I was thinking how wonderful you are."

"I am happy, Peter . . . because we are together."

The small bus climbed slowly up the winding road leading to the lookout point. There were six other tourists aboard, all elderly couples. Peter wondered if the bus could have safely accommodated any more weight, it seemed to be straining in the lowest gear available.

When they reached the lookout point, the view was spectacular. Below were the towns they had left, looking much like intricate toy models. Beyond were the Rhine Valley and the river itself, its course winding majestically into the horizon to the north and south of them. It was a bright clear, crisp, day. There were a few puffy white clouds in the otherwise blue sky. The lack of haze gave clarity to the view, enhancing one's vision, so that Strasbourg and the mountains beyond stood out sharply. Holding Han's basket between them, they were humbled by the sheer scale of the area they were privileged to gaze upon.

Peter was distracted by Helga's sudden search under the folds of the blankets in the basket, trying not to disturb Hans who was sound asleep. Finding what she was looking for, she triumphantly held up a camera, the one item that he was already regretting that he hadn't brought with him.

Helga took pictures of him and the baby. Hans was now wide awake, having been awakened after all by Helga's hunt for the camera. He took similar pictures with Helga holding the child and then she prevailed upon another tourist to take a group snapshot.

They turned away from the view below them to face into the forest rising above them. There were paths in among the pine trees and they climbed to an open area. Sitting on a fallen tree stump, Helga proceeded to feed Hans. Peter watched, feeling rather helpless, regarding her with increasing desire. When she had gently revealed her breast and offered it to Hans he wanted to possess her. He moved closer, and putting his arms around her he kissed Hans lightly on the forehead, Then he caressed her soft skin with his lips. He felt his arousal and he could see her own desire rising to match his.

It was agonizing to wait for the completion of Han's leisurely repast, and when he was done and was safely asleep in his basket, they moved further into the woods and made love among the towering trees, inhaling the scent of pine, witnessed by unseen choristers, twittering and chattering with gay abandon up in the branches through which the wind sighed.

They were oblivious to the presence of other humans, but there was no need for concern as the few tourists who had accompanied them were unable or unwilling to climb the steep woodland paths.

When they got back to the lookout point, the bus had gone and they were alone. The next bus was due to arrive within the half hour, so they sat on the wooden bench enjoying the sun and the immensity of the silence.

Peter thought of the morrow and the necessity of his departure, but he was reluctant to allow it to intrude upon their pleasure.

"It's a beautiful country, Helga."

"As beautiful as England?"

"As beautiful as England," he repeated, adding. "But it is different. I feel the presence of history here, just like I do at home, but . . . "

"Victor Hugo loved this area," she said. "I think he said that it moved him to come face to face with great natural phenomena that are also part of history . . . something like that."

"It's what I regard as a spiritual experience, like the sea," he said. "But then I'm influenced by you, Helga. I find beauty whenever I'm with you."

She leaned forward and kissed him.

By the time the bus could be seen making its way up the steep incline, a few clouds were gathering. The sun's rays became visible as they poked through the breaks between them, patterning the valley with shadows and creating a moving mosaic of light and colour. The bus came to a stop, but no one got off. This was the last run of the day.

When they reached the hotel it was close to the dinner hour so they went upstairs and cleaned up. With no movement to induce sleep, Hans was awake, in need of changing and hungry.

Helga sat up on the bed nursing him while Peter lay beside her. How different life was with a child? He had not foreseen the constant attention that an infant required and the realization gave him no comfort as he thought of her, alone, bringing up his child. He wanted to help her. Stay with her. What a terrible dilemma it presented? Whichever way he turned desertion loomed. Desert the navy or desert Helga? He could stay and take the consequences. Become her husband and live in Germany? Fight for Germany if need be? But they both had their commitments, to their families and their countries. Could he really be happy if he deserted England and would Helga wish him to? Perhaps she did?

"Helga. What if I stayed with you?"

"Stayed here, in *Deutschland?*"

"Yes."

"It would fill my heart . . . but I don't think it would work. We cannot, either of us, sacrifice our identity with the land of our birth. If we come together as man and wife, it must be as two people with complete identities, only then can we face our son with the honesty he deserves."

"What if those identities are challenged by war between us."

"Not war between us, Peter. Between our leaders. But we are caught in the web of history. The only solution is to be true to ourselves and to our love for each other. Whatever happens that cannot fail, but we must not arrange our relationship by defying or denying the course of world events."

"We are sacrificing our love for something we don't understand."

"Perhaps we are, but perhaps we are putting our love to the ultimate test. Is there anything wrong with that?"

"I don't know."

He got up and peered out of the window. The sun was beginning to cast long shadows on the garden at the back, the garden like his own father's garden, a world away from this place. What madness is it that intervenes to threaten the love of two human beings? He hoped his pessimism was ill-founded but he felt a terrible foreboding.

Dinner restored his optimism. It's remarkable what a full stomach can accomplish, he thought. They lingered over the coffee talking of inconsequential personal things like the scent she favoured. She asked him if he had ever fancied another woman, and, thinking of Harriet he said he had. "But not since meeting you," he added.

"How about you?", he said.

"I went with boys. We had fun. But then I met you."

She reached out and touched his hand.

They went up to their room. Relaxed now, enjoying their precious time together, they made love and Helga was soon asleep. Peter remained awake, resisting the onset of slumber. He liked to admire her beauty when she slept, it re-enforced another of the images he wanted to carry away with him.

They awakened early and joined the elderly couple in the dining room for breakfast. Peter was silent. He was unable to bring himself to risk a conversation. He was fighting mounting sadness. Everything seemed so hopeless again. Time seemed to be their constant enemy. Perhaps it was everyone's enemy? Perhaps England and Germany were running out of time?

The car arrived precisely at nine. The soldier-driver opened the door and they all walked towards it. He kissed Helga and Hans and the tears came and they both wept unashamedly.

"Take care my love," he said to Helga, and then reaching down and dropping tears on Han's head, as though he were baptising him, he said. "Goodbye, dear Hans-Peter."

He hugged her and kissed her again and then he climbed into the car.

150

The door closed and within seconds he was alone. Helga and Hans-Peter had become an image, a memory.

He was escorted to the centre of the bridge by two German soldiers. It was a repeat of the French action of a few days before. Was this a provocative act? A retaliatory gesture of genuine menace or, as he had wondered before, was it all just a game?

No French soldiers came to meet him. They watched like the Germans had done with rifles at the ready. But this time he didn't care.

They cleared him through the border check and he made his way into the town. It was only then that it struck him that he hadn't taken advantage of John's offer, hadn't phoned him in Zurich. But then he was glad he hadn't. He just wanted to be alone. He had no desire to confide in anyone, least of all John. In fact, he really hadn't liked him a whole lot. Too upper class perhaps?

10.

Peter got off the bus in Portland and looked at his watch. It was nine o'clock. He was due to catch the returning liberty boat to the Sarum the next morning at eight, so he had lots of time. He decided to head for the pub. In that way he could collect his uniform and perhaps even prevail upon George for a bed for the night.

The pub was practically empty, there were just a few locals, older men he had seen there before. George spotted him as he entered.

"Wondered when you'd get back, son. They recalled your mates, day 'fore yesterday."

"What!" Peter felt a wave of nausea.

"Been quiet around here."

A customer came in and George drew a glass of beer and set it on the counter. The recipient deposited some coins and walked off.

"I reckon a few ships have left." George appeared to want Peter to confirm his conclusion, but all he could think about was getting out of his civvies and down to the dockyard.

He passed the guard at the gates and entered the Regulating Office.

"What ship, mate?" The crusty looking Petty Officer, probably a reservist, Peter thought, was a disturbing reminder that he was back in the navy again.

"Saram."

"Saram, is it. Seems you have a problem. She left yesterday."

Although the news was expected, he still felt the sudden shock of being abandoned by his crewmates.

"I'm not late," he protested.

"There was a recall. Suppose you didn't hear it. Like the other blokes who'll be surprised in the morning. You're to report to barracks. You know where that is? They'll give you your orders."

Three days later, when he reported to the Saram alongside the docks in Greenock on the west coast of Scotland, Tom seemed to be vastly relieved to see him. But Peter wanted to deal with his fear.

"You give Jimmy my letter?"

"Hell no." Tom sounded indignant. "We left before your leave was up."

"Thank God!" Peter dumped the valise on his locker and sat down.

"I think you're slated to see Jimmy though. Probably wants to know why you didn't hear of the recall. Wasn't on the wireless or anything. Local police went after everybody."

"Christ!" Peter reacted to the unexpected complication. That meant his father would have been contacted.

Bruce-Hallet fixed Peter with his now familiar stare. Then he glanced at the single sheet of paper in front of him on his desk.

"You reported in on time, Gray. You're not on a charge. As a matter for the record I'd like to know why you missed the recall?"

"I was in Germany, sir," the words spilled out as if he had no control of them.

"You did say, Germany, Gray?" Bruce-Hallet appeared to have momentarily lost his composure.

"Yes, sir."

"Ah, well, I suppose you had a reason?"

"I went to see my son. You see his mother lives in Germany."

"She is German then?"

"Yes, sir."

Bruce-Hallet's face had a trace of a smile he thought. Peter blinked to dispel what could only be a false impression. It was as though he was facing the German official at the border again.

"I admire your resolve, Gray."

Peter couldn't decide whether it was an admonition or a compliment, but he felt that a weight had been lifted. He had the distinct impression that Bruce-Hallet had already guessed where he'd been. Probably the whole ship's company was in on his secret.

"That's it, Gray. You're dismissed."

Peter stood up. His legs felt weak. A slight shaking marred his salute.

"Aye, Aye, sir," he said, happy to have confessed the truth.

11.

*G*ünther made a surprise visit to Munich during the middle of the afternoon, some ten days after Helga's return from Kehl. It was Eva who answered the door. Helga recognized her brother's voice and she came out of the living room to meet him. She was carrying Hans who had been cranky all night. Even his afternoon nap had been shorter as he had awakened earlier than usual. But now she was glad her son was up as she could immediately confront Günther with the reality of his existence.

"Helga!" He walked forward and then stopped as though uncertain how to greet her. The baby, dozing now in her arms, prevented a simple hug or kiss.

"This is Hans-Peter," said Helga proudly. "Would you like to hold him?"

She thought he would retreat, and she could see that he knew she thought that. He looked at her and then at the baby and smiling, nodded his head.

He took Hans in his arms, looking awkward, his eyes appealing to her for help.

"Like this." Helga arranged the baby, directing Günther's hands so that he adopted a more comfortable position.

"He's quite heavy," the surprise registered on Günther's face.

Helga led the way into the kitchen and Günther followed carrying Hans.

Eva was already in the kitchen. There was a homemade raspberry torte on the table and the coffee was brewing. Helga sat across the table from her brother, watching the intense expression on his face, amused by his attempts to cope with his unexpected task. A perfect opportunity, she thought.

"I met Peter . . . Just over a week ago."

Günther looked startled.

"It's not possible!"

"It happened Günther. Exactly as I've said."

He looked at Eva, hoping for some confirmation of his doubts, but she nodded.

Smiling now, enjoying the benefit of her advantage, Helga waited. Günther said nothing, but looking down at the baby started a gentle rocking motion. He looked up with a smile of satisfaction as Han's eyelids began to drift shut with sleep. Eva brought him a plate of torte and a cup of coffee. Günther freed a hand and added cream and sugar, oblivious to everyone except the child in his arms. He slowly lifted a piece of the torte to his mouth and took a bite, his expression conveying satisfaction. Then he took a sip of coffee.

"It's no good fighting your instincts is it?" He looked earnestly at Helga.

She thought the question could equally well have been directed at himself as to her.

"We all have our own needs and desires, Günther," she said, enjoying the equality she had achieved in her response.

"He's a very nice baby," he said, as if he'd made a surprising discovery. "You must be very gratified?"

"I am, Günther."

He appeared to want to extricate himself from the embarrassment of his changed attitude. She could sympathize with his difficulty. Giving up his condemnation of her association with the Englishman would go against all that he had come to believe.

As if on a sudden impulse, his demeanour changing, he handed Hans back to her.

"I've been posted to a battleship, the *Schlosstern*," he said.

Helga felt disappointed. She had hoped for an admission of error in his past attitude, or at least a more genuine sign of support, but he had chosen to avoid the subject altogether.

"You must be pleased."   She almost said 'gratified,' the lack of enthusiasm showing in her voice.

"I'll be going aboard at the beginning of August."

"Have you told Father?"

"Not yet."

Altogether, Günther stayed three days. Helga found him more subdued than on the last visit.   Something seemed to have happened to temper his arrogance and she wondered if life in the *Kriegsmarine* was responsible. He seemed to want to be with her more, sharing some of the pleasures of the past. They talked of the growing up years in Blankenese, the happy years. Most satisfying to her was his acceptance of Hans. He helped with the everyday tasks associated with parenthood, and his fussing over the child often brought Helga to the point of tears.

"You must take care of him, Helga," he said on the day he left.   He hugged and kissed her and held the baby s hand in his, caressing the small fingers, deep in thought.

"I hope there won't be war . . . ," he stopped short of a further qualification, but then, as if reaching down inside himself for the necessary courage, said, "I want you to be with Peter again."

He turned quickly away. She drew him back and kissed him.

"Thank you," she said. It seemed the simplest and most appropriate thing to say, for the magnitude of the gesture had overwhelmed her capacity to express the emotion she felt.

THREE

SUNDAY, SEPTEMBER 3RD, 1939

1.

The Sarum was at sea, off Scapa Flow, the Royal Navy's far northern naval base in the Orkney islands, when the Prime Minister, Neville Chamberlain, came on the wireless. He sounded dispirited, his voice tired.

> This morning the British ambassador in Berlin handed to the German government a final note stating that unless we heard from them by 11 o'clock that they were prepared at once to withdraw their troops from Poland, a state of war would exist between us. I have to tell you now that no such undertaking has been received and that consequently this country is at war with Germany . . .

His words continued but Peter didn't hear. All he was conscious of was the humming of machinery which had suddenly become an active weapon. A weapon to be directed at Germany and Helga. She was the enemy now. Perhaps his father had been right after all.

He looked across at the impassive faces of his shipmates standing, sitting, and squatting in front of the loudspeaker. He caught Tom's attention. Tom got up, stretching his arms above his head, as if to break through the gloom, coming over to sit beside him.

"Least we know where we stand, Pete."

"You sound like you wanted it to happen." Peter was irritated by Tom's apparent acceptance of a decision that spelled potential disaster for his relationship with Helga.

"Come on Pete," he said. "Let's make a cuppa."

The news was received in Blankenese and Munich with utter disbelief. As much as England was always an enigma, and France the traditional enemy, the thought of actual war was not something that had been seriously contemplated by the population at large.

Rolf was the most resigned, having felt for some time that it would happen eventually. Ilse was stunned, not yet wishing to accept the dangers that now faced the family.

Eva, so seldom resigned to the worst, had difficulty too, but at least she could invoke the mantle of previous experience, believing that the visitation of such horror was the predicament of those that lived to a ripe old age, the repeating of the recurring cycles of history. Helga wept, for her child, for Peter, and for herself, caught up in a series of events that she had never had the misfortune to experience before, hoping that she could acquaint herself with the strength and fortitude to survive and enjoy a future with Peter.

Günther, on board the battleship *Schlosstern* at Kiel, received the news with a feeling of jubilation. So, the English were going to fight after all. They would soon find out that Germany was ready. It was now a matter of honour, the honour of the Fatherland, and he felt totally committed to a cause and a belief that had its origins in the *Hitler Jugend*. Now he was aboard one of Germany's most modern warships, ready to fight for his *Führer* and his country.

FOUR

1943 - 1944

1.

Peter found an empty table in the railway restaurant at the Bristol railway station; an en route stop on his way north from Plymouth. He placed his kitbag on a chair to reserve a place, and dropped his hammock beside it, returning to the counter to pick up a cup of tea and a Cornish pasty. He was barely settled into his modest lunch when he was joined by two other sailors in transit like himself.

"Been abroad, Mate?" It was the older of the two who spoke, a regular service able seaman, with probably at least six years of service Peter reckoned.

"Two years in the Indian Ocean." Peter was aware that his deep suntan still set him apart from the pale faces in the crowds milling about the station.

"Not much action there?" The response contained a note of sarcasm, as if he'd been at war while Peter was idly soaking up the sun in some tropical paradise.

"Convoys mostly," Peter ignored the gibe. "Up the east coast of Africa, bound for the Med."

"My mate and me," he glanced towards the much younger ordinary seaman, "We were in the *Graf Sprezen* do, off Montevideo. The Jerries scuttled the bleeding ship instead of coming out to fight."

His friend nodded. "Served on the Amander, we did."

Peter froze, remembering the calamitous letter from Stephen's mother informing him of her son's death on board the Eurander in that same action.

"You all right, mate?" The older sailor caught his reaction.

"I had a friend . . . we were in training together . . . he died aboard the Eurander."

"Badly hit she was." The younger sailor, seemingly unaware of Peter's shock, was more intent on recounting the facts.

"Must've got a load of the *Graf Sprezen's* guns."

"It's rough when you lose a mate." The older sailor commiserated and Peter was thankful for that. "Want another cuppa?" he said.

Peter nodded, staring stoned-faced at the young face before him. Perhaps denial is his answer to death, he thought.

The express train hurtled northwards from Bristol. The light was fading as the evening gave way to the compelling darkness of the blacked-out landscape. There was an inevitability about the transition, a blurring and then a loss of outlines. It was like his own life, everything disappearing into nothingness. Helga was somewhere out there in a place beyond his reach.

Ever since arriving back in England his thoughts of Helga and his son had intensified. There had to be some force that could bridge the darkness, he told himself. His own love reached out but without validation. He hoped in vain for some sign or sound or image, knowing in his heart that waiting was all that was offered him. The feeling of helplessness was not new; it had been his constant companion since the end of peace and the beginning of war, but being back in England the geographic closeness of Germany had the effect of underscoring how near and how far was the prospect of their coming together again. Furthermore, the war didn't show any signs of abating and the cost it was extracting in human lives was not something spared the living.

He got up and left the crowded and stuffy compartment and went into the corridor. He wanted fresh air, so he lowered a window and looked out at the countryside.

Cows were still grazing in the darkened fields. There was something reassuring about that. The train thundered on. It had not yet reached the towns and cities of the industrial

Midlands, now given oven to war production, that would come later, before his destination, Newcastle-upon-Tyne, was reached in the early morning hours of another day.

He looked out ahead as the wind of movement assaulted his face. The train was rounding a curve, approaching a station, but there was no slackening of speed. And then a large speck of soot lodged in his eye and he closed the window, cursing himself for his stupidity, returning to the compartment and rubbing his eye.

"What's up?" A pale-faced able seaman was sitting opposite.

"Soot . . . in my eye."

"Let's 'ave a look . . . Yea, plain as day," He pulled out a dirty handkerchief and removed it.

"Big sucker," he said, holding it up for Peter to see.

"Thanks."

"Spot of leave then?"

"No," he looked around at the other servicemen, and then satisfied that his secret was safe, he said, "No, a new ship . . . How about you?"

"Home for me . . . Yorkshire. Fourteen days of beer and sex!"

Peter managed a smile. Sometimes the crudity of his shipmates appalled him. He hoped he hadn't shown his displeasure but the conversation died, and he leaned back and closed his eyes.

He thought of his last meeting with his father during the Christmas just passed. He had arrived home during the third week in December. There had been no mother to greet him at the station and he was gripped by the pain of her loss. When he reached the house in the dark of early evening, made more sombre by a blackout he was still trying to get used to again, he didn't look forward to sharing his grief with his father.

"Hello, Peter, " his father had said, as though his unannounced arrival after an absence of more than two years was a commonplace event. He had aged dramatically. The familiar dark hair was prematurely grey.

"I have some leave," Peter said. "I got back from the tropics last month."

He followed his father into the living room. A fire was burning in the old grate topped by the mantlepiece on which stood the clock given to his mother by his grandfather. On the table were the remains of what must have been his father's supper. The whole room looked untidy.

"I'm sorry. I . . . I didn't. I couldn't get home for mother's . . . " Peter began a faltering attempt to introduce the matter of their mourning.

"The police were here," his father said, abruptly.

"When was that?" Peter wondered if he was referring to a recent event, or whether it was the long ago recall of the crew of the minesweeper, Saram, in the days of peace, the summer he went to see Helga in Germany.

"You have to go back to your ship." The words came absentmindedly, as if they had been stored up, awaiting release irrespective of their relevance.

"But that was, well, before I went abroad, wasn't it?"

"Yes, that's right. You're looking fit, son."

"Thanks," He had no idea how to react to his father's rambling

"I've had a bit of rheumatism. The damp weather you know . . . " His voice trailed off.

Peter felt a dampness in his eyes as he thought of his mother. She had been the driving force and now that she was gone his father had been reduced to a pitiable state of confusion. The loss of her must have been a crushing blow and he could appreciate now why her death and funeral had passed before his father could even bring himself to put pen to paper and inform him.

"Are you home long?"

"Till just after Christmas."

The leave had not been a celebration of Christmas, but a sad reuniting of father and son. Peter had gone on long walks with his father in the countryside he loved. He had attended church with him on Sundays, and afterwards they went to the cliffs to look down on the now inaccessible piers and beaches, sown with landmines and crisscrossed with barbed wire. It had been like taking his father through the pattern of his relationship with Helga, as if seeking some sort of unspoken endorsement of his action, but it didn't seem of relevance now; his father never spoke of Helga; the subject seemed buried deep in some inaccessible corner of his mind.

The garden was quite another matter. He never tired of talking about his plans for planting and harvesting his vegetables. It was his substitute for painful memories and it even intruded upon the divergent conversations, like when Peter announced that his leave would be ending the next day and, after a pause, his father had said.

"Had a good crop of runner beans this year."

The train jolted violently as it pulled out of yet another station. He was back in the present with his burden of sadness and disillusionment. His fellow traveller had gone. He was probably already standing at some bar, regaling everyone with his naval exploits.

The electric train out of Newcastle stopped at every station on the south bank of the Tyne. He looked out upon mile after mile of shipyards. The early morning was grey and dismal, and the rising sun could do little to enhance the view. Rather than brightening the outlook, the sun's rays created vast pools of shadow in which men laboured on ships hulls, rivetting and welding, appearing to exist in some forbidden valley, cut off from light and air.

He approached the dockyard gates and a worker in a grubby

wcrk suit emerged from the gatehouse.

"What number?" he said.

"Number?" Peter questioned, "I'm looking for the Sandrake?"

"New destroyer, Job number thirty six, straight ahead and turn left when you get to the wharf. She's tied up alongside."

He was glad to reach the gangplank. He was looking forward to some rest. The Sandrake was far from completed, dockyard workers were everywhere and there was the constant rat-tat-tat, of rivetting, a piercing metallic sound that drummed at the ears. And then there was the smell, salt air mixed with coal smoke and the acrid fumes generated by electric welding. He was greeted by a Petty Officer in clean well-worn blue overalls.

"Welcome aboard . . . Leading Seaman Gray is it?" he said, consulting a list of crew members.

"Yes, got into Newcastle this morning."

"Good, not much point staying here. Nobody living on the ship yet. Let's see. You have a shore billet. Mrs. Reynolds, 45 Dock Street. Out of the gates and turn right."

Mrs. Reynolds, Dottie as she liked to be called, was a fussy little woman who reminded him of a long departed aunt whom he had hated. But Dottie seemed friendly enough and she soon had him installed in his own bedroom.

"You're lucky. My husband's bolted so you can have his room. Never slept together, we didn't. Breakfast at seven thirty, dinner at six. Don't stay out after ten thirty or you don't get in."

With that she left him wondering if he had fallen into the role of a surrogate husband, a thought that he hastily dismissed. He collapsed on the bed and dropped off to sleep. Some two hours later he was awakened by a rapping on the door. It was Dottie.

"It's six fifteen. Are you coming to dinner?"

He managed to confirm that he was and, still struggling with sleep, already regretting his tardiness, he stumbled downstairs.

The other boarders, a Chief Petty Officer and an Able Seaman, were already finishing their main course.

"Bit of shut eye then?" said the Chief sarcastically.

"I didn't sleep all night. Left Plymouth yesterday morning."

"It's a lousy journey," said the seaman sympathetically.

Dottie came in with his dinner while the others dug into their pie and custard. In between her popping in and out, taking and bringing things, and generally conveying an air of impatience with lingerers, Peter managed to elicit from the others an idea of the routine. Lunch was not provided and after breakfast, around about seven thirty, the earliest he could expect to return was late afternoon. Still, it all seemed very simple, a far cry from the discipline of basic training which he had shared with Stephen. It was hard to accept that Stephen had gone; his youthful, lively friend blasted to oblivion by German guns. He shuddered at the recollection as he prepared to leave for his first day on the Sandrake.

2.

$\mathcal{G}$ ünther stood on the upper deck of the *Schlosstern* berthed alongside the dockyard in Gotenhafen, in occupied Poland. New crew members were expected and he looked forward to meeting with Siegfried for the first time since they had left the old anti-aircraft training ship, the *Mullenburg*, in 1939. As Günther waited, he instinctively scanned the clear blue summer sky for enemy bombers. The *Schlosstern* had been moved to Gotenhafen to escape the heavy RAF raids which they had been subjected to in Kiel and which had severely damaged the *Schlosstern's* sister ship, the *Gnosseneau,* resulting in her being de-commissioned. There had been rumours that the *Schlosstern* would suffer the same fate, with many of her crew members being transferred to the U Boat service, a fate that would have befallen Günther too, but fortunately, the present indications were that the *Schlosstern* was to remain in service.

They came in a single file up the gangway and Günther spotted him. It was hard not to. The tall muscular frame and the slightly rounded face and above all, the same confident smile when he saw Günther, left no doubt of his identity.

"Siegfried!"

They shook hands with an awkwardness born of a long absence.

Günther studied Siegfried's face, noting the lines that now furrowed the once smooth skin. He knew his own features must also be reflecting the strain of almost three years of war.

Without a further word, they went below to find Siegfried's mess. When they got there some of the other new crew members were already stowing their gear.

"Get settled in and we'll talk," Günther turned to leave,

and then stopped. "Let's go ashore later and have a drink?"

Over steins of beer, in a quiet corner of a local bar, Günther felt relaxed, able to share confidences.

"You were on the *Prinz Otto!*" Günther was surprised. " . . . In the dash up the Channel from Brest to Wilhelmshaven with the *Schlosstern?*"

"Yes." Siegfried's reply was muted, contrasting sharply with Günther's enthusiasm.

"Remember how we shot down all the British torpedo bombers!" Günther recollected his surprise. "Don't know how we did it."

"I was afraid, Günther . . . I was at my post in the engine room. I only heard explosions . . ."

Günther hated to admit it, but he too had been fearful. Hunched over the Radar displays - watching the echoes of enemy aircraft - all thoughts of the *Führer* and the Fatherland had been overtaken by a compelling dread of death. That death hadn't come was his most memorable reminder of their experiences, but he wasn't about to admit it. " . . . It was a victory Siegfried

"Was it? I suppose it was. Need lots of those don't we?" Siegfried was reflective, brooding. "It's not going well, the war."

Günther disapproved of Siegfried's unexpected pessimism. It was so unusual that it caused him to struggle with his own doubts, trying not to succumb to reminders of all the military reverses and the increasing number of bombing raids on German cities. He felt he had to do something to break the gloom and his mind sought a more cheerful subject. He held Siegfried's eyes.

"Hear you have a girl friend?" he said, pleased when he saw a slight blush come to Siegfried's face.

"It was your sister, Helga, who brought it about." He sounded defensive. "I phoned the house in Munich one day to see if you were there and she invited me for coffee. Frieda happened to be visiting at the time."

"I've never met Frieda." Günther tried to imagine what she was like. "Helga has talked of her."

"She's a nurse at the local hospital. We've been keeping in touch."

He envied Siegfried although he was annoyed to think that he had snatched Helga's friend from under his nose.

"I must go to Munich," he said, thinking of his sister and her child. Helga had tried to get him to go out with Frieda, but it had never happened and now the opportunity had passed him by.

"Let's go together." Siegfried was eager now, too eager, Günther thought. He hardly wanted to be reminded of his stupidity in not acting on Helga's suggestion. Of course, if it hadn't been for his initial opposition to her pregnancy?

"It's a happy ship, the *Schlosstern*," Günther said, surprised by the irrelevance of his remark, but too embarrassed to stop. "We've all been through . . . It's been hard the war . . . but we are confident in our ship, it's a lucky ship."

Siegfried didn't answer. He appeared to be trying to understand Günther's strange behaviour.

"I'm sorry," Günther said, trying to explain. "I haven't talked about any of this for a long time. It's hard to separate life in the *Kriegsmarine* from life at home these days. It's all war, isn't it?"

"Why don't we take the next leave together?" Siegfried, persevered with his idea.

Günther nodded absentmindedly. He didn't want to consider the subject any further.

3.

*J*he *Schlossstern* was to stay in Gotenhafen longer than expected. Even though it was still understood that the ship was to remain in service a great deal of uncertainty still existed about her future. As a result, a large number of her crew members were billeted ashore, many being sent on training courses. Only a bare minimum of personnel was kept on board.

Günther and Siegfried were members of a group assigned to a refresher course in Kiel. The course lasted three weeks and at the end of it they were given two weeks of leave.

Günther decided to adopt Siegfried's idea for a joint visit to Munich. However, he elected go to Blankenese first, for a few days, then spend time with Siegfried on his parent's farm in Neuengamme, and after that, during the last week of their leave, they would both travel to Munich to see Helga and Frieda.

They caught the early morning train out of Kiel. They soon learned that there had been a devastating air raid on Hamburg the night before. The news, mainly by word-of-mouth from people at the station in Kiel and on the train, was sketchy and contradictory and it was impossible to get a reliable picture of what had actually happened.

It was when they reached Bergedorf, some fifteen kilometres east of Hamburg, that the train stopped and the conductor went along the platform informing passengers that they couldn't go further.

"Let's see if we can hitch a ride," said Günther, standing up and collecting his belongings. Siegfried followed.

When they reached the platform and looked towards Hamburg a pall of smoke covered the sky. It was not a static cloud but constantly moving and reshaping itself, as if fed from below by some demonic force.

"My God." Siegfried stood stunned, his eyes staring at the spectacle.

"Come on!" Günther laid a hand on his arm and he flinched. "We've got to go."

Günther thought of his parents. Had the raid touched Blankenese? There was every indication that the damage was extensive. What if his father had been in Hamburg, working in his office at the docks?

"We've got to get there, Siegfried. I must find out about my parents . . . "

"I . . . " Siegfried hesitated, and Günther looked back, urging him on, and he fell in step with Günther, moving quickly into the street. There were few vehicles about, but most were coming from Hamburg; all of them were crammed with people carrying personal possessions. Occasionally an emergency vehicle would rush by heading towards the city.

They soon encountered a few people making their way out of the city on foot and carrying what little belongings they could manage. As they strode forward, for the sight added to their determination to see what had happened, the numbers got larger, with family groups very much in evidence. Meaningful conversation with them was out of the question. Often their clothes were torn and bloodied. They all had the same vacant stare, as if the horror had robbed them of feeling or identity and they were possessed only with the desire to put as much distance between themselves and the city as possible. Within a very short time the numbers had grown to overwhelming proportions and with their abundance came a frenzy of movement, frightening in its scale and intensity, a human tide with its own momentum, a tidal wave of terror.

"We must go on!" Günther, who had moved ahead of Siegfried again, waited until he caught up.

"It's no use, Günther. We can't get through."

Günther dismissed any thought of giving up, and he

dragged Siegfried forward.

As they moved closer to the city, the extent of the destruction loomed larger. High shooting flames seemed to reach up to the heavens as if the Devil himself had deposited the fires of hell in this place. And with it all came the choking, acrid, smell of smoke which assaulted the lungs and created a feeling of imminent suffocation. The marvel seemed to be that so many had survived.

It was now impossible to move against the human stream so that soon they were being propelled backwards. There was little hope that they could reach Hamburg and even if they did it was already clear that there would almost certainly be a major dislocation of communication and transportation services. The chance of travel beyond Hamburg to Blankenese was most unlikely. Besides, the jostling, desperate flow of humanity had become an unassailable force which was carrying them along with it, determining their path over the ground, taking them away from Hamburg.

"Let's get out of here?" Günther, his eyes watering with the effects of the smoke and the emotional strain, and barely able to keep his footing, had lost the will to go on.

"We'll go to Neuengamme!" Siegfried shouted, trying to remain erect.

The suggestion upset Günther. He had been so preoccupied with his own troubles that he had completely forgotten about Siegfried's family. No longer capable of rational thought, he fell in with Siegfried, going with the flow, heading towards the south and Neuengamme.

They reached the farm by mid-afternoon, having finally managed to separate themselves from the crowd which seemed intent on moving south and east of the devastated city.

Sitting in the large kitchen with cups of coffee brought by Siegfried's mother Lisa, Günther found it hard to accept what they had experienced. Yet he couldn't erase the visual horror he had witnessed nor the smell of smoke which still inhabited his clothes. Several attempts to get through to his parents in Blankenese from a telephone at the adjoining farm had been unsuccessful.

"I must go back, Siegfried," there was a reckless urgency in his voice.

"It's crazy, Günther, you can't get through."

"But if I cross the Elbe and go up the west bank, I should be able to cross to Blankenese by ferry. It's unlikely that the trains on the other side of the Elbe have been disrupted."

"I'll come with you." Siegfried volunteered. "Let's do it in the morning."

Siegfried's mother made them an early breakfast and packed sandwiches, and with knapsacks over their shoulders they started walking south to the Elbe. They found a fellow who was willing to ferry them across and by late afternoon they were at the nearest railway station. They caught the first train out, heading north up the west bank of the Elbe. Upon leaving the train, they were able to get a ride on an army lorry heading to the ferry which crossed to Blankenese. As the ferry made its way across the Elbe everything on the far shore seemed peaceful, only the thick clouds of smoke billowing up from the fires still burning to the south, over Hamburg, gave any hint of what had happened.

Günther felt cautiously optimistic, a feeling which strengthened as they got closer to the dock at Blankenese and there was no apparent evidence of any damage. The houses, neatly arranged on the slope up from the shore, seemed out of another time and place and only the still persistent smell of smoke from their clothes reminded him of the other certainty so close at hand.

His parent's house looked as it had always looked. From the front, two stories faced the road, with the cupola soaring above the roof line. The ground was level here, at its highest point before it dropped down sharply towards the river. There was the large well-manicured lawn in front enclosed by flower beds bright with colours. To the left was a large group of chestnut trees and to the right, the drive, lined with poplars, led to the garage. Günther heaved a sigh of relief when he saw that the Mercedes was parked there. In fact, he began to feel embarrassed at what now appeared to be an undue concern for the fate of his parents.

Minna let them in and his mother came running out of the kitchen.

"Günther! What a surprise. I was worried that you'd been caught in the bombing. Oh! Hello . . . Siegfried? He nodded. "So nice to meet you Siegfried."

"Is father all right?" Günther wondered if his mother's enthusiastic greeting masked more sinister happenings.

"He's upstairs resting . . . "

"What happened, Mother?"

"He's fine . . . "

Günther didn't wait to hear any more. He vaulted up the stairs.

His father was sitting up in bed. His left arm and hand were bandaged and there was sticking plaster on the left side of his face and neck, below his eye and under his chin.

"Günther!" His father extended his uninjured hand in welcome and Günther took it in his, feeling a slight but unusual tremor in the fingers. He looked at his father's gaunt face, not knowing what to say, aware of a crushing look of defeat.

"It was the day bombers," his father said, as if welcoming the opportunity to share what was on his mind. He paused and when he continued his voice faltered.

"Heinrich . . . Heinrich was killed," he said turning away to look out of the window. "Twenty years he drove the Mercedes for me . . . "

Günther couldn't digest the words. He closed his eyes

179

ard put his hand over his forehead as if to shut them out. It was all so wrong. Then he sat down allowing the truth to claim him; becoming obsessed with the thought that his father was probably lucky to be alive.

"He insisted on going outside to watch the bombers. A bomb fell close. It shattered the windows in the office. I was cut by flying glass . . . Heinrich was killed by a bomb fragment. It went through his chest. Death was instantaneous."

His father brushed his hand across his eyes, then regaining his composure, and re-inhabiting the persona that Günther knew said, with a louder and stronger voice. "Your mother and I, we wondered how you were?"

Günther struggled with his memories. Heinrich dead? Dear kind, gentle, lovable Heinrich, who helped him and his sister build sandcastles on the beach and create make-believe houses in the garden. The Heinrich that smuggled them chocolates. Chocolates that they were not normally allowed to eat, except on special occasions. The Heinrich who had expressed pride in Günther when he first appeared in the uniform of the *Hitler Jugend*, but whom Günther knew had expressed that pride with a tinge of visible sadness which had bothered Günther for several weeks afterwards.

"We wondered about you," his father repeated. "Did you get to Neuengamme, Günther?"

"Yes. I came back to see how you were . . . Siegfried is with me."

"You must go and see your sister, Günther. Tell her we're in good health . . . "

For a brief moment he thought his father might say 'And tell her we love her' but if such an emotion existed it didn't find expression although Günther was convinced that it had been there, and he celebrated that.

Siegfried poked his head around the door.

"Excuse me, sir . . ."

Rolf motioned him to come in and they all talked until

Ilse called them to dinner. Rolf stayed in bed, insisting that Günther and Siegfried dine with Ilse. The meal started on an unhappy note, the demise of Heinrich casting gloom over them all, but as they talked they turned to the happy memories of youth and innocence, and they laughed and cried with joy and regret.

"It occurs to me," said Siegfried, looking at Ilse, "If you need food, you must let my family know. Being on the farm has its advantages and I know my parents would be pleased to help in any way they can."

"That's very kind of you, Siegfried." Ilse seemed to struggle with the thought of accepting help from strangers, but as she was the one who faced the daily reality of growing food shortages, Günther was convinced that it wasn't his mother that would object to Siegfried's offer of help but his proud father, Rolf.

Günther was alone with his mother for a brief period and he wanted to raise the possibility of her going to Munich, but the idea was soon abandoned when he realized the condition of his father would preclude any such possibility. She would stick by her ailing husband. If ever there was a chance of her agreeing before, it was now overtaken by events beyond his capacity to reckon with.

"Do you think Father will be all right?"

"Yes, he's strong, he'll be fine," and then, as if anticipating his next question, she said, "Go to Munich with Siegfried. See your sister. Don't worry about us."

The doorbell rang in the early evening. Helga, still reeling from the news out of Hamburg, the devastating air raid, the death of Heinrich and the injuries suffered by her father, suspected that more grief was to be visited upon her and her grandmother. She opened the door slowly, not wanting to find out who was on the other side.

"Günther! Siegfried!" She dived into Günther's arms and hugged and kissed him and then, taking Siegfried by surprise, she hugged him too.

"You must call Frieda. Give her a nice surprise. Phone her now," she said, pointing to the telephone in the hallway and Siegfried, needing no further inducement, hurried off.

She turned back to Günther, worried now.

"Did you see Father? Mother told me you went to Blankenese after leaving Neuengamme. "Is he . . . ?" She feared his answer.

"He's cut and bruised, but he's fine. It's mother that worries me. She is still as stubborn as ever. I thought about getting her to come here . . . "

"But she'd want to stay with him," she said, surprised that her brother hadn't accepted that. She studied his face and saw his sadness.

"Oh, Günther. I can't believe . . . "

A spasm of emotion caught her words.

" . . . Heinrich . . . "

She saw in her brother's face a reflection of her own memories of warm summer days, when they were young together and Heinrich drove them to picnics on the beach with their mother and father. Heinrich was always considered a member of the family, more so than Minna who tended to be more conscious of her position. Heinrich was like a grandfather they didn't have, lovable and wise and with a great sense of fun. She hugged her brother and the tears came.

"Why Heinrich?" she wailed.

"The English bastards!"

She broke away from her brother, upset by what he had said, unwilling to accept that his hatred encompassed a whole race and not specifically the father of her child.

"I'm sorry . . . I didn't mean . . . "

She hated Günther's attempt at an apology. He was capitulating now and it was out of character. It was no use, he had said it and she was angry. She strutted off towards the kitchen and Günther followed. Of course, Günther was right really, the English were the enemy, she couldn't deny it, however much she wanted to exclude Peter. Their actions were despicable. They had killed Hienrich and she hated them for that. She wished she could talk to Peter, reassure herself that he didn't deserve to be called an 'English bastard'.

"I had a feeling you were coming," said Eva, looking up at Günther as he entered the kitchen where she sat at the table nursing a cup of coffee.

"*Omi* . . . really." Günther proffered a mild rebuke. "You're clairvoyant, are you?".

He leaned over and pecked her on the cheek.

"It was just a feeling," she said.

Siegfried came in, his face wreathed in a wide smile.

"Frieda's coming over."

"Wonderful!" Helga welcomed the good news. "Would you like a coffee?"

Siegfried shook his head.

She turned to Günther. "How about you? Coffee? . . . or something stronger," there was a frostiness in her voice.

"No thanks." Günther, spoke warily.

Helga allowed a trace of a smile, as she felt her anger subsiding.

Nothing was said for a while, then Günther broke the silence, leaning back in his chair, adopting a more familiar posture.

"So, how is everything in Munich . . . How's young Hans?"

"You just missed him," said Helga. "He's fast asleep. We were just enjoying some relaxation when you arrived. He's lively all the time."

"He had a cold over Christmas," said Eva.

Helga laughed. "It didn't seem to slow him down. Anyway, we missed you at Christmas. Just make sure you're here this year."

"I'll make sure of it."

"We heard all about your exploits," said Helga. "It was on the wireless. I'm glad I didn't know about it until it was all over."

"It was exciting," said Günther. Siegfried grimaced.

Helga looked at Eva and they shook their heads in unison. Helga knew that it was pointless to try and elicit any further information; she only knew that it was not the kind of excitement that reduced her worry about his welfare.

The subject changed to the tragic death of Heinrich, and then to life in Munich, the increasing food shortages, and the mounting concern about air raids. So far Munich had been spared but there had been innumerable false alarms.

"It's bound to happen at some time," said Eva. "The English will retaliate for the bombing of their cities."

"The war might be over soon," said Günther suddenly, and they all looked at him, dumbfounded at the naïveté of the remark. Helga disliked this tendency of his to equivocate by making light of serious matters, yet she wondered if it had something to do with what he had seen and heard in Hamburg, especially the loss of Heinrich.

Eva sighed. "I think I'll go to bed."

She got up and rinsed her cup and Günther went over and

kissed her.

"Good night, *Oma*."

The doorbell rang and Helga answered it. It was Frieda. She was tall and dark with deep brown eyes, the exact opposite of Helga in colouration, but in personality she was almost alike. She was not quite as outgoing as Helga but not lacking personality and charm. Siegfried came bustling out of the kitchen to give her a hug and Günther followed. Helga could tell he was curious, especially as she had tried so long to get them together. She introduced him and he blushed profusely when she gave him a kiss.

Anxious to get away on their own, Siegfried and Frieda left and Helga returned to the kitchen with her brother

"So, what's going on?" he said. "This friend of yours? The one you wrote to me about?"

Helga had hoped the subject would not arise, but now that it had she would tell him all.

"I met him when I was shopping. He invited me for a snack. And then it became a regular thing. He's very nice."

"He's in the *Wehrmacht?*"

"Yes, a lieutenant."

"Where's he from?".

"He's from Aachen. His parents are here . . . "

She paused and looked away. This was going to be the difficult part.

"And? . . . "

"There's a complication . . . "

She paused again, and then she stood up. He waited.

"I know you're not going to like this . . . you see he's married."

"Damn it Helga . . . what are you doing?"

She flopped onto the sofa. He got up as if wanting to detach himself from her presence. He paced up and down, then he stopped.

"Have you been intimate?"

She started to cry but then gained control.

"Yes . . . just once," she said firmly.

"My God! What made you do this?" He was shouting now, beside himself with anger.

"Günther . . . please keep your voice down. You'll wake Hans."

He ignored her.

"Does Eva know?"

"She's met him . . . I imagine she has drawn conclusions."

"Of course."

He continued pacing.

"I can't believe this . . . Why, Why, Why? Tell me Why?"

"I don't know. I was lonely, bored. It just happened."

"How about your child . . . and his father, Peter . . . did you think of them?"

She looked up, wiping the tears from her eyes. She felt defiant now. After what he had said about the English, the remark was absurd.

"Stop it Günther . . . you don't have to rub it in. I'm carrying enough guilt."

He sat down.

"Is it still going on?"

"No . . . he was posted to the eastern front."

"The Russian campaign?"

"Yes."

"God!"

"I know . . . it looks bad."

She added abruptly, "He's dead."

"Then it's all over?"

"Yes." She lowered her eyes, avoiding his gaze.

There was a silence as she waited for him to respond but when he didn't she looked up.

"Günther I still love Peter. It's just the waiting, the uncertainty. How do I know he's even alive?"

He got up and sat beside her, cradling her in his arms, and she felt again their love for each other, a love she felt she had lost.

Two days before Günther was due to return to the *Schlosstern,* he was sitting in the kitchen with Helga and Eva when the telephone rang. Helga answered it and talked for a while to the caller. Günther couldn't hear the conversation because the phone was in the hall, but he could hear her laughing. When she came and tapped him on the shoulder, he was startled.

"Call for you," she said.

"Hello," he said cautiously.

"It's Siegfried. Didn't Helga tell you? Frieda and I want you to join us for dinner and a film. Will you come?"

"Is Helga coming?"

"No, no. She's, ah . . . busy."

It sounded strange. Surely Eva could look after Hans? He deliberated for a moment.

"Sure, I'll come."

They met in a restaurant in the theatre district on the *Maximilianstrasse.* It was crowded, and a carefree atmosphere prevailed, a dramatic contrast to the situation in Hamburg. Siegfried astonished Günther by introducing him to Anna, a friend of Frieda. The subterfuge to get him to the restaurant had been masterminded by Helga and Frieda to provide him with a companion. Embarrassed at first, Günther soon fell for Anna's tranquil charm. Anna, who worked in the same hospital as Frieda, was happy to participate in the ruse and her hazel eyes sparkled with infectious merriment. Of medium height and build, with a placid face and brown hair, Günther was immediately captivated by her.

Over the remaining hours of his leave, Günther spent most of his time with Anna. Her congenial disposition made him realize how lacking in fun his past existence had been. They walked in the *Englisher Garten*, the large park which dominated the eastern part of the city, went boating on the Isar River, and took in an evening of Mozart. The time faded away so quickly that it was a shock when the time came to think of returning to the *Schlosstern*. On the last night, Günther, fighting his shyness, asked if he could keep in touch.

"I'll be very annoyed if you don't." Anna kissed him on the cheek and responding to her initiative; he embraced her.

"Come on," she said, happily, I'll take you back to the *Sunderstrasse*. Frieda and I have to work tonight.

After the girls had left, Günther sat in the living room with Siegfried.

"I think you like her?"

"Yes, yes. She's fun to be with." Günther felt his face flush as Siegfried smiled contentedly.

5.

$\mathcal{A}$t the shipyard on the Tyne, Peter began his new routine. He was responsible for all of the electrical systems that controlled the gunnery and torpedo apparatus. It was inspiring to be on a new ship and he was serious about the responsibilities that he had assumed. Furthermore, the work provided an antidote to the depression which he had experienced since returning from the tropics. He worked long hours, immersing himself in the intricacies of the ship's electrical systems. But there were still the difficult hours, when he was off-duty and alone with himself and his memories. He thought constantly of Helga and his son, but whereas the hope of a reunion remained alive in his heart, its intensity was waning. As much as he tried to fight it, he felt its presence like an evil shadow. His optimism, which had held up well throughout his period of foreign service, had suffered a marked decline when he returned to England and the immediacy of the war. He hated what it was doing to people, yet he too felt its corrupting influence. He felt angry and helpless, devastated by the loss of friends and family. Particularly calamitous had been demise of his maternal grandparents in an air raid on London. It had occurred early in his term abroad and, as if trying to atone for his thoughtless letter about the death of his mother, his father had written a lengthy account of the raid, and the devastation it had caused to the centre of the city, leaving no doubt that they were killed instantly. It was this tragedy which more than any other made Peter scornful of those who could still find a high moral purpose in death and destruction. He felt a ruthlessness that he had not known before, a self-centred desire to live for himself, seize the moment, live life to the full without regard for the consequences. Yet he was still, in the odd quiet moment, able to lament the absence of the kind and considerate side of his character. But these reflections did not overcome his conviction that the war gave one the right to live in the present.

The Dance Studio was quite near the main railway station in Newcastle. It took just less than twenty-five minutes to get to and from his lodgings in Holiburn. It all began when he decided to enrol in a modern dance course, part of a determination to improve his chances with the opposite sex. It was the fourth night, one of two nights per week, a total of ten sessions in all. He had finished Dottie's generous supper and had caught the seven o'clock out of Holiburn, a routine that had become firmly established. He bought a newspaper on leaving the station in Newcastle. A quick coffee and a review of the latest news preceded his lesson at eight thirty.

She was a new arrival. She was tall and slender with a nice body. Great legs he thought, and the first time he danced with her and she moved in close it was all he could do to contain the excitement stirring his thighs. It wasn't long before they were dating regularly. Unlike Helga whose grace and beauty and strength of character had created a deep and loving relationship between them, his new companion radiated a primitive sensuality which matched his desire for immediate pleasure. She was completely uninhibited and he was, from the first, at the mercy of her advances.

Her name was Sarah and he soon learned that she had been engaged to a fighter pilot. She told Peter that it had lasted three years and then had just faded away. "Oh, there were others, but nothing serious," she said.

If he had any doubts about his sexual prowess it was soon dispelled. During the four months in Holiburn they met every time that he was able to get ashore for an overnight leave, usually at least three times a week. He would rush to catch the train from Holiburn, drawing knowing glances from his fellow boarders as he rushed to finish his supper.

On every occasion the mutual desire for copulation was so strong that it usually took precedence over any other activity. One look at her with her low-cut dresses, slim figure, and sensuous lips, and his arousal couldn't be delayed. And he not only enjoyed the sex; it became a passion. He was hooked, and thoughts of Helga faded further into the background of his mind. It did become something of a physical marathon, however, which brought forth comments from his crewmates about his heavy eyes and a tendency to sudden afternoon naps.

Jonathan Saunders joined the Sandrake about three weeks after Peter. He was a *hostilities only* seaman called up for the duration of the war. A tall studious type who appeared out of place in the general confusion which accompanied the final stages of the ship's construction, he had just tripped over a welding cable, incurring the verbal displeasure of a burly worker, when Peter happened by.

"Sorry," he was saying in a polite cultured voice.

"Welcome aboard," Peter said, amused by his attempts to make amends. "I'm Peter Gray. Saw you come aboard yesterday."

"It's quite a mess isn't it?"

"Thank your lucky stars we're not living on board."

"Oh sorry, Jonathan Saunders, pleased to meet you."

"You've got a billet?"

"Yes, not far from here, on Leslie Street."

"Feel like a cuppa?"

"Yes . . . Yes I would."

They went to a wooden shack in the dockyard where a happy-go-lucky middle-aged woman was dispensing tea and buns. And then they walked back to the ship.

"How long you been in . . . the Navy I mean?"

"About six months, I've just got out of training."

"What did you do before?"

"I was working in my father's law firm. I was hoping to

get back to my studies when it all started. Are you a regular?"

"Volunteered in nineteen thirty six . . . didn't expect to get into a bloody war."

It wasn't long before Peter struck up a friendship with Jonathan. He was the first of the regular crew members, seamen who were to provide the basic human resources to man the torpedo and gunnery equipment and whose contribution would be critical in the months ahead.

At first, their friendship was limited to work activities; Peter was too busy with his amorous activities to tolerate a third person on his trips ashore. But they did get to a cinema to see 'Gone with the Wind' on one of the rare occasions when Sarah was indisposed. Over coffee afterwards Peter learned that Jonathan almost went into the RAF but at the last minute changed his mind.

"Why was that?"

"Somehow, I couldn't see myself in the RAF and the manning officer obviously agreed."

"Hope you made the right choice!"

"I just happen to believe in fate."

Peter was silent. He wondered if it was fate or lust that made him decide to go out with Sarah.

By the end of September the sea trials of the Sandrake had been completed and they sailed for Scapa Flow.

The last night with Sarah had been one gigantic marathon of physical gratification, and in the morning, arising early to return to the Sandrake, Peter felt exhausted rather than emotionally fulfilled. They hugged and kissed outside the dingy hotel which had been the scene of so much of their consorting.

"I love you, Peter," she said, as the tears came to her eyes. "You must write to me. Please promise you will?"

"I will . . . I will write."

"You do love me, Peter?"

"Yea . . . yes, I do." He hated his hesitation and his

192

words sounded hollow as if he was overcome with the urge to escape, which he was. They kissed again and then he just left, not even looking back.

As he walked up the gangway, he felt an immense sense of relief.   No longer would he have to face the demanding sexual encounters and he was thankful for that.

6.

Scapa Flow, a barren group of islands enclosing a large natural harbour, had been the Navy's wartime base in the 1914-1918 war. It offered little in the way of shore amenities for the crews who were stationed there. Unless one liked hiking, there was little else but the canteen which dispensed beer to thirsty sailors. Deprived of the normal social opportunities of the large ports in the south, it offered a way for them to escape the seaboard routine during the few hours they were allowed ashore.

Shortly after arriving in the Flow the crew of the Sandrake was informed that they were to be part of a large force being assembled to protect a new round of convoys to Russia. Furthermore, the Sandrake was to be one of four destroyers which would be providing an escort for a battleship and a cruiser, the whole force constituting a Battle Group.

One sunny but cool afternoon Peter and Jonathan strolled among the scattered clumps of heather, having rejected the smoky atmosphere of the canteen with its crowds of ratings becoming more convivial as the beer flowed, in favour of the open air. The peaceful scene had an unexpected impact on Peter who succumbed to a sudden impulse to reveal his relationship with Helga.

"I thought you had a girlfriend in Newcastle?"

"Yes, well, I don't know what possessed me. I needed a woman, I guess . . . the sex I mean." He blushed, feeling exploitive now, as if Sarah had been a sexual convenience, not a focus for genuine feelings of regard. Yet he had relished being with her, he couldn't deny that, and she obviously sought his company if not his deep affection. He felt dismayed by the

194

shallow feelings he had expressed when he left her behind.

"Nothing wrong with wanting sex, It's just normal human desire. My father always said, "Sow your wild oats while you're young - get it out of your system, then you can love and know what it means.""

"Your father said that?"

"Yes. He suggested I find a prostitute, so I spent a weekend in London . . . "

"London! London, you said?" Peter felt suddenly giddy.

"Yes, lots of whores around Piccadilly . . . I shagged the whole time. It was a bit boring really."

"Christ! I don't believe this!"

"You just got it the wrong way round. You found love before you got to know your sexual aggression. Still, I don't see that any harm's been done."

Peter stopped walking and sat down. This apparently naïve youngster - he seemed younger than himself even though he was about the same age - had more worldliness than he guessed. Jonathan sat down beside him. "Don't look so shocked and uncomfortable. You seem like a perfectly normal human being to me and obviously you are very much in love with Helga."

He studied Jonathan's bright and open face, envying his confidence, and then he thought of London again.

"They lived in Rotherhithe," he said.

"Who did?"

"My grandfather and grandmother."

"I see . . . you go there . . . to London . . . often?"

"They're gone. I was away. It was a bomb . . . They were killed?"

He paused.

"Yes, Jonathan . . . Killed. I haven't wanted to accept it. You see I loved my grandfather. I was only with him a short time, before I joined the Navy, but he taught me self-confidence, gave me the capacity to find excitement in the world around me ard to listen to my own thoughts and intuitions. It was like, well, if he was dead, then part of me was dead too. As long as he lived, I had a father . . . I couldn't cope with his loss. Do you understand, Jonathan?"

"Yes . . . Yes, I do," he paused. "But you do have a father?"

"Funny isn't it . . . he's my real father but I don't really know him. Grandfather understood me in a different way. Made me realize what a father could be . . . made me understand what I must be to **my** son. It's like the difference between sex and love. If you get it right, they can exist together, but if you don't you're not really living are you?"

"Maybe we need a drink after all?"

"I think we do."

Peter felt there was a new confidence in his stride as they headed to the canteen, and he liked the feeling.

"Thanks, Jonathan," he said. "You've helped me a lot."

7.

$\mathcal{T}$he *Schlosstern* swung at her anchorage in Altafjord in Northern Norway. It was a desolate location, a complete contrast to life in a German port with its promise of leave with family and friends. Although it had only been a few months since leaving Gotenhafen, to Günther it felt like a lifetime away. The only contact with the family was by post and that was uncertain at the best of times, now it was affected by the constant threat of Allied raids from the air and sea. The battleship *Tirzen* had already been disabled by British midget submarines. Nevertheless, the continued flow of Allied convoys to North Russia, carrying vital supplies of weapons, had to be countered and a surface attack by a German warship like the *Schlosstern* was one way to cause maximum damage and destruction.

Günther and Siegfried went down to the messdeck. They had just returned from a short spell ashore; a welcome interval from the almost continuous training exercises. Skiing in the fresh snow had been invigorating, bringing colour to their cheeks and highlighting their appreciation of the cups of hot coffee which they cradled in their still chilled hands.

"It was good to get ashore," Günther said.

"If only we could get to sea though . . . take a shot at the enemy," Siegfried expressed a sentiment universally shared by the crew.

"It'll happen soon enough." Günther, sounding remote, didn't find the prospect too appealing although he too was bored with waiting for something to happen.

"What's the matter?" Siegfried reacted with surprise. "I thought you were eager for action?"

Günther shifted uneasily. "I am, but . . . well, they'll have the whole British fleet waiting."

Siegfried's initial surprise turned to a look of consternation.

Funny, Günther thought, when Siegfried's optimistic I'm pessimistic, we have a habit of adopting opposite moods, but he didn't care what anyone else felt. It was when he encountered the bombing of Hamburg that he became aware of a cynicism which had been growing over time, resulting in an erosion of his original enthusiasm for the *Nazi* regime. At first, he tried to deny his feelings, but the loss of Heinrich and the continued reverses in Russia, highlighted by his sister's indiscretion with the married Lieutenant serving there in the *Wehrmacht,* beset him with grave doubts about the future of the *Third Reich.*

He desperately wanted to see Anna again and each letter exchanged between them increased his feelings of loneliness. Even his devotion to the *Führer* seemed self-serving now, selfish even. Today, when his boots had crunched in the pristine snow, the joy of just being alive seemed infinitely more precious than succumbing to the lure of ideologies. The little things counted. The time he had just spent together with Siegfried, enjoying the simple beauty of natural things, was so much more consequential than the dispassionate strategies created by distant authorities with little concern for ordinary people.

"My God! Cheer up, Günther, It's not like you to be this way."

Günther gazed wearily at Siegfried, not wanting to be reminded of what he was supposed to be, only conscious of how he felt. He got up.

"I need to be alone for a while."

Siegfried was silent, but his face showed concern. Günther, aware of it, didn't want to linger. He got up hastily and left, making his way to the upper deck. He strode forward until he reached far up into the bow of the huge ship. It was dark now, the short hours of daylight displaced by the almost perpetual darkness of night at this latitude at this time of the year. The Northern Lights brightened the sky, creating majestic

198

ever-changing patterns. There was a cool breeze blowing in from seaward and a suggestion of snowflakes danced in the wind. The hairs stiffened in his nose as he breathed the cold Arctic air. Everything was peaceful. It must have been this way for hundreds, thousands of years, he thought, before man brought his insanity to the world.

8.

The approach to Akureyri, a small port on the northern coast of Iceland, was through a long narrow fjord. The British Battle Group entered it in line-ahead, the battleship leading. It was here that they were to refuel, ready to take up a protective position west of a northbound convoy en route to Russia.

By mid morning they were safely anchored off the town and a short spell of leave was announced. Peter and Jonathan, together with Mike Struthers, a leading signalman, went ashore at noon. It was a pleasant surprise to find that Akureyri was caught up with pre-Christmas activities. And then there were the girls. Every one of them seemed to exude the healthy Nordic vitality. Even in the freezing temperatures they were dressed in skirts and their apparent immunity to the cold was a source of wonder to the sailors so recently pressed into adopting the rigours of Arctic weather. Children skated on a nearby rink as the trio browsed in the shops, looking for presents that they knew would be late for family and friends. Peter chose a brightly coloured hand knitted scarf for Helga, convincing himself that the act would somehow bring nearer the chances of a reunion. Mike bought the same for his wife, while Jonathan decided on a number of exquisite Christmas tree decorations for his mother, a reindeer, sleigh, and a Father Christmas, crafted from wood and painted in red and white. Finished with their buying spree, they sat drinking coffee and eating sticky cakes, and trying to make conversation with the pretty waitress, but they did more laughing than talking as language difficulties precluded their attempts at verbal exchanges and gestures became more successful.

Akureyri turned out to be more fun than Peter could ever have guessed. It reminded him of another life, a life that he had lost to the demands of war. He felt both deprived and strangely reassured. There was, after all, some calm in a world of idiocy, and he had rediscovered it in the remoteness of the frigid north.

As the motor launch made its way back to the Sandrake, darkness was falling and he looked back at the Christmas lights, supplemented by the lights of the town, a town unaffected by a blackout, and he felt sadness. He turned away reluctantly, back towards the darkened ships, back to the unknown, back to the prospects of another day yet to be born, and he found himself tensing, an involuntary preparation for whatever might soon be demanded of him.

An hour before midnight, the ships of the Battle Group cast off their moorings. The smooth waters of the fjord were sliced by the bows of the ships, in line-ahead again, heading towards the open sea. When they cleared the shelter of the fjord, the full force of a worsening gale assailed them, sending the Sandrake into a vicious rolling and pitching motion.

"We've had our fucking Christmas." Peter struggled to sling his hammock in his usual billet above the mess table.

Jonathan eyed his swaying Christmas tree decorations that he had hung from a ventilating shaft.

"At least we had a chance to be reminded of it,"

Peter, along with the rest of the crew, were called to Action Stations at four in the morning. The Admiral, flying his flag in the battleship - determined to keep his crews in fighting trim - had ordered a night action. The object of the exercise was to practice a torpedo attack on a battleship, and no one had any doubts that the battleship he had in mind was the *Schlosstern*.

The destroyers were detached with the aim of executing an attack on the cruiser accompanying them - the cruiser having been assigned to represent the *Schlosstern*. Using their Radar, the destroyers located the target and then moved into two formations, two ships in each, moving in at high speed, zigzagging to avoid the simulated fire from the larger ship, and then turning broadside to launch their torpedoes. It was a great success, executed with the precision that the Admiral demanded, bringing the crews to a heightened state of battle readiness.

It was during the early evening that Peter received the news from Mike. He had just come down from the bridge.

"Skipper just got word. The fully-loaded northbound convoy is being shadowed by enemy aircraft."

"Shit! That means that Jerry already knows what we're up to."

"Fraid so."

9.

$\mathcal{I}$n Altenfjord, Günther and Siegfried, together with their crewmates, prepared to celebrate Christmas in the time-honoured tradition. The *Schlosstern's* living spaces had been decorated with Christmas trees hung with lights and ornaments. The gloom of inactivity was forgotten as the merriment raised morale, bringing a feeling of even greater camaraderie to the crew. There was also a mood of anticipation. Something was in the wind and everything pointed to a major operation of some kind. The logical objective would be an attack on the next heavily-laden northbound convoy.

It was the afternoon of Christmas Day. Günther had just refilled his glass from the bowl of punch sitting on the mess table when Siegfried joined him.

"Heard the latest rumour - we're going to sea . . ."

"Oh sure," Günther advertised his disbelief, but just then the 'notice to sail' was announced over the loudspeakers.

"So, they want us to believe it **this** time, when the weather is the worst it's been for days," he said, trying to justify his scepticism. "Don't get your hopes up."

"I wasn't getting **my** hopes up." Siegfried was irked. "They'll be waiting for us . . . just like you said."

"Ah well, the eternal pessimist," Günther was dismissive. "We're the lucky ship, remember? If they send us out, we'll get them."

In a mood of suspense they went to their stations, preparing for sea at last. Out beyond the anchorage, the effects of a southwesterly gale, which stirred the waters of the Barent's Sea into mountainous waves, was already being felt on the *Schlosstern's* upper deck as a biting wind. Ringed by mountains, the normally placid surface of the fjord was being assaulted by wind gusts, mixed with snow and creating a haphazard choppiness, all the more frustrating for navigation because snow and spray reduced visibility in the Arctic darkness.

During the early evening, the crew of the *Schlosstern* was ordered to assemble on the quarterdeck.

Günther hurried aft with Seigfried, joining others emerging from the bowels of the mighty ship, a throng of eager souls, imbued with curiosity, eager to learn of their mission.

They stood in silence as the First Officer began to speak. Soon, there was no mistaking their task. The *Schlosstern* had been ordered to attack, and if possible to destroy, a heavily-laden convoy on its way to Russia. The *Schlosstern* was to be accompanied by five destroyers. The overall objective of the sortie was to disrupt the supply of war materials to the Eastern Front and in this way assist the *Wehrmacht*.

The crew cheered as the short address ended. Günther and Siegfried joined in, caught up in the excitement of the moment. At last they had the assignment they had expected when they moved north to Norway.

The crew returned to their stations, and the *Schlosstern* weighed anchor, heading down the fjord towards the barrage ships guarding the entrance. The five escorting destroyers joined her. When they cleared the sheltering land, to begin their foray into the Barent's Sea, the full force of the gale hit them. Steaming at twenty-five knots, a course was set to intercept the convoy. The effect of the southwesterly storm was to create a steady rolling and pitching motion sending loose items adrift in the messdecks.

"Oh to be at sea again," Günther yelled, picking up the pieces of a plate which had come whizzing past his head to disintegrate on the deck.

The *Schlosstern* and her escorting destroyers continued at their planned course and speed. Somewhere ahead was the convoy and if all the information they had received was accurate they had a good chance of intercepting it and completing their mission.

10.

On the morning of Christmas day, as the Battle Group continued to steam eastwards towards the convoy, the weather deteriorated further. Peter, preparing for the likelihood of action, decided to make a routine check of the gunnery control systems. It had been a wild night. The mountainous seas had sent the Sandrake plunging and rolling so violently that it was virtually impossible to sleep. Water seemed to find its way in everywhere and loose objects were flung about defying any attempt at securing them. When Peter arrived on the bridge, he climbed up to the Gunnery Director Tower, asking the crew if all the instrument lights were working.

Jonathan, in his post on the starboard side of the tower, turned to Peter. The ship lurched, and the structure around them creaked and groaned with the strain of resisting the turbulent sea.

"Maybe, I should have joined the RAF?" Jonathan grinned.

"Too late now, mate . . . How're the instrument lights?"

"Hard to tell in this light, wait till it's dark - they seem OK."

He closed the door and climbed down the ladder. Mike was looking up at him.

"Ready for a night action?"

"It's the instrument lights . . . always a problem, a little vibration . . . " He threw up his hands in despair.

Peter looked to port, towards the battleship. Large waves were coming over the bow, running the whole length of the ship, and depositing tons of water on its superstructure, sending great clouds of spray into the air.

"Big bastard thinks **we** can't take it." Mike, following Peter's gaze, sounded annoyed. "Said she had to slow down because of us . . . "

Just then, the Sandrake heeled over at an alarming angle and Peter found himself standing at a slant of about fifty degrees to the deck. The ship held this position, shuddering, as if trying to decide whether to roll completely over, or recover and try again on the other side.

As the Sandrake righted itself, Peter offered unspoken praise to some unknown marine architect. However, the danger still existed and every roll repeated the possibility of capsizing.

"Bloody 'ell!" Mike's hands were still gripping the side of the bridge.

"Think I'll stay on deck for a while." Peter had visions of being trapped below decks if the worst happened.

That evening, Peter and Mike cradled cups of hot cocoa. They were alone in the mess. The majority of their mates were at action stations.

"If the *Schlosstern* comes out now, we'll be too far from the convoy to be of any help," Peter ruminated.

Mike nodded. "Don't forget the Cruiser Force . . . They're coming down from the northeast. They'll be closer to the convoy."

Peter lapsed into silence. The time was passing slowly. The combination of bitter weather and all the waiting to get into position for an attack gave him a feeling of unreality. Was there even a ship called the *Schlosstern?* Could it be that it was all a hoax? He experienced a curious lack of interest, as though he was becoming disassociated from the tactical dispositions generated by all the reports, the reports that had two opposing forces coming together in anger somewhere in the Arctic darkness.

"Worried?" asked Mike.

"Scared shitless."

"I think of my wife, sitting at home, waiting. It's gotta be worse . . . You married Pete?"

"Ah . . . no." He hesitated. For a brief moment he felt like confiding in Mike, but then he drained his cup and, leaving Mike, went to the galley to get a refill.

Early on the morning of the next day, as the Battle Group continued its drive towards the convoy, Peter was stowing his hammock. The loudspeakers started humming and he waited for a message. It wasn't long in coming. A cheer erupted as the Captain announced that the Admiralty had confirmed the *Schlosstern* was at sea.

He was jolted back from the unreality that he had experienced the day before. It was now clear that the possibility of action loomed large. If the *Schlosstern* reached the convoy its superior speed and firepower could cause untold damage. The Battle Group was still too far away to be of any help. Everything depended on the cruisers. If they could attack her before she reached the convoy some time might be bought. But the cruisers had inferior armament. The Battle Group was the only sure way to provide heavier opposition.

Peter sat silently, admiring Jonathan's Christmas presents for his mother - the reindeer, the sleigh and the Father Christmas - hanging above the mess table, teetering back and forth as the ship continued its endless rolling and plunging. The Battle Group raced to intercept the *Schlosstern*.

11.

𝒯he *Schlosstern* steamed westwards at full speed. The destroyers, which had been detached to search further south, were also steaming westwards. The whole force was fanned out to maximize the possibility of intercepting the enemy ships. If all the estimations were correct, interception of the convoy was imminent.

Suddenly, without warning, shells burst in the sea ahead of the *Schlosstern*, raising menacing spouts of water, exploding dangerously close to the ship's hull. Gunther, at his post in the Radar room, heard the sound and felt the vibration, but he kept his eyes glued to the displays, looking for the telltale signs of echoes that would announce the presence of the convoy.

"Echoes dead ahead!" He yelled into his microphone.

Günther had barely completed his report when there was a tremendous explosion above him and the sound of falling debris. The Radar displays flickered and the images disappeared.

The *Schlosstern's* own guns opened up. An interception had been achieved, but not with the convoy's merchant ships. Enemy warships were firing at the *Schlosstern*. Then other reports came in. Enemy shells had hit the port high-angle director which was wrecked. Worst still, it was the same hit that had put the main Radar out of action.

The *Schlosstern* turned away, breaking off contact with the cruisers. Günther was baffled by what was happening.

> This is the Captain. A second attempt is being made
> to attack the convoy. We are going to approach from
> the north. The destroyers from the south.

Günther, still shaken by the suddenness of the enemy attack, pondered what they were up against. He hoped they wouldn't have to spend too much time finding the convoy now that the *Schlosstern* had been discovered.

As the night gave way to the beginnings of another fleeting period of daylight, snow squalls persisted. The emptiness of the sea and the isolation of the *Schlosstern* stood out starkly, and he wished they were being accompanied by the destroyers, but they were well away to the south. Somewhere ahead lay the convoy with its cargo of war materials and they alone had the best chance to reach it.

Another announcement broke the stillness.

> From the Captain. Information has been received
> from our aerial reconnaissance. What appears to be
> a British Battle Group has been located several
> hundred miles to the west of us. It is too far away to
> be of any danger to our operation.
> We are continuing with our plan to attack the convoy
> from the north.

Attempts to fix the main Radar having failed, Günther reported to the First Officer on the bridge. One of the lookouts had been seriously injured by falling debris and Günther was given a temporary assignment to take over lookout duties, there now being a need for a heightened visual scan ahead.

As he lifted the binoculars to his eyes, Günther looked out at the grey, lonely, stormy sea and he thought of Anna and Helga and the pleasant days of leave spent in Munich. He wished he was with them all - sorry again that on this Christmas, the Christmas he had promised to be home, that fate had dictated otherwise. But the reality of the present soon intervened.

Around noon, Günther heard reports coming in from the after Radar - which was still operating - which indicated that contact had again been made with enemy vessels and he redoubled his watch ahead.

At first, he was uncertain. What he saw looked like storm clouds on the horizon. But then the port lookout yelled.

"Dead ahead! Ships!"

The alarm bells shrilled, and the *Schlosstern* opened fire. Enemy starshells burst overhead and shell splashes erupted around them. Then the *Schlosstern* heeled over, guns firing. It wasn't the convoy, but enemy warships again.

Günther continued to observe the action from his position on the bridge. Eleven inch shells from the *Schlosstern* were soon straddling and hitting the enemy. Clearly, the *Schlosstern* could outgun them and when, free of any hits herself, she turned away, Günther was surprised and disappointed. Why hadn't they continued the attack? And where were the destroyers when they were needed?

The Captain gave the crew another report.

Our second action has been with the same British cruisers. Those we encountered this morning. We have inflicted heavy damage and they have withdrawn. However, the weather is worsening and the destroyers have been ordered to return to Altenfjord. Having failed to engage the convoy we are also returning to Norway.

The abruptness of the decision to return to their base astounded Günther. He felt betrayed. The Schlosstern had seemed to hold the initiative, so why would they break off the action now? In spite of all the optimism which had attended their sailing, the sortie was failing. Still, they had survived and perhaps the decision was the most prudent given the difficulty of reaching the convoy. He barely had time to ponder the implications of their strategy when word reached the bridge that they were still being shadowed by one of the cruisers.

By mid-afternoon, relishing a welcome break from the exposed bridge, Günther was down in the mess enjoying some hot soup and coffee. Siegfried appeared and sat beside him.

"What's happening?"

Günther disliked the implication that he should have the answers.

"You heard the announcement."

"Why didn't we sink the cruisers?"

"I don't know, Siegfried,"

Seigfried waited.

"I don't know," Günther repeated angrily. "Besides, the bastards put our main radar out of action."

"We could have outgunned them?"

"Look, Siegfried, I don't get to hear everything. To tell the truth I'm more worried about the British Battle Group."

"Captain said they were too far away to be of any danger."

"But that was . . . " He looked at his watch. "More than three hours ago, perhaps more, allowing for the time it took us to receive the information."

"My God . . . You don't think?"

"Yes I do. Why would the cruiser be shadowing us? Probably keeping the Battle Group informed of our position?"

They drifted into a silence broken only by the sounds within the ship as its main engines sped them eastwards towards Altenfjord and the safety of their base.

12.

*A*board the Sandrake Peter was closed up at his action station in the Gunnery Transmitting Station. From here he could follow the unfolding events and be ready if any problems developed in the complex electrical system used to train and fire the guns.

"Message from the bridge," the able seaman yelled. "The cruiser force has been engaged in two actions with the *Schlosstern*. She appears to have abandoned the attempt to attack the convoy. They are now shadowing her by radar."

Although the gale had slackened somewhat, the Sandrake continued to roll and pitch as it pressed forward at high speed, hoping to intercept the *Schlosstern* before she could return to the safety of her base at Altenfjord.

Peter went to the mess and poured himself a cup of strong tea. He found a book and tried to read but he was too anxious. As the time dragged on, his mind flitted about, alternately thinking of Helga and his son, the stupidity of his affair with Sarah, and the loss of his mother and his grandparents. Always though, the more immediate circumstances imposed themselves over everything. Any time now, he could experience combat for the first time.

It was late afternoon, after he had returned to his post in the Transmitting Station, when the Captain announced that the battleship's Radar had located the *Schlosstern* at a range of about twenty-two miles.

Peter felt his pulse rate climb. It was actually happening. He steadied himself against the bulkhead trying to accustom himself to his racing heart. He worried that his crewmates might see his discomfort, but they were all busy dealing with the rush of commands from the bridge.

"No destroyers!" said the able seaman stationed at the gunnery plot.

Peter let out a sigh of relief. Still, while the absence of destroyers might lessen the dangers of attacking the *Schlosstern*, he hadn't any doubts that she would prove a formidable foe. As much as to calm his nerves as to attend to a necessary task, he decided to go down to the Generating Room to check the all-important power supplies and the backup batteries. He had no reason to suspect any problems but he had to occupy his troubled mind.

He heard the guns open fire as he descended the ladder.

At a range of some six miles, the Battle Group illuminated the *Schlosstern* with starshell.

13.

At the house on the Sunderstrasse, a Christmas tree adorned the living room. It was decorated with trinkets and ornaments from many past Christmases, from happier times before the war, when family and friends gathered around to celebrate.

Outside it was a cold grey day with a strong wind which had the few pedestrians drawing up their coat collars. Helga turned from the window to watch Hans playing with his presents, a bright red fire engine from Eva, a puzzle from Frieda and a tool set from Anna. Ilse and Rolf had sent a model car. Helga knew it was Ilse's doing even though the card said, 'From Ilse and Rolf.' But the best present of all was the package of wooden building blocks from Günther.

Frieda and Anna had joined them on Christmas Day and they all hoped that Günther and Siegfried would arrive, honouring the promise that Günther had made to Helga earlier in the year that he would be home for the festivities. Even as the day had advanced with no sign of either of them, and the rest of them had grown sceptical, Helga had held onto her belief that they would arrive unannounced. But now, a day later, after Frieda and Anna had departed, she was forced to concede that her hopes were not to be realized. In her loneliness, some news from Günther would have also helped her deal with Peter's absence. It was as though Günther's safety enabled her to believe in Peter's survival.

Eva was, as usual, comforting but realistic. "I'm sure he would be here if he could," she said.

"But why didn't he write?"

"Perhaps it was impossible. After all, we're sure that they're somewhere up in Norway, so even if he did write it would take time to get here."

Helga thought of Anna's stoicism, how she had argued that no news is good news.

She looked at Hans playing happily, oblivious to her concerns, not even comprehending that he had a father, even though Helga tried to make him understand that it was Peter's photograph that stood by her bed. "Father," he would say, repeating the word without meaning, smiling because he was pleasing his mother.

Later that day, after Hans had settled in for his afternoon nap, Helga opened a box containing the shingle she had collected on the beach with Peter. She found it comforting to run her hand through the multicoloured stones, allowing her thoughts to return to that day by the sea. She could hear the waves advancing and retreating and the gulls' sharp cries, and she felt again the warmth of Peter's hands in hers. She picked out a single stone admiring its smoothness and its colours and she thought of the eons of time that had produced it. It was a humbling perspective but it was reassuring too. Time and patience created beauty just as time and patience would restore her relationships with Peter and her brother.

14.

$\mathcal{T}$ime was now one asset missing from the *Schlosstern's* mission. She was speeding towards home when three starshell burst overhead, rending the darkness, stripping away the last vestige of anonymity

Then a salvo of heavy shells landed off the port side sending up gigantic fountains of water. Günther shivered. These were heavy calibre shells - much heavier than those carried by a cruiser. The *Schlosstern's* guns opened up, returning the fire which was now coming at them in rapid sequence.

A cacophony of sound assaulted Günther's ears while the thud of near misses sent shock waves hammering at his body. He felt helpless and vulnerable, his task of vigilant observation now replaced by inactivity.

A blast knocked him to the deck, and dazed and disorientated he struggled to his feet, unable to decide whether he was injured or not. When he looked ahead, smoke arose from a gaping hole near A Turret. He picked up his binoculars and his earphones, only to learn that A Turret was out of action and the ammunition supply to B Turret interrupted by a fire below decks.

The large calibre shells kept coming. Helped by the continuous starshell, the enemy was able to keep up a ferocious barrage. Günther had soon recovered enough to establish that he had escaped injury but this was small consolation as the shells rained down and the *Schlosstern* kept up a steady fire with her remaining heavy guns.

Günther gripped the side of the bridge, trying to assure himself that there was something solid amidst the smoke and the din of shouted commands and the closeness of enemy shells.

Nevertheless, the incoming shells seemed to be slackening. Could the *Schlosstern* be pulling away from her attackers? The answer was not long in coming.

> From the Captain. The enemy is falling behind. We are outrunning them. The Schlosstern has proved its superiority.

Günther wanted to join in the Captain's optimism but this time it seemed ill-placed. It began to appear inconceivable to him that the enemy would allow them to escape. As in the sinking of the *Bistroden* some two years earlier, the enemy would surely concentrate all their forces to try and sink the *Schlosstern*. He caught himself shaking as he brought the binoculars up to his eyes. He couldn't decide whether it was fear or excitement. And then he heard a dull thud. It seemed to come from further aft, yet nothing appeared to change. They maintained their course and speed.

He felt it first as a decrease in the spray thrown up by the bow wave. Then the bow wave itself became less pronounced. The speed was definitely dropping. The Captain confirmed his worst fear.

> We have sustained a shell hit in the boiler room. This has resulted in a loss of speed. We hope to resume normal speed soon.

Günther thought of Siegfried down below decks, wondering if he was all right. Because he was in the engine room - which was physically separated from the damaged boiler room - he was probably unharmed. Nevertheless, the loss of steam had already reduced their speed; it would be tough down there, trying to restore the lost power.

Günther felt jubilant when the speed of the *Schlosstern* increased again. The engine room crew must have performed another miracle? Shortly after, the *Schlosstern's* main and secondary armament opened up again as more enemy starshell burst overhead. He strained to see what was happening through the smoke and the shell bursts.

§

Aboard the Sandrake, Peter listened to the answering fire from the *Schlosstern*. As each German salvo landed amongst the Battle Group there was a terrific *cru-ump* leaving little doubt what the effect would be if hits were scored.

He tried to concentrate on the task at hand. His eyes roamed over the switchboards, gauges, and the machinery. Everything was fine. A steady hum permeated the small compartment. He went over to his small workbench and checked his tool bag.

He was about to leave when his eyes were caught by a copy of a National Geographic Magazine. He picked it up and thumbed through the pages, looking at the glossy pictures, but his hands were shaking and he couldn't concentrate. The firing of salvoes and the crash of enemy shells continued. He had not thought when he joined the Navy that he would ever have to fight. But this was the job he was trained to do, this was the job the Sandrake was designed for, to kill enemy warships with torpedoes.

He started up the ladder but, having forgotten his bag of tools, he went back to get it. He was leaving the Generating Room when an announcement came over the loudspeakers and he ducked into the empty Cook's Mess opposite to hear what it was. It was the Captain's voice.

We have been ordered to close and attack the
Schlosstern with torpedoes as soon as possible.

He looked at his watch. Some twenty minutes had elapsed since the *Schlosstern* had been located. The high-pitched whine of the main turbines increased as the Sandrake worked up to full speed, zigzagging to port and starboard to upset the aim of the German gunners.

He sat down at the empty mess table, trying to grasp the implications of what he had heard. And he thought of death and the odds of survival. He became acutely aware of the predicament he was in and he felt a terrible fear. He got up and paced up and down but after several minutes he started up the ladder again. The corridor was empty and he returned to the Transmitting Station. The Able Seaman caught his eye.

"We're going in," he said.

Peter moved his mouth to speak but his throat was dry and no words came. Instead, he nodded his head.

The German shells rained down as the Sandrake continued to run into the target under heavy fire. It was obvious now that the German gunners were ranging on the Sandrake and each salvo felt like the preliminary to the last. A hit with one salvo and their headlong rush would end in disaster.

Suddenly the Sandrake turned sharply, getting into position to release its torpedoes. At that moment she would be beam-on to the *Schlosstern*, presenting an easy target.

There was an extra large bang. The ship shuddered.

"Lost contact with the Director Tower," shouted the Able Seaman.

Peter watched him as he pushed his headphones closer to his ears and he wished that he too could shut out the sound of the exploding German salvos.

"Message from the bridge," he said. "Director Tower out of action. Guns to fire independently."

He looked across at Peter.

"Illumination out. Instruments on the forward gun position."

Peter picked up his tool bag and started on his way to the upper deck. He had to ascertain on which side the Sandrake's guns were firing in order to avoid being caught in the blast. Confirming it was to starboard, he moved around to the port side and peered out from under the superstructure. Starshells illuminated the scene and shrapnel from shells bursting nearby splayed the upper deck. The noise was shattering and he was momentarily transfixed by the sight. He adjusted his tin hat and pulled his anti-flash gear closer around his face, then made his way slowly towards the forward gun. A shell exploded off the bow and shell fragments whizzed by his head. Another shell exploded and another shower of fragments rattled around the superstructure. He felt a tug as a piece of hot metal tore a hole in his tool bag. He started to run, seeking to reach the safety of the forward gun. By the time he reached it the crew had been ordered to check fire and the Sandrake was pulling away from the *Schlosstern*. He replaced the burnt out lights, and then waited until the enemy shelling slackened before returning to the Transmitting Station. It was then that he realized that his left sleeve was ripped and a trickle of blood had spread to his hand. When he reached the corridor below decks, he saw Mike Struthers ahead.

"Jonathan?" he called, his voice strained.

Mike stopped and turned.

"They're all gone." Mike said. His face was like a mask. "Whole crew in the Director Tower . . . wiped out!"

"Christ?"

"Shell went right through. Nothing left."

Peter looked at Mike with his tin hat askance and the sweat pouring off his face and as he looked he realized that Mike was covered in what looked like sawdust, but which was in reality minute parts of a human body, perhaps several bodies, the crew of the Director Tower - all that remained of Jonathan.

"What's happened to your hand?"

"Oh . . ." Peter's thoughts were still on the fate of

Jonathan. "It's my arm. Just a small scratch. Piece of shrapnel. I was lucky."

"You'd better get to the Sick Bay."

"Jonathan! . . . I can't believe it, Mike."

§

The torpedo hits came in quick succession, one . . . two . . . three. Günther scarcely had time to register the underwater explosions before salvo after salvo of heavy fourteen inch shells straddled and then hit the *Schlosstern*. Reports of damage were soon coming in and were so numerous that it was difficult to comprehend what was happening. But still the *Schlosstern's* guns kept firing. Another fourteen-inch shell hit the bows and, as had happened before, Günther was knocked to the deck by the force of the explosion. Struggling to his feet, he felt that he was in the midst of a roaring inferno. He seemed to float in space while the awful din continued unabated and flames and smoke surrounded him on every side. He picked up the earphones and put them on, responding automatically, carrying out his assigned task, not caring where he was or what was happening, trying to add his contribution to the last efforts of a dying ship. Yet was it dying? Guns were still firing and reports were still coming in. They were still steaming at speed. And his mind went into another dimension where they were winning the fight, destroying the enemy against all odds. The *Schlosstern*, the lucky ship, pulling it off again, returning in triumph to the Fatherland. Günther returning to family - to Helga - to Anna.

How long he remained in a detached state of mind he couldn't say, but he was suddenly aware again of the continuing and overwhelming barrage of fire. Through it all isolated groups kept the armament firing and the ship steaming, as damage control parties worked to patch and repair.

Günther saw broken bodies everywhere, blood oozing from

mutilated flesh and bone. He stepped backwards and realized that he was looking at an exposed abdomen, the entrails looking like the residue from a butcher's chopping block. He felt sick and unsteady. Casualties were increasing by the minute. The slaughter couldn't continue, not for a lack of courage or gallantry but because the ship was becoming a burning wreck. Then came more torpedoes, more hits, more wounds into the dying ship. Günther remained at his post, numb now, without feeling, carried along by events, waiting for the end. But still reports kept coming in, less regular now, but still reflecting the determination of each member of the crew to keep fighting. It was a losing battle though and communications became erratic, coming in from isolated groups trying to maintain some semblance of control in their own surviving sectors of the great ship. And then the inevitable order came . . .

> From the Captain: Don life jackets and assemble on
> the upper deck. Prepare to abandon ship.

He made his way down from the bridge. When he reached the upper deck it was tilting at an alarming angle, the starboard side was already at sea level. Many of the crew were in the water grabbing at bits of wreckage for flotation. He looked at the faces mirroring shock, or horror, or fear, or perhaps all of these, and he thought of Siegfried in the engine room. Had he escaped? What had happened to him? And then someone took his hand.

"We've got to get out of here."

They moved down the sloping deck towards the starboard side where the water was lapping at the edge, but before they could jump, a wave hurtled them into the ice-cold Arctic sea.

15.

Hans was still asleep when Frieda and Anna arrived in the middle of the afternoon. Helga greeted them at the door.

"I've come to cheer you up." Frieda gave her a hug.

"I'm coping." Helga voice was guarded

"But you need to get out. Look, there's a dance at the hospital tonight . . . why don't you come?"

"How can I? . . ."

"Of course you can," Anna said.

Eva appeared behind her. "I can look after Hans. He'll be in bed after supper anyway."

"There, you see, it's arranged." Frieda reacted with delight.

"I suppose I can't refuse?"

"No," Frieda and Anna spoke in unison.

Most of the participants at the dance consisted of patients and nurses. Although there were a goodly proportion of civilians, by far the largest number were service personnel transferred from other hospitals. Many of them were members of the *Wehrmacht* from North Africa.

Helga found herself dancing with a young major who was due to return to duty within a week. He told her that he had been shot in the arm. He was a tall bronzed handsome fellow from Mannheim. He was also a fabulous dancer. As he whirled her around the floor, she realized that she was enjoying herself. Being close to a man again restored her sense of femininity. She even found herself flirting a little.

"Can I see you again?" he said, as the evening drew to a close.

"I don't think so . . ."

"Perhaps a lunch, or just coffee. I'm only here for a few more days."

Helga looked at the boyish face, thinking suddenly of Peter and Günther. He looked more like Siegfried she thought as she scanned the room looking for Frieda. But Frieda was dancing, talking and laughing with her partner.

"Would you come?" His question jolted her out of her daydream. He drew her close and she caught the scent of him, but she thought only of Peter and she pulled away.

"I can't . . . You see, I have a son."

"You're married?"

"Well, no, I don't think . . . "

"I'm married. I have two sons."

Helga, felt distressed. What am I doing she thought? It's Erich, the other lieutenant, all over again.

"It's no use. I can't."

"I'd just like someone to talk to . . . "

At that moment Frieda and Anna appeared, each with their dancing partners, both of whom were soldiers.

"We were just going to get a coffee," Frieda said.

"Want to join us?" Anna took her Helga's hand.

"Yes." Helga reacted quickly, with obvious relief.

There was a room off to the side of the dance floor which offered light refreshments. The three girls found a table as the soldiers went for coffee and sandwiches.

"Looked like you needed rescuing." Frieda eyed Helga with a smile.

"He's very nice."

"They're all nice." Anna said.

"They're all leaving in a few days." Frieda lowered her voice. "Off to the Russian front I imagine."

Helga watched them as they smiled happily, bringing the treats to the table, and she thought of Peter and Günther and Siegfried. For a moment, she imagined it was actually them, home again, freed from the prospect of injury and death.

16.

Siegfried was alone in the icy water, amongst the oil and wreckage. At the order to 'Abandon Ship' he had made his way up from the engine room. Shells were still landing on the ship, shells that were heard as dull thuds in the depths of the engine room, but which exploded in sound and fire and smoke and mangled bodies as he reached the upper deck. A shell blast knocked him over and he rolled down the sloping deck into the sea. His first instinct was to swim away from the ship to avoid being sucked under when she went down, but the *Schlosstern* was still afloat, heeled over on her starboard side with her funnel level with the water. Visibility was limited by snow squalls and only when lifted by the crest of a wave could he see very far. There were many survivors in the water. Some had already found pieces of wood or located some of the rafts that had been cut adrift before the ship was abandoned. He tried to swim towards a raft but progress was difficult and when he got near he realized that it was already overcrowded. In the end he found a large piece of wreckage and he clung to it. Soon he felt a growing numbness in his whole body, his hands were freezing and he had difficulty holding on. He looked back towards the *Schlosstern*; she had turned turtle and some crew members were standing on the bottom.

After about three quarters of an hour Siegfried was covered with foul-smelling fuel oil which stung his eyes and got into his mouth. He was virtually incapable of feeling and immersion in the freezing water was draining his body of heat. He had to get to a boat or a raft. It was more by luck than deliberate intent that he found himself near a raft. There were already four crew members lying on it and one of them, seeing him in the water, reached out and grabbed him, hauling him on board.

Searchlights pierced the darkness. It was a British destroyer. Siegfried tried to raise his body and to free an arm to attract attention. The sea was still rough although ironically the fuel oil had calmed the surface. Nevertheless, the wind was still strong and snow blanketed the area. The destroyer had seen their raft and was inching towards them. It was a difficult manoeuvre which heightened Siegfried's fear that he couldn't last long enough to be rescued. When, at last, the destroyer was alongside he looked up towards the deck as the British sailors lowered a net.   But he had difficulty grasping it and even more trouble climbing. It took several attempts before, dazed and frozen, he was hauled aboard.

The British sailors wrapped him in blankets and took him and other survivors to the crew's messdeck.   Four of the survivors, those that were seriously injured, were taken to the sickbay for treatment.

He was given warm cocoa and food. The destroyer men did their best to make him comfortable and to restore some heat to his frozen limbs. The events of the preceding hours were still hazy and he had great difficulty in determining where he was.

As he began to recover, all he could piece together at first were images of broken limbs and blood, and the terrifying ripping and tearing of metal caused by exploding shells. He put his hands to his head to quell the noise which gradually subsided to be replaced by a wave of cold. He could feel a rocking motion, but this faded too as the cold intensified, slowing movement and urging a capitulation to sleep and death.

As he drifted out of semi-consciousness, he saw the face of Günther and he smiled in a look of recognition. But Günther disappeared and, engulfed with an overwhelming desire to get him back, he called out, startling those around him.

"Günther! Günther!"

A British seaman rushed over but he pushed him away. "Günther!" *Mein Freund!* He yelled.

Other survivors came over, and as he began to regain full consciousness his panic left him. Chastened now, he asked what had become of Günther. No one knew. It was then that the stark realization that the majority of his crewmates must have perished hit home. Only the awareness that the other survivors were suffering a similar experience kept him from complete collapse.

17.

The Sandrake limped away from the battle zone. One of the two main turbines was out of action reducing the speed to ten knots on one propeller. Eleven lives had been lost, including Jonathan, and there were eleven wounded on the foredeck with varying degrees of injury. For the doctor and his assistants it was a daunting task. To make matters worse, the wind had freshened again and mountainous seas faced the Sandrake as it made its way to Polyarnyy in Northern Russia. The forward messdeck was an ever present reminder of the cost of victory. The doctor worked hard to ease the pain of the wounded, a task which was made more difficult by the constant rolling and pitching and the lack of equipment to effect major surgery.

En route to Polyarnyy the Sandrake committed its dead to the sea. Peter and Mike were part of a small group assembled, crewmates of the departed, standing by the rail, feet well apart as the ship continued to roll and pitch, waiting for the neatly stitched white canvas shapes to be released into the Arctic Sea. The Chief Petty Officer draped a white ensign over each body as it was placed on a rough wooden chute. The Captain intoned the last rites for each.

> Forasmuch as it has pleased Almighty God of his great mercy to receive unto himself the soul of our dear brother
> **Jonathan Arthur Saunders**
> here departed: we therefore commit his body to the deep, looking for the resurrection of the body, when the sea shall give up her dead, and the life of the world to come, through our Lord Jesus Christ . . .

There was a muffled 'Amen' and then the chute was lifted. There was a small splash as Jonathan's body hit the water, a splash which was carried swiftly aft as the Sandrake forged ahead. The next body was laid on the chute and the process repeated.

When it was all over, Peter and Mike made their way back to the mess. Mike watched while Peter, his left arm still bandaged, took down the reindeer, the sleigh and the Father Christmas.

"Will you send them on?" said Mike.

Peter nodded as he remembered the day in Akureyri.

"He was like a child - rediscovering Christmas," he said, as he felt his eyes watering. Mike got up.

"I'll get some char," he said.

It was Peter's first experience of death in combat and the shattering wounds inflicted by naval firepower. It was still hard to believe that forty eight hours ago they were browsing in the shops, thinking of Christmas. His thoughts returned again to the few hours that he and Mike had spent with Jonathan in Akureyri. How innocent they all were then. How unaware of what fate would befall them. He thought too, of the enemy and the terrifying losses they had sustained. There couldn't have been many survivors. Those who had avoided the overwhelming firepower of the British forces faced death in the icy waters.

Mike's voice disturbed his reflections.

"Get the cups Peter. It's good and hot. Freshly brewed."

Peter tossed and turned all that night. It wasn't just the relentless pounding of the sea and the cries of the wounded. He thought of Jonathan again and the eruption of a shell that brought instant death to a life barely lived, a promising life prematurely ended by war. When will it all end he thought, and what of Helga - was she even alive? Yet he was still alive, spared by some trick of fate which allowed him to exist for now, for the next minute, the next hour, the next day - perhaps?

18.

$\mathcal{D}$ue to her damage, which had slowed her speed, the Sandrake, escorted by a sister destroyer, reached Polyarnyy considerably later than the main force. The sombreness of the place dulled the ecstasy of victory. There were no plaudits from the Russians, even the bare necessities like fresh provisions and fuel oil were provided with a noticeable reluctance. In this cold and cheerless place it was hard to feel elation. Instead of joy Peter felt a deep depression. Jonathan was gone and with him the optimism that they had shared during their walk among the heather in Scapa. What was the use of believing in anything when life was so precarious? In a mood of recklessness he buried thoughts of Helga. One had to live now he persuaded himself, never mind what might be or could be. Never mind the future, the present moment was all that mattered. He wrote a letter to Sarah.

> Dear Sarah,
>
> I should get some leave soon. I've missed you all these weeks away. (It was less than six weeks since they had left the Tyne for Scapa yet it felt like a lifetime) Did you have a good Christmas? I'm sorry I didn't send you a card, we've been so busy, it's hard for me to express how much I miss your company.

He stopped writing. Images of Helga floated before him. What was he doing? What perverse motives caused him to be writing to Sarah? He pushed all thoughts of Helga aside as though dreams and hopes were but unrealizable fantasies. Better to live now, before death intervened, like it did so unexpectedly with the tragic loss of Jonathan. Life was fragile. He desperately wanted a woman he could touch, someone to share his experiences with. He needed a sympathetic ear, and he wanted sex - passionate sex, the kind that had consumed them both and which blotted out all the memories. But he wasn't about to write about that, not with censorship by one of the Sandrake's officers.

I'm looking forward to seeing you again.
Please take care of yourself.

Peter

He couldn't think of anything else to say. He wrote out the envelope, sealed the letter and posted it. Feeling restless he looked for Mike.

"Going ashore, Mike?"

"First chance I get."

"Fancy a pint or two?"

"I thought you didn't drink?"

"I'm learning."

They went ashore that afternoon to the hut that masqueraded as a beer canteen. It was full of smoke and crews from the fleet sat at rough wooden tables. The beer, such as it was, was dispensed from wooden casks behind a long narrow table where the customers lined-up to be served. Peter and Mike joined a group from one of their sister destroyers. A seaman was holding forth in a loud voice.

"Picked up about twenty-one of them. Frozen they were. Couldn't even grab a line? Some didn't make it."

"Don't they even have any brothels around here?" said another.

"I don't believe they have sex."

"Too bloody cold."

They all laughed. A seaman looked at Peter.

"You had casualties then?"

232

"Yes . . . my friend - he was one of them."

"Killed?"

"Yes."

"Sorry," he said.

A silence descended over the group.

"Want another round?" said another.

"You paying?"

"Sure, nothing else to spend it on."

The morning after, Peter nursed a throbbing head, but just talking about things had been a help and he understood much better why his crewmates went a bit wild when released from the routines of life at sea. Thoughts of Helga returned, pleasant thoughts, but the memory seemed less real, more distant, more elusive, less attainable than ever before.

Out in the harbour, Siegfried and the other German survivors were being transferred by a Russian tug from the rescuing destroyers to the battleship. As soon as they arrived aboard, they were given a list of their crewmates who had been rescued. The list was painfully short and Siegfried perused it with dismay. Günther's name was missing.

He joined the small silent group, huddled together, trying to understand why they were the fortunate ones, the few that had miraculously survived. They were now prisoners awaiting their fate. Nevertheless, there was universal relief among them at being saved from internment by the Russians.

Siegfried moved to a quiet corner of the mess and sat down. He tried to piece together the events since leaving Altenfjord, but nothing made sense. His head spun with ghastly images. He felt terribly alone, forfeited to fear and foreboding. He thought of Frieda and his family, and of Helga and Anna, only to become even more depressed. He couldn't believe that he would ever see them again.

19.

The news of the sinking of the *Schlosstern* reached Blankenese and Munich on New Year's Eve. Günther's father Rolf phoned his wife Ilse, and then wired Helga in Munich immediately after obtaining the news from a source in Hamburg. By all accounts there had been a terrible loss of life and everything pointed to the fact that Günther and Siegfried were probably dead. Coming after so much tragedy on the Eastern Front, it sent a pall of gloom over the whole family. With Rolf's maritime connections he was able to talk to a high official in the *Kriegsmarine* in Kiel, but there was little he could tell him. There wasn't any information about survivors, even if there were any. The devastating news had the effect of bringing the family together both emotionally and geographically. Rolf and Ilse travelled to Munich to stay for a few days with Eva and Helga. Frieda was already with Helga, and Anna joined them after they had arrived. It was a strange reunion, sad in the reason for its happening, but unassumingly satisfying for Helga in its reuniting of her with her mother and father. And young Hans became the centre of attention. Gone was the bitterness occasioned by the surprise pregnancy as Hans drew the affection normally lavished by a father and mother on a grown son. Helga delighted at the return of her father as she watched him playing with her son. Still, the present tragedy hung like a cloud over it all. The first night, as they assembled around the dining room table for dinner, with Hans clucking in his high chair, there was an oppressive silence as they took their places. Helga was the first to speak.

"Father? . . . do you think there's any hope they could have survived?"

Rolf shook his head.

"From everything I hear, and it isn't much, the chances

seem remote . . . "

He stopped and wiped his eyes with the back of his hand.

Anna began to sob and Frieda slid an arm around her shoulders, but Helga felt anger rising above her sadness. "So, they've gone then," she said fiercely, "Just like that?"

"We've always known the possibility existed," said Ilse, sounding unnaturally calm.

"It's my brother, your son . . . " Helga wailed, closing her eyes and placing her head between her hands. But the personal darkness she created only intensified the spectre of loss.

"Peter! . . . Peter!" She cried out, her thoughts now carried to the father of her child.

Ilse got up and put her hands on her daughter's shoulders. "You miss him don't you?"

In her confusion, Helga wasn't sure whether her mother was referring to Günther or Peter.

"Yes . . . Yes, I do," she said, taking her mother's hand, embarrassed by her outburst.

She looked at her father and there was sadness in his eyes, so much sadness that it seemed enough for both Günther and Peter, but instead of lamenting it she felt content, content because there appeared to be hope that an acceptance of Peter had replaced the long held animosity.

Frieda was quiet, directing her attention to Anna who was unable to quell the flow of tears. Helga thought of Siegfried and how Frieda's composure made it hard to believe that she too was facing a loss. She showed no visible signs of her feelings, having submerged them in a concern for Anna whose time with Günther had been so pitiably short.

"It's hard to know what fate holds for us," said Eva. "I don't think any of us should jump to conclusions. They might well be safe . . . prisoners, but safe . . . but if they're with the British they'll be well cared for . . . I'm sure of that."

"What if they are with the Russians?" said Rolf.

"Don't be so negative." Eva was becoming impatient

with her son. "There is nothing to say they're not alive."

With that the mood seemed to lighten and Helga wondered, as she always did, how it was that age could bring so much wisdom and balance, and above all, acceptance.

Two days later, after Frieda had returned to work and Anna had gone to her parents who lived nearby, the doorbell rang. Before Helga could answer, it rang again, and then again. Feeling irritated by the impatience of the caller Helga prepared herself for an angry confrontation, but when she opened the door it was their neighbour, Gertrud. There was a wild look in her eyes and she opened her mouth as if to speak but there was only silence.

"Gertrud! What's the matter?" Helga was worried now.

There was no response and Helga motioned her in. Whereupon, Gertrud rushed into the living room and collapsed on the sofa as the tears streamed down her face.

"Good Heavens! Gertrud. What is it?"

"It's Günther. He's gone . . . I heard it on the BBC. They mentioned the names of the survivors . . . Günther was not one of them."

Helga sat beside her. Her first thought was that listening to the BBC was illegal, as though this invalidated what she had heard, but then she remembered that most people who listened thought the information was accurate.

"Are you sure, Gertrud?"

"They read the names twice. Yes, I'm sure."

Helga looked up to see her parents and Eva. They must have heard the commotion and the grim news.

"My God!" Ilse shouted. "It's not Günther. They would have told us. It's all untrue. You shouldn't listen to the BBC." She waved her arms randomly in the air as if trying to sweep away what she had heard. Eva embraced her, comforting her, and she became suddenly quiet.

"Did they say anything else?" Rolf seemed to be searching for confirmation.

"Just that the *Schlosstern* had been sunk . . . "

"Was there anything about Siegfried, Siegfried *Holmann*?" In her concern for Günther, Helga had forgotten about Frieda's boyfriend.

Gertrud shook her head. "I don't remember that name."

There was a mournful wail from Ilse. "He was drowned," she said. "My boy! My Günther! Drowned!"

Eva helped her to the other sofa while Rolf sat beside Helga and Gertrud. Helga was dazed and disorientated. The possibility of her brother's survival had left hope, but now that hope had been dashed. She took her father's hands in hers, the strong hands with the long fingers, the gentle hands that had once held her and her brother, the hands that once worked the ropes of cargo vessels, but which could render the gentleness of Beethoven on the piano in the study at Blankenese.

"I'm going to make some coffee," said Eva.

"I must go," Gertrud said.

"Please stay awhile," Rolf implored.

Helga thought it a strange request until she felt as her father must have felt, that Gertrud's presence appeared to bring Günther closer, as if hearing and bearing the news connected her in some spiritual way with her brother.

"We must have a service," said Ilse, as if she had captured the same sentiment.

Rolf went over and hugged his wife, taking her hands and kneeling in front of her, a gesture that surprised Helga.

"Yes dear," he said, a deep concern reflected in his voice. "All in good time."

It was two weeks later that an official notification of Günther's death arrived at the house in Munich. Shortly after, Frieda phoned Helga to tell her that Siegfried's family had been notified that their son had been saved and was now a prisoner of war.

Although expected, the news of Günther's death catapulted the

Jansen family into a repetition of the shock they had experienced when the word of the tragedy first reached them. It prompted a return to Ilse's thought about a more public expression of grief.

Because of the risk of air raids and the difficulties of travelling, it was decided that any kind of memorial service for Günther, in Blankenese, would be delayed until circumstances had improved. It was not clear to Helga what this meant inasmuch as it was hard to see how anything could improve in the foreseeable future. However, at Eva's suggestion, on the following Sunday the pastor offered special prayers for Günther and his fallen shipmates during the regular service. Anna and Freda sat with the family, sharing a common mourning. It was a simple but moving tribute given in the old church that had seen the passage of time and history, and which carried an honour roll of those who had died in the 1914/1918 War.

A few days later, Frieda decided to travel to Neuengamme to visit Siegfried's family.

The visit was a particularly happy occasion, not only because Siegfried had survived, but because Frieda hadn't met Siegfried's family before, even though they all knew that he had a girl friend in Munich. They insisted that she stay overnight and they were soon showing her photographs of Siegfried's growing-up years.

It was at breakfast on the second day, the day that Frieda had planned to return to Munich, that Siegfried's mother, Lisa, spoke of Günther.

"They were great friends, Günther and Siegfried. We've all been praying for Günther's family."

"They've taken it quite hard, especially Günther's mother, Ilse. I'm quite worried about her."

"How is Helga?"

"She was very close to her brother, although they disagreed on many things. . . ."

"Her association with the Englishman?"

"Yes, and now it's Peter's navy that has caused her brother's death."

Lisa became quiet and her eyes searched Frieda's face.

She touched Frieda's hand. "Helga must not let bitterness destroy her love for her husband."

Frieda was unprepared for the force of Lisa's opinion. Her implication that Peter was in effect, if not in fact, Helga's husband, seemed so right that it swept away the issue of ambiguity. She wished that Helga was able to hear Lisa's endorsement of the power of love.

Frieda wiped away the suggestion of a tear. "It's not a war between individuals is it?"

"Unfortunately it is . . . individuals caught by the insanity of the majority. We are all victims of this."

Frieda looked into the clear blue eyes set in the rugged face with its strong angular features.

"Thanks, Lisa. I'll do my best to help Helga."

As Frieda prepared to leave Neuengamme she felt reassured. The experience of the country and these uncomplicated hard-working people had provided a sort of spiritual renewal, a revival of a faith in the common decency that resides in every individual.

Helga's parents left to return to Blankenese on the day that Frieda left Neuengamme. It was a sad parting, not only because of the loss of Günther but because, during her parents' visit, it had been divulged that her father's future had become uncertain. The *Third Reich* wanted his expertise in the *Kriegsmarine*. The likelihood was a posting to Berlin or Cuxhaven and neither location had any appeal for Rolf nor Ilse as it meant shutting the house in Blankenese. The mere thought of vacating Blankenese pushed Helga into a greater depression. As if the loss of Günther wasn't enough, now the family home was in danger of being sacrificed.

But there was another thing that was troubling her. As

time went on she began to see the loss of her brother as a punishment for her liaison with Peter. After all, he was in the Royal Navy, the same Navy that had killed her brother, a navy populated by those 'English bastards' that Günther had held responsible for the slaughter of civilians in Hamburg.

Some three weeks after the news of the sinking, Anna came to see Helga. Normally an affable person with a zest for life - who Helga thought provided a good compensation for Günther's tendency to a self-absorption - the change in her demeanour, so evident at the family gathering, seemed even more pronounced as she sat beside her on the sofa in the living room.

At first, Helga was only conscious of her blank stare but then, without a word, she handed her a letter. Helga hesitated, and Anna nodded, and she drew the single page from the envelope.

> Dearest Anna,
>
> Siegfried and I have just come back from a few hours ashore. We had fun. I like Siegfried and we have spent many good times together.
> I miss you very much and I can't wait to see you again. The days seem long and empty without you.
> Take care of yourself always, knowing that I will always love you and will cherish our getting to know each another, if even for a short time.
>
> All my love,
>
> Günther.

Helga studied the gently flowing handwriting which she knew so well and which always seemed so strangely out of keeping with her brother's strident beliefs. If ever there was a premonition embedded in a censored letter, this was surely it. It was like reading a fond farewell. She held her gaze on the letter, not wanting to lift her eyes to Anna. And when she did, tears were dimming her vision. Anna was crying too and they embraced, sharing again the loss of a loved one who had contrived to send a message from beyond a watery grave.

20.

As the Sandrake steamed slowly down the Tyne, ships' sirens blared and dockyard whistles shrieked. It wasn't until the din had been going on for a few minutes that the crew, mustered on deck for entering harbour, realized that it was intended for them. When they reached the narrower parts of the river, they could see the crowds of men and women in overalls lining the shore. It was their ship, built by them on the Tyne, proving itself capable of the job it was built for, and they were showing their pride.

Shortly after securing alongside, at the same jetty where they were fitted out prior to sea trials, the first liberty men were piped ashore. Peter was one of them. He had phoned Sarah at work and she agreed to meet at the dance school.

Sarah was sitting quietly, watching the couples on the floor, the men in uniform, clumsy and vulnerable, and the women patient and coaxing, ignoring their partners' embarrassment. He spotted her immediately and he hastened over, standing in front of her, a tall lanky blond sailor. She looked as he had remembered her, the same sensuous features with the moist lips and the coaxing eyes. She got up and slid into his arms. Still snuggling, they eased onto the floor, holding each other tight.

They didn't stay long on the dance floor. The desire for sexual intimacy was too strong to ignore. Peter booked a room in a nearby hotel, and they were soon giving expression to their passions. Afterwards, as they lay together, arms around each other, the deeper implications of the reunion crept into Peter's consciousness.

"A penny for your thoughts," said Sarah.

He turned and looked at her, searching, looking for something beyond the immediate experience.

242

"What's wrong, Peter?"

He continued to hold her eyes in his and she leaned over and kissed him, a long lingering moist kiss, her tongue exploring his mouth. They were soon in the throes of intimacy again. Peter, overcome by her overt sexuality, was swept along hungrily, his appetite wanting satisfaction.

Again, as they lay together, the same concern entered his mind.

"Sarah . . . has there been anyone else?"

She responded quickly - almost too quickly, he thought.

"I told you . . . there was the pilot. You know. He was lost."

"Lost! . . . I thought you said the relationship 'just faded' something like that?"

"Well, he was lost to me," she said, and there was no doubt about the guilt that accompanied the lie.

"There have been others?" Peter persisted.

"What's gotten into you . . . no, of course not?"

There was no point in encouraging more lies, he thought, as she tried to match his stare.

"I'm hungry," he said. "Let's go down and get some dinner."

Peter had to stay aboard the Sandrake for the next few days as the new director tower was being installed. As it was lowered onto the new pedestal, his thoughts turned to Jonathan and the irreplaceably of a human life. He knew that the servicing of the gun control systems would never be the same. Just then, Mike appeared, and as he turned towards him, in a moment of memory, he saw again the particles of blood and flesh that had covered his face on the day that Jonathan had died. He swayed slightly and Mike reached out a hand.

"You OK? You're white as a ghost?"

"Sorry, I . . . "

"Jonathan?"

"Yes."

"Come on Pete. Let's get a cuppa."

It was a Thursday and he was back in the hotel of the first night ashore. The bed creaked as the intensity of their intercourse advertised itself. He felt more aggressive than usual, but it only seemed to add to Sarah's satisfaction. When at last he had reached his climax he felt a gratifying physical relief. He rolled over onto his back and Sarah plastered his face with kisses.

"Jesus that was great," she pushed herself up on his chest.

He held her eyes. "I needed it," he said.

"I wouldn't have guessed."

She kissed him, exploring his mouth with her tongue.

"I'm available anytime," she said, and then she avoided his eyes as if regretting the possible wider implications.

He turned away. "Got a cigarette?"

She stared back at him.

"I thought you didn't smoke?"

"I want one."

"Then we'll both have one."

He puffed away, furiously, choking on the unfamiliar irritant.

"What's the matter . . . you mad or something?"

He stubbed out the cigarette.

"Let's get out of here . . . I think I'd like to eat?"

"That's always your answer . . . let's go and eat."

"Look. I'm hungry, OK?"

He got up and started dressing and she followed.

They had fish and chips, sitting at one of the few tables as people came in and out ordering and picking up orders. It was the perfect spot. He didn't feel like talking. Then they went to an Alice Faye musical at the Odeon. Afterwards, they went for a coffee.

"Good film?" she said.

"Yes . . . it was OK." Bunch of crap, he thought.

"Peter, what's wrong. You don't seem yourself?"

"I don't know . . . it's well. Jonathan was killed . . . "

He stopped and turned to her with moist eyes and she moved close to him and put an arm around his shoulders. He stiffened.

"I'm OK. I don't want to talk about it now."

"There's something I want to tell you," she said, drawing closer. "My mother and father have invited us for the weekend. Would you come?"

He shifted uneasily.

"Oh come on Peter. It'll be a nice change."

He looked at her and she kissed him.

"I want you to come," she said.

It was the last thing he wanted, but unprepared for the idea and not wanting to argue he convinced himself that it might be a polite way to begin to extricate himself from her clutches.

"OK then," he said.

Too late, he wondered what he was letting himself in for.

21.

Frieda came regularly to Eva's house on the *Sunderstrasse*. Helga looked forward to her visits as they had become a form of catharsis, helping her to mourn the loss of Günther.

Frieda had told her about the meeting with Siegfried's mother, Lisa, in Neuengamme and while Helga appreciated hearing of Lisa's view of her relationship with Peter it hadn't alleviated her confusion. In fact, to her, Lisa's helpful advice seemed more like a device to appease her guilt rather than to expunge it.

Spring had already arrived on the day that Frieda came with further news of Siegfried. Helga could feel Frieda's happiness as she walked in through the door, and she was surprised and delighted when she waved Siegfried's letter. Perhaps, she thought; something good has come out of the loss of Günther's ship after all?

"I want you to read this, Helga. It might surprise you."

Helga, intrigued, took it eagerly.

My dearest Frieda,

First of all, let me assure you that I am safe and well. We are well treated here although the days go by slowly and we all wonder how our families are faring with the bombing.

Please tell Helga that Günther and I remained good friends until the end. We shared all our delights and fears and the loss of him has affected me deeply, as it must have his dear family. He was always talking about his family and how he had promised to see them all for Christmas, and he remained hopeful until it became certain that leave would not be possible.

I want Helga to know that I was rescued by the Royal Navy. I have nothing but praise for their actions after the battle. They took us into their care and treated us as they would their own. It was only when I left the Royal Navy ships that rescued us that I realized that I was a prisoner, such was the camaraderie that we developed with the crews. I understood then that seamen all over the world share the same respect for the sea and ships - share the same feelings and hopes that also dwelt in our hearts and minds - irrespective of what ideology commands their deeds.

I think it is important that Helga know this. It must be doubly difficult for her to accept that the man she loves is on the enemy side, but it seemed appropriate to me that Helga would have picked a companion from a service that showed so much generosity and kindness in our defeat.

Oh, Frieda, how much I long to be in your arms again, to savour the scent of your hair and to enjoy the sight of your smile. You see, I can easily remind myself of you, for I somehow managed to save a photo of you and Helga and Günther and young Hans. It was in my wallet which was returned to me by the British.

I hope you are well. Please have faith that we will be reunited. In the meantime, take care of yourself and your wonderful family.

You can write to me at the address on the envelope.

Love and kisses,

Siegfried.

Helga breathed a deep sigh, if only Günther had been saved. How strange it was that fate played tricks with friends, close friends. She told herself that she was beyond crying as she became conscious of Frieda's eyes watching her reaction. But she couldn't find the words to express her feelings, all she could do was to fall into Frieda's outstretched arms. Then she cried, loudly and without restraint, expressing her sorrow and her joy for the gift of Siegfried's revelations.

When at last she had recovered enough to speak, all she could say was, "Peter! Dear Peter! May God keep you safe?" Yet the spontaneity of the remark did not erase the questions. It was still Peter's navy that had killed her brother and she had no idea how time would allow her to deal with that.

Helga and Frieda spent the rest of the day together. Frieda had managed a day off, and with Hans alternately walking and demanding to be carried, they made their way to the nearby park where they sat picnic-style with sandwiches and a flask of coffee.

"How are your mother and father?" said Frieda, taking the strands of grass that Hans was offering her. "Thank you, Hans."

Helga took a bite of her sandwich. "Not too good." She swallowed and took a sip of coffee. "I had a letter from mother a week ago. Father has been called to Berlin," She looked around to see if anyone was listening. "He is to become a member of the naval staff there."

"Quite an honour, is it not?"

"That's apparently what he says. I talked to mother on the phone after getting her letter. She told me he called it an 'honour' to be selected, but I gathered she had the impression that he didn't want to go. You see, he loved working at his own company in Hamburg and then, well, he and mother have lived in Blankenese since they were married."

"Your mother didn't want to go to Berlin?" Frieda leaned forward to redeive another offering of grass from Hans.

"Thank you, Hans."

"I think she would have gone, but father insisted that she come here. I think father felt it would be safer from the bombing."

"It will be nice to have her with you."

"Yes, but . . . " She spoke in measured tones. "I've got used to my independence, Frieda."

Helga thought of the difficulties that could easily erupt between her and her mother. Ilse had very definite opinions about how things should be done, and removed from the responsibility of caring for her husband and the large house in Blankenese, she could imagine all that energy being directed to giving her advice on how to bring up Hans. Of course, she could try and apply her influence to the running of the house in Munich as well, but she couldn't see Eva submitting to that. No, it would be to her and Hans that she would turn for fulfilment.

Oh, how she wished Günther were here. She wished they could have talked more, put their differences aside. She never knew how Günther really thought about many things. He was so caught up with serving the Fatherland. But then, she hardly helped to achieve a relaxed atmosphere between them. She particularly regretted her failure to be completely open with him and the last incident, before he left on the fatal assignment, was especially troublesome.

"What are you thinking about?" said Frieda.

"It was something I told Günther. It was untrue at the time."

Helga struggled to deal with her lie.

"You see. I told him Erich was dead. I wanted him to forgive me for what I had done."

Frieda looked confused.

"Erich. He was the lieutenant," Helga said, embarrassed that she had to repeat it. "We had a brief affair. It was wrong of me and I regret it. He was married."

"Of course I remember. I just don't remember you telling

me his name."

"I'm sure he's dead now . . . I think I willed it."

She saw Frieda bristle. She always did when she intended to counter Helga's tendency to heap blame on herself.

"Would you have wanted to hear from him? Wanted to see him again?"

"No," said Helga, with unwavering conviction. "It was a spur of the moment thing. It couldn't last. But so many deaths, so many partings."

"You loved him did you?" There was a note of sarcasm in Frieda's voice, a deliberate challenge.

"Of course not," she blushed. "I was lonely that's all. But that's what war's about isn't it . . . loneliness."

"Yes . . . it's about loneliness," said Frieda despondently. "And living for today."

22.

Sarah's parents lived in Seham, a coal-mining town on the northeast coast below the Tyne estuary. Peter and Sarah left Newcastle by train on the Saturday afternoon. It was a dull day with a cold wind blowing in from the North Sea. The towns en route appeared to consist of row upon row of council houses, perhaps once contributing to the efficiencies of the industrial revolution. But now it was just depressing, more depressing than the wild, barren expanses of the Orkneys and the huge anchorage at Scapa. At least it had a primitive natural beauty, so absent in the conformity which he now gazed upon.

If he expected a relief at Seham, he was greatly disappointed. It was a typical northern mining town with great slag heaps and smoking chimneys. Her parents lived on one of the streets of council houses which dominated the town. As they walked along it on the way from the station, he could feel the eyes looking out from behind the faded curtains. Children chided him as he walked by.

"Got any gum sailor?" they would say, until one discriminating urchin yelled.

"He's not a Yank!"

"Have the Yanks been here?" said Peter, looking towards Sarah.

She coloured a little.

"I suppose they must have been."

Sarah's parents, Mabel and Bob, were in their late forties. They were a jovial couple, belying the hard life they led. He was still in the mines, a reality reflected in the deep rasping cough.

"You like the navy then?" said Bob.

"It's OK. I'm glad I chose it over the Army or the Air

Force. Of course, I won't be sorry to get out when it's all over."

"No thoughts of staying in then?"

"No."

"Good occupation though.   There's going to be unemployment after this lot."

Peter had a distinct impression that his credentials as a potential suitor were being weighed. Stable job, steady income, responsible parent. It all added up. Besides, as the afternoon wore on, with endless cups of tea and home made cakes, Peter began to see behind the joviality to a repressive family atmosphere not unlike his own. He could understand a little better why Sarah had 'escaped'.

"Sarah's told us so much about you," said her mother.

"Oh, Mum, you're embarrassing him."

Peter was indeed embarrassed as the whole visit began to take on the nature of an event in a serious relationship. He tried to get out of the house, and away from the constraints of being with her parents, by asking her to dinner and a film, but when she told her mother of their intentions she would have none of it, protesting that she had already prepared a dinner for them.

Seated around the table, Bob intoned a solemn Grace, including a prayer of thanks for Peter's delivery from harm, and then he carved the roast as Mabel filled plates with generous helpings of potatoes, vegetables and Yorkshire Pudding. How they had circumvented rationing to put on such a spread was best left unchallenged.

It was a very hearty dinner, finished off with gooseberry pie and custard, and it occupied them all in serious eating, a fortuitous preoccupation which discouraged conversation, much to Peter's relief. After dinner he and Sarah went for a pint at the local pub. It was obvious that Sarah was a well-known patron and he thought he saw knowing glances exchanged as she entered on his arm. But everyone was prudent, confining their remarks to not having seen her for a while.

They sat in a corner, away from the centre of the crowd.

"Look, Sarah, you've got to tell me what's going on . . . what you've told your parents?"

"That we're very much in love," she said, without hesitation.

"You've got to be kidding?"

"Well, isn't it true?"

"Aren't you confusing lust with love?"

"Do you think I would have given myself unless I felt close to you?"

He was too stunned to make any immediate response. Either she was completely naïve or she was manipulating him in the most unconscionably way. But she was continuing.

"After all - would I risk having a child?"

He felt slightly weak and he held onto the edge of the table to steady himself.

"Are you pregnant?"

"I don't think so."

"Christ!" he shouted, and a hush came over the crowd. Humiliated, but not caring, he continued in a low menacing voice. "What do you mean, you don't know?"

She smiled, but it looked more like a sneer.

"Let's go," he said, grabbing her by the arm and propelling her to the door.

Peter was determined to end the visit as quickly as possible. Sunday morning being a time when the family was accustomed to sleeping-in, he eased himself out of bed, moving as stealthily as possible. His caution received a setback, however, when the pebbles that Helga had given him - the ones he had promised to protect - fell out of the pouch on his belt and scattered across the floor. He froze, listening for sounds of movement, but no one stirred. He knelt down and collected the stones, each one adding to his thoughts of Helga and the love they shared. When at last he had collected them all and restored them to his pouch he was overcome with remorse. The affair with Sarah felt tawdry and demeaning, a betrayal of Helga's trust.

He packed his things and crept silently downstairs. It was only six o'clock and he penned a note to his hosts.

Thank you for your kind hospitality. I have to get back to my ship. Sorry for the rush.

Peter.

It was the best he could do. No explanation was better he concluded than a lengthy attempt to defend his actions.

He made his way down deserted streets, feeling that what little noise his shoes were making on the pavement was enough to wake the neighbourhood. When he reached the railway station, it too was deserted. But he did find a lonely porter who told him that the first train was not due out until ten a.m. - more than three hours to wait - "Sunday, you know," he said.

"Is there anywhere I can get a breakfast?"

"There's a café down the road. You can't miss it."

It was a small café whose patrons were shift workers from a local munitions factory. He managed to get scrambled eggs and toast, and he chatted amiably with the girls with kerchiefs around their heads who crowded around to talk to a real sailor. After numerous and leisurely cups of coffee, he made his way back to the station. It was still only nine fifteen.

He felt her presence before he saw her. She had seen him first and she rushed out of the shadows as his eyes were trying to accustom themselves to the dark interior of the station.

"Peter! Oh Peter!" she cried. "What are you doing?"

"I'm going back to the ship."

"Why?" she said, unable to conceal her anger. "You've upset my parents. They feel insulted."

"I'm sorry, but . . . "

"And how do you think I feel?"

"Sarah, it's not going to work. It's better that we end it now."

"What if I'm pregnant?"

"Look, don't lay that on me - it's not going to work."

"So - you're going to abandon me?"

He was grasping at straws now, hoping his intuition was right and that she was not pregnant but was trying to trap him. Yet he couldn't know for sure and he could tell that she knew the uncertainty would eat away at his conscience.

"Come back home . . . with me?" she said, appearing desperate now to atone for her actions, trying to win him over.

"No, it's no good. I told you. I'm going back to the ship."

"Come and sit down. Talk to me."

"No," he said, and he pushed her away.

The train was still not in, but he walked onto the platform through the open gates, past the empty ticket collector's box, and she didn't follow him, as far as he knew, for he didn't look back to see. He felt disgusted by his behaviour. Not the sudden desire to escape, but the way in which his actions had been dominated by lust. What happened, he thought, to the so-called sensitive caring person, the shy awkward teenager who had fallen in love with Helga and who had fathered her child?

It was as though only in uncaring selfish desires of the flesh could he push away the reality of a war which showed no signs of ending and the grief and loneliness that he could not bear to face. He was unsettled now, as distressed by what Sarah had revealed to him of his anger and aggression, as he was by the power of the deeper and more sincere feelings about Helga which he had been trying so hard to avoid.

23.

*N*ight after night the bombers came to German cities. It was a clear moonlit night when they came to Munich. The gunfire started in the distance as the beams of searchlights swept the sky. The anti-aircraft fire gradually became louder and closer, tracking the bombers as they droned in over the city. And then the flares came, blinding lights, hanging in the sky like fireworks.

Helga and Eva stood in the back garden watching, fascinated by the spectacle, until the bombs came and it seemed more prudent to head into the cellar. Young Hans was already there. More often than not he slept there now even though Helga worried about the damp atmosphere not being good for his health.

It was just after midnight and while Eva brewed some coffee, Helga checked Hans. He was sound asleep, so far the din above had not disturbed him.

"Do you really think we can win?" Helga tried to warm her hands on the fresh cup of coffee.

"It doesn't look good!"

"I'm afraid. Afraid for mother and father . . . afraid for Peter."

"I"m sure Peter's fine . . . "

"How can you say that?" Helga turned on her grandmother, venting her frustration. "How do you know? He might be lying at the bottom of the ocean like Günther."

"It's no good distressing yourself, Helga. We can only live each day and hope for the best . . . "

Just then a particularly loud explosion shook the house and bits of plaster fell down from the ceiling.

"We're all in danger," said Eva, continuing as if nothing had happened.

Helga was frightened, but her anger was still in control.

"Don't lecture me, *Oma*. I just want it to be over." She was sobbing now and Eva went over and tried to comfort her as the sirens announced the 'All Clear' and relative silence returned to the city. A city now faced with the inevitable casualties and damage. Miraculously the house was unharmed, just shaken up like its occupants, that is except Hans who remained fast asleep.

"I'm sorry," said Helga, as if apologizing for the raid as well as trying to make an amends for her outburst. "It's just that I miss Peter. It's hard not knowing whether he's even alive or whether he even thinks of me. Do you think he does *Oma?*"

"Who knows? You can only hope." It seemed like an uncaring reply, but her grandmother could always be counted on for the truth.

"Yes . . . keep hope and memories." Helga felt resigned. "I have lots of those," then she brightened. "But I also have Hans." She looked at the small form, wrapped in a blanket, sleeping the sleep of innocence.

The doorbell rang and Helga went upstairs to answer it. It was Frieda. Her face was white and covered with what looked like soot. Her nurse's uniform was torn and dirty. She swayed and Helga caught her and helped her into the house.

"The Hospital . . . it was hit . . . I don't know . . . " Frieda's voice faded and her eyes glazed over.

"Eva! Eva! Come quickly!" Helga yelled.

They managed to get her into the living room and onto the sofa.

"I'll get some water," said Eva. "We'd better not give her any alcohol. She's probably in shock."

Frieda lay on the sofa, her eyes closed. Her breathing was shallow, but her pulse was strong. When Eva arrived with the water, they tried to lift her into a sitting position. Awakening suddenly, and with terror in her eyes, she stared at Helga.

"Helga! You're Helga!" She seemed to doubt her

identity.

They managed to get some water into her.

"Yes, yes . . . it's Helga. You're safe now."

Frieda closed her eyes and slumped back on the sofa. They examined her for injuries and apart from a few bruises on her hands and legs she seemed fine.

"Should we let her sleep?" said Helga. Then moderating her hasty conclusion. "What if she has a concussion?"

"There's no sign of that kind of injury. Besides, there's no way we're going to get a doctor now. I think we should let her rest for a bit. We can wake her up again in about an hour and see how she is."

Covering her with blankets, they left her to sleep.

"How do you suppose she got here?" said Helga.

"She must have walked."

"But it's a long way!"

"I doubt she'll remember it."

"I'm going to stay with her." Helga eased a pillow under her head.

"No, you're not. Go and look after Hans, I'll stay here."

In the morning when Helga awoke to the sounds of Hans playing happily in his crib, the rest of the house was quiet. It was seven thirty and Eva was usually up at this time. Worried now, she rushed down to the living room. Eva was dozing in her favourite chair from where she had promised to watch Frieda. Helga made a move to wake her, but she was distracted by movement from the sofa.

"I'm hungry." It was Frieda's voice.

Helga sat by her side, studying the smooth lines of her features, her face having taken on a more healthy glow. She laughed, relieved to see the change.

"Well . . . that's a good sign."

"How did I get here?" she searched Helga's face for an answer. "I was lying awake, looking around, trying to decide where I was . . . then I recognized this room, and I saw you sitting there . . . "

"It was last night, after the raid, you came to the door."

"I only remember . . . there was a flash . . . and then things falling down . . . people were shouting and I walked through this hole . . . I kept on walking. I had to find you . . . It was horrible . . . "

"Frieda! I'm so glad you're all right," she gave her a hug.

"Ouch!" Frieda grimaced. "I still have some sore spots."

"Can you get up?"

"I'll try."

She managed to stand erect and walk a few paces.

"Mostly stiffness. I think I survived."

They both looked at Eva, sleeping soundly, unaware of the happy twosome laughing at her.

Frieda stayed with Helga and Eva for just over a week before returning to her work and her apartment near the hospital. Helga accompanied her to the apartment, passing the ruins of the wing of the hospital, marvelling that she had survived. The apartment, which was nearby, was intact, the only signs of the raid being a broken window pane which they covered with a piece of wood. They were so occupied with fixing the window that it was a while before they realized that the post had arrived. There was a letter from Siegfried from a prisoner of war camp in Canada. Frieda ripped open the envelope, reading it standing up.

Her eyes wet, she handed the letter to Helga.

Dear Frieda,

It is still cold here. We are all hoping for spring but it is late April now and no sign that the snow will soon be over. It is quiet here, too quiet. It gives us too much time to feel homesick. We get news here and xxxxxxxxxxxxxxxx.

(The censor had presumably decided that this was too

sensitive).

Mutter wrote to say that the farm is busy and she wanted Helga's parents to know xxxxxxxxxxxxxx Dear Frieda, I'm glad we met if only for a little while. We had a lot of fun didn't we. Perhaps it is too much to ask, but I hope that you will wait for me. Surely the war xxxxxxxxxxxxxxxxxxxx Please take care of yourself.

Love and kisses,
Siegfried.

"He's lonely, Helga, and there's nothing I can do about it."

Helga was annoyed. "Why don't they black it all out instead of leaving bits of sentences for you to wonder about?"

"I'm sure it was censored in *Deutschland,*" said Frieda, bitterly.

At the house on the *Sunderstrasse*, the phone rang early one evening and Eva answered it.

"It's your mother, Helga," she shouted up the stairs. "She wants to speak to you."

Helga turned away from her sleeping son and went downstairs.

"Hello, Mother."

"Helga, I want you to listen carefully," she sounded conspiratorial, as though she was planning a public statement of some kind that could get her arrested. "I've rented the house here to an older couple. Friends of father and me who wanted to get out of the city. Eva knows I'm coming to Munich though. In fact, she has always encouraged me to come. I'll tell you more about this when I arrive."

"When will you get in?"

"I don't know. The trains are uncertain." She sounded impatient, wanting to conclude the conversation.

260

"How's Father?"

"He's well. He writes to me every few days . . . now I must go. See you tomorrow."

Before Helga could enquire further, she had hung up.

24.

Peter stood on the East Cliff gazing down at the piers. Although they were no longer accessible to the public - the way to them was blocked by barbed wire and concrete blocks - the local fishermen still took out their boats from the small harbour, passing in and out through the narrow channel between the piers, seeking cod and mackerel and plaice and crabs.

It was through this entrance that the *Joachim* had come, and he thought about it more than ever now, after experiencing the loss of family and friends and the desperate desire to live now, in the moment, trying to block out memories, trying to avoid thinking of an uncertain future. It was this attitude which had brought about the unfortunate relationship with Sarah, yet that experience had, he now realized, strengthened rather than destroyed his love for Helga. He needed her memory to go on living with the fear and uncertainty. It reminded him that some things are precious and that war and destruction cannot erase love and understanding, only frustrate its fullest expression.

He had arrived home on the south coast the day before. The ship's company had been given leave.

His father was more active now, even though the house was still in a deplorable mess. He had joined the Home Guard, proud of the opportunity to serve his country again. But the old hatreds from a previous war still punctuated his comments on the progress of the new one.

"You did us proud," he said. "Sinking the *Schlosstern* . . . just like we sank them at Jutland. Every Jerry we kill brings the end of the war nearer, son."

It was not the time for Peter to talk of the heroic adversary who fought to the last in the icy waters of the Arctic. That would only take him closer to the subject of Helga, and he had no intention of risking that.

Still, Peter valued the opportunity to be with his aging father even though he tried to limit the number of occasions, preferring to be alone when he could get away. He saw few friends and those friends that he did see were mostly passing faces in crowds or the subject of a brief encounter on walks or trips to the shops.

His desire for loneliness became a passion. He found himself deliberately avoiding people, preferring to seek out quiet country lanes and paths along the seacoast, although even this was difficult as the whole area had now become a staging ground for units of the United States Army assembling in Britain for the expected invasion of Europe.

Being alone with himself became an important part of his coming to terms with the experiences of the last few years. He could see now that his uncharacteristic sexual adventures were not only a delayed reaction to a family not comfortable with their emotions, they were desperate attempts to come to grips with the death and destruction that lurked everywhere. He wanted to feel alive, to prove to himself that he was not dead physically or emotionally. It was an attempt to feel when all feeling was being repressed, a selfish attempt at gratification. Perhaps the only defence was that it was an equal contest with Sarah since they exploited each other. He had not heard from her since the day of his hurried departure and he had no intention of restoring that relationship.

One bright and sunny day he retraced the route of a walk he had taken with Helga, and as he walked he became more aware of his surroundings, the snapping of small twigs under his feet, the song of birds, the rustle of the undergrowth disturbed by a gentle breeze, small animals foraging for food, and the aroma of the country. As he became more sensitive to his surroundings, he became more in touch with himself. In this place there was no need for a state of constant alertness, it was not necessary to prove anything, to erect barriers against the exposure of his sensitivity or to fight to keep control of his emotions.   He could allow himself to feel, and as the discovery of his feelings reached deeper he felt both elated and vulnerable. He wanted to shout and he did, and then he wanted to cry and he sat on a tree stump and the tears came freely.   He shed tears that he never knew he had, and he thought of his mother and his grandparents and Jonathan and Stephen, and he wanted Helga to be there with him to share his grief and his fear and to acknowledge that it was permissible to know such things.

What he had experienced with Helga was a genuine love, given freely, coming from within.   He got up, possessed with a wholeness he had not felt for a long time, and he went to the Tea Room where he and Helga had gone.   And as he walked towards the pleasant old building with its thatched roof and white walls, he picked wildflowers from the hedgerows.

It was the same owner that had greeted him. She seemed puzzled at first, but then she asked.

"Hope you don't mind my asking, but haven't you been here before?"

"Yes, before the war."

"Ah, yes . . . I remember.   You were with a companion."

Peter nodded and he felt his eyes moistening.   She caught his unease and motioned him to follow her, prudently directing him to a table in a quiet corner and giving him a menu.

"Take your time," she said. "No rush."

He appreciated her concern for his feelings and when she returned to take his order after a noticeable delay she anticipated his wishes.

"So, you'll have tea, scones, jam and Devonshire cream?"

He smiled and indicated approval, delighting now in the memory it evoked, transported for a moment back to a time that was, holding to a hope that he would see Helga again.

He lingered over his tea, lost in thought and recollection, and when he got up and paid his bill he felt ready to return to duty.

FIVE

1945

1.

$\mathcal{H}$elga, carrying her shopping basket, was returning from her morning trek to forage for food. She felt tired and her face showed the results of months with fitful sleep, interrupted by air raids and reports of Germany's collapse. The strain of the last few weeks, waiting for the end, waiting for the armies to occupy her homeland, was more demoralizing than the air raids.

Helga walked slowly. Her limbs were tired. It was more mental tiredness than the result of physical exertion. There were large gaps in the rows of houses along the street. She could already see her grandmother's house in the distance, its four intact stories, rising above the rubble. It was remarkable that the house had survived. There were broken windows on one side. It was impossible to find glass, let alone to find someone to repair them. She thought of Peter and whether he had survived the war and where he was.

When she entered the house, Eva and Ilse were in the kitchen drinking coffee, so she poured herself a cup. Hans was playing happily with bits of wood collected from ruined buildings and earmarked for firewood.

"Two loaves?" Ilse noticed immediately.

"Supplies are a bit better . . . I think." Helga remained cautious. One never knew from day to day what to expect. "I saw Frieda . . . She had a letter from Siegfried. He's being sent back to England soon . . . "

Ilse cut her off.

"Why doesn't Günther write to us? We're his family?"

Helga sighed. It was a continuing problem. How to deal with her mother's loneliness. She had never recovered from the news about Günther and her mind acted unpredictably, one day she would talk of his imminent return, then on other days she behaved as though she had never even borne a son. Maybe she *was* convinced that he was dead and this was her way of dealing with the pain? But her actions were also influenced by the loss of contact with her husband, Rolf. With news that the Russians were already in the outskirts of Berlin, there was little cause for optimism. Even if he had survived the intense bombardment, there couldn't be much chance of an escape. The best to be hoped for was that he had been taken a prisoner, but if captured by the Russians Rolf had himself doubted that any German could hope to survive.

Helga brushed her mother's hair from her face and she didn't resist. She just smiled, as if the touch of another hand provided reassurance and understanding.

As the Allied armies moved ever closer, there was an announcement one morning on Munich Radio stating that the Bavarian Freedom Movement had taken over control of the city from the *Nazis*. However, no changes were evident on the *Sunderstrasse*, and two more days were to elapse before the American troops entered the city. When they came, in vehicles of every description, there was relief, and even a little restrained cheering.

For Helga's mother it was a time of increasing anxiety. Hope of ever seeing her husband was dwindling. His letters had ceased abruptly after the news of the Russian advance on Berlin.

Eva, beyond eighty now, lived on by her indomitable will and unshaken optimism that problems can be faced and overcome. Still, Helga disliked leaving Hans in her company for too long, fearing it would tire her, even though this was the only opportunity she had to get away, to be on her own for a while.

It was a time of waiting, just like it had been for most of the war, except now that the war was nearing its end an even greater degree of uncertainty enveloped them.

2.

*R*olf *Jansen* moved slowly along the country road avoiding the main routes south. He was dressed in a torn and grubby suit taken from the body of a civilian killed during the Russian drive on Berlin. When the offices of German Naval Staff were certain to be overrun, he had volunteered to join with some of his colleagues to oppose the Russian Army, but his unit was quickly decimated by Russian shelling and bombing, becoming widely scattered with each man fending for himself, hoping to escape capture. To deflect unwelcome attention he had removed all the obvious signs of his connection with the *Kriegsmarine*. After several days on the road, sleeping in fields or in deserted buildings, and scrounging for food wherever he could find it, he had acquired a scruffy looking beard which added to his dishevelled appearance. Gone was any sign of the dapper officer, or the confident former owner of a shipping company. All he could think about now was getting home to his family. He didn't have much time. The invading armies from the east were hot on his heels.

He struggled along a winding street in a small town close to Dresden. He had avoided Dresden itself after hearing of the terrible devastation wrought by the bombing, but this town had not been spared either and there were ruins everywhere. The distraught faces of the people he passed showed exhaustion and fear. He looked in vain for a place to rest but there was nothing but rubble and he trudged wearily on. He felt strangely calm about it all. It was as if a numbing sense of defeat had removed his capacity to feel deeply about anything. He had convinced himself that he was so used to bad news that while he hoped to see his family he was already prepared for their death.

A voice startled him. It was a female voice and for a

moment he thought it was Ilse. Realizing his mistake, and feeling suddenly alone, suddenly vulnerable, the false calm that had been his shield against despair now shattered, he sat down on the rubble and wept. Just trying to survive, struggling to reach Munich, had become too much to endure.

"It's all right. I'm a nurse . . . was a nurse. I'm trying to help."

He looked at her suspiciously.

"Come with me. I'll find you a meal, a place to sleep. I'm trying to help people in need."

Reassured, he stood up unsteadily, and resting on her arm, accompanied her along the street.

Her house was undamaged but shoddy, and he was unaccountably bothered by the peeling paint. She must have noticed his look of censure.

"Impossible to get paint," she said, "And it's not something I can do."

"Your husband?"

"Hans was killed . . . in Russia. Nine months ago."

"I'm sorry . . . "

She looked at his civilian clothes.

"My unit was destroyed . . . Those of us left. We had to escape from the Russians."

"I don't know where to go," she said. "My home is here . . . I intend to stay."

She opened the front door and led him into the kitchen.

Rolf stood by the table, uncertain what to do.

"I know you want to go, but first I insist . . . a cup of coffee."

"A cup of coffee," he repeated, his voice sounding distant and preoccupied. He looked around furtively, as if unwelcome visitors would arrive at any moment.

When Rolf reached the outskirts of Munich, he was near collapse. He had covered the last ten miles comparatively quickly, having hitched rides on farmers' carts, or the odd vehicle that was moving, avoiding military transport for fear of being apprehended. However, fatigue was robbing him of even a basic level of energy. He was now in an area occupied by the Americans. The landscape showed its battle scars. From Nurnberg south it had been especially depressing. There were wandering multitudes of homeless confused people, showing the strain of the loss of relatives, possessions and self-esteem. Drifting back into his protective shell, made him view it all dispassionately, as though he was a detached observer of a massive performance, like a Nuremburg Rally in the years before the war gone terribly wrong. Then it entered his consciousness that he, too, was a player, a ragged disillusioned member of a scattered people - the survivors of a dream that had failed.

A Jeep drove up and stopped.

"Where ya going, old man." The driver was a young American corporal.

Rolf started to walk away, fearing what might happen to him, but he swayed slightly and the other soldier came after him.

"Careful," he said.

"*Nein! Nein!*" Rolf shouted and pushed him away.

"Stupid old bastard!" The soldier pulled out his gun, yelling. "How's it feel to be like one of the poor suckers you butchered?"

Rolf didn't hear. He was running, expecting any second to feel the impact of a bullet.

"Let him go!" The corporal yelled.

Rolf heard the Jeep drive away and he slumped to the ground, his heart pounding, not sure whether he was glad to be alive or whether a quick death would have been preferable.

Helga thought she heard a knock on the front door but when it wasn't repeated she turned back towards the kitchen. It came again, stronger this time. There was no doubt there was someone there. She opened the door to see an old man leaning against the door frame. His face, that is what she could see of it under the heavy beard, was wizened, skeleton-like in its appearance, and he was stooping, looking as though he might fall at any moment.

"Hel - ga!"   The voice was barely audible.

She looked again at the old man, striving to look past his appearance, until suddenly the clarity of recognition formed in her brain.

"My God . . . Father! . . . Father!"

She dived at him, hugging the skin and bone that he had become, almost knocking him over.   She helped him into the house, lowering him onto the sofa in the living room.

"Mother! . . . *Oma!*" she shouted. It's Father . . . Father!"

"Are you out of your mind Helga?"   Her mother appeared first and stood eyeing the dishevelled figure on the sofa as if to imply that Helga should throw him out.

"It's Father," said Helga, annoyed at her mother's insensitivity.

Ilse's face went white and she collapsed on the floor. Eva was standing behind her, looking.

"It's my son . . . it's Rolf . . . God took care of him." Eva went over and sat beside him and put her arms around him, nestling him like a baby, her baby, in her lap.

She looked up at Helga.

"We'll need to feed him."

"What about mother?"

Eva looked at Ilse as if she were a minor player in the drama.   For an instant Helga had the impression that her only thought was that **she** had reclaimed **her** son.

"She'll be all right . . . just a faint that's all . . . get the smelling salts."

"Mother knew I was alive," said Rolf, his voice, stronger now, and Eva smiled with deep satisfaction.

3.

The Sandrake was in the Indian Ocean steaming towards Ceylon, when news was received of the end of the war in Europe. Peter and Mike were lolling on the rail looking out at the vast expanse of warm ocean, a spectacle of some absurdity after the chilling Arctic seas.

"Just like us to miss the fucking party," Mike said.

"Shit" Peter kicked the stanchion holding the guard rail. He turned to Mike, giving him an angry stare, and then he looked at the far horizon. The reality of the situation pressed in on him. He had to find out about Helga but now he was committed to a new war. It was shortly after supporting the D Day landings that the Sandrake had been sent to the Far East. He felt cheated out of a victory he believed he had earned, and more grievously, an opportunity to be with his love. Besides, this war, in the Far East, didn't seem like his war.

The Sandrake glided across the surface of a smooth sea as the porpoises played around the bow and the occasional flying fish fell stunned on the deck. Peter drifted away from Mike and made his way below. His deeper thoughts, those so long in limbo, were only of Helga, wondering if she and his son had survived. The fear of their demise loomed large, yet the end of the war in Europe also brought the prospect of their survival. He decided to write.

Dearest Helga,

I want you to know that I am alive and well. The news makes me want to believe that you and our son have survived. May God grant that I am right? I must hear from you if only to confirm that you have not perished in the conflict. I want you to know that

I love you with all my heart and that it is hard to believe that these six years of waiting are finally over and that the possibility of a reunion has returned. I am desperate to see you and to hold you in my arms again and to have young Hans-Peter at our side. I don't feel very coherent. I write struggling with my emotions, hoping and praying that all is not lost. Please darling, write to me, tell me that you are safe and that we can soon be together.

All my love,

Peter.

He read the letter over and over as all sorts of doubts assailed him. So much time had passed that his expectations began to seem unrealistic. Even if she had survived, she may well have married or entered into other friendships or liaisons. After all, had he not found the strain of waiting too much to bear? He shuddered to think of Sarah and their wild sexual escapades.

He sealed the envelope and dropped it in the postbox knowing that it would now face the ship's censoring officer and that it would not be on its way until they arrived at their next port of call.

At Trincomalee, the main naval base on the east coast of Ceylon, a large force of ships was being assembled to bolster the offensive capacity in the region. It was a vast area, stretching westwards to the East African coast and eastwards to Malaya and Singapore, the latter already captured by the Japanese. As well, there was the unprecedented loss by bombing at sea of two British battleships. There was much to avenge, and a considerable area of Japanese-held territory to recover. The war here was far from over.

In the weeks that followed, as Peter tormented himself with

thoughts of Helga, the Sandrake, accompanied by her three sister destroyers made sorties to bombard Port Blair in the Andaman Islands, east of Trincomalaee, and to the north coast of Sumatra, opening fire on coastal defences in the small port of Sabang.

It was on one of these sorties that it happened. Peter was on the bridge when a Japanese cruiser and destroyer were reported off the coast of Malaya, and the Sandrake and her three accompanying destroyers were ordered to attempt to locate and attack them. A considerable distance separated them from the reported enemy position. Full speed was ordered to close the distance as rapidly as possible.

Peter went down to the Transmitting Station, going over in his mind the checks he would do to make sure that the fire control system was in good working order. It was like the *Schlosstern* business over again. It would obviously have to be a torpedo attack, not only because the cruiser's guns would be more powerful, with longer range than the British destroyers' guns, but also because there was no heavy warship with the British force. They were on their own this time and their chief weapons were their torpedoes. A torpedo attack? Peter imagined how it would be. After the *Schlosstern* sinking it was no longer an unknown. Steaming in at full speed, getting in as close as possible, risking a hit from the enemy's weapons, hoping one could get in, turn, and fire, before becoming disabled. A suicidal mission really.

Peter felt nervous; the thought of repeating the *Schlosstern* episode wasn't exactly appealing. He wasn't sure which was worse - knowing what could be ahead or going blindly, innocently, into the fray. Besides, the thought of risking his life, or becoming seriously hurt in some way after having survived the war in Europe, became a bizarre twist of fate, negating the belief he had placed in it being the end of all the waiting for a reunion with Helga.

Tom Thompson, Jonathan's replacement, who Peter found difficult to accept, for he triggered too many memories, came in.

"The phone line. It's dead."

"Which fucking phone line?" Peter's brusqueness brought a mellowed answer.

"The director end."

"Hang on here. I'll go up and check."

He picked up his tool bag and made his way onto the bridge to the new director tower which had replaced the old, the one which was shattered to bits with its crew, with Jonathan and the others. He climbed into the empty space, trying to picture what it must have been like then, on that cold Arctic night in December.   They couldn't have felt anything.   It would have been over in a flash - only those left bear the burden of grief, he thought.   The phone rang. It was Tom.

"You're there?"

"Yes, can you hear *me*?"

"Very faintly . . . your voice is breaking up."

Peter pushed back the memories. "Hold on. I'll change the handset . . . " (louder) "I'll change the handset."

"OK," Tom's voice blasted back.

Peter disconnected the old handset. As he did so, the nearby loudspeaker came on, humming. He waited.

This is the Captain speaking. We expect to be in an
area of possible contact with the enemy units by late
tomorrow afternoon.   I'm going to keep a 'standby'
state of readiness until then.

Peter connected the new headset and gave the call-up lever a twist.

"Tom? Tom? D'you hear that?"

"I heard we have a shindig tomorrow . . . with the Japs."

"You can hear me then?"

"Loud and clear."

It was not until three in the afternoon of the next day, after they had been closed up at action stations for an hour, that the Captain made a further announcement.

> This is the Captain.   I expect to make contact with the enemy force after dark.   I have decided to make this a night action, giving us a greater chance of surprise.   Make sure you wear your life vests and that your locator lights are working.   If we get into the water, someone will be along to pick us up. Good Luck.

Peter was walking aft, along the upper deck, when the announcement was made. As they steamed through a placid sea, it was hard to believe that they were once again on a risky venture. The tropical heat was still oppressive even though there was now a light breeze. When he reached the rearmost torpedo tubes, the Captain's announcement had already influenced the banter among the crew.

". . . if the sharks don't get us first!"

They all laughed, uncomfortably.

"What's the problem?" Peter yelled and the laughing stopped.

"Dirty contacts on the firing switch," said the Leading Seaman.

Peter got to work.

In the early evening, Peter was in the Switchboard Room below decks when Tom shouted down the hatch.

"We've got Radar contact - just came through from the bridge!"

"I heard you."

He felt resigned, philosophic even, whatever happened would happen, there was nothing he could do about it. There were no further reports from the Captain, they were not necessary anyway, the plan was clear, and as the whine from the main turbines increased he knew they were going in. He tried to concentrate on the task at hand, but he felt his body tense, waiting for the explosions. Which would come first, the Sandrake's guns or the eruption of enemy shells?

The steady hum of the turbines continued, punctuated now by the Sandrake's violent turns as she zigzagged in towards the targets.

The time ticked on, every minute seemed like an age. Still, nothing. Was the enemy unaware of their presence?

The Sandrake's guns started firing and he waited for the crash of incoming shells. The minutes ticked away. Still, nothing.

Then the onslaught came. Salvoes dropping in quick succession. They continued their headlong rush towards the enemy. Peter winced as a louder explosion sent shrapnel fragments rattling against the hull. The enemy was finding the range.

The Sandrake heeled over and he grabbed at the top of an electric generator to steady himself, almost burning himself on the hot casing. This turn was longer and he knew the critical moment had come, the moment of greatest danger as the ship turned broadside to the enemy to release its torpedoes.

There was a loud bang, followed by the shriek of metal resisting the penetration of shell fragments. There was a whoosh of white smoke as steam began filling the compartment.

He checked switches and power supplies. Everything was in order. There was no doubt; the steam was superheated steam from the forward boiler room.

The temperature rose rapidly and visibility was decreasing. He made one final check as the heat attacked his unprotected skin. He fumbled for the ladder and rushed up to the deck above, closing the hatch behind him. Damage control parties were already trying to get into the forward boiler room but the heat was so intense that access was impossible.

"Anyone down there?" Peter yelled to the Leading Seaman in charge.

"The whole bloody boiler room watch!"

In the early hours of the morning the Sandrake steamed back towards Trincomalee its mission accomplished. The Japanese cruiser and destroyer had been sunk. Peter sat in the mess drinking tea, trying to calm his nerves. Above decks the anti-aircraft crews were on the alert in case of a Japanese air attack. Mike Struthers came into the mess and flopped down beside him.

"The poor buggers didn't have a chance - scalded - all of them - superheated steam - you were lucky mate."

"They found them then?" Peter winced. It was already obvious that all that would be found would be lifeless bodies.

"Opened the hatch this morning . . . "

Peter felt a wave of nausea. Fighting it, he poured himself another tea.

"I didn't think about it, Mike," his voice felt remote, different somehow. "All I thought about was me. Me getting out of there. Shit, I didn't think of the other poor sods on the other side of the bulkhead."

"Nothing you could do . . . the shell went aft . . . even with the small hole it made in the bulkhead, your compartment got steam . . . "

"Only thought of myself, Mike," he said. His muscles tightening.

Mike brushed the perspiration from his forehead.

"We sank both of them, Peter . . . the cruiser *and* the destroyer . . . "

"Somebody always dies, Mike."

With the sea duty crew assembled in their best whites for entering harbour, the Sandrake and her accompanying destroyers steamed down the line of warships, their crews waving and cheering, a victorious force returning to Trincomalee.

Not long after they were anchored, the post arrived and

Peter waited as the names were called. Mike received a letter from his wife, but there were no letters for him. Still, he consoled himself with the fact that it would take time to get mail in and out of an occupied Germany.

The next day the ship was alive with a new buzz. They were to be sent to Durban, in South Africa, for repairs.

4.

$\mathcal{I}$n Durban, the modern port on the east coast of South Africa, the afternoon sun shone in the clear blue sky. There was a light breeze but it did little to reduce the humidity. It had been a welcome sight to see a modern city spread out before them as the Sandrake rounded the Bluff - the promontory that shielded the inner harbour - in the early hours of the morning. They tied up alongside the busy quay and immediately the dockyard workers came aboard to attend to the damage. At the same time, the usual naval advance parties were sent ashore, one rating assigned to collect the mail and a group of three ratings needing urgent dental attention.

Peter looked out upon the clean white buildings and the traffic flowing along the palm-tree-lined street near the docks, and he turned away. Not knowing quite why, he didn't want to go ashore.

"You coming, Pete?" Mike was getting out his best whites.

"Don't feel like it." He wanted to say, 'Bugger off!'

"Thought you had a piece of crumpet here? . . . when you were here in forty-one?"

"Yea . . . Don't want to see her."

"What the hell's the matter?"

"Said goodbye the last time. Don't want to do it again. It's all goodbyes. See you later and all that. But there's no later." There was a bitterness in his voice.

Mike finished dressing and combed his hair.

"Well . . . I'm off."

As soon as Mike had left, Peter felt remorse. He hadn't intended to upset Mike but that's what he felt he'd done. He waited until he was sure that all the liberty men had left and then

281

he went to his locker.   He found the picture of Helga, his favourite, the one taken outside the Tea Room.   He stared at the happy face, the fair hair and the blue eyes.

"We'll be together . . . soon," he said, talking to the picture. And then the tears came, warm streams reaching his chin, dropping onto his hands, giving expression to his longing and his fear.   He returned the photograph, making sure that it wouldn't get bent out of shape. He stretched out on the lockers with his hands behind his head and gazed up at a spider's web being blown about by the ventilation system.   A stupid place to spin a web he thought.   His gaze was caught by the dark spot at the edge of the waving filaments.   It was the spider, patiently waiting, seeming confident that the gamble would work.   Peter closed his eyes.   He had to get to Helga.

The hammering of a dockyard worker disturbed him and he sat up, his mind occupied with all the options he once considered as he sought to enter Germany. He had done it before and he could do it again, only this time he was thousands of miles away on the southeast coast of Africa. He stood up and looked out of the porthole. A slight breeze ruffled his hair. Along the extensive dockside were cargo ships loading and unloading their cargoes. Maybe one of them was heading back to England?

It was two days later when the news broke. The damage to the forward boiler was more serious than expected. They were to return to England as an urgent refit was now required which could not be handled by the local shipyard. This enforced return had its difficulties as they would probably need to steam on one boiler, greatly reducing their speed.

Peter was ecstatic. Fate seemed to be on his side and a return to peace and Helga at last within his grasp. His only disappointment was that there was still no letter from her. They sailed from Durban in the early hours of the morning, turning southwards past East London and Port Elizabeth, following the gently curving coastline, setting a course to round the Cape of Good Hope. Although their normal speed could not be maintained, they were able to hold a steady course against a strong westerly gale which sent mountains of water over the bow. Through it all, graceful albatross swooped and dived over the stern as if they were oblivious to the force of the gale - spectators to the discomfort of those who would dare to venture into their world.

There were half of the distance towards home, one day at sea after a refuelling stop in Pointe Noire on the West African coast, when Peter was summoned to see the First Lieutenant. It began when Mike came rushing into the mess.

"Buffer's looking for you."

"What for?"

"How the hell should I know."

Peter grabbed his cap and headed for the Master at Arm's office.

"Ah, Gray." The Buffer was a burly Chief Petty Officer who had served as a Boy Seaman in the First War. "Come with me." He got up and headed aft.

Peter, fearing the worst, followed. Perhaps his letter to Helga had been seized and he was about to be charged with communicating with the enemy - well, at least a former enemy. He had little time to ponder his fate.

"Sir, you wished to see Leading Seaman Gray?"

"Come in Gray. That will be all Chief."

"Yes, sir." The Buffer saluted and left.

"Sit down, Gray."

The Officer opened the file in front of him and extracted a small sheet of paper.

"I've received some bad news . . . " Peter gulped, his thoughts turning to Helga.

The officer handed Peter a telegram.

H.M. SHIPS,
ADMIRALTY
WHITEHALL

I WOULD BE GRATEFUL IF YOU COULD
INFORM LEADING SEAMAN PETER ARNOLD
GRAY THAT HIS FATHER, HARRY ERNEST GRAY
HAS BEEN ADMITTED TO HOSPITAL SUFFERING
FROM A SEVERE CASE OF PNEUMONIA   STOP
ACTING AS MR. GRAY'S SOLICITOR I STRONGLY
RECOMMEND THAT HIS SON BE GRANTED LEAVE
TO ATTEND HIS FATHER WHO IS RESIDING IN
THE LOCAL HOSPITAL   STOP

HUGH WILLOUGHBY
REDFERN AND SHEARDON
BARRISTERS' & SOLICITORS

Peter stared blankly at the brusque message, thankful it wasn't Helga. He couldn't believe that his father, who always prided himself on his excellent health, could be facing a serious illness.

"I'm very sorry, Gray."

He looked up. The Officer was studying his reaction.

"It's all death, isn't it." Peter mouthed the words as if by rote.

"Your father's not dead Gray. He's ill."

"Yes, thank you, sir."

"Are you all right, Gray?"

"Yes sir."

"If you need further help, I expect you to let me know."

"I will sir."

"It's fortunate that we're bound for home. As soon as we dock, I'll authorize some leave."

"Thank you, sir."

Peter saluted, and left.

In the days that followed, Peter felt lost in a deep well of depression. Mike's attempts to coax him into a more optimistic mood were to no avail. It was when they arrived off the coast of England that he brightened a little.

"Be glad to be ashore, Mike." Peter looked out the porthole above the mess table. It was the morning that the approach to Plymouth hove into view.

"You just need a break, that's all. Too much fucking sea time. Besides . . . " Mike hesitated, unsure about raising the matter. "Your dad . . ."

Peter felt a stab of guilt. He hadn't thought much about his father. Mike looked uneasy.

"I want to be out of this lot, Mike."

"Don't we all?"

The loudspeaker blared, 'Prepare for entering harbour'. The turbines slowed, the steady whine dropping to a low hum as they entered the channel into the harbour.

Peter and Mike left for their stations. Their time aboard the Sandrake was nearing its end. In a matter of weeks the ship would be decommissioned - taken out of service for a long refit. The crew would be disbanded and sent on leave before taking up new postings.

5.

$\mathcal{I}$ was Gertrud who came to Eva's house on the *Sunderstrasse* with the latest gossip.

"The Allies are starving our prisoners of war. My neighbour told me she knows someone who tried to get food to a prisoner of war camp and she was threatened with death. Did you know there is also an order forbidding civilians to deliver food supplies to prisoners of war? She also believes the Allies are deliberately reducing our food rations."

"It can't be!" Helga, disbelieving, turned to Eva for support.

"It's going to be like the last war." Eva's words were measured and her voice was steady. "They're going to bleed us again."

They were in the kitchen, sitting around the table. Hans was playing with his grandparents in the living room.

"I thought . . . " Helga began.

"That this time it will be different?" Rolf appeared in the doorway having heard the conversation. "After all the news about concentration camps . . . the brutality? No, we're to be punished, all of us."

"All of us. We didn't know." Helga sought some reason for clemency.

"We didn't know?" Rolf repeated angrily. "Didn't we know of the mistreatment of the Jews . . . the mysterious disappearances of former friends? Don't you remember how we knew people were Jews . . . the stars sewn to their clothes . . . did we not see this?"

"We didn't wish death," Helga said.

Rolf frowned. "No it turned out to be worse." His voice was despondent. "We condoned it by our silence."

It was a month later when Rolf and Ilse decided to try and return to Blankenese. Helga and Eva tried to dissuade them.

"How do you know you can even return to the house?" Eva put the question to Rolf.

"I don't know, but I have to regain my life . . . to try and find what's left of what I worked to achieve. Perhaps it's all gone?" He pulled himself erect. "If so, I must start again . . . I will start again."

"How will you find food?" Her father's determination was all very well, Helga speculated, but it was bad enough finding the bare necessities to stay alive in Munich. What must it be like in Hamburg where the bombing had wreaked far greater destruction?

"Maybe we'll go and visit Siegfried's parents on the farm in Neuengamme. He did offer to help," said Ilse.

At first, Rolf appeared dismayed by the idea, but then, as the reality of the situation sank in, said, "Yes, perhaps we'll do that." Sounding more resolute, he continued, "We must find a way to rebuild our lives."

Eva sat silently, a look of satisfaction on her face, and Helga thought how sad it was that so much of this family spirit had been absorbed by wars and destruction.

6.

$\mathcal{A}$ taxi brought Peter to the local hospital. The pleasant buildings sat on top of a hill overlooking the town. It must have been where his mother had been brought before she died, and the sight of the modest single story building, nestling among mature trees and surrounded by well-tended lawns and flower beds, gave a feeling of tranquillity. Peter liked that. He felt comforted.

Sitting by the bed, he looked down at the frail form, unable to believe that now, when the war was finally over, his father had become incapacitated. He felt that he was partly responsible. He could tell by his letters that he had been unwell for some time, and he blamed himself for not being forceful in urging him to seek proper medical help instead of giving way to his insistence that he was in good health. 'Fit as a fiddle,' he would say.

Peter pushed such thoughts away, persuading himself that he could have done little to arrest the effects of his father's decline.

Just then a doctor arrived and taking him aside informed him that the prognosis was not good. His father was breathing heavily, drifting into long bouts of semi-consciousness and capable of accepting only fluids which were being administered by a kindly nurse.

He wondered as he sat by the bed whether his father even recognized him, for he would stare blankly, as if unseeing, not responding to Peter's attempts at conversation. He took his father's withered hand in his, hoping for some sign that he felt his presence, but it remained limp and unmoving.

Late on the morning of the third day, as Peter maintained his vigil by his father's bedside, it seemed as if some part of him - perhaps his soul, he thought - had vacated the worn out body.

It was as though he had waited for his son's return. In his passing there had been only peace, a peace which challenged Peter's own fear of mortality.

It was a modest service with few mourners, held in the old church where he had been a sidesman for the past twenty five years. The church to which Peter had come as a youngster with his father, having failed to enlist the support of his mother to stay at home with her. The church to where he had dutifully accompanied his father whenever he was on leave.

The service seemed distressingly short to honour a life that had spanned two World Wars, but it was dignified by a reading from Tennyson's, Crossing the Bar.

> Sunset and evening star,
> And one clear call for me!
> And may there be no moaning of the bar,
> When I put out to sea . . .
>
> Twilight and evening bell,
> And after that the dark!
> And may there be no sadness of farewell,
> When I embark;

Peter wiped a tear from his eyes. Not a bad send off for an old sailor he thought.

At the cemetery a cold wind blew, swaying the trees and ruffling the hair of the mourners. As the coffin was lowered into the same plot that had received his mother seven years before, Peter saluted. It was a spontaneous gesture which seemed to disturb the minister as he intoned the words of the burial service. For Peter, it was a mark of respect, not only for a father disciplined in the Royal Navy he knew, but for a man of simple tastes, a countryman who had served his masters faithfully and honestly - even though the subservience he displayed towards authority had always bothered Peter. How he wished that his father could have found the capacity to express what he really felt. It was sad. Sad because in his declining years, Peter had begun to see another side of him, a gentleness manifested most in a love and respect for nature which, he became convinced, revealed a deep sensitivity that his mother must have known. Perhaps it was this that had attracted her to him when they first met?

7.

*W*hen Peter awoke the next day in the house he once shared with his parents, he lay staring at the ceiling. The sun was up and its rays, caught by the larch tree, danced myriad patterns on the walls and ceiling, just like it had seven years before on the day he had prepared to meet the *Joachim* and Helga.

There was no sound from the kitchen below, yet he imagined them there, his mother cooking the bacon and eggs and his father buried in his newspaper. It was like a time warp, not of this century. Some bizarre event that came from a past life. He got up and made himself some coffee. Sitting alone in the kitchen, bathed with memories, it seemed disrespectful to accept that it was his house now, or would be when the legal niceties had been settled.

When he had first arrived home after the funeral, he found it difficult to concentrate. He wandered around the empty house, alternately trying to read or listen to the wireless. It wasn't until the third day that he walked the one and a half miles to the seashore and to the harbour.

The pier was accessible now, the barbed wire having been removed, and the amateur fishermen were out in force, casting their lines with noticeable awkwardness, out of practice after five years of war.

Standing there, gazing out towards the distant horizon, intensified his thoughts of Helga - thoughts that were never far from his mind even during his worst anxieties. As well, being home again, back in the pleasant countryside and the small harbour entered through the twin piers, brought all the old memories flooding back. Things were so different now, the war was over and he, instead of celebrating the return of peace, was struggling with demons whose origins he could not begin to understand. Just that morning he had seen some of the first pictures showing the horror of the German concentration camps. It was hardly a situation that offered hopes for a satisfactory reunion, even if Helga was alive, or still unattached, or even remotely interested in him.

In this mood, which was worsened by the dark low clouds and the persistent drizzle, he gazed out upon a barely discernable horizon and lamented the loss of a dream. Perhaps, he thought, it was only the war and the desire for a vision of eventual happiness that had sustained the illusion all this time. For it was unrealistically romantic, a few days together which he had amplified into a long-term relationship. Yet Helga had acted the same way, but then she too could have been the victim of teenage naïveté. In the penetrating cold of this day, at the end of the familiar piers, facing a sea he now knew swallowed men and ships, a callous unforgiving sea, it was hard to recapture an idealistic vision of a relationship that was now just a memory.

He sat on one of the weathered piles surrounding the pier. He felt uncharacteristically relaxed in spite of the disappointment which he felt. It was as though the acceptance of the end of a dream had resolved a conflict between what was and what he imagined might have been; 'What might have been?' no longer capable of being sustained in the light of the reality of this moment, this time in history.

He walked home, deciding not to stop at the small café near the harbour mouth. He wanted to get home, to be alone with his thoughts for a while.

He unlocked the door and hung his coat in the hall. He didn't notice it at first but there was a letter lying on the floor. He picked it up casually, thinking to himself that the twelve thirty p.m. post was still operating as it always did. He dropped the letter on the kitchen table and went to see what he could find for lunch. It was only then that the unexpected existence of a letter occurred to him. He raced back to the table, picked it up, turning it over to look at its origin - it was postmarked *München*. His heart began to race. He opened the letter with trembling hands.

Dear Peter,

This is Helga.

I wonder if you remember me, or if this will ever reach you. I'm worried that you might be dead but I pray that you might have survived the horror. This is the only address I have, other than the navy address but I assume that you must be out of the navy now, so it is all I can use. It is very hard to know how to begin or even if you will want to hear. Maybe you are married or about to be married. The only thing I can do is to tell you about me.

There was a time when I hated you Peter, hated you for leaving me when I most needed you. The visit we had in 1939 still haunts me, not only because we renewed our love then but because it made that second parting so much more difficult and if I had known what was to come I doubt whether I would have had the courage to go on.

He put the letter on the table. He was shaking so violently that he had to rest his hands.

Peter. You still have a wonderful son. Hans-Peter is big and strong and I wish you could see him even if you don't want to see me.

Peter brushed a hand across his eyes.

I stayed in *München* throughout the whole war and now that it's over we are experiencing the aftermath of our folly.My brother Günther went into the *Kriegsmarine* and was one of those who were tragically lost in battle. His friend Siegfried, who is in love with my girlfriend Frieda, survived, and is still a prisoner of war.

My God, her brother dead - at the hands of the Royal Navy? He had never entertained such a possibility and it cast a pall over the happiness he had felt with the arrival of her letter. He read on.

We thought my *Vater* had been killed in the battle for Berlin and the strain of it all took its toll on Mutter's state of mind, but that's over now and he is safe and with the family again, recovering from his ordeal. *Mutter* and *Vater* are hoping to return to the old house in Blankenese.

I still remember our time together in England and *Deutschland*. If only we had known what was to come. The innocence of the young. We were young then and full of hope. The *Joachim* is no more. It was bombed and sunk during the war.

Was that why, today of all days, he lost hope on the pier? The *Joachim* would not come anymore. Would not fulfil those promises they made so long ago?

I would like to see you, Peter. I'm not married or anything - I wanted to wait for you in spite of everything that has happened. But perhaps you are married - maybe you are not even alive - perhaps your parents will open this and tell me - I have to find out.

Parents die, everyone dies, but not Peter, he survives to live a hell he has found for himself. Death is simpler, it's memories and guilt that kill the spirit.

Whatever your circumstances could you

294

write? I would so much like to hear from you.

Helga *Jansen*

He placed the letter on the table. It was hard to believe. Helga was alive, having brought up his child, their child, through all the horror. The memory was alive after all, but what was he to do now?   They were both older, changed by war. He had been in the Royal Navy, the navy that could have killed her brother. How could she forgive that? He noted how she was careful to avoid any suggestion of a lasting affection. It was just an enquiry. She was right though, how did they know how they would feel about each other?   But didn't he have a responsibility for what happened? She had given birth to his child and brought him up, in spite of everything, family rejection and war.   The thoughts assailed him, entered his head and thrashed around. He was confused, unable to cope with the meaning of it all.

He did little for the rest of the day and when at last he went to bed, he struggled with his conscience before he fell asleep.

When he awoke the next morning, he felt refreshed. Gone was the gloom of the day before. Helga was alive and he was alive. Whatever had happened in the preceding years was already history. It was the present that mattered.

It was a sunny summer's day. He walked briskly along the familiar footpaths on the way to the coast. He would spend the morning on the cliffs and take his lunch in the small café near the harbour. He stopped now and then to gaze upon the fields of tall grass awaiting its transition to the sweet hay of late summer. Butterflies flitted above the slender stalks and red poppies and clover gave colour and fragrance to the warm pleasant breeze. For a brief moment a touch of sadness, even guilt, invaded his happiness. It was only a few days before that he had bidden farewell to his father.

Entry to the beaches was still banned due to the presence of mines, so he walked along the old promenade and sat looking out upon the calm sea only gently agitated by the diminishing wind.

In a few days he would be back aboard the Sandrake, and then would come the disbanding of the crew and a spell in the dreaded barracks awaiting a new assignment. He was all too aware that he could be posted to the Far East again and with it would go the prospect of an early reunion with Helga. He had to do something and fast. He began to ponder his options.

It was disappointing that there was no indication that Helga had received his letter. She had posted hers shortly after VE Day. Perhaps she had written it as they were being occupied by Allied troops. Still, the immediate problem was to let her know that he was alive. He would try and phone. His first thought was to try the local dentist but the more he thought of this, the less the idea appealed to him. The last thing he wanted to do was to get the local gossip going at a time when feelings towards the Germans were gripped by loathing. He would wait until he returned to the Sandrake. By this time he might have a better idea of his future. In the meantime he would write to Helga.

*B*y the beginning of August the relief that had accompanied the end of the war, and which had lifted Helga's spirits, had been replaced by despondency. She found it increasingly difficult to find enough food. The situation was worsened by the reality that there was still five mouths to feed, Rolf and Ilse having found it impossible to find a way to return to the house in Blankenese. She was particularly concerned about young Hans who was not receiving the nourishment that his young fast-growing body needed.

Herr Welt, his *Kaffeehaus* badly damaged, still managed to provide her with a morning cup of weak coffee. It was here that she met with Frieda when she could sneak an hour or so away from the hospital where she still worked. They were overloaded now. There were so many cases of injury and malnutrition that only the worst could be cared for. It was exhausting work and Frieda, like Helga and all the others, was showing the signs of strain.

One morning, after a particularly sleepless night, she was dozing at a table in the *Kaffeehaus* when she was startled by a shout. It was Frieda.

"Helga!" she shouted, waving a letter. "I've heard from Siegfried."

Frieda joined her, sitting down at one of the small tables among the rubble.

"What does it say?" Helga said.

"I haven't read it yet. I'm so excited. I wanted to read it with you."

She tore open the envelope and spread out the pages.

Dear Frieda . . . she read on.

We are being transferred again. The rumour
is that we will soon be going back to England. It is
hard to believe that this is actually happening after so
long.

She rushed over the next part, mumbling to words to
herself.

Dear Frieda, I've missed you so much. I've
wondered how you are and what you are doing and
whether you will want to see me again? I will
understand if there is someone else. You have to
live your own life. As for me I only know that I think
of you always and want to be with you again.

She started reading aloud again.

How is Helga? Are you still good friends?
All things considered, they have been good
to us here. It's a very interesting country and I would
like to see more of it. We have never been short of
good food. I fear, that as a prisoner, I have fared
better than all of you.
I don't know about defeat or victory, I only
know that such a catastrophe must not happen again.
I believed in the *Führer*, I suppose we all did, and
the way he brought our country back to prosperity.
But it also brought us war, a war that caused millions
to suffer. I'm very confused about it all and I'm glad
it's nearly over.
I worry a great deal about you and all my
family. We get regular news on the radio and in the
newspapers, and I can only try and imagine what you
have gone through and are still going through, and
what it must be like there. I wish I could be there

now, to help. I feel so helpless, so powerless to help
my friends and family. If I had ever realized what
terrible suffering . . . *Gott sei Dank* . . . soon it will be
over.

She skipped over the last part.

> Please take care of yourself Frieda.
> All my love,
>
> Siegfried

Frieda put down the letter and sipped on her coffee.
"Siegfried home! It's hard to believe," Helga said.
"It may be some time yet."
"Do you want to see him again?"
"Yes, very much . . . I suppose we've both changed . . .
maybe we'll be different people . . . it's a bit scary isn't it?"
"Very scary."
Frieda studied Helga's face, quickly reading the signs.
"Peter?"
"Yes Peter. Is he even alive and if he is alive, would he
even want to see me?"
"Do you want to see *him*?"
"I don't know. Sometimes I hate him . . . hate him for
all that has happened . . . but then I feel the longing . . . my desire
to be with him again is so strong . . . "
There were whistles as an American Jeep went by.
Frieda looked at the retreating Jeep and then looked back
at Helga, shaking her head.
"What went wrong. Why did we trust the *Führer?*"
"Life was good for a while. He made it good for us."
"You sound like Günther."
"We all believed, didn't we?"
"We had doubts too."
". . . that we didn't listen to."

9.

*P*eter's attempts to phone Helga before he left the Sandrake were unsuccessful. He would get through to Germany only to find himself connected to some office of the occupying armies and to be told in a blunt and offhand manner that contact with German civilians was out of the question.

After the Sandrake was decommissioned, he spent some ten days in barracks before being transferred to a torpedo training school for a refresher course. It was during this period that Atomic Bombs were dropped on Japan. The Far Eastern War was over! Peace had returned.

By early November, upon completion of his training course, Peter was assigned to a new destroyer, HMS Gratton, nearing completion in a shipyard in Birkenhead, across the Mersey River from Liverpool. In many respects it was to be a repeat of the process he experienced on the East Coast and another river of maritime commerce, the Tyne, when he lived in lodgings ashore until the Sandrake was ready to receive its crew. However, this location had an advantage which he was quick to explore. Mike Struthers, his old shipmate from the Sandrake days, lived in West Kirby, across the Wirral Peninsula from Birkenhead, easily accessible by electric train. Mike had worked for the Post Office before the war. He specialized in telephone services which were allied to the postal service.

Peter dialled Mike's telephone number.

"Hello," A pleasant woman's voice answered.

"Hello," he said. "I . . ."

"It's you." The voice became excited.

"It's a friend of Mike's . . ."

300

"I'm sorry, I thought you were Mike."

"No, I . . ."

"Is he all right? I mean, have you word?"

"No, you see, we served together, the Sandrake . . . '

"He's . . ."

Peter felt terrible. It was all starting badly.

"I was hoping to see him. We haven't been in touch for some time."

He heard a gasp of relief.

"My apologies. I always dread the worst even though I spoke to him just last week. I try to tell myself it's all over, but I still can't believe it . . . I didn't get your name?"

"Sorry, Peter, Peter Gray."

"Joan Struthers."

Her voice lightened.

"Mike's waiting for his demob. Can't wait to get out."

Lucky sod he thought

"When do you expect to get out?"

Unprepared for the question he faltered.

"Ah, I'm a regular . . . "

The very truth of it shattered his composure. It made his task of reuniting with Helga appear more distant than ever.

"Mike's still in Plymouth. He's expected home for Christmas. Look, could you join us for Christmas dinner? . . . I'm sure Mike would love to see you?"

The prospect of seeing Mike again and to experience a Christmas in a home was very appealing and he said he would see what could be done. She promised to have Mike contact him, and he left feeling buoyed by the prospect. Besides, it had occurred to him that Mike might be of assistance in the search for a way to reach Helga.

10.

*H*elga received Peter's letter - sent so long ago from Ceylon - at the end of November. The envelope was soiled and festooned with the imprints of rubber stamps and pencilled notes and when she went to open it she could tell that it had been opened before. She felt a stab of anxiety. Could her father have read it? But it was Eva that had handed it to her after answering the doorbell's ring.

She went to her bedroom and closed the door.

As her eyes took in the words she felt her heart begin to pound and tears came to her eyes. She looked at the date, realizing that it had been sent ahead of hers, realizing that her letter may have faced the same delay, even if it had reached him.

She wiped the tears from her eyes and lay back on the bed, staring at the ceiling. After waiting all these years, the shock of knowing he was alive made her swing from joy to consternation. She tried to recall what she had said in her letter and whether it had been too guarded. Perhaps he had received her letter and was troubled by her caution? She remembered then how she had tried to balance her hopes with the reality that he might not only be dead or married, but uncaring of her existence.

She put the letter away and went downstairs to find Eva.

Eva was sitting at her usual chair in the kitchen, She locked up as Helga entered.

"Coffee?"

"Thanks."

"It was Peter?"

"Yes."

Helga grasped Eva's hand.

"He's alive!" Sharing the knowledge brought back the

enormity of the occasion and the tears started again. Eva didn't attempt to soothe her and she was thankful for that.

"I'm happy . . . but I'm also afraid, *Oma*."

"Of course you are. It's only natural. Six years. It's a long time."

Helga dried her eyes and her grip on Eva's arm intensified.

"Mother and father mustn't know."

"Is this wise?"

"Nothing must interfere. I must work this out with Peter."

"They will find out soon enough."

"But not now? Please *Oma?* Not now?"

Eva smiled.

"Please promise me you'll not tell them?"

"I promise."

Helga leapt up and hugged her.

A week later, Rolf announced that he and Ilse were to make a further attempt to reach Hamburg and the old house in Blankenese. For the moment, Helga's concerns about her parents were lessened, and she began to think of ways to devise an effective contact with Peter.

11.

It was good to see Mike again even though it had only been five months since the Sandrake had been decommissioned. Peter joined the group at the Christmas table, Mike and his wife, Joan, together with their parents. The presence of the parents put Peter in a reflective mood, thinking of his lack of family and engendering an unwelcome loneliness. However, the feeling soon passed as the happy conversation, enlivened by the wine and the delicious spread that Joan had prepared, swept away his melancholy.

It wasn't until much later in the evening after the parents had departed and Joan, sensing their need for privacy, left Mike and Peter in the living room.

Now that they were alone, Peter found it difficult to go through with his intention. Mike broke the silence.

"How about a brandy . . . perhaps a liqueur?"

"Brandy'll be fine."

When he returned with the drinks, Peter took a generous mouthful.

"I've got to see her, Mike."

"Who?"

"Helga." No sooner had the word left his mouth than he felt embarrassed. He'd never confided in Mike. It was always Jonathan that he had turned to or, before that in the Saram days, to Tom.

"I'd forgotten. I thought I told you."

Peter took another gulp of brandy before revealing his secret.

It was another half an hour before Peter had completed his story.

Mike had listened with rapt attention, his face showing more amazement by the minute. At times he appeared to convey the thought that it must be a joke, some kind of bizarre dream that had invaded Peter's mind and turned into a conviction that it was all real. When he had finished, Mike got up.

"Like a refill?"

"Yes, thanks."

Mike refilled their glasses. As Peter waited, he realized that Mike was taking his time, no doubt struggling with his thoughts. He handed Peter his drink, but when he sat down he offered no comment.

"I've got to get to Germany. She wrote to me. She's OK. I want to marry her, Mike."

Mike smiled, and then leaned back, clasping his hands behind his head.

"Cagey bastard, aren't you? You certainly fooled me. I always thought you were an opportunist. A girl in every port."

"It was always Helga. She never left my thoughts . . ." He blushed. "Sarah," he mumbled. " It wasn't serious . . . "

Mike ignored his discomfort.

"Helga has your child?"

Peter nodded.

"He must be . . . "

"Six now."

"Can't you get some leave? Compassionate Leave?"

"I've put in a request. A week ago."

"Why did you wait so long?"

"I got her letter after my father's death . . . "

"Your . . . ?"

"Yes . . . It was very sudden."

"I'm sorry. It must have been hard for you?"

Peter felt irritable. He didn't want Mike's sympathy, not at this particular time.

"I'm thinking of desertion," he said. He felt relieved to get it out at last.

"You can't be serious?"

"How else am I going to get out?" There was a resentment in his voice. "I'm not like you, waiting for demob. I'm in for the long haul."

Mike was silent. He toyed with his drink.

"Surely there's some way to get out?"

"I signed up. Well, my parents signed for me. Twelve bloody years from the age of eighteen!"

"Christ!"

Bothered by Mike's discomfort, Peter turned to his immediate objective.

"I've been trying to reach Helga by phone. Every time I get bogged down with the bureaucracy. Some pompous military sod. I've been wondering if you could help, you being in the telephone business?"

Mike appeared relieved to move away from the threat of some risky action.

"It could be that the telephone system is damaged. Wouldn't be surprising? All the bombing."

"Could you give it a try though?"

"Sure. It might be a good time. All the brass will be celebrating. Let's have a go - first thing in the morning?"

It was after breakfast, after a night of wakefulness and a morning when his appetite, even with Joan's hearty plate of bacon and eggs before him, failed. Mike, all too aware of his discomfort, took his coffee and went to the telephone. He had closed the door behind him so that Peter couldn't hear. He heard the murmuring though, with Mike's voice alternately soft and loud, interspersed with long pauses. Then he came bustling in through the door.

"She's on the phone!"

Peter shot out of his chair, racing past Mike. The phone lay on a small table in the hall. He hesitated, then picked it up.

"Helga?"

"*Ja* . . . Peter, *Mein* Peter!"

His heart was pounding and he felt a tightness in his throat. For a moment he was incapable of speech. The shock of hearing her voice again after an eternity of silence was like some dream, a fantasy that had no connection with the present.

"Peter"

"Oh Helga! Dear Helga! I must see you. Are you well? Is Hans-Peter OK?"

"Hans-Peter? He is big now. Can you come, Peter?"

"I will, but . . . it's complicated. I am still in the Navy. I have to get leave."

"Oh Peter, please . . ."

There was a desperation in her voice, an entreaty. He had to give her reassurance.

"Don't worry. I'll come. Soon. I will come."

She fell silent and he struggled to keep the conversation alive.

"It's Christmas there?"

"*Ja*, Christmas. We try to be happy. It is difficult."

"I will come, soon. I'll let you know."

"I am in *München*. You will come here?"

"Yes. Yes. I will come there."

"Oh Peter. It will be soon. *Ja*?"

"Soon, Helga."

There were sounds of sobbing.

"*Auf Wiedersehen* dear Peter."

He barely had time to give a quick, 'Goodbye' before the phone went dead.

SIX

1946 - 1947

1.

Siegfried dozed in the crowded railway compartment on his way south to Munich. He was appalled by the extent of the devastation which he had seen since arriving back in Germany; the suffering of the people as they struggled to put the past behind them. He had left a confident Germany, infused with a sense of invincibility, and he felt cheated, betrayed by an ideology that he had believed in. Yet he couldn't find the anger that Horst, a fellow prisoner, had felt. Horst, who had served in U Boats and was captured by the Allies in the later stages of the war, believed that Germany should have won, which assumed that their mission was right. Siegfried remembered how he had suffered twinges of doubt even before the war began and his questioning had always upset Günther who, like Horst, was imbued with the demands of unfailing loyalty to the *Führer*. Yet he, Siegfried, had also reached a point where he had suppressed his doubts and accepted the validity of their actions. But he could no longer deny those earlier misgivings as they came back to haunt him. He now believed that their cause was indeed flawed from the start. No matter how much history might argue for the settling of an injustice - he remembered the results of the harsh reparations imposed by the victors after the First World War when his parents struggled to make ends meet - Hitler's methods had resulted in untold suffering. It had all started innocently enough, for Hitler had restored to the people a belief in their country's future. Hitler **had** brought Germany out of poverty and made them all proud to be Germans again. But he, like Günther and Horst, had not foreseen the price to be paid, had not comprehended the implications of Hitler's intentions? Only now did he know of the existence of *Mein Kampf*. Even if he had read it in the heady days of the *Hitler Jugend*, he would probably have endorsed its goals, even as it might have heightened his doubts.

It was early afternoon when he arrived at Frieda's flat. He had not warned her of his arrival and he had no idea if she would be in. He rang the bell. At first there was no sign of any life so he rang again, and then again, before he began to consider going directly to the hospital. He had begun to walk away when the door opened.

"My God!" she yelled as she fell into his arms.

They hugged and kissed and she pulled away.

"I'm sorry. I was asleep. I'm on the night shift. What a way to greet you," she said, frantically trying to arrange her hair and rubbing her eyes.

He stroked her hair and kissed her, denying her the chance for more apologies, and the familiar broad smile lit up her face.

"Oh, Siegfried, you should have told me you were coming."

"I wasn't certain . . . "

"What a wonderful surprise . . . " She motioned him in. "I want to hear all about your experiences."

He chased her down the hallway and into the bedroom.

It was late afternoon when Siegfried was awakened by Frieda's sudden movement. She sat up hurriedly, glancing at the clock.

"I have to be at work in an hour!"

Siegfried, blinking, barely awake, observed the dark hair falling haphazardly over her shoulders and face. She turned towards him, her eyes mirroring her concern. He loved those eyes set within the slightly angular face. She is beautiful, he thought, as he pulled her down beside him and kissed her.

"Siegfried! It's serious. I have to do something."

He couldn't resist a smile and she smiled too.

"Just you wait there," she said, mischievously.

He tried to think of ways to delay or prevent her

departure but when she returned she was jubilant.

"My friend Gerda will take my shift."

She leapt back into bed and his excitement blended with hers, making up for all the loneliness of the last few years.

Over dinner in the flat, Siegfried told her of his visit to his family in Neuengamme, how his father and mother seemed to have aged prematurely and how his brothers and sisters had grown, how his mother Lisa had talked excitedly of her meeting with Frieda, hoping that she would see her again. He talked of his experiences in the POW camps and how he feared he would never see her again.

"Were you with Günther at the end?"

He knew that the question would arise and he hoped he would have the courage to deal with it, but now he felt nervous. He took a deep breath.

"It was horrible, the end . . . " He didn't want to go on, but then he remembered that she was a nurse who had probably witnessed as much death and destruction as he had.

"The shells kept coming, ripping the ship to pieces. Then came the torpedoes and we knew we were finished. There were bodies everywhere. When I came up from the engine room, I was shocked by what I saw. There was such terrible damage to the superstructure. It was then that I felt that Günther, in his position in the forward Radar Room, was probably already dead. A shell landed nearby and I was blown in the water. I don't know how I survived the cold sea. I must have been near unconsciousness when they hauled me aboard the British destroyer. It was a few days later that I realized that very few of us had survived and that Günther was not one of us . . . "

The sadness seemed to well up from his feet and legs like a warm irresistible current of energy gone out of control. His whole body shook with its intensity and when it reached his head he felt borne away by an emotion so great that he couldn't contain his actions. He rapped his fists on the table and the tears flowed, streaming down his face in torrents as his whole body shuddered in deep sobs.

"I should have looked for him!" He cried out in anger and dismay. "I should have saved him!"

He felt Frieda's arms around him and she half-carried him into the bedroom. He must have cried himself to sleep, for when he awoke it was dark outside. No doubt she heard him stirring as she came in with a cup of warm coffee. He sat up and she kissed him.

"I'm sorry," he said.

They spent the next day together, Frieda having arranged for some time off. It was a day in which they got to know each other again. A happy day which he had come to believe might never happen. In the evening they went for a walk in the nearby park. It was a bright moonlit night, a night of peace.

"Remember this park Frieda? . . . I thought about it often."

"Me too . . . I even remember it was a night just like this . . . we hadn't had air raids then."

"It's good we didn't know . . . "

"Did you want to see me again?"

"Yes. Yes . . . Why do you ask?"

"I wanted to hear you say it."

He kissed her on the cheek and she turned and embraced him, her kisses showering him with devotion.

They sat down on a park bench, silent now as he struggled with another issue he had yet to face.

"What's the matter, Siegfried? Why so quiet?"

"I feel I should see Helga."

"It's been on my mind too but I thought it best if you decided when you're ready."

He felt blessed with the presence of her. All the time she had harboured the same thought, yet she had waited, knowing that he would tell her when he was ready.

"I love you, Frieda."

She moved over and kissed him, a long lingering kiss.

"I love you too, Siegfried."

She held his hands as she broke away.

"Shall we go together?" she said.

"I'd like that."

They met Helga at the *Kaffeehaus..* Frieda had told her beforehand that Siegfried had returned. Helga greeted him with a hug and a kiss. She looked older, he thought, but it wasn't from any physical aging. She was a mature woman now with a son, Hans-Peter, the Englishman's son, but the changes in her life seemed to have added to her inner beauty. The athletic physique was there too in spite of the signs of emaciation that was a common sight now. The warm smile was, however, touched by an indefinable sadness, yet there was strength in her face, a determination, all the more gratifying because it existed without any hint of rancour.

"It's wonderful to see you, Siegfried," she said, her blue eyes capturing his. She looked at Frieda.

"I'm happy, very happy," Frieda caught the question in Helga's stare. She felt proud to have Siegfried by her side.

Helga turned to Siegfried.

"I have to ask you about my brother . . . "

He shifted uneasily, even though he was prepared for the question.

"I'm sorry, Helga . . . "

"I'm comforted to know that you were his friend."

"We enjoyed good times together. I only regret I never saw him at the end."

"It must have been horrible?"

"Yes, it was, but I think Günther, even more than me, was proud to fight for the Fatherland."

He wished he hadn't revealed his own doubts.

"Günther was a true believer," Helga said. "I was often

bothered by his commitment, but I never doubted it. That was my brother . . . never willing to compromise, uncomfortable about any suggestion that the cause might have faults."

He wanted to say that he was the one who should have died, not Günther. That it was he that doubted and should have paid the price for that doubt.

"In a strange way, I'm comforted that he died without seeing the ultimate end." She spread out her arms to indicate the devastation around them.

"He died a hero," Siegfried said, but it sounded hollow, meaningless now.

"Yes, a hero. It's how I'll remember him." Helga toyed with her hair.

Siegfried ordered coffee, an interruption which broke the awkward silence. He could feel the relief; facing what needed to be said, even though it added to memories burdened by the years of conflict, had freed them to turn their attention to the present and the issues yet to be faced.

Siegfried looked up to find Helga staring, as if willing him to catch her gaze.

"I've been in touch with Peter. I wrote to him and then he phoned me. I hope to see him soon."

"You must be very happy?"

She gave a fleeting smile.

"I am."

She toyed with her hair again.

"The Royal Navy rescued you?"

"Yes, they were good to us."

"Frieda told me." Her face accentuated the determination he had observed earlier but now it had a tautness to it.

The coffee came and Helga cradled her cup in her hands.

"They killed my brother," she said.

"Yes."

"Can you understand that I cannot forgive that?"

Siegfried was trapped. He wondered where it was all

316

leading to, yet in his heart he knew and he was afraid.

"Peter, the father of my child," she intoned. "He was our enemy?"

Siegfried thought of his experiences with that enemy. He recalled his first realization, on the British destroyer, of the common bond which unites all sailors. He thought of the insanity of war. He searched for an answer to her hatred.

"He *happened* to be on the enemy side," he said, trying to stem the emotion that had possessed her, but she would have none of it.

"You're playing with words, Siegfried."

He became more determined.

"I fought that enemy," he said, "and when we had fought, we found our humanity again."

She seemed to drift out of her pool of disdain. Her eyes brightened and she regarded him with a suggestion of hope.

"What can I tell my child, Siegfried?"

"That he has a father . . . "

"I don't even know that. I. . . I . . ." Her voice failed and she collapsed in tears, her strength of will overcome by deeper emotions.

Siegfried watched helplessly as Frieda comforted her, observed now by a sea of faces, the outburst having attracted the attention of the other patrons.

"He must come back to me . . . "

"Let me take you home, Helga," said Frieda, passing him the keys of the flat, her eyes imploring him to go there and wait.

After they had left, Siegfried sat for a while, oblivious to the eyes of the customers at the adjoining tables. He wished he had met Peter. Wished he could assure himself that Peter was gifted with the same humanness that his rescuers had shown him.

At the house on the *Sunderstrasse*, Frieda sat on Helga's bed. Helga was calmer now, more ready to talk again about her fears.

"You were so happy when you talked to Peter . . . "

"I love him. It's when I think of Günther. The terrible conflict returns. I try to fight it." She stiffened. "I will fight it. Oh, Frieda. I love Peter so much."

Siegfried said goodbye to Frieda at the station the next day. He hated to leave but he had to get back to Neuengamme to honour a promise to his parents that he would return.

"I'll be back in two weeks," he said.

"Take care, my love."

He climbed aboard and stood in the open window and she held his hand.

"I love you," he said.

"I know," she said, and her knowing was all he needed to lighten the time of their parting.

2.

$\mathcal{I}$t was early March when Peter stood looking over the rail as the small cargo vessel entered the port of Hamburg. He had been given three weeks compassionate leave. The Captain of the Gratton had decided to allow the leave, leaving it to Peter to make his own way to Munich. He had made one stipulation which had the nature of an order, 'Wear your uniform at all times.' Nevertheless, Peter had packed his civvies as well.

While the effect of the uniform was to cause him to stand out above the predominance of army personnel, it had already proved beneficial in passing without hindrance through check points on the British side. How it would work when he disembarked at Hamburg was another matter entirely.

The complexities of entering Germany were soon overtaken by a more distressing preoccupation. By and large the British occupying authorities, although varying in their attitude to his intentions, did not obstruct him, in fact he was soon finding it relatively easy to obtain transportation in military vehicles, more often than not their drivers anxious to hear from the Royal Navy. It was the extent of the damage that far surpassed anything he had imagined. His route took him through many of the badly bombed cities. Hamburg was only one example of many. Most of the centre of the city had been reduced to rubble and among it were hordes of homeless people scavenging for food and shelter. The faces haunted him. Devoid of hope, emaciated by hunger, there was a hopelessness about it all that spoke only of approaching death.

"They're paying for their God-damned war," the driver spoke with bitterness. "And for Belsen and Dachau and all the other concentration camps."

"Is there no food?"

"Precious little, mate. But that's their problem, ain't it?"

"You think they should starve?"

"Christ, I dunno. We try to help. Especially the children. It's a God-damned mess."

That night, resting in an army billet, Peter couldn't sleep. Meeting with Helga had taken on an entirely different connotation. Could he really expect that circumstances would be any different in Munich? He saw himself being regarded as the victor coming to look upon the vanquished, hardly an atmosphere in which their love could be rekindled? And then there was the matter of her brother killed by the navy whose uniform he wore. He was glad he had the impulse to bring his civvies. Somehow he would have to change before Munich. He thought back to their telephone conversation and the excitement they shared, but the closer he moved towards Munich the more he was overtaken by doubts, not by any weakening of his determination to see her, but the growing recognition that they had both changed during these six years of madness. There was also the matter of her parents. In a Germany brought to her knees, as members of a proud and once prosperous family who had lost a son to the English and who had borne the shame of a daughter with an illegitimate son by a member of that same hated race, how could he expect anything from them but anger and rejection.

He got another lift to Hanover and then hitched a ride with a lorry going south. The driver, a happy-go-lucky corporal, Sam from Manchester, told him he'd take him to Munich. They reached the US Zone some way north of Nuremburg. There was a small guardhouse by the side of the road and the sergeant said, "Jesus. It's the Limey navy!" But he let them through, the Corporal having concocted some story about an important liaison meeting in Munich.

They slept in the lorry that night, hoping to get some sleep before entering Munich in the morning.

Peter, sitting beside Sam, scanned the view ahead. Dressed in civvies now, having accomplished an awkward change in the back of the lorry, he raised some eyebrows - his sports attire contrasted sharply with the army outfit worn by Sam - as they cadged cups of coffee and toast from an US Army kitchen on the outskirts of Munich. They also managed a wash and a shave

The buildings in the suburbs seemed to be devoid of damage and it wasn't until they reached the centre that the results of the bombings and the final assault took on the familiar signs of devastation. Nevertheless, the ruin seemed less severe than they had witnessed in the more northern cities.

There was one constant though, the faces of the dejected inhabitants. Often pathetically thin, they wandered aimlessly as though looking for lost homes or relatives, or for the most basic necessity of all - food.

It proved to be difficult to find the *Sunderstrasse* and even when they found it, to locate the house. It was a large house, looking shabby but little damaged, sitting on its own piece of ground as were the other houses on the street. Some houses, less fortunate, showed the effects of what must have been heavy raids, with shattered walls and missing roofs next to gaping holes in the ground and piles of rubble.

"Well, this looks like it, matey?"

Peter stirred but had little inclination to move. Now that he was here the immensity of the occasion pressed in on him. He fumbled with his jacket and smoothed his hair.

"Good luck, then."

The Corporal held out his hand and Peter grasped it.

"Thanks, thanks for everything."

The Corporal nodded and turned on the ignition. Peter alighted and stood gazing at the house. When he turned, the vehicle was almost out of sight.

He walked up to the door and rang the bell. There were footsteps, someone running, a loud cry, and the door opened.

Helga was there, restraining Hans.

"Sorry, he always runs . . ." She stopped. Her eyes widening with recognition. "Peter, *mein* Peter."

She collapsed into his arms.

He lost all of his apprehension about meeting her again after so long an absence and was swept up in a wave of emotion. For the first hour he couldn't leave her. He sat by her side in the living room, occasionally stroking her hair or kissing her, oblivious to the furtive peek by Eva who, seeing them so happy, slipped quietly back to the kitchen.

Helga had remembered him as somewhat reserved; now he was delightfully uninhibited, showering her with kisses and hugs. She felt loved as never before, experiencing a surge of sadness and joy that filled her heart with almost unbearable happiness.

Young Hans observed it all, his eyes filled with wonderment. At first he hung onto Helga, then gradually he eased towards his father, encouraged by his prompting.

"You're so big! . . . Peter struggled for a word, raising his hand to emphasize his height.

"Tall?" Helga suggested.

"Yes, Tall."

Hans faced his father; his eyes unblinking.

Helga watched.

For the first time since arriving at the house, Peter felt uncomfortable. During his long absence his thoughts were always on Helga. His son was not forgotten, but he had existed as an indistinct image, a very young baby who had not assumed an assertive role or personality. It was a shock to be greeted by a grown boy with a questioning stare.

"How are you, Hans . . ." The question sounded unnatural, a frantic grasp at words with which to break the silence.

322

Hans looked at his mother, seeking understanding.

"*Wie geht es dir?*"

He turned back to his father and smiled.

"*Mein Vater!*" he said.

Peter felt the blood rush to his cheeks. He was surprised by his embarrassment, but he took Hans-Peter's hands in his.

Helga reached forward and placed her hands on theirs.

The gesture brought a surge of pride as Peter felt the strength of the bond they shared. But the feeling was fleeting as other thoughts intruded. Hans-Peter, their son, his son, was still a stranger, a healthy growing boy whom he didn't know and who didn't know him, a son who spoke another language making it difficult to have an intimate conversation, even though Helga had made impressive progress in teaching him English.

As if sensing his anguish, Helga stood up.

"You must meet my *Grossmutter.*"

When Eva greeted him, he was immediately charmed by her. The wise and placid face put him at ease in the large house which must have survived so many memories. It was one of those buildings which had an atmosphere of permanence, as though it would survive whatever the whims of time decreed.

Helga showed him to a vacant bedroom at the rear of the house which overlooked a garden containing an apple orchard. The open area was largely overgrown except for a rectangular space which was, Helga said, given over to vegetables. She turned from the window.

"Eva wants you to have this room."

He placed his valise on the armchair by the window.

"Come," she said, before he could ask where she slept, "We must look at the rest of the house."

Throughout the tour, Peter sneaked sideways glances at her and once or twice their eyes met to trigger a smile. She looked thinner, he thought and there were signs of weariness in her face. But there was a trace of the familiar mischievousness in her eyes and the flaxen hair still reached down over her shoulders. Her clothes were worn and shabby but their condition failed to hide the strength of spirit that gave her a commanding presence.

The tour over, they arrived back in the kitchen.

"We're going for a walk *Oma*. Would you look after Hans?"

Eva nodded. Hans was already playing happily with what looked like stones from damaged buildings.

They walked hand in hand towards the *Kaffeehaus*, Alone at last, he squeezed her hand to show his happiness. She snuggled up closer and pecked at his cheek.

As they walked, the signs of war, destruction, and surrender created a different reality. When they had met before, peace was still intact and war an unknown prospect. People lived with apprehension but not with misery and defeat. Now, here in a country once full of a belief in its impregnability, there was only material and human devastation.

A US Army jeep speeded by and there were whistles and catcalls. Helga stiffened.

"Some of them are nice," she said, "but others . . . "

He drew her closer.

Sitting with weak cups of coffee in the remains of the *Kaffeehaus*, they began to share experiences.

"I wasn't sure I would ever see you again," Helga said.

"I think I gave up for a while . . . "

"There was someone else?"

"There were others. It was madness. Live for the day."

"I . . . " She looked down at her cup. "There was a lieutenant in the *Wehrmacht*. I think he was killed."

Peter took a sip of his coffee.

"In my dreams you always came back to me. I had to believe you would be waiting."

Tears came to her eyes.

"It was difficult. When my *Bruder* was killed. I hated you then. There is still some of that resentment. You have to be patient Peter. I do love you but it is hard to forget the brutality." She waved her arms. "All this destruction."

He felt a twinge of guilt but the rightness of his cause overcame it.

"It was not what we wished."

Her face flushed, but she waited, toying with her cup, taking a sip. Putting her cup down she said.

"We are all victims."

"No one really wins, Helga."

She shook her head.

"My *Bruder* was proud to be in the *Kriegsmarine*. Proud to serve on the *Schlosstern* . . ."

Peter stared in disbelief. The last thing he could ever have imagined was this. He felt the blood draining from his face and his heart began to race. For a moment he felt sure he was going to faint.

"Are you all right?"

"I . . . I . . ." He stood up and walked around and then feeling a little calmer he sat down.

"I was serving in one of the destroyers which helped to sink the *Schlosstern*."

She closed her eyes, not saying anything. It was as though she wanted to blot him out, remove him from her life now, this instant.

"I'm sorry. I didn't know," he said.

"Siegfried was on board the *Schlosstern*," she said. "He was a survivor."

"Siegfried?"

"My friend, Frieda's fiancee."

God he thought. Siegfried must hate me too.

She must have read his thoughts for, looking him straight in the eyes, she said, "Siegfried said that the Royal Navy treated him well."

"I don't know what to say," he said.

"It's difficult, isn't it Peter?"

"How can you feel . . . anything but hate?"

She leaned over and touched his hand.

"I wanted *Peter* to have his *Vater* back . . . and I have my wish."

That night Peter experienced a distressing dream. He was on the deck of a ship, kneeling over a sailor lying on the deck. He had his hands around the fellow's neck, a German sailor, and he was choking him. Helga was standing nearby and shouting.

"Peter! Peter . . . don't . . . It's Günther . . . he's my brother."

But he ignored her pleas, shouting.

"He's the enemy! The enemy! Don't you understand . . . if I don't kill him, he'll kill me?"

And then he stopped. Helga was pointing a gun at his head.

"Stop! Or I'll shoot," she said, but he ignored her and she fired.

A door banged and he sat up in bed. His heart was racing and he was bathed in perspiration.

Helga rushed to his side and hugged him.

"I had this dream. I was killing your brother and you stopped me."

"Oh, Peter, Peter, you must not torture yourself."

She went into the bathroom and brought a towel and a glass of water and she daubed his head. He drank quickly, relieving the dryness in his throat and then, seized by desire, he drew her down onto the bed.

When he awoke, her hand was lying across his chest and her face was turned towards him. He remembered those nights before, in that small town across the border from Strasbourg, when he had savoured her beauty as she slept, as he did now. He lay contented as the early morning light announced its presence, and his thoughts drifted to back to his dream and a contradiction he was unaware of, or if aware of, he had long since dismissed. The phrase 'fraternizing with the enemy' came back suddenly, prompting questions.

How does one define an enemy? Is it someone who is hated because of birth, race or beliefs? Sort of like saying, I disagree, so you are my enemy? You threaten my life, my property, my country, therefore you are my enemy and only your death can remove the threat? Is it a simple credo for all peoples, civilized or uncivilized - there being no distinction when it came to deciding enemies? To deal with an enemy one needed hate, aggression, superiority, a reason to kill, so as to lift killing from murder, to make it respectable, a legitimate act of self-defence, bravery even.

Of course, it required a rejection of humanness, an enemy had to be inhuman, a beast, a premeditated killer. But this surely was a matter of perspective. One's own position had to be right, upheld by the State and the Church, then one could kill without fear of guilt. Each side, in reality, the enemy of the other. Each side carried the hate and aggression necessary to be an effective enemy.

An enemy became human in defeat. You saw faces like your own. Fears like your own. Pain like your own. Humanness was still there if you could experience defeat. And you could share the humanness you regained. The Royal Navy which rescued survivors saved human beings from death. The enemy was gone and in its place were human beings in need of care.

Peter felt saddened. If only Günther had survived.

Helga, awake now, leaned over and kissed him and he smoothed her hair. He held the blue eyes in his, recapturing the past they had shared.

"I love you, Helga."

"I love you, *mein* Peter."

327

"We must be married, Helga?"

She kissed him, her tongue exploring his mouth, and they made love again. When he awoke, she was fully dressed, standing by the bed.

"Shall we try and find some breakfast?"

He sat up.

"How did you get into the room last night?"

She pointed to the connecting door behind her.

"I sleep in there. You see; Eva thinks of everything."

3.

$\mathcal{E}$ach day, Peter accompanied Helga in the search for food. It was a long and frustrating process. Some days would be more successful than others, but most meals would be bowls of watery soup and dry bread. Coffee was a luxury and the grains were used over and over. The weather was cold and damp, often with wind and driving rain, but through it all Helga managed to remain optimistic.

"It will soon be spring," she would say. "Then we can plant things in the garden."

Peter, all too aware of the toll it was imposing on everyone's health, especially the young children like Hans-Peter, was determined to act. Besides, time was running out. He had to return to his ship.

It was on the third day, when they had stopped at the *Kaffeehaus*, that he revealed his intentions.

"We must be married, Helga. I want you to return to England with me - as my wife."

She was quiet for a while. It was if he had proposed some sort of impossible dream, then the tears ran down her face and she grasped his hands in hers, but she didn't speak.

Will you marry me, Helga?"

"*Ja*, yes. I will, Peter."

"And come to England with Hans?"

At that, she released his hands and took a sip of coffee.

"I worry about *Oma*, about Eva, she is old now, she cannot be left alone."

He expected her reaction, yet he hoped it was something they could resolve. It also renewed his concern about her parents who, being absent, had not, thus far, blighted their reunion.

"Will your parents object?"

"My *Vater* will, and *Mutter* will support him." She became pensive. " My *Bruder's* death. He cannot forgive that. He has accepted Hans, but not so completely that he has forgiven me and, if we marry . . ." Helga tensed. "But I intend to marry you, Peter . . . " She stopped, as though regretting her impulsiveness. "I will tell them after we are married."

"Are you sure?" Peter, overjoyed by her reaction, was still troubled by the implications of a break with her parents.

"They're in Blankenese now?"

"*Ja*, but they also spend time in Neuengamme at Siegfried's familys' farm, food being scarce in the Hamburg area."

Helga fell silent avoiding his eyes. When she turned to him again, her face bore a serious expression.

"If we go to England . . ." She stopped, as if gauging his reaction. "If we go to England, where will we live?"

It was an issue that continued to haunt him and it was made more difficult by his uncertainty about being released from the navy.

"I wanted it to be on the south coast. My parents' old home."

Helga appeared confused.

"Your father will agree?"

Peter was unprepared for the question. He looked away, trying to collect his thoughts, the memories of the difficulties with his father crowding back.

"He died . . .'

"Died?" She was astonished.

"Yes."

"Oh, Peter . . . When?"

"A year ago . . . it was quite sudden . . . pneumonia."

She took her hands in his.

"I'm so sorry."

"He had a full life . . .'

He stopped, uncertain how to deal with the contradiction

- the loss of a father who was bitterly opposed to Helga. But it was not a real issue now; it only existed as his own guilt, and he shrugged off the thought.

"Living in the old house, well, it's not too practical at the moment, my being in the Navy, the ship being in the north."

He brightened a little.

"I've talked to my friend, Mike, and his wife Joan. They live near Birkenhead, where my ship is. They'd like you to stay with them. Then I can visit you."

Helga toyed with her cup, avoiding his gaze, looking down at what was left of her coffee.

"You'll still be in the navy?"

"Yes, but it shouldn't be long . . ."

She looked up, her clear blue eyes holding his.

"Peter, I want to be with you . . . but wouldn't it be best if I stayed here until you have been released?"

"I . . ." He wanted to try and reassure her, but she was continuing.

"We also have Hans to think about. He will be unhappy away from his friends. He is still trying to get to know you. It will be hard. We both need you with us, to help us. It will be a new country Peter."

Damn the navy, he thought. It's going to ruin everything. I've got to get out. Somehow, I've got to get out,

"Peter. I love you. We will be married. Then we can work things out."

She leaned over and kissed him.

"I love you too," he said.

They finished their coffees and made their way home. Although the matter of her going to England was still unresolved, it seemed neither the time nor place to pursue it. Marriage was the first step. He glanced at Helga walking beside him, head down, deep in thought. He squeezed her hard and she smiled and drew closer.

They were married in a registry office at the beginning of the following week. Eva, Frieda and Siegfried were present, Siegfried having arrived from Neuengamme the day before. Everyone was dressed in their customary clothes. Frieda, whose easy manner delighted Peter, had managed to find some flowers for him to give to his bride.

Afterwards, they all walked back to the house on the *Sunderstrasse* where even the meagre lunch failed to dampen the joy of the occasion. And they talked and shared experiences and Peter soon developed an easy rapport with Siegfried.

It was the next day, when Helga and Frieda had gone for a walk with Hans, that Peter and Siegfried had an opportunity to talk. It was a dullish day with occasional glimpses of sunlight filtering through the worn curtains in the living room. They had brewed a fresh pot of coffee and were sitting comfortably on the sofa.

Siegfried took a sip from his cup.

"Strange, is it not. We meet as friends?"

Peter looked at the strong face, lined as his must be with the strain of war.

"It was all so ridiculous."

Siegfried nodded his head and a sadness grew between them.

"Six years of our lives . . . gone." Siegfried's voice wavered. "The best years . . . for what?"

"So many lives lost too?"

"We both lost friends . . . young friends, just like us with our innocence."

"Did you believe in Hitler?"

"*Ja* . . . I believed. The *Führer* was like a God to me . . . tc us."

"Helga told me . . . when we first met, in England. She told me how good the *Führer* was to Germany. It was hard for me to understand."

"I hated the English . . ."

Peter thought of bursting starshell piercing the Arctic night.

"We were never in doubt about your courage," he said. "We knew you would fight hard. I was scared when we attacked the *Schlosstern*."

"We thought we might escape. Then it became certain it was no use. *Mein Gott*, it was terrifying."

Peter was silent.

"I was below. My shipmates told me we had been hit." Siegfried got up and looked out of the window, parting the curtains, as if peering back towards another time and place. After a while, as Peter remained seated, he left the window and returned to the sofa.

He held Peter with a friendly stare.

"The Royal Navy rescued me." He paused. "And I discovered that all sailors have a common bond. We're all humbled by the sea."

"It must never happen again, Siegfried?"

"No . . . never."

Peter sipped his coffee.

"What was Günther like?"

"He was very committed. We all were." His face lightened. "We were good friends. We had good times together . . . He didn't like Helga's relationship with you though."

"Helga hasn't talked much about him."

"It was hard for her. They were very close. He was harsh about you and that hurt. It all changed though when Hans was born. He adored the baby . . . and he wanted you to come back . . . for Helga's sake."

Peter toyed with his cup, trying to deny the tears forming behind his eyes.

"You've all been so good to me."

"I'm glad you found Helga. Glad the war didn't destroy what you have."

Peter brushed a hand across his eyes.

Siegfried cradled his cup. "Have you met her parents?"

Peter shook his head. "They will be difficult?"

"*Ja* . . . but Helga's very determined."

"They've been staying with you?"

"*Ja.* I don't think Rolf will approve of your marriage. Ilse would, but she won't oppose Rolf."

"Just what Helga said."

"Rolf is a very proud man. Very strict and uncompromising. He was never a *Nazi* but he did believe in duty and responsibility. Helga's pregnancy was a bitter blow and then when Günther died I think he felt it was the penalty for Helga's indiscretion. And the fact that you were in the navy . . ."

"I would like to meet him."

"For your sake and Helga's, I'd give it time. Perhaps he will find the compassion to forgive. I know he loves his daughter very much. It's a feeling I get when I hear him talk to his wife, nothing specific, just a sense that under the tough exterior there is a caring father."

"Thank you for telling me this. It helps a great deal."

4.

*A*s the days passed, bringing Peter closer to the time he would need to depart to rejoin his ship, a discernible tension gripped him. He had to know if she was coming with him. It was after Helga had put Hans to bed that Peter decided to broach the matter again.

"I've given it much thought." Helga anticipating his question, spoke before him. "I think it's too risky to take Hans away from his *Grossmutter* unless we can all be together. We are a family now, a family getting to know each another. It will take time. We must do it together. You must be with us. I want you to be my husband every day, not just when the Navy decides you can have leave."

Although he had hoped for a different answer, in his heart he knew she was right. It was not difficult to place himself in her position. Going to a strange country, a country which had only a short time ago been at war with them, was a daunting prospect. He needed to be with them. Be by her side to help. It wasn't just a case of becoming a newly married family growing and adjusting together. She and Peter would be in a country that was still hostile to Germans and all that they had stood for. No matter how like them individual Germans might be, there was a collective guilt that fell upon the German race, a guilt that had to be confronted. The people of Britain had faced a determined enemy imbued with an ideology that had caused death and suffering to millions of people. Adding to the complication of postwar healing was the stark revelation about the concentration camps. He could demonstrate his love for his new wife and his son, but he couldn't guarantee the sort of reception they would encounter in England. He had to proceed cautiously and with the deepest concern for the welfare of his family.

He reached over and took her hands in his.

"I'm very sad . . . but you are right."

"I don't want you to go. But it is best . . ."

"Yes, it is best."

5.

*W*hen Peter arrived back aboard the Gratton, he presented his request to be discharged from the service, arguing that his personal situation could no longer be reconciled with life in the navy. The trouble was that this did not, in the minds of the Admiralty, constitute grounds for his release. Unless he was physically or mentally impaired, he could not expect to break his - or more correctly, the promise his parents had made - that he would serve for twelve years from the age of eighteen. Consequently, to officialdom, he had at least two more years to serve.

Mike was demobilized in the summer, returning to his old job in Post Office telephones, an event that intensified Peter's longing to be released. He visited Mike and Joan as often as he could, usually at weekends and, if he was lucky, on the occasional weekday. Mike and Joan were wonderful, helping him to keep in touch with Helga by telephone. But as the weeks and months dragged on Helga's frustration increased.

"Don't worry, Helga. Soon I'll be out of the navy . . . "

"But when, Peter?" She was angry now. "It's always soon. I don't know what it means. Soon, soon, always soon."

He could tell by her reaction that she knew that he didn't know. That it might be months, maybe years?

"Tell me honestly. Do you really know?"

"No, no, I don't."

He was dejected. Surely she understood that he was doing his best?

"If I'm not out by Christmas, I'll desert. I'll come back to Germany."

"Peter. I'm sorry. I don't want you to do anything foolish. It's just . . . I need you, Peter. I love you."

"I love you too."

The Gratton, left the builder's yards and started her sea trials in late September, completing them and moving to Portland. This had one major advantage inasmuch as Peter could get home more frequently. He installed a phone so that he could continue to converse with Helga. Nevertheless, it was a difficult period for both of them. It was already clear that he would not be able to rejoin Helga by Christmas as he had pledged. He postponed thoughts of desertion because there was a good chance that he would be released, under a special 'Buyout Plan' early in the New Year. He phoned on Christmas Day.

"I'm worried," Helga said. "My *Bruder* Günther promised to be home for Christmas . . . he didn't come. He never came home at all."

He was alarmed by her recollection. It seemed to open all the old wounds, Günther's death at the hands of the Royal Navy and the hatred she admitted she still felt towards him as the relentless enemy.

"It's not like that. I'm certain that I'll be with you within a few months . . ."

"A few months! Peter, are you trying? Do you want to see us?"

"Of course I do. I want to get it right. As you've said, it's important we reunite here as a family."

"I will come there. I cannot wait."

"We agreed, Helga. Please, just a little longer."

There was silence and for a moment he thought she would hang up.

"Don't . . . Look, Helga, I will get more leave and come over?"

"*Nein, Nein.* You are right. I must wait."

"Helga, I love you."

She was sobbing now.

"*Ja*, Peter. I know."

338

She hung up, leaving him to wonder what she really felt, compounding all his worries about realizing a dream they had fashioned so long ago.

6.

Peter boarded the train in Portsmouth. Officially released from the Royal Navy, he still wore his uniform. Up on the rack above his head was a cardboard box containing his new wardrobe. A grey suit, a white shirt and a red tie, socks, underwear, and a pair of black shoes. He had discovered that a demob outfit was like his first navy issue, specific sizes and no tailored adjustments. It all came down to the fact that if he was to eventually get something which he liked he would have to buy it himself - finances and clothing coupons permitting. At the moment, everything felt loose on his slender frame.

"Glad to be out of that lot."

He recognized the face of the fellow opposite him. He had been in the same queue for kitting-out in the large hanger-like building. An assembly line, that's what it was - in one end in the service, and out at the other end in sloppy, standard-size civilian issues.

"How about you?" he persisted when Peter didn't answer.

Peter was taciturn. He didn't feel the comment warranted a definitive response.

"I'm Larry Olpen," he said.

Peter took his outstretched hand.

"Peter Gray."

"Pleased to meet you, Peter."

He continued.

"Kept my old job, they 'ave . . . waiting for me to get back . . . the old firm."

"What sort of work do you do?"

"Accounting . . . "

"Going to be quite a change. Being on civvy street?" said Peter.

"The Missus is happy and the kids, well . . . babies when I joined. Be hard to recognize now."

Peter thought of Helga and his son. He would phone her as soon as he got home. He imagined her receiving the news. At last it had happened. He smiled, a contented smile, and then realized that Larry was eyeing him. He felt he should be making a better effort at conversation.

"How long have you been married . . . if you don't mind me asking?"

"Course not . . . Got spliced at the beginning of the war . . . nineteen thirty nine. Sally and me. Met at a dance . . . the Hammersmith Palais."

The information hit him like a blow to the stomach. Oh yes, he knew all about dance halls. The image of Sarah was suddenly before him. He recoiled at the thought of the sexual gymnastics.

"Too draughty mate? . . . looked like you shivered?" Larry reached for the window.

"No, I just thought . . . "

"Someone walking over your grave like?"

"Perhaps."

"You married mate?"

Peter nodded absentmindedly, and his new acquaintance, getting bored with Peter's reclusiveness, searched amongst his things and found a newspaper. Peter felt relieved as the paper effectively covered Larry's face. He could read the front page headlines, *Thousands Returning to No Jobs,* they said.

As soon as Peter arrived home he phoned Helga. She answered quickly, leading Peter to speculate that she must have been anticipating his call.

"You were waiting?"

"Peter. I wait every day. Is it today, the good news?"

"Yes! Yes!" He succumbed to the excitement which followed the months of despair.

"Oh, Peter! It has happened. I'm so happy. When will you be here?"

"Well, I have to . . ."

"But you are out of the Navy?"

"Yes, It's just that I want to check out a job first. My friend Mike has given me a good connection."

She gave a long sigh. "How long, Peter?"

"A week or so. As soon as I can."

"You're at home now?"

"Just arrived."

"I love you, Peter."

"Love you."

"Come quickly, we're waiting."

"I will."

It was a personal contact, given to him by Mike, that lead to an interview in London and a job starting in October. It was to fill a vacancy occurring in a radio transmitting station some fifteen miles north of his home on the coast. He could barely believe his good luck. There was little else in the area which would have suited his experience or offered so much potential. Not that he was fully qualified, but a training course was to be provided and ex-service personnel were being given a preference.

So, he had his wish. The chance to be with his family and to be able to stay in his parents' old house on the coast. Within a couple of weeks he had acquired a motorcycle. It would facilitate a more efficient means of getting to and from the remote location; the transmitting station was situated on a hill in the rolling Dorset countryside.

He was ready to return to Germany.

7.

Peter's return to Germany was essentially a duplication of the first trip except that, not being in uniform, he had to resort to civilian transportation. The ship docked in Hamburg again and he took the train south. It was a long and tedious journey. The effects of the bombing and the shelling were everywhere and the rail system had been a prime target.

When at last, he reached the house on the *Sunderstrasse* and collapsed into Helga's arms, he realized that he was desperately in need of sleep. Nevertheless, the excitement of the reunion kept him awake for a few hours.

Helga had already planned for the journey to England. Eva, as usual, had countered Helga's doubts about leaving her by inviting Frieda to stay with her. 'And Siegfried can come and stay for as long as he wants,' she had said.

Hans-Peter's impending separation from his grandmother was a much more difficult problem. Both Helga and Eva had explained what was to happen and Hans had apparently taken the news quite calmly at first, but when Helga announced that his father would soon be arriving to take them to their new home it provoked an outburst of crying that was only silenced by a promise that he would be able to talk to his grandmother on the telephone.

The night before they were due to leave, Helga told Peter that she intended to phone her mother to inform her of their intended departure and, more dramatically to tell her that she was married. The news that she had not told her mother took him by surprise. While he knew that she had steadfastly refused to communicate with her mother immediately after their marriage and before he left for England, the matter had not occupied his thoughts since then. It had slipped from his mind, an issue that he assumed had been resolved.

Predictably, Ilse was furious that she hadn't been told and insisted that they stop off in Hamburg. Helga argued against such a meeting, pointing out that if Rolf came, the sight of Peter would prove too much for him. In any event, Peter had intended to try and avoid Hamburg, returning to England via Bremerhaven, but such enquiries as he was able to make pointed to Hamburg as a more logical departure point, there being more shipping using this route.

On the day of their departure, Eva accompanied them to the station. It was an emotional parting, perplexing for all of them, but especially difficult for Hans-Peter. He loved his great-grandmother and that love was reciprocated. He resisted leaving her, his crying rising to shrieks of despair as they boarded the train.

The journey from Munich to Hamburg was even slower than Peter's trip south. There were frequent stops and many diversions. It was two and a half days before they reached their destination.

Weary and disoriented, having had little sleep and precious little to eat, they were moving down the platform when Helga spotted her mother. She seemed barely able to stand and there was a wild look in her eyes as she tried desperately to identify her daughter among the milling crowds. Helga called out and she turned and rushed towards them.

Ilse held out her arms and Helga fell into them. Hans-Peter hung onto his mother's skirt casting backward glances towards his father.

"What have you done, Helga?" The tears rolled down Ilse's face. "Why are you doing this?"

Peter stood helplessly, watching the outpouring of emotion. He felt isolated and responsible, forced to remain silent lest his intervention aggravate the hostility her mother felt. Helga was quick to confront her.

"Peter and I love each other. You've always known that. Now we are married."

Ilse looked towards Peter, her eyes were glaring and he waited for the onslaught.

"You . . ." Words failed her and Helga motioned her to a bench.

"*Mutter*. You must calm yourself. It is a happy time. Hans-Peter is with his *Vater*."

"Rolf must be told." Ilse had calmed a little but when she turned again towards Peter, her eyes were filled with resentment and he felt sure she was poised to leap up and spit in his face.

"*Mutter*," Helga was saying. "I'm not a child. It's my decision."

Peter walked forward. If he was to assert his position, the time was now.

"I love your daughter. Why else would I have waited as she has waited for me. I intend to look after her and my son."

Ilse looked up at him. Looked into his eyes as if searching for some sign of his sincerity. Then she turned to Helga again.

"You must all come home to Blankenese."

"*Mutter*. We have no time. We have to get to the docks immediately."

Ilse insisted on accompanying them to the docks. It was midmorning when they arrived. The next ship to England was leaving for Harwich in two days. Whether they could obtain a passage, depended on the Captain. It was a Dutch ship that had brought food and supplies and would be returning empty to England. The Royal Navy Lieutenant, acting on behalf of the Military Port Authority, saw no difficulty with their papers. Peter had his passport and the marriage certificate. As well they had Hans-Peter's birth certificate.

"Let's see if we can find the Captain," he said.

Ilse stayed behind.

The Captain was in his cabin. He appeared somewhat taken aback when he was presented with eager passengers.

"I don't have space," he said. "This is a cargo vessel."

He was a formidable character, heavy set, with a well-trimmed beard. He looked as though he had been at sea forever and Peter couldn't help thinking of his likeness to *Kapitain Hopp* of the *Joachim*.

Nothing was said. The Lieutenant conveyed the impression that he was not about to argue.

The Captain looked at Helga and then at Peter. He leaned back in his chair.

"It's important you get to England?"

"Yes sir. I want to take my wife and child home."

The Captain held out his hand and Peter gave him the papers.

If he had any opinions, it was impossible to deduce them. He gave the papers back to Peter.

"I'll take you," he said. "We sail the day after tomorrow, at noon."

They worked out a price for the passage and Peter paid him.

They rejoined Ilse, sharing the good news.

"Now that you have to wait, you'll have to come to Blankenese with me," she said, unable to hide her look of triumph.

8.

Peter, hand in hand with his son, followed Helga and her mother as they walked up the drive to the house in Blankenese. The sun had come out and the wind had dropped, but it did nothing to lessen Peter's nervousness. Meeting Ilse had been traumatic enough, but it paled before the imminent meeting with Helga's father. It conjured up the kind of apprehensiveness he had felt at the prospect of action with the *Schlosstern*.

Ilse introduced Peter to their faithful housekeeper, Minna, who greeted them at the door and took their coats and luggage.

Rolf didn't appear and Ilse took them to the living room on the second floor. Then she excused herself, leaving Helga and Peter alone for the first time since their arrival in Hamburg.

"*Mutter's* gone to get *Vater* out of the cupola. It's his lookout point on top of the roof. It's where he watches the ships steaming up and down the Elbe."

Peter felt disheartened. All his plans were falling apart. He hadn't counted on meeting her parents so soon, fearing that they would find some way to frustrate his intentions. After the years of waiting there were to be more delays. And to make matters worse there was the risk that Helga might be swayed by a concern for her parents' welfare, just as she had been for Eva's. Besides, they were against the match from the very beginning. He had little time to ponder the matter as Ilse, followed by Rolf, were descending the stairs.

Peter stood up.

"My husband, Rolf," Ilse said.

Peter looked at the tall trim figure, the weathered face and the grey hair, only to be held by the piercing blue eyes. He exuded an unmistakable authority and Peter felt ill at ease.

Rolf extended his hand and Peter took it. For a brief

moment he was reminded again of his first encounter with the Captain of the *Joachim*.

"Let's go to the study."

It seemed more like a command than an invitation.

"Ilse will join us," he added.

They sat around facing each other. Each of them occupying an individual chair. Peter grew more agitated and it was the arrival of Minna with coffee which offered a welcome interlude.

Rolf's first question was not what Peter expected.

"You served on a destroyer that helped sink the *Schlosstern?*"

"Yes, the Sandrake."

"Did you pick up survivors? Siegfried told me a destroyer rescued him."

"No, We suffered damage and casualties."

"You lost crew members?"

"Yes, eleven dead and the same number wounded."

Peter toyed with his hands.

"I'm sorry. Your son . . ."

He was stopped by Rolf's resentful stare.

Rolf Jansen looked at the tall, lanky, fair-haired boy and thought of his son, Günther. Why was this person spared the death that came to my son? The question tormented him He was the enemy that killed him. He is the *Engländer* who caused my daughter to conceive an illegitimate child. How can I forgive?

He took a sip of coffee and his hand was shaking.

It was in this very room that he had argued with Günther. Günther who disliked his misgivings about the policies of the *Third Reich*, Günther who had enthusiastically accepted the doctrines of the *Führer*. What a waste it had all been. So much suffering. But Günther was gone and now he had a son-in-law.

"You have left the Navy?"

"Yes."

"You have employment?"

"I start in October."

"How will you look after my daughter and grandson?"

Peter became irritated by his questioning. Was he not the enemy he had spent the last six years of his life to defeat? All right, Peter thought, he had lost a son, but I have lost family and friends. Besides, there was an arrogance that was unacceptable.

"I intend to pursue a career in electrical engineering." The words were uttered with a forcefulness which reflected his anger and his determination to resist the growing feeling of intimidation.

Ilse, appearing to sense the beginnings of a confrontation, stirred uneasily.

"Perhaps, Peter and his new family would like a rest?"

Peter wasn't sure if it was sarcasm or a hint to Rolf to accept the situation and find some compassion for his daughter, if not for his son-in-law. Nevertheless, Peter was quick to accept the opportunity.

"Yes, we're feeling quite tired."

Helga and Peter were given Helga's old room, with an adjoining room for Hans-Peter. They had rested in the afternoon, saying little and soon dozing on the comfortable bed. Dinner was quite formal after the relaxed atmosphere of Eva's house. The conversation was polite but restrained with Ilse doing most of the talking. She mentioned the kindness of Siegfried's parents and how they had stayed in Neuengamme for over a month after leaving Munich.

After dinner they sat in the living room with cups of freshly brewed coffee.

"Tonight's dinner wouldn't have been possible without the generosity of Siegfried's family." Ilse looked at Rolf, seeking his agreement, but he was looking towards the window, out to the Elbe, reduced now, in the gathering darkness, to the lights of buoys marking the channel.

"I think there'll be rain tomorrow," he said.

Peter was moved to venture a question.

"Sir," he began. "Do you still run the Shipping Company?"

Rolf turned sharply, holding Peter's stare, giving the impression that it was an impertinent question.

"I intend to rebuild my company," he said, proudly. "The war only interrupted my operations."

An uncomfortable silence fell over the group and Rolf stood and moved over to the piano. He lifted the cover off the keys and started playing.

Peter whispered to Helga. "Beethoven, isn't it?"

"*Ja*," she said.

They went up to their room early. Peter sat beside Helga as she read to Hans-Peter. Then she put him to bed and they were on their own.

Helga glanced at Peter and smiled. "You are disheartened by my parents, aren't you?"

"It's your father. He seems so angry."

She looked at the once boyish face, lined now by the stress of war. He had matured and she liked the result. If ever she had any doubts about her love for him, they had left her. She took his hand, stroking it gently, regarding the contours of his skin, speaking in a low voice.

"My *Vater* is still trying to deal with the loss of a son. He is not sure how he feels, only that he is possessed by sadness. He feels guilty and angry and very alone. When you asked the question about his Company, all he could think about was the loss of his male heir. I know how he thinks. He is a very caring *Vater*, but he finds it difficult to deal with his emotions."

"I was very foolish. Very insensitive. I shouldn't have asked . . ."

"No matter what you may have asked, it would have

350

probably brought a similar response."

"It reminds me of my father. I wish he could have shared his deeper feelings."

Helga felt the blood rushing to her face. She wanted him, her husband. She kissed him and they rolled over on the bed.

"Don't let this house intimidate you either," she said, "No one will hear a thing."

As their departure approached, Peter and Helga attended to their packing. Not that there was much to pack, Peter had travelled light and Helga had selected a minimum of clothes, but with Han's things as well, it still represented a considerable bulk to carry, as they had found out during the train trip north. As well, returning to Blankenese had added to Helga's personal items. There were the various extras that Ilse pressed on Helga. A few toys and sweaters for Hans, and for Helga, a skirt, blouse and shoes. The end result was another extra heavy suitcase.

On the day of their departure there was a mood of tenseness. While Ilse fussed, Rolf carried a disinterested air. Meals had already become polite exchanges of little significance, and breakfast that morning was no exception. Except for the constant stream of questions from Hans, which even Rolf couldn't ignore, little was said.

When it came time to leave, Rolf declined Ilse's suggestion that he come with them to the docks. He hugged Helga, and Peter was sure he could see the tears forming in his eyes. He picked up young Hans - tickling him and bringing forth a merry chuckle. He stroked his hair and let him down gently. It was a revealing moment, the first occasion on which he had seen Rolf display any emotion. Then, as if overcoming a compelling reluctance, he turned to Peter and shook his hand.

"*Auf Wiedersehen,*" he said.

Peter, caught off guard, managed a nod, and Rolf turned,

heading back to the house, not looking back.

Ilse accompanied them to the docks. It was a dreary day with low clouds and rain. A strong wind added to the discomfort of having to walk to the departure point. It was a tearful parting on the quay, and when they arrived on board they all waved to her from high in the stern, away from the bustle of last-minute departure preparations.

They left just after noon, tugs easing them away from the quay. Ilse remained standing and waving, a small figure, becoming smaller as they turned and headed down the Elbe.

They remained on deck, determined to locate the house in Blankenese, confident that the ship would be spotted by Rolf. It was not difficult to locate the large house and the rooftop cupola and they waved in the expectation that they would see him. But they were too far away to be sure and without binoculars they saw no signs of life. They turned away sadly as Blankenese disappeared astern.

By the time they had reached the North Sea the wind had reached gale force and the empty ship plunged and rolled. Yet for Peter and Helga it felt good to be at sea again. Even Hans-Peter was immune to seasickness.

Their cabin was small but comfortable and while most meals were brought to them, on the second day, the day before they expected to arrive, they had dinner with the Captain. He turned out to be a lively fellow, one of those professional sailors who had been hardened and mellowed by the sea. He had a sort of rough-hewn sensitivity that avoided awkward questions and which kept the conversation to life at sea as he had known it. But he avoided any reference to the war, beguiling them with tales of his experiences in the Dutch East Indies before the war when he was a young seaman learning his trade.

Hans-Peter was excited by all the new experiences. Arriving in England he listened to the strange new sounds, gazing eagerly out of the train window as they headed to London and then westwards, to the Dorset coast.

9.

By September, four months after arriving in England, Peter's new family was well settled into the house on the south coast. In a few days' Hans-Peter was to start his studies at the local school. Helga was in the living room at the back of the house. Outside the window, the larch tree, which Peter had planted as a young boy, sported a swing hung from one of the lower boughs. But it wasn't in use today, Hans-Peter was working with his father in the garden. They were putting the finishing touches to a playhouse which they had worked on during the summer. It was close to the hedge at the side of the property. Next to it was a large rectangle of turned earth, the site of the old vegetable garden which Peter planned to replant in the spring.

Helga sat in the bay window stitching the hem of a curtain, one of the many changes she was making to the windows on the lower floor. Her efforts were prompted by the discovery of the material in an old trunk in the upstairs bedroom, probably a project which Peter's mother had failed to finish before her untimely demise.

Helga was happy. Since arriving in England she had enjoyed her husband's undivided attention for four months. It had been a time of renewal and adjustment, going back to the places she remembered from her prewar visits on board the *Joachim*. As well, it had been a time to get to know the small town, becoming familiar with the complexities of shopping with ration cards and clothing coupons. And there was the sheer delight of having their own house, to be able to enjoy a personal intimacy with her husband uninhibited by the presence of others. Above all, there was the confirmation of their love for each other. The more she had got to know Peter, the more she had celebrated his gift for caring, his thoughtfulness and his concerns about the difficulties of adapting to life in England, a subject soon to be sorely tested.

Helga got up and put on the coffee. She opened the window and called.

"Coffee's brewing. There's lemonade too."

Satisfied that her husband and son had heard, she returned to her sewing. There were things she had to discuss with Peter, urgent things, and maybe this was the morning to do it?

Hans-Peter came in first for some lemonade and a biscuit. He didn't stay long as he wanted to take his snack to the playhouse. Peter washed his hands and joined her.

"Will they fit on the existing rails?" Peter looked at the curtains.

"They'll be the same size as the old ones. It's just that the others are worn and faded."

Peter took a chocolate digestive from the plate in front of him.

"Is everything OK? You look serious."

"Some people aren't very friendly."

Peter was puzzled.

"Even people you introduce me to . . . they show hostility when they discover my nationality."

"Are you sure?"

"It's worse when I'm on my own. Sometimes people cross the street to avoid me."

It was the kind of reaction that Peter had always worried about, but until this moment he had assumed it hadn't materialized. He had no doubt though that Helga's concerns were legitimate.

"Why didn't you tell me?"

"I didn't want to get you upset."

"What about our next-door neighbours?"

"Even them, at first. Now I feel there's more of an

acceptance."

At least that was some sort of progress, he thought, but he was angry, annoyed that his countrymen were upsetting his wife, particularly when she was by herself.

"It makes me very lonely." Helga's voice was tremulous now. "I get homesick for Eva and Frieda."

He took her hands in his.

"I'm sorry," he said. "You must tell me these things."

She put her arms around him and held him tightly.

"I feel better now I've told you."

The first weeks at school were particularly difficult for their son, and Helga had several meetings with the headmaster to find out how he was progressing. However, it was at the beginning of November when a most upsetting incident occurred. Peter had started work in his new job, leaving early in the morning and usually returning around six for supper. Hans-Peter was at school, but in recent weeks it had been evident that he was having further difficulties. He wasn't sleeping well and he was listless.

On this day, Armistice Day, November the eleventh, Hans-Peter returned home from school with a cut lip and a bleeding nose.

Helga hastened to his side.

"What happened?"

"I fell . . . I tripped . . ."

"Where?"

"In the *Wald*."

"In the woods?"

"*Ja*."

Helga read the lie, but went to work to stem the bleeding. It was a matter that needed more probing, but she would wait for Peter.

It was just after six when Helga heard the sound of Peter's

motorcycle. She greeted him at the door with Hans. Peter picked up his son and hugged him, then he noticed the cut lip.

"What happened here?"

"He fell . . ." Helga answered before Hans cou'd react, looking at Peter, qualifying her answer with a slight shake of the head to prevent further enquiry.

After supper, Peter gave his son the usual bath and then went to the bedroom in order to read him a story before tucking him in. Helga came up and joined them. She had already told Peter of the problem at school.

"Hans, I want to ask you a question," he said.

He looked at his father and then turned away.

"What happened at school today?"

Hans looked at Helga and then lowered his head.

"You didn't fall, did you. Something else happened?"

There was no answer.

"I think you should answer your *Vater*," Helga said.

"You didn't trip in the woods?"

He shook his head.

"Was it the boys at school?"

No answer.

"I think you should tell me the truth."

Hans sneaked a glance at his father and then the tears came. He broke into turbulent sobbing and Helga tried to comfort him. She looked at Peter and shook her head.

Peter, defeated now, got up slowly, handing the storybook to Helga as he made his way downstairs. He poured the last of the coffee and sat thinking.

Tomorrow he would meet with the headmaster.

It was early morning. Peter had driven his son to school on his motorcycle, a rare treat, and had left him in the playground with his fellow students. He went to the headmaster's office.

"John Rutherford," the headmaster extended his hand and

Peter grasped it with a noticeable reluctance.

"Peter Gray."

He motioned Peter to sit in the chair opposite his desk.

"Would you like tea?"

John Rutherford was a short robust-looking type, with an energetic bearing, much younger than he had expected, most likely in his late thirties. Probably avoided being in the Armed Services Peter thought, unable to curb a twinge of vindictiveness.

"Yes, thanks."

He got up and went to the door. Peter heard him asking his secretary to get a pot of tea. Then he returned to his desk, facing Peter with a serious expression.

"I think I know why you're here. You see we had a rather nasty incident here yesterday which involved your son."

The implication appeared to be that Hans-Peter was in some way responsible and it angered Peter, causing him to jump to the defence of his son.

"He came home with a cut lip and a bleeding nose. If he was involved, I'm sure it was defensive."

The secretary arrived with the tea.

Peter took milk and sugar, not waiting for an invitation. He took a sip. "Furthermore, he wouldn't tell us what happened. All he'd say was he tripped and fell."

"I'm sorry if I gave the impression that your son was in some way the perpetrator. He was very much the victim. He was the focus of what I can only describe as a spiteful attack. Shouting, 'Heil Hitler' and making rude gestures, four boys bullied him. It was one of our teachers who put a stop to it."

Peter moved to speak, but the headmaster continued.

"To make matters worse, it occurred after our Armistice Day commemoration."

"If you knew all about it yesterday, why was our son not taken care of. Why weren't we informed?"

"Hans-Peter ran away and the teacher, who didn't

358

recognize him, only reported it to me early this morning."

"Isn't this a serious lack of concern for a young child that has been hurt?"

Peter began to suspect that the matter may not have come to his attention at all if he hadn't complained.

"I must apologize. I intend to speak to my staff about the matter."

"These boys. You know who they are?"

"Yes, and they'll be punished. Their parents have been informed. I'm determined to ensure that this sort of thing won't happen again."

"It's been very traumatic for my son. Adapting to life here is difficult enough without this."

"I want to assure you that this will not be tolerated. Your son is doing well considering the difficulties he has been faced with. I mean becoming familiar with our studies. However, his English is remarkably good . . . "

"Thanks to my wife."

"Yes, I've had several meetings with your wife. I know she is concerned about his welfare. I think I was able to assure her that Hans-Peter is trying hard. Until this happened, his confidence had been improving daily. I intend to require the boys to make a personal apology."

Although not entirely convinced that all had been done to prevent the incident, Peter nevertheless accepted the Headmaster's explanation.

"Thank you."

They shook hands and Peter turned to leave.

"If there is any more difficulties, Mr. Gray, I urge you to contact me immediately."

"I hope it won't be necessary."

Peter strode out into the sunlight and his motorcycle.

Before setting out for work, Peter returned home and told Helga what had happened. However, he didn't convey any of his reservations to her, feeling that perhaps he was overreacting to the widespread public rancour towards Germans. He simply told her what the headmaster intended to do.

"Well," Helga said. "It doesn't remove the effects of the incident on our son but at least it's an acknowledgement of unacceptable behaviour."

"I think we should encourage Hans to talk, but only when he is ready."

"I'm proud of our son, Peter."

"So am I. I only wish we could help more."

"He has to work through it himself."

A few days later they had a visit from one of the fathers of the boys involved. He had been in the Royal Navy and knew of Peter and his experiences on the Sandrake.

"I couldn't believe a child of mine would do such a thing. It won't happen again. I'll see to that."

He didn't stay. He seemed embarrassed by the whole business.

"Thanks for coming." Peter said.

"It was the least I could do," he said, as he turned and walked out to the road.

SEVEN

1948

1.

𝒯hey strolled out onto the pier, a happy threesome, Helga, Peter and their young son, Hans-Peter, now nine. It was a late spring day, the eleventh anniversary of Helga's first meeting with Peter in 1937. The day that the *Joachim* came over the distant horizon to this small port on the south coast of England.

Helga was now feeling more comfortable in the community. The hostility that beset her in the early months after her arrival had lessened. People were more friendly, more accepting of her presence among them. She believed that part of the reason for the change was her work as a part-time teacher at the Grammar School. She ran a series of lectures on the great German philosophers. She was even able to get neighbours to look after Hans on the days that she was likely to be late getting home or was committed to evening classes.

Peter had acquired a sidecar which he is able to attach to his motorcycle to provide seating for Hans, or for Helga when Hans insisted on riding the pillion behind his father. They were ardent travellers. They had toured the coast as far as Land's End and inland, northwards to the Cotswolds. They had even made a trip to see Mike and Joan in West Kirby. But most of all they loved the Dorset countryside and the seacoast, the area where they first met.

They reached the end of the pier and sat down on the piles which supported the sides of the antique structure. The spring sun had a warmth which moderated the chill of the stiff breeze off the sea. Peter, feeling contented, sneaked a sideways glance at his wife. He still marvelled at his good fortune to have met and married her.

"Don't get too near the edge!" Helga shouted at young Hans who was peering over the edge of the pier, looking down to where the fishermen s' lines entered the water.

"*Nein,* Yes *Mutter,*" he replied with a look of mischievousness in his eyes.

"Do you think he'll welcome a sister?" Peter looked at Helga, waiting for her reaction.

"Peter!" Helga feigned surprise. "How do you know it will be a girl?"

"It will be . . . I'm sure of it."

"*Ja, Ja,* but, well, I prefer to believe it when it happens."

"We could call her Eva?"

"You like Eva, don't you?"

Peter remembered his first meeting with Eva in Munich. Helga's grandmother was in her early eighties then and as bright and as alive as someone half her age. It was Eva who helped and supported them as they contemplated marriage. 'You two love each another, that's all that matters,' she had said.

"Yes, a grand lady."

"She was my saviour. I don't know what I would have done without her. My parents virtually disowned me when I went to live with her in her house on the *Sunderstrasse.*"

Helga's recollection of Eva's generosity gave great pleasure and she smiled at the memory.

"Come on Hans, Hans!" she said. "We're going now."

They turned and made their way towards the inner harbour.

"My *Mutter* would like a granddaughter." Helga laughed as she took Peter's hand.

"You see. That's proof it will happen."

"Shall we go to the Tea Room?" Peter grinned, knowing what the answer would be.

"Of course," Helga tightened her grip on his hand.

"*Vater,* can I have a cream tea?" said Hans as he ran to join them.

364

EIGHT

1953

1.

$\mathcal{I}$t was a blustery winter's day, December 26, the tenth anniversary of the loss of the *Schlosstern*. Helga and Peter, with their two children, Hans-Peter and Eva, had spent Christmas with Helga's parents in Blankenese. Now, they were all assembled at the local church to honour the memory of Günther. Sitting in the first pew was Rolf, with his wife Ilse and his mother Eva. Next to Eva sat Anna. Helga and Peter were seated behind them with Hans-Peter and Eva. Young Eva, now four, had already demonstrated a persistence worthy of her great-grandmother, insisting on attending the service, and this had been allowed providing she behaved herself. Next to Peter and his family were Siegfried and Frieda with their son Klaus, and Siegfried's mother and father, Lisa and Konrad.

Other survivors of the *Schlosstern* sinking were in the congregation, friends of Siegfried and Günther who had come to Blankenese from other parts of Germany.

Harold Parkin and his wife Janet had journeyed over from England. It was Harold who had served aboard the Royal Navy destroyer that had rescued Siegfried, it was he who had saved him from the icy waters of the Barents Sea. Siegfried and Harold had corresponded for some four years now, but this was their first meeting since that tragic day.

There were also friends and neighbours, a modest group, quietly reliving a past which most wished had not become a part of the history of the Fatherland.

Framing an engraved brass memorial plate which adorned the wall of the old church, and which had been placed there by Rolf and Ilse the year after Günther's death, were sprigs of holly remembering the Christmas of 1943, the Christmas that Günther had promised Helga he would be home. On each side of the chancel was a flagpole, the first displaying the flag of the old German Imperial Navy with its black vertical and horizontal bars, centred by a heraldic symbol, and bearing in its upper left corner the Iron Cross. The second bore the White Ensign of the Royal Navy with its vertical and horizontal red bars, with the Union Jack in its upper left corner. This latter addition was suggested by Siegfried and, after some initial reluctance, endorsed by Rolf.

As the service drew to a close, the minister intoned a requiem,

> We are here today to honour the memory of Günther Otto *Jansen*. A former member of this congregation, who on this day, December 26, in the icy sea off *Nordkapp*, gave his life for his country. He and his comrades aboard the *Schlosstern* went forth bravely to defend, what they believed to be, the honour of the *Vaterland*.

> It was on a day on which many died and few survived. A day on which the crew of the *Schlosstern* fought bravely against a courageous enemy.

> This is a day when we can look back with sadness to the horror and insanity of war and remember a common humanity. In this congregation there are no enemies, only friends. A living testament to the power of love and forgiveness.

> May we never again be called upon to put aside our common humanity and succumb to the brutality and horror of war.

There was a palpable stillness as the minister left the pulpit. Then came a gradual swelling of voices as the choir, with members of the congregation joining in, sang the German sailors' song:

Auf ei-nem See-mannsgrab, da blü-hen kei-ne
Ro-sen.
Auf ei-nem See-mannsgrab, da blüht kein E-del
- weiß.
Der einz'-ige Schmuck, das sind die wei-ßen
Mö - wen _ und Trä-nen, die ein Mä-del weint
so heiß.
Der einz'-ige Schmuck, das sind die weißen
Mö - wen _ und Tränen, die ein Mä-del weint so
heiß.

(On a sailor's grave no roses bloom.
On a sailor's grave no flowers bloom.
The only decorations are white seagulls,
And the many tears a girlfriend weeps.)

From the front pew came a loud and sustained sobbing which continued through the closing prayer. It was Anna. Anna who had enjoyed such a pitifully short time with Günther before he left to make his last voyage. It seemed as if she grieved for the entire congregation, her public outpouring of emotion being sufficient for each. And from many there was evidence of silent envy for her lack of constraint.

The recessional hymn, the carol, *Stille Nacht! heilige Nacht!*, sung with fervour by all, transformed Anna's mourning into an exaltation of the spirit of the Christmas season, offering a further reminder of Günther and Siegfried's celebration of that fateful Christmas aboard the *Schlosstern*, before they sailed on their last mission.

As the doors of the church were opened, a breeze moved through the nave, reaching the chancel and rustling the two flags. It was if unseen hands had transported them to where ocean winds blew, to their stations on the sterns of once proud ships with their gallant crews - German and British.

After the service, they all strolled through the quiet churchyard. Even the children captured the solemnity of the moment, and were unusually quiet. It was cold, with a strong wind blowing, and Peter looked across to Siegfried hand in hand with his family. Catching his gaze, Siegfried turned and Peter could see that his eyes were moist. He knew that he too was remembering the cold evening in the Barents Sea when sailors fought and died, the dead forfeiting their youth, and the living forever committed to memories of death and destruction and the stupidity of war.

As the group dispersed, Peter noticed Rolf and Siegfried in earnest conversation. They were standing under one of the ancient yew trees that surrounded the church. At one point he thought he saw Rolf glance in his direction. At the time he and Helga were talking to Gertrud, Eva's neighbour from Munich, but Peter became so absorbed by the thought of what Rolf and Siegfried might be discussing, as well as being envious of their obvious friendliness, that he heard little of what Gertrud was saying. His lack of attention increased when Siegfried and Rolf were joined by Rolf's mother, Eva, and Günther's friend Anna.

Peter admired Anna and he had gone to great lengths to answer her many questions about the last hours of the *Schlosstern*. She showed no hostility about his part in the tragedy, only the terrible grief that Günther's loss had brought to her life.

Ilse's voice claimed his attention.

"We should all be getting back to the house. I'll go and collect my husband," she said, walking towards the group gathered around Rolf.

The day after, Helga and Peter and their children were still at the family home in Blankenese. Grandmother Eva was also present, intending to stay for a few days before returning to Munich and her house on the *Sunderstrasse*. A strange atmosphere prevailed. Rolf was unusually quiet, shunning conversation, and Peter was convinced that his unhappy demeanour was caused by his continuing animosity towards him. Yet he sensed a difference, hard to define, but nevertheless a difference. Time and again, in unguarded moments, Peter caught Rolf eying him with a questioning look.

It was mid-afternoon when Rolf beckoned Peter aside, surprising him by leading the way up to the cupola. They climbed the steep narrow staircase which opened out into a circular room with windows covering the entire circumference. An ingenious system of blinds could be lowered or raised to block out the light or to define one's chosen viewpoint. It was a large room with three comfortable chairs in the centre. Around the edges, under the windows, were bookshelves topped by a convenient shelf area. They stood and looked out over the Elbe. Two large freighters were steaming by, one upstream to the port of Hamburg, the other, downstream to the North Sea. Rolf looked at Peter with a friendly gaze.

"I have a small fleet again now," he said. " Not as large as those," he pointed to the huge ships which were already moving out of their view. "Coastal vessels like the *Joachim* . . . in fact the next one I will call the *Joachim*."

He motioned Peter to a chair.

After Peter was settled, he rang for Minna, and then reached for some papers. He selected a sheet for Peter.

"This is the fleet and the routes they serve. You'll notice that we are resuming our run to England."

Minna came up the stairs.

"Some *Kaffee,* Minna," said Rolf.

He turned back to Peter. There was a prolonged pause before he spoke. Appearing uncharacteristically embarrassed, he said, "You're a good man, Peter . . . I've been blind to many things . . . people tell me . . . it has been difficult. I wanted . . ."

He stopped, unable to continue, and for a moment Peter thought he might be ill. It was excruciating to watch Rolf try and deal with his contradictions. Peter, wanting to respond, but

371

unable to think of an appropriate reaction, remained silent.

Rolf went to the window, staring out across the Elbe. After a long delay he turned.

"Peter," he said, taking a deep breath, "I've given this a great deal of thought . . . "

He hesitated again and then, straightening, irrevocably committed to his objective, continued in a firmer voice.

"I'd like to ask you to join my company. You have experience in electronics and wireless and I need someone from my family to look after this?"

Rolf sat down, obviously relieved to have unburdened himself. Peter, however, was dumfounded as he continued.

"Siegfried's already with me. I'd like you to join us."

Minna came with the *Kaffee* and a light snack.

As she departed, Rolf called, "Minna, bring some *Schnaps,* please."

Peter felt his heart thumping, and he sensed the beginnings of a trickle of perspiration on his forehead.

"I . . . I don't know what to say . . ."

Peter remembered how Helga had warned him that when her father had an idea he was determined.

Minna arrived with the *Schnaps*

"Does Helga know?" Peter said.

"No, It's between us."

"But . . . I would like to discuss it with her."

"I understand."

Peter, overwhelmed by what was happening, felt the intrusion of some misgivings. He shifted uneasily and Rolf was quick to sense his discomfort.

"Is something wrong?"

"No . . . No, it's just . . ."

Rolf waited.

"Will I be accepted in Germany?"

Rolf smiled. "You have my word."

There was no opportunity to pursue the matter as Rolf

reached for the *Schnaps*.

"Come, we must drink to your joining my family."

They drank and chatted amiably as Peter struggled with the consequences of Rolf's change of heart. He wondered if the memorial service hadn't represented a sort of exorcism, a final reconciliation with the loss of his son. If it was, Peter could well understand it, for the simple, dignified service had also enabled him to come closer to peace with the past and his role in the death of Günther and the *Schlossstern*. It had also offered him the occasion to honour the memories of Stephen and Jonathan.

When, still bewildered, he hastened to impart the news to Helga, he realized that he was breathless with excitement.

Helga greeted the news with happiness.

"Will you take it?"

"Do you want me to?"

"You must decide."

"I'll take it." His voice was firm, lacking any doubt.

"Oh Peter, *mein* Peter. I love you."

They fell into a long lingering embrace.

"We can live in Germany," Peter whispered.

"But we'll holiday in the house in England?" Helga effused.

"We must be there when the new *Joachim* arrives," he said.

"*Wunderbar!*"

They drew closer, slipping into another embrace, kissing tearfully. And then they held hands and went to find Hans and young Eva, and to tell great-grandmother Eva of the good news. And when they found her, she smiled, that understanding smile which suggested foreknowledge. But it wasn't a time for questions, only happiness, which they all shared.

Acknowledgements

Grateful acknowledgment is given to Minerva-Music, Frechen, Germany, for permission to use the refrain from the song, *Auf einem Seemannsgrab...da blühen keine Rosen.* Copyright © 1954 by Minerva-Music.

Many books and reports assisted me in my research concerning the conduct of the war, both from British and German points of view. Especially useful were: The Bomber Command War Diaries - An Operational Reference Book 1939-1945, by Martin Middlebrook and Chris Everitt, published by Harmondsworth-Penguin; Fraser of North Cape, by Richard Humble, published by Routledge & Kegan Paul; The Drama of the Scharnhorst, by Corvette-Captain Fritz-Otto Busch, published by Robert Hale Limited; Supplement to the London Gazette, August 5th, 1947; The Death of the Scharnhorst, by John Winton, published by A. Bird Publications; The Loss of the Scharnhorst by A.J Watts, published by Ian Allan; Hitler's High Seas Fleet, by Richard Humble, published by Ballantine Books Inc; Illustrated London News, circa 1936; The Gathering Storm, by Winston S. Churchill, published by Houghton Mifflin Company.

Numerous individuals have also helped me. Most especially, I'd like to record my appreciation for the perspectives and the documentation provided by Helmut Feifer, Helmut Backhaus and Ernst Reimann in Germany. Their personal experiences of life in the Kriegsmarine and as crew members of the Scharnhorst were most valued Also, John Baxendale and Tom Bethell in England, for Royal Navy points of view on the battle off Nordkapp. However, I would not have been successful in contacting any of these individuals without the assistance of the German Embassy in Ottawa and the staff of Marine-Ehrenmal-Laboe, who kindly introduced me to Wolfgang Kube, the chairman of Bordkameradschaft Scharnhorst.

I am particularly indebted to Asta and Herwig Leuders. Asta read the text and provided me with a valuable appreciation of the circumstances prevailing during the time the story takes place. An especial mention must go to Julia Mendzigall who provided the numerous translations required and who was meticulous in her comments and criticisms of the text.

Anne-Lise and Rudolf Schultzf were not only gracious hosts, but provided valuable guidance while my wife and I conducted the extensive research in Germany. Hans Stutz gave us an insightful preview of Munich before we left Canada. My thanks also to Eva Rimmele of the Institut für Zeitgeschichte in Munich for pre-war viewpoints concerning border crossings into Germany.

Editorial suggestions were also provided by Munro Scott and Rachel Wyatt, and additional story comments by Hilda Scott. The matter of story continuity was methodically examined with the assistance of Patrick Spearey.

Many others helped; Margaret Fraser provided additional research material; Ron & Dorothy Searle sent pictures of German survivors on a British battleship; Norah Walker was generous in her account of her husband's life in the Royal Navy; Nancy Smith was my first and most forthright critic.